# A
# JOURNEY
# TO
# ORASSIA

CALIBER
BOOKS

Also from ALAN CAILLOU

**CABOT CAIN Series**
    *Assault on Kolchak*
    *Assault on Ming*
    *Assault on Loveless*
    *Assault on Fellawi*
    *Assault on Agathon*
    *Assault on Almata*

**TOBIN'S WAR Series**
    *Dead Sea Submarine*
    *Terror in Rio*
    *Congo War Cry*
    *Afghan Assault*
    *Swamp War*
    *Death Charge*
    *The Garonsky Missile*

**MIKE BENASQUE Series**
    *The Plotters*
    *Marseilles*
    *Who'll Buy My Evil*
    *Diamonds Wild*

**IAN QUAYLE Series**
    *A League of Hawks*
    *The Sword of God*

**DEKKER'S DEMONS Series**
    *Suicide Run*
    *Blood Run*

*The Charge of the Light Brigade*
*A Journey to Orassia*

*Rogue's Gambit*
*Cairo Cabal*
*Bichu the Jaguar*
*The Walls of Jolo*
*The Hot Sun of Africa*
*The Cheetahs*
*Joshua's People*
*Mindanao Pearl*
*Khartoum*
*South from Khartoum*
*Rampage*
*The World is 6 Feet Square*
*The Prophetess*
*House on Curzon Street*

A JOURNEY TO ORASSIA

For further information visit the Caliber Comics website:
www.calibercomics.com

Cover image by: Dubya2x

*In these Books is Written the Way of a man with a woman*
*That he shall Enjoy her.*
*Through her, he will find the only God,*
*For all that woman is, God made for him alone.*
*There is no other Truth,*
*There is no other way to Find it.*


Introduction to the thirteen volumes of the Kandit Oras
of Raiden el Darrah, poet, philosopher, voluptuary, and
soldier, born A.D. 514, died A.D. 632 at the age of one
hundred and eighteen.

# CHAPTER I

ROGER SEQUOYAH looked at the long tree-shaded roar ahead of him and was happy.

It makes no difference, he thought, however much you travel, the excitement is always there once you hear the first foreign word and sense the first little inconformity; it may be only a gesture, an idea, a nuance of inflection, but when first you notice it, that is when the sensation begins. The color of a tree, the curve of a road, an unexpected view...or it could be just the knowledge that the foreign accents all around you were not really foreign anymore, but native, that you were the foreigner now, a man apart from all the others and therefore somehow more free.

He had rented a car in Paris, and the man from the American Express had gone with him because he was from Oklahoma too, and the two of them had carried the Oklahoman ambience about with them like a blanket over their heads that would not let him see, or feel, or hear anything that was alien.

And it was not until he was clear of the city, driving alone on the wide concrete road that cut its way through the silent green forest of Fontainebleau, that the blanket began to lose its shadow over him; and that was where the first true inconformity came to his senses, a charming alien scene, quickly gone but absorbed in a moment, that impressed the color of the country on him, as though all that had gone before had been nothing more than a transition from one world to another.

By the side of the road, under the scented shadows of the trees, a French family had parked their Citroen and were taking their midday meal; they had set up a folding table that was covered with a neat white cloth, and there were knives and forks and long-stemmed glasses, and a tall bottle of red wine, and four aluminum saucepans nesting one on top of the other, out of which a cheerful woman was spooning meat and vegetables. The man was carefully tucking a napkin into his collar...they could have been in the dining room of their St. Cloud home; and when Sequoyah saw the man sniff carefully at the cork he had drawn from the wine bottle and nod his approval, the picture was already flashing by with the speed of the road; but the image of it stayed to remind him.

Sequoyah grinned. He drove on a few hundred yards and then pulled under the trees himself, to let the historic aura of the forest seep into his imagination.

He climbed out of the car and stood in the broom and heather with his arms akimbo, his back to the road in a conscious effort to lose it, while he stared at the pines and the oaks, at the spruce and the chestnut trees, at the hornbeam and the beech and the birch, trying to identify them one by one, because the forest was almost a part of him and he loved its silences and its bird-sounds, its sunlit leaves and the mottled shadows the branches threw on the moss of the ground.

He took off his jacket and laid it down, outside up, and lay there for a while, staring up at the sky.

It was May, and buds were bursting into yellow-green.


He came from Oklahoma, and he was thirty-five years old. His professorship at Kemah University (Ph.D. Geology) had given him a certain slackness of muscle, but he moved easily and quickly on the balls of his feet like the athlete he once had been. There had been a time when the shouts of the fans had been important to him, when nothing had been of more consequence than making All-American; and although that had been a long time ago he had never lost the desire for a constant, driving physical fitness. There was a latent energy even in the way he rested now, with his shoulders back and one knee carelessly raised, and his long arms spread out on the heather.

A car went by, moving fast and tooting its pipsqueak horn, and he sat up quickly and looked, and there were a crowd of college girls crammed into a little convertible, five or six of them, their long hair blown by the wind, turning and waving at him and shrieking their laughter; he put his arms round his knees and watched the car recede into the distance, amused by the masses of swirling, varicolored hair that seemed to him somehow to accentuate the sensual aspects of the warm sun.

And then he lay back again and thought about Maxwell Christie and the careful obscurity of his offer, an obscurity that would have seemed strange in a man of Christie's forthright artlessness had it not been for one salient fact—the fact that oil, like gold and diamonds and hidden pearl beds, was something you kept quiet about until the leases were signed and the drills were down; there was just too much money involved to allow any careless talk.

"You wrote me," Christie had said on the phone, "now come and see me." And that was all. When Sequoyah had protested the short notice, Christie had answered impatiently: "You like the London weather? I'll expect you in Marseilles tomorrow."

*The hell with Christie*, be thought, and it was a conscious abnegation of the urgency in him. *Sure,* he thought, *I'm in a hurry, but when a man like Christie whistles, a man like me doesn't jump, not too fast anyway. I need his money and I need his help, but let's not join in the yes-sir, no-sir, not too fast... Besides, he needs me too, and for what?*

He stood up and put on his jacket again, and drove south at speed, and soon the gently rolling hills of Provence were spread out graciously around him, with bright green vines and sudden, unexpected patches of brilliant purple where the bougainvillea was flowering.

He drove till the sun went down, and now the air was sweet with the scent of hidden flowers where the market gardens were, and there were warning signs for the motorists outside the towns...AVIGNON, A TOWN THAT LIKES NEITHER NOISE NOR SPEED. And ARLES. PEACE AND QUIET OBLIGATORY.

Then the traffic was thicker and slower and the scent of the sea was stronger, and then Marseilles was there, noisy and crowded and full of life, and when he reached the three-sided square of the Vieux Port where the yacht would be moored, the dinnertime crowd was already sauntering among the sidewalk restaurants, looking at the piles of oysters where the ice chips dripped, studying the langoustines and the plump prawns and the lobsters that slowly crawled in their glass-walled tanks; the Provencal couples walked arm in arm, and sometimes they stopped walking and kissed, and all around him there was a lazy air of indolence, as though nothing mattered because it was dinnertime and the smell of the food was ripe and enticing.

He parked the car and sat at a table and ordered a bottle of wine, looking out at the yacht that he knew would be Christie's even though its name was obscured by the prow of the fishing boat that had just come in, knowing that it could belong to no one else because of its size and the sheer majesty of its trappings. He wondered if Christie was on board, impatiently waiting for him, angrily wondering why he hadn't arrived on the morning's plane.

And, while he was sipping his third glass of Beaujolais, a heavily built man in white duck trousers and a striped shirt came over and looked at him for a while and then moved forward and said cheerfully:

"Yes, it must be you. Roger Sequoyah?"

"Yes?"

"I'm Breck. I work for Mr. Christie."

"Sit down. Have a drink."

Breck looked at him, half smiling, enjoying a secret joke that he did not want to share. The smile was sardonic, almost (but not quite) derisive.

"I won't, if you don't mind."

Was there a touch of overt hostility there? Breck's handshake was strong and friendly, and the smile showed strong white teeth, but the eyes were veiled. He said: "We were rather expecting you this morning."

Sequoyah nodded. "But I decided to drive down from Paris."

"Yes, I know."

It was a flat statement that said a lot more than that. It said also: *I called London and they referred me to the American Express, who referred me to Paris, who gave me the number of the car; it's a gray*

8

*Peugeot sedan, and it's parked round the corner on the Canebière.*
Breck looked at the half-empty bottle and said:

"Why don't we go on board, Mr. Sequoyah?"

"If you're sure you won't join me?"

"I'm sure."

When Sequoyah looked round for the waiter, Breck said: "I'll take care of it." He pulled a roll of bills from his pocket and threw down twenty francs, and they walked across the Quai des Belges and down the steps to the water's edge. They walked without talking, and Sequoyah thought: *My God, it feels like an abduction.* A small outboard motorboat was waiting for them with a cheroot-smoking sailor squatting in the stern. The sailor looked at Breck and grunted: "*Enfin.*"

Sequoyah said mildly: "Why doesn't he moor alongside the quay?" And Breck said: "I wonder?"

Sequoyah looked at him sharply, but his face was expressionless. The motor started with a roar, and the prow rose up as the twin screws churned up the water behind them; and soon, ghostly white in the moonlight, the steep sides of the yacht rose high above them.

Christie was waiting, and the legend took on life and became a man.

He was still young, not much more than fifty, Sequoyah thought, with black hair that was streaked with gray and cut close to his head. His features were sharp, almost rodent-like, and when he moved it was with quick, sudden gestures, as though the motion he was making had been planned long ago and was annoyingly late in execution; as though there were no time left for even so simple a thing as shaking hands.

Christie's grip was firm but quickly gone, and then the hands were at his shoulders, gripping him, and the sharp, alert eyes were peering into his own as though the secret of his strength or his weakness were there to be plainly seen by any sharply observant man. The grip at his shoulders tightened, and Christie said:

"I've followed your career, young man. I think we can do business together."

Sequoyah said, smiling: "I'm glad to hear it. When you didn't answer my letter earlier, I almost gave up."

"Almost, but not quite."

"Not quite. I would have written again."

"Good. I like persistence. Let's go to my cabin."

Looking around him admiringly, Sequoyah said: "Quite a ship you have here."

Christie said: "Get to like it." It was almost an order. "It's going to be your home for a while."

"Oh?"

"For quite a while. If you have any other commitments..."

"No, not really."

"Good. Where's your baggage?"

"Locked in the trunk of my car at the moment..."

"Breck will take care of it. Give him the key."

The order was sharp, staccato, expectant of instant obedience. He sighed, and Breck was behind him, silently holding out his hand, and while he fumbled for the keys he saw that Christie was already striding away, moving in quick short steps towards the companionway. He turned there and smiled, as though he were trying not to show the impatience, but he said:

"Are you going to stand there all night?"

The lamplight shone from the walls of the corridors, and he felt himself touching the paneling with his fingertips as he followed Christie, enjoying the delicate patina almost sensuously; it was like alabaster, and the dark blue carpet under his feet was the thickest he had ever trodden on. The corridor was long and brightly lit, and when he came to the cabin he was astonished at the size of it. The portholes were cut square, like the windows of a house, and the walls were lined with leather-bound books; wherever he looked, there were bookshelves, heavily laden, and the only vacant space on the walls was filled with three fine paintings. He recognized a Manet and a Seurat, but it was the third which caught his attention, and for a while he stared at it, conscious that Christie had turned and was waiting for him to speak, his eyes bright with something that might have been pride.

It was a painting of a minutely detailed desert that seemed to carry its horizons far beyond the confines of the cabin, far beyond the water itself and across to the other end of the world; and once the eye had been carried there, it was abruptly bounced back, with cruel speed, to the foreground, where one side of the frame was filled with half a young girl's face, staring out into emptiness with almost a look of fear. When he went closer and peered at it, he could see a Greek ruin, no bigger than a postage stamp, so intricately painted in such architectural precision that he was reminded of the Persian miniatures he had seen in the museums of Baghdad. It was suspended in space, and he turned to Christie and said:

"No one but Dali... Who's the girl?"

"My daughter Candia. My only child."

"A commissioned portrait? That's rare, isn't it?"

Christie merely grunted, and Sequoyah said dutifully: "She's a lovely girl."

"She takes after her mother. Same eyes. Same skin. Same temperament too. What are you drinking, scotch or bourbon? Rye?"

"A little scotch, please."

Christie opened a small cupboard and handed him a pewter goblet. It was ice-cold to the touch, lightly frosted, and he said casually:

"If you'd rather have a glass..."

"No, this is fine. Marvelous."

"You know about pewter?"

"Nothing. Nothing at all."

"If you look inside, you'll see the bottom has been etched. They stopped doing that in 1680. That one came from Nuremberg and was made by Peter Flotner in the fifteen-nineties. You know the secret?"

Sequoyah looked at him, amused, and said nothing.

"The secret is to take yourself back in time...1590 was the year when Nuremberg was the center of the witchcraft trials, the year when they anticipated the Nazis of the twentieth century and roasted forty-two women and girls, in ovens, on charges of heresy. It was the year when von Dernbach of Fulda discovered he could prompt confessions from his young witches by thrusting red-hot skewers into them as they hung from the ceiling-beams in strappado."

He was pacing back and forth, like an animal in a cage, moving restlessly as though seeking a way back to a time that was gone and had left its imprint only in memories and pewter goblets.

"The secret," he said again, "is to take yourself back with the touch of antiquity. Touch a piece of pewter, and hear the sounds made by the hammer that formed it, feel the warmth of the open fire where the lead boiled... You know about von Dernbach?"

Sequoyah shook his head.

"The witch-hunter of all time. That was once his goblet. The whisky's in the cask there, help yourself."

"Do I detect a longing for the good old days?" Sequoyah turned the wooden spigot of the small oak cask and said: "But you didn't bring me here to talk about witches."

"No, I didn't." Christie went to one of the windows and looked out at the floodlit mass of Notre Dame de la Garde that stood sentinel over the city. He said slowly: "You know all the oil fields of the Middle East, and you know that there are still some deposits that haven't been located. I want to talk about one of them, and I want your word that what I say won't go out of this room." He swung round suddenly and said: "And I mean just that, your words, and pay promise that I can trust it."

Sequoyah felt his spirits sinking. He said:

"I had hoped, rather, that you wanted to talk about my letter. About oil in Oklahoma."

"Your letter is important too, if your scheme means as much to you as I think it does."

"It means a great deal."

"Why? Well, why does anyone want to look for oil? Money, of course, but in this case it's something else as well..."

"In Oklahoma? The area you're interested in was examined inch by inch, years ago. Some of the best men in the world. If there'd been anything there they'd have found it, take my word for it."

"No, I won't take your word for it."

Christie was startled, as though he were not accustomed to having his word doubted, and for a moment there was a trace of anger on his face. But he smiled quickly and said:

"I looked at the map, and the epicenter of the area you're interested in is the place where you were born, the place where your father died of nothing but poverty... Yes, that's what it was and don't interrupt me when I'm talking. Inch by inch they've been over that land, and there's no oil there, and if you insist there is, then I'll tell you that your thinking is not objective. And if you still insist I'll say you're an idiot, which I know you're not. That makes it an obsession."

"It's not an obsession." He put down the witch-hunt goblet and looked at Christie and said clearly: "I came in answer to your message, hoping that I could talk you into financing something which is very important to me. If all you wanted was to say no, you could have told me that on the phone. So, if you don't mind..."

Christie said: "You're a stubborn man, Sequoyah, and that's all to the good." He snorted and said: "And I'm prepared to finance you, I'll give you all the money you want, so keep your shirt on."

Sequoyah stared. "You mind if I sit down?" He took his drink to one of the leather armchairs and stretched his long legs out in front of him, sipping his whisky from von Dernbach's goblet and looking at Christie.

"Just like that? On nothing more than the basic facts I gave you? And in spite of your disbelief? You must want something mighty substantial in return."

"Your thinking is muddy, Sequoyah. What'll it cost, a million? Two, perhaps? That's a lot of money in your world, isn't it?"

"In anybody's world, I'd say."

"Not in mine. In exchange for your services on a project of *mine*, I'll put up the money for yours, and I don't give a damn whether it turns up or not."

"That's a pretty rash promise, Mr. Christie."

"I'm not a rash man, as you'll find out. Is it a deal?"

"In principle, it's a deal, but..."

"Then that's all there is to it."

"For God's sake, there are a thousand details we have to discuss..."

"We will, when the time comes. Meanwhile you can take my word."

"Yes, I know I can. All right, what do you want me to do?"

"First, your confidence."

"I can keep a secret."

13

"Ever been to Orassia?"

"No. I only barely know where it is."

"That's where we're heading in a few days' time. I need an expert in tideland oil, and I need him now. I need you. For as long as it takes. We make a survey, and we make a report, and it's got to be in secret."

In the silence, Sequoyah could feel the almost imperceptible motion of the yacht as a barge went by, heading out to sea. He said at last, worrying about it:

"Are you implying that the government of Orassia mustn't know about it?"

"The Shah of Orassia will know. No one else." It was a gentle correction, but insistent, as though there were a fine point somewhere in the distinction, a distinction that merited some thought.

"Why not? Presumably the Shah's the only man who can grant the leases..."

"He is. But Orassia is a feudal state, and that's the way the Shah wants it. His family have ruled there for a thousand years, and by Arab standards he's a hell of a good ruler. But the mass of his people are poverty-stricken, and like most of the Middle East, it's no longer easy to maintain the *status quo*. There are factions that want to take over the country, democratic factions I suppose you'd call them, and there are only two things that have prevented a democratic revolution. One, money. Two, outside help. If we find oil, and the secret gets out too soon, those two things will be readily available. A close look at recent history will show you pretty clearly just where that money and outside help might come from if certain elements *outside* Orassia feel it might be advantageous to offer them to certain elements *inside* Orassia. You see what I'm driving at?"

"No."

"Then let me put it like this: the people there have nothing to fight for, nothing to prompt them to overthrow the government. Let them smell oil, and they'll have a purpose; and there are plenty of forces outside the country who will give them the arms they would need, and then... You've seen revolutions used before. I make myself clear?"

"Excellently clear."

14

"Good. Are you with me?"

"Yes, I am."

"We leave in three days' time. If you have to let anyone know where you are, tell them you're in Aden. We'll be in contact with Aden constantly."

"There's no one."

He was aware, suddenly, that he had said something of relative importance, even if it were only because this was something not even Christie could possibly know about him; inexplicably, it gave him a certain amount of satisfaction.

Christie said: "You'll like the Shah, a good man. A rich man too, even by my standards."

"A good, rich ruler, and a poverty-stricken populace." He should have known it wasn't much of an argument for a man like Christie. "Yes, precisely. There's a good deal of money in the country and it's all in the hands of the Shah's family, but slowly he's trying to improve their condition. He just doesn't believe that democracy is necessarily the best way to do it."

"That might be construed as a weakness."

"Or as a strength, take your choice. The fellahin in Egypt are no better off under presidents than they are under kings. They just pay taxes instead of tithes, and maybe they wash more often in the name of a newly found arrogance. The great masses of Orassia are nomads, and if you give a nomad a little power, the first thing he wants to do is to destroy the cities, because that's where he believes the corruption is..."

Sequoyah said, interrupting the smooth flow: "And, of course, he's right."

Christie sighed. "Yes, I suppose so. But it's also where the progress is, and he'll never learn to separate the one from the other. That was Genghis Khan's trouble; if he'd been a townsman instead of a nomad, his descendants would probably be ruling the world today. Orassia's not the kind of place where the masses can be given free rein, they need a strong and constant control on the bridle or outcome their swords. Don't make the mistake of thinking that what's good for an Oklahoman farmer is necessarily good for a desert camel-herd. In time, Orassia will be a wealthy country and the wealth will be better

15

ALAN CAILLOU

distributed; but don't weep if we don't live, you and I, to see that time. And first, we've got to find it for them."

He spoke quickly, as though consciously not permitting too much thought on a specious argument. Sequoyah brushed the thoughts aside.

"And if we do?"

"The European Oil Amalgamation is prepared to pay the Shah for a long lease of mineral rights, if our survey shows that it's worth their while."

"And if it doesn't?"

Christie shrugged. "You'll have gained a bit of experience, and you'll have the financing for your damn-fool Oklahoma project. You can't lose, can you, either way. Have you had dinner?"

"Not yet."

"We'll eat on board. I hope you're fond of good food."

"Within limits."

"Some time in the next few days, give my chef a note of the things you like and the things you don't like. You'll find it will be worth the trouble. And if you've finished your drink, I'll show you just what we've got here."

He swallowed his drink and threw open the door. He said impatiently: "Well, are you coming?"

She was a fine looking ship, with a well-raked, rounded stern, a cruiser stern, and two raked masts; the funnel was oval and raked, and a broad red band circled it. She weighed in at 8400 tons, with a gross of 5800 and her draft was 35 feet; she was equipped with electric steering gear (with telemotor control from the wheelhouse), gyro compass, automatic helmsman, radar, and diesel-engine aluminum lifeboats. Her Doxford diesels gave her a service speed of fifteen knots and a maximum of eighteen and a half, on just over seventeen tons of fuel a day.

Sequoyah was impressed with the accommodation on board—two self-contained master suites, eight single cabins, and enough room for twenty-two deck officers and men as well as the sixteen engine-room personnel and the catering staff of twelve. The main cabins were paneled in honey-colored sycamore, and everywhere he looked there was evidence of quality; in the furniture, the fittings, the

16

spotless polish at which, always, somebody seemed to be working. It was not a ship, Sequoyah thought, that any Tom, Dick, or Harry could own; but then, Christie was obviously not just anybody; he was a man who knew what he wanted and could afford to pay for it.

Her name was *Abaris*, and when he asked the question, Christie said, smiling: "An obscure Scythian from the age of Croesus. Apollo gave him an arrow which would take him anywhere he chose, at speed, and silently." He patted the railing affectionately and said: "She'll go anywhere, Sequoyah, quickly and smoothly. As you'll soon see."

Sequoyah looked over the four decks, gleaming in the Mediterranean moonlight, and knew that the *Abaris* was not just a wealthy man's toy; it was a home, a workshop, a research center, and the core of Christie's whole life.

And when he went to his cabin that night, after a dinner that left him drowsy and overfed, he found Breck there with a big, heavily built seaman in a dark sweater, stowing his gear. He said to the seaman: "Put the briefcase over on the table, I'll be working on some papers..." The man looked at him blankly and Breck said: "Tagos, a Greek, he doesn't speak English." He took the briefcase from him and stowed it away in the table drawer and said: "A replacement, one of our men went down with malaria and we had to ship him ashore. Is there anything else I can do for you?"

Sequoyah shook his head, and later, when they had gone, he opened a package that had his name on it and found inside a heavy gold cigarette case. He flipped it open and saw that it had been inscribed inside, in letters so delicate he could hardly read them: "R.S. IN AFFECTION, M.C." He shrugged; it looked like a good beginning. *At least,* he thought, *Maxwell Christie sure as hell needs me...*

He went to bed and started planning about Oklahoma. His thoughts began: *And when this is all over...*

# CHAPTER 2

CHRISTIE WAS SHORT-TEMPERED that morning.

When Sequoyah came out of his cabin to look at the equipment that had been stored in the bulkheads, he heard him saying sharply: "...and the fact that your opinion is inconsistent with mine automatically makes your opinion manifestly absurd. If we leave by eleven, we'll have a foot or more to spare."

He heard Breck say: "Yes, sir," and then Breck was coming along the deck, smiling a little to himself, and when he saw Sequoyah he grinned and said: "We leave at eleven." He dropped his voice a little and added: "If the gods are kind to us."

When he had gone, Sequoyah went up to the bridge. Christie was staring across the harbor to the wharf, where the restaurant waiters could be seen in their shirt sleeves, hosing down the pavements and setting out the tables for the early morning coffee and brioches. He said cheerfully:

"Good morning. So we sail at eleven?"

"Yes. If we don't leave by then we'll never get out of the harbor."

"Oh? Is something holding us up?"

For a while, Christie did not answer. He said at last: "I was about to say nothing will hold us up, but it wouldn't be true. If she's not here by then, we'll lose a day."

Sequoyah took the telegram that Christie handed him and read:

*Just to give you the satisfaction of knowing you are right, I*

*am coming to Marseilles. Will arrive early in the morning.
The animal is showing his claws and I would like to know
what made him unsheathe them. Candia.*

He looked at Christie and said: "The animal?"

"An animal named Fenton. She thinks she's in love with him."

"And you don't think so."

"No." He turned to look at him and said: "When you get to know me better, Sequoyah, you'll realize something you ought to know about men in my position. Our enemies say we've got where we are by ruthlessness, and perhaps they're right. But that's only half the story; the other half is the careful application of it in the right direction and nowhere else. Fenton's a harsh man, but he hasn't channeled his harshness where it could do some good; he's like an animal, lashing out in every direction but the right one, wasting his strength and getting nowhere. He's the wrong man for a daughter of mine." He took back the telegram and looked at it and said: "Maybe she's learned, maybe she hasn't, but that's something I'll soon find out."

"If we're leaving by eleven, you won't have much time to find out anything."

"She'll come with us."

"At such short notice? We might be away for a long time..."

"She's an impetuous young woman, Sequoyah, and if she doesn't like Orassia she'll radio for a plane and fly back to New York, it's as simple as that. But we'll try and keep her with us. If she can get that damned animal out of her system, and all the others too..." He broke off, and Sequoyah thought he could detect a latent savagery there, something rather more than parental disapproval. He was wondering about the painting in the cabin, remembering the fear that was in the eyes. Fear of what? It was the kind of fear that does not easily show, the fear that can be seen only by the discerning eye of an artist, and when you looked at the painting for the second time, it had gone, and in its place there seemed to be a wide-eyed acceptance of the empty desert that stretched away behind her in Daliesque perspective, reaching back to a horizon that might, or might not, really be there, towards the tiny, meticulously detailed ruin of an ancient splendor a shattered dream? He could not guess.

Christie was saying, misunderstanding his reverie and mocking it: "Are you worried about having a young girl on board, Sequoyah? Don't. Candia knows how to take care of herself, it's her worst fault. She might even be useful to us."

He smiled. "No. I was wondering how she'd find the Middle East. Has she been there before?"

"The Middle East has none of the social graces nowadays, so she hasn't been there. A generation earlier, Candia would have spent her winters in Cairo, Luxor, Alexandria. But now...now it's Nassau, Rome, and Palm Springs, a new generation and a new concept of the graces. Orassia will be good for her."

Still smiling, Sequoyah said: "You sound as though you want to teach her a lesson."

Suddenly, the latent anger had been pushed away to the recesses of the mind. Christie laughed out loud and said:

"Yes, that's what it amounts to, and by God, that's what she needs, a spoiled brat who needs her bottom spanked once in a while to teach her she's not as grown up as she thinks. Twenty-four years old and still a goddam baby. Only...a lesson like that is too easy to run away from, isn't it? Maybe I should take away her allowance and make her stay there. The trouble is, she'd spend two days and no more in examining the problem, and then she'd come up with the right answer; Candia's the kind of girl who'd soon remember the penchant of the Oriental despot for the kind of thing she excels in. She'd trade my money for the luxury of the palace, and that's one thing we can't allow, can we?"

"No, I suppose not. Is it really so luxurious?"

Christie shrugged. "You must have read in the papers, the Shah has just voluntarily cut his personal salary down to twenty million dollars a year. What it was before, God alone knows, but he's not exactly a poor man, and in his palace...it shows. Believe me, it shows."

Sequoyah said carefully, exploring: "I also read about the Awlad Yussef there."

The anger was there again, controlled but ready to be shown if it should be necessary to show it. Christie said casually:

"The Sons of Yussef, I'm surprised you've even heard of them. They're just a handful of agitators, controlled by sources outside the country, and not very well controlled at that. In the Arab states, the pattern's a pretty constant one. The dream of Arab solidarity, an empire stretching from the Persian Gulf to the Atlantic Ocean, with a single ruler, a single government. Trouble is, no one can decide just where that ruler ought to come from. An Egyptian? An Iraqi? A Moroccan? Or a true Arab? That would limit them to a Hashemite, wouldn't it? The Arab world embraces a hundred states, and each one hates the guts of all the others. And, take my word for it, the Awlad Yussef don't even know who they are working for. Some of them think their money comes from Nasser, and some are sure it's from Russia. In actual fact, it's more probably from the Saudis."

"Or the CIA."

Christie threw back his head and laughed loudly. "Or the CIA. You might just have a point there." Serious again, he said: "No, I think we can discount these gentlemen. The Awlad Yussef are too miserably paid and too miserably organized. The Sons of Yussef...and no one seems to be sure who Yussef really is. Or was. I asked for a briefing once, from one of their own committee members. He told me gravely that Yussef was a great national hero who was killed in the seventeenth-century wars with the Yemenis. That would make him Yussef bin Hakara, but Hakara was a Royalist, so the Awlad wouldn't be making much sense if they followed his teachings. The Awlad want the overthrow of the Royal Dynasty; someone has taught them the specious delights of democracy, and they have assumed that it might solve the problem of Orassia's acute poverty."

"And just how strong are they?"

Christie shrugged: "Fortunately, too weak to be any sort of a threat to the Shah."

"And therefore, by association, to us?"

"Exactly. Provided the confidential nature of our mission is clearly understood."

"So it's the Awlad we're hiding from?"

"No. We're hiding, as you choose to put it, from everyone except the Shah, and that might include even his immediate family. The Awlad lack organization and power because they lack money.

21

But the promise of oil revenues might be enough to persuade what the press likes to call 'a foreign power' to invest considerable sums of money in the Awlad's fortunes. It wouldn't beg the first time. So, in case I haven't made the point clearly enough, this undertaking remains a secret undertaking, Sequoyah. From everyone. Not just the Awlad. From everyone."

"You made it clear enough. But you won't be able to hide a vessel like this, not even out there."

"Where we'll be working, we will. And in the capital city, its presence will arouse no comment. It's well known that the Shah and I are personal friends. When we leave Aden, we head for Arkan, which is the capital and principal port... Hell, it's the only port, if that's what we're going to call it. We'll stay a few days at the palace, and then head down the coast on a fishing trip, the best fishing in the Middle East. Drop a hunk of meat on a six-inch hook, and you'll come up with fish the like of which you've never seen. Shark as big as whales, barracuda more than ten feet long, and sting rays you could almost build a house on... Did the charts come in?"

"Yes, they did. I noticed some of them are stamped 'TOP SECRET.'"

"British naval charts. Those are the ones I particularly want to see. Let's take a look at them."

They went down to the chartroom and found Breck poring over a large-scale map of the sandy coastline of Orassia. Christie said to him sourly:

"Hadn't you better be getting over to the airport?" Breck shrugged: "I checked the passenger lists, Mr. Christie. She's not on either of the next two planes."

"You can't be sure. Get over there."

"Yes, sir."

"Did you return Mr. Sequoyah's car?"

"Yes, sir."

"If she's there, bring her straight here. Don't tell her where we're going."

When Breck had gone, Christie shook his head and said: "One of these days I'll get rid of that man." He was shutting the charts, unrolling them, spreading them out, flat on the huge table. He found the one he was looking for and laid the flat of his hand on it, his fingers spread wide. He said:

"Here, this is where we start the soundings. We'll set up a camp on shore, a fishing camp. We'll hunt for shark and put out the story we're after their skins. There's a man in Aden who makes shagreen, and I've promised him a supply of hammerheads, so that's the story. While we're working, some of the men can fish, and we'll send the skins down the coast by dhow, the monsoon is just right for us. Once we leave Arkan, that is our ostensible reason for being there, and no one except the men on board this vessel must ever know anything else."

Sequoyah nodded. "I take it the crew's reliable?"

"They'd better be, they're paid enough to keep their mouths shut."

"I know a couple of outfits that would be interested in you as a matter of automatic principle. Wherever Maxwell Christie goes, there's oil, and if it's not yet been discovered..."

Christie grinned. "If there were only a couple of them...! That's one of the advantages of a vessel like this. It's not only a private oceanographic ship, it's a damn fine yacht too; and everyone knows I spend most of my life on board her."

There was a drumming overhead, the chop-chop-chop of a helicopter, and Christie looked up and frowned. The drumming grew to a roar, and he said angrily: "We're being inspected. Let's get up there."

They hurried on deck, and the helicopter was hovering over them. Christie squinted up at it and snorted, and Sequoyah saw that the door of the hovering craft had been slid back and that an agreeable-looking girl was peering down at them; it was low enough for him to see the long fair hair that was being blown back from her face. It was the girl from the painting, and he heard Christie say: "My daughter, I might have known. Now we're going to have to send for Breck, goddammit."

Sequoyah pointed to the shore. "There he is, he's coming back."

The outboard motor had just reached the wharf; now, making a wide sweep, it was heading back towards the *Abaris*.

Watching, Sequoyah could see that Breck was standing up in it, staring up at the helicopter and waving. He turned his attention back to the girl in the sky above him, and saw her climbing delicately out of the cockpit. She was strapped in a harness, and as someone up there began to winch it down, he heard Christie's sharp intake of breath. She was clutching at the cable with one hand and waving at them with the other, and he saw that she was laughing. He said mildly:

"I hope she knows she's liable to break a leg doing that."

Christie snorted. "She doesn't know anything of the sort, and if she did it wouldn't make one bit of difference. Not to Candia."

The harness swayed dangerously as an air pocket caught the helicopter and brushed it to one side, and then the cable came down with a rush and she was suddenly standing on the deck beside them. She gave him a cursory glance of no more than passing interest, and then her arms were round Christie's neck, hugging him, pulling him tight to her. He heard her say: "You didn't think I'd let you sail without me, did you? Did you get my telegram?" She spoke quickly, all in one breath, rolling two sentences into one. He had the impression of urgency again, the same urgency that her father displayed in his quick, erratic movements.

He stood back and waited, and then Christie disengaged himself gently and said: "I would have given you one more day, just one more. This is Roger Sequoyah, my daughter Candia."

She held out her hand and said, laughing: "I don't know who you are, Roger Sequoyah, but I hope my entrance impressed you."

He said gravely: "It impressed me. I was ready to run for the splints and bandages. Is that your baggage up there?"

The harness was poised above them again, swinging wildly, and three or four brightly covered suitcases were netted to it. She said, looking up at it: "Just the essentials." The line of her throat was smooth as marble.

He wanted to see her eyes, to look for the emotion that he knew must be in them, and suddenly she saw that he was watching her and knew exactly what he was looking for; she held his look, and there was an intimacy there that said it pleased her. Momentarily, her face was grave and only those frightened eyes were alive; but it was not fear now, it was something else, something like an awareness of thoughts which she believed he must be thinking. There was a cool acceptance in them, as though she were noting something he was offering her but putting it away for future reference.

And then, the look had gone, and she was laughing with her father again. Impetuously, Christie took her in his arms once more and kissed her, and then held her out from him and looked at her and said: "You look well." It was a question, and for a moment there was almost a touch of hostility on her face, but she said calmly:

"I'm well, and in good health, and relatively happy."

"Only relatively?"

"Not as happy as I was yesterday, happier than I will be tomorrow. Relatively."

Christie said lightly: "Then we'll have to try and take your mind off whatever it is that's worrying you, won't we?" Before she could reply, he turned to Sequoyah and said: "She's too proud to admit it, but she's running to Papa because it hurts."

He felt uncomfortable because he could sense the beginnings of a fight in the sudden tenseness, and he said nothing, but looked up instead and watched the helicopter wheel away like a dragonfly, keeling over to one side and swooping off quickly, down to the water's surface, almost, then up again so that it seemed to brush the masts of the fishing vessels; he heard an angry fisherman shout in the peculiar Marseilles patois. He heard Candia ask abruptly: "Can I come with you?"

"Of course. I was hoping you would. We're going to Aden."

She brushed it off with a shrug. "Aden. And then Arkan, they told me in Paris."

To his surprise, Christie was smiling gently. "Who told you that, Candia?"

"Oh, I don't know, someone I ran into in the hotel."

"And did he say why?"

"Yes. He told me that too." There was something in her voice that was final, as though that was all there was to it.

But Christie was still smiling. He said: "And you don't approve."

The shrug again. "Why should I not approve? Another book, another picture, every man should have a hobby."

Sequoyah was wondering what the hell they were talking about. Christie put a hand on his shoulder and said, almost gaily: "I made a parental mistake once. I once left this child alone in my cabin and quite forgot her natural curiosity. She found a book I'd put aside for study, not quite the kind of book a young girl ought to read, or even see. That was a long time ago, and ever since then..." He said, mocking: "Do you, too, disapprove of pornography, Sequoyah?"

He said shortly: "No, not particularly. Must serve a purpose of some sort."

Christie was mocking him again: "Oh? And what purpose might that be?"

He hated the trend of the conversation. He said shortly: "If it doesn't you've got to discount... Hell, one way or another, it's been with us a long time, hasn't it? In some circles, it's even gained a sort of...respectability. Doesn't mean a great deal to me because I've never been exposed to it very much, but I'm damned if I'm going to disapprove of it to satisfy so vague a principle as...as current morality."

"A pity. I do. But, without getting into the thorny problem of semantics, there is a difference, you know. A couple coupling...dug up in the ruins of Pompeii, it becomes a priceless masterpiece; in the corner drugstore it brings the vice squad, panting. My books, Sequoyah, are in the former category. The second finest collection of erotica in the world. The finest, of course, by popular consensus, is the one in the Vatican Library, and I suppose that gives us a kind of vicarious respectability."

Needling him, Sequoyah said: "I'm surprised you speak of their collection with so little envy."

But Christie only smiled and said dryly: "They've been collecting longer than I have. Much longer."

He was aware that Candia was watching him again, almost surreptitiously, as though this were a game that she often played, as though this were one of the things, that by past experience, might be a guide for her, a guide to a stranger's character; it was as though her approval of him—or her contempt—hinged on what he would say now. And he could sense that Christie, too, was probing, looking for...for what? *Does he want to know so much about me,* Sequoyah thought, *so soon?* He thought: *the hell with him,* and said: "There's nothing harder to define than pruriency, and I suppose it's a question of quality."

"The courtesan costs more than the street-corner whore, is that what you mean?"

*All right,* Sequoyah thought, *if you like this little game.* He nodded: "Something like that. At least, the courtesan has left her mark on history. And don't forget, it's only recently that an appeal to the sensual appetite has become associated with immorality. There was a time..." He looked at Candia and said to her, rather than to Christie: "The men who carved those statues on the temple porticos in Konarak were highly regarded craftsmen; their philosophies were founded in flesh and blood rather than in tinsel and chromium plate. Just because our morality has changed...I wonder if our values are any greater than theirs were? I doubt it."

Candia said: "Then you must read me some of the poems of...who was it, Advayavajra? The man who wrote: 'Putting aside her robe in the lotus garden... Where the gentle sound of the water came to their ears... She took Duvaji's hand, loving, laid it...'"

Christie interrupted her. He said coolly: "You will have time to interest Mr. Sequoyah in your limited Hindu learning later on. Right now we'd better get you installed."

Breck came up over the side from the launch and Candia turned to him with enthusiasm. Her motion towards him was only half arrested as he put out his hand and said politely: "Miss Christie. It's good to see you again."

When she shook his hand, she said: "You're putting on weight, darling. Daddy isn't making you run as hard as he used to, is he?"

The smile was still there, still only at the mouth. "Just as hard as ever, and it's good for me. And I'm not getting fat."

"Not fat, darling. Just heavy around the paunch."

Christie said irritably: "If we can dispense with the little courtesies, we'll get under way. Shall we? Take her out to sea, Breck. Keep an eye on the depth sounder, we won't have much to spare."

Breck nodded, smiled at Candia, and turned away. She laughed soundlessly.

There was always the feeling there, Sequoyah noted, a feeling of restrained hostility which was made more noticeable by a servant-master relationship; and yet, Breck had neither the manner nor the appearance of a servant. There was something in his reserved stolidity, in his untroubled acceptance of Christie's goading, that was more than a little disturbing. *One day,* he thought, *there's going to be trouble between these two...*

One of the crew came up and took Candia's suitcases, and when they had gone he said to Christie curiously:

"Does that mean the secret's out? Already? If someone in Paris knows what we're doing..."

"Someone in Paris knows what I want him to know, Sequoyah."

When he was over satisfied with himself, Christie always spoke softly, as though making the point of his cleverness more acceptable by underplaying it. He said:

"The Shah has a book that I've long wanted, a book that is as important to Orassia as the Doomsday Book is to England, and one of these days..."

Astonished, Sequoyah said: "The Kandit Oras? I don't believe it..."

"You know about it?"

"Yes, I do, vaguely." Somewhere at the back of his mind a memory was stirring, a not too recent memory. He said slowly: "It must have been ten, twelve years ago, I was in Bahrein with the Standard people, and the whole of the Arabian Peninsula was in an uproar because someone had tried to smuggle the Kandit Oras out of Orassia. I seem to recall it was recovered just as it was leaving the country, on a dhow that was heading for Aden, but meanwhile... Wasn't there a great deal of rioting over it?"

Christie was delighted. He said happily: "The Shah was never really convinced that I wasn't behind that little scheme, but I assure you, I wasn't. It was a French archaeologist named Gramont who had organized a highly paid team in Egypt to get it for him, three men and one woman. He paid them a million dollars plus a considerable sum in expenses, and they took eight months to get their hands on the book, and then...the woman betrayed them at the last moment, and if you ask me, it served them right; she was a personal present to the Shah, a Turkish woman who had lived most of her life in Cairo, and she was to live with him as part of his harem until such time as they had their hands on the book, and then..." He laughed shortly. "Then she was to escape, with her accomplices and the Kandit Oras, and return to Gramont, who had meanwhile gone back to Paris; he knew the Arab world wouldn't be safe for him. But the Shah chose to remember her original offense rather than her expiation of it, and decided that the lesson would have to be taught... I understand she was a woman of remarkable sexual capacity, and it's a pity, isn't it? She was executed along with the others, all four of them, publicly beheaded in the compound outside the Shah's Palace in Arkan. The story is that she fell in love with the Shah's son, that this was the reason for her betrayal, but the Shah chose to believe that she reneged on them because she was afraid she wouldn't get her share of the money."

"Four people executed? Over a book?"

Christie said sardonically: "Four people? More than eight hundred were killed in the rioting."

"For God's sake, over a book?"

"Not a book, an institution. The Kandit Oras is the original manuscript of Raidan el Darrah, the philosopher-poet who died at the age of a hundred and eighteen, on June 7, 632, the same day that the Prophet Mohamed died. In fact, el Darrah was a close relative of Abu Talib, who was the Prophet's uncle and tutor. He was not only a philosopher, but a warrior too, and when the Abyssinian King Elsebaan was overrunning Arabia and forcing Christianity on the Homerite Empire, el Darrah led his men to the coastal oasis which is now the city of Arkan and held out there against all comers—not only against the Abyssinians, but the Persians as well. And when the Persians overran the Peninsula and secured the principal ports, el Darrah still held out, and the state of Orassia was born. Now he is regarded as more of a god than a man. June the seventh begins a national holiday, and the entire philosophy of the country's ruling classes is founded on el Darrah's teachings, which were set down in thirteen volumes..." Christie sighed. He said again: "Thirteen volumes! Can you imagine the value of them if they were still extant today? But they were all destroyed in the wars of the sixth and seventh centuries, with one exception—the Kandit Oras. And that survived only because of its erotic theme. An obscure panderer to the

Arabian Prince Muhandali who glorified himself by the title of Head Eunuch found it in the burning palace and took it to his master for his stimulation. It is said that it was el Darrah himself who led a small party of men in a raid on Muhandali's camp and put every man there to the sword, except Muhandali, and him...el Darrah drove an iron spear shaft into his body, and lit a charcoal fire over the other end of it, and at last Muhandali told him where the book was hidden, and it was recovered."

His eyes were gleaming, and somehow the sight discomforted Sequoyah. But he listened, fascinated. Christie went on:

"It was stolen again by a raiding group of pagan Gallas in the fifteen-hundreds, passed into the hands of the Turks, then the Portuguese, and finally a zealous Christian missionary seized it and tried to take it to Rome... I'm happy to say he got his come-uppance too when his dhow was sunk, fortuitously, less than a mile offshore— off the Orassian shore, and if that isn't poetic justice, I don't know what is. It had been out of the country for less than six months. Ever since, it's more closely guarded than the crown jewels in the Tower of London."

Sequoyah leaned on the rail and watched the pointed sails of the fishing boats in the harbor dropping back behind them; the ten o'clock excursion boat to the Château d'If was just heading out to sea, more than an hour late, crowded with gaudily dressed tourists. Christie stood beside him, watching the land recede, watching the green and the gray of the hills and the tree-lined sweep of the coastal road where the cars raced on their way out of town, heading for the tiny villages of Provence; the sound of a klaxon came clearly to them over the water. He turned to Christie and said:

"You really hope to get this book?"

"One day, perhaps. In Paris they think I'm after it now, because that's the story I allowed to get around. That's why it's safe, even watched as I am, for us to go there. No one in the civilized world is likely to believe that we're really fishing. But they will believe that I'm after the Kandit Oras again. Under a cover story, a cover story."

Sequoyah was troubled. He said slowly: "Do you mean you are going to steal it?"

"No. I am not a thief, Sequoyah."

30

"Seems to me it's the only way you'll get it."

"Maybe," Christie said moodily. "For twenty years I've dreamed of acquiring that book, but perhaps... I don't know, perhaps I'd be satisfied with just a look at it. If it came to a showdown, if I actually saw it in front of me, could touch its pages, smell the scent of the parchment, wonder over it for a while... I don't know. We never really know how much we need a thing till we get our hands on it, and then, like a demanding woman, it can sometimes be too much to bear. I just don't know..." He broke off, frowning, worried.

"You've never seen it?"

Christie began to laugh. "Never! Three times I've begged the Shah to show it to me, but he's afraid that the sight of it will be more than I can tolerate and maintain my honesty, and to give him his due, perhaps he's right. But this time... This time, Sequoyah, he needs me. And this time..."

"Do you read Arabic?"

Christie sighed. "I wish I did, if for that and nothing else. Parts of it were translated into French about four hundred years ago, a group of poems that tell the story of the God-King Dvandusi and his nine favorite concubines, each of whom was ordered, on pain of death, to keep him sexually stimulated over a twenty-four hour period; each stanza recounts in great detail the methods these women chose to use, and there's a comment there, either on their ability or on their desire to stay alive, in the fact that only one of these women lost her life. The last one. Seems hardly fair, really. In my collection, I have the French translation and a version in English that was made by an anonymous Hindu. One of these days I'll let you see it." Frowning, he said: "This was the item that Candia stumbled on that day."

Breck came up the companionway and he was grinning. He said cheerfully: "We're over the bar with nearly three feet to spare, just as you said."

"Good. Set your course at forty-eight. We'll head for Punta Caprara and go through Bonifacio."

"Yes, sir."

"Give the skipper my compliments and tell him I said to push her a little. I want to reach the canal on Friday."

The noise from the shore was diminishing, and the sounds of

31

the wheeling gulls came to them over the rush of the water and the steady thrum of the engines. And when midday came and the sun was hot on their faces, the shoreline was faint and obscure, half-hidden in a gray haze, and ahead of them there was nothing but open sea, bright blue and topped with the white of the breakers.

Down on the lower deck, a French seaman was singing a gentle air as he slopped his mop around, and the melancholy words came to him over the screech of the gulls: *Nous n'irons plus an bois, les lauriers sont coupés... No more we'll go to the woods, the laurels have been cut down...*

Sequoyah looked over the taffrail to see who was singing, and there was Candia, coming up on deck in a bright yellow bikini and an open robe flopping around her long legs, her hair hanging loosely down over her shoulders. She looked back towards the sound of the singing, then turned again and waved when she saw him, and when he waved back she called out:

"Are you doing anything?"

He called back to her: "Nothing that can't wait."

"Then come and sit with me." When she approached, she looked back to the singing sailor and said, laughing: "You know the song?"

He nodded. "Vaguely. A nursery rhyme."

"Grist for your argument."

"How's that?"

"If you know its significance. The respectable pornography you spoke of. The laurels they cut down were the laurel twigs on the doors of the brothels, which were ripped off when Louis the Fourteenth shipped all the whores off to Quebec as wives for the settlers there. As you say, today...a nursery rhyme."

Sequoyah laughed. "I find it extraordinary that anyone should even know a thing like that."

"I'm full of useless bits of knowledge. Now come and join me in a sun bath."

"Give me half an hour first? A couple of things I should see to..."

Behind him Christie said: "Another thing you'd better know, Sequoyah. She'll hound you till she gets her own way. Better give in to her, it saves a lot of trouble."

"There's the diving gear to check out..."

"Breck can see to it. And we've time on our hands, six days at the least."

Candia was standing there looking up at him, waiting. He called down to her: "Then five minutes to get into something cooler."

"And tell the steward to bring some drinks!"

He nodded to her and went down to his cabin to change into a bathing costume, and when he returned she was stretched out on a bath towel, wearing huge sunglasses while she rubbed lotion over her shoulders. She took off her glasses to look him up and down for a long time while he stood there, and she said at last, admiringly: "You keep yourself very fit, Roger Sequoyah."

She patted the towel beside her, handed him the lotion, and said: "Sit close beside me. You can do my back for me." She put back her glasses and rolled over onto her stomach, then reached behind her with one hand and flipped open the catch on the top half of her bikini. He poured a little oil into the hollow at the small of her back, and gently began to rub it over the smooth skin.

He could almost hear her purring.

# CHAPTER 3

THE SKIPPER was pushing her indeed. The well-raked, rounded stern cut its way into the waves and threw up a white spray which the wind hurled back over the bow; it fell on them from time to time in refreshing drops, and when the ship rolled heavily, Candia sat up and twisted round to face him.

She said irrelevantly: "You know about welded plates?"

Surprised, Roger said: "Good God no! Should I?"

"It's a point of honor with Father. When he bought the *Abaris*, it was a cargo boat, a tramp, and a bit of a wreck too, but it was exactly what he wanted except for the speed. So he had all the rivets taken out and the plates welded, it put the service speed up from twelve to fourteen knots, and then he had fifteen-foot fins fitted to the propeller boss, which gave him another half a knot, and a few other odds and ends which only the shipbuilders know about gave him another half. Now she does fifteen under normal circumstances, and for the first day or two out he always does the same thing—pushes her. Eighteen and a half is his maximum so far, and he's trying to break the twenty, a point of honor."

"She's a fine-looking ship."

"Uh-huh. He likes a little luxury around him."

"Any idiot can be uncomfortable. It's the easiest thing in the world."

"I suppose so." Candia lay down on her back and he sat up to look at her, surreptitiously admiring the tight line of her stomach. She said casually: "What are we really going to Arkan for?"

The question made him uncomfortable, and he said lightly: "Fishing, book-hunting, there are a dozen stories, take your pick of them."

"Fine I will. Just tell me what you're doing on board? For the sharks? Or the pornography?"

"I'd rather talk about you. What are you doing on board?"

Her shoulders moved ever so slightly. "Oh...I had an affair going, and Father broke it up. He's always doing that. So it seemed the natural thing to do, on both counts. When a girl's in trouble she runs home, didn't you know? And when you're hurt, you run to the man who hurt you, right?"

"Isn't that a bit involved?"

"But at least I've changed the subject for you." She said airily: "He'll tell me why we're going there, of course. I just wondered if you would."

"I'm an employee, nothing more. It wouldn't be right, would it?"

"Not if it's a secret."

"Not a secret... I just have to respect his confidences."

She twisted onto her side and moved the brassiere a shade. As though dismissing the subject, she said: "You're a bit of a bloody prude, aren't you, darling, but we'll soon change all that. I'm getting hungry, what time is it?"

"One o'clock."

"Two bells."

"Is it? I don't even know port from starboard."

"So you're not a fisherman."

"No, I'm not."

Sequoyah turned at a sound behind him and Christie was there. He had changed into white slacks and a blue blazer, and he said cheerfully:

"No, he's an oil man, like me, only perhaps a little better."

Candia said blithely: "I was pumping him, but he won't tell me a thing."

"I admire your discretion, Mr. Sequoyah." He squatted down on his heels beside them and said: "There's nothing you need not know. Sooner or later, everyone on board will know precisely what we're up to. And I didn't get a chance to tell you, my dear. You're looking extremely beautiful."

"Well, thank you, Father. When are we eating?"

"Now, if you're ready."

Sequoyah got to his feet. "In that case, I'd better change. I feel guilty, sitting around in a bathing costume in the middle of the day, it doesn't seem right."

"That's because you work too hard," Christie said. "But we've six days of nothing to do ahead of us, so enjoy yourself."

"If you'll excuse me..."

When he walked away, he was conscious that they were both looking after him, father and daughter. And later, when they were sitting at the table in the long sycamore-paneled dining room, he knew that they had been talking about him, a long, heart-to-heart talk; and somehow, the knowledge left him faintly disturbed. It seemed to him, too, that Christie, once he had made the cursory introductions to the ship's officers, was ignoring him, but he shrugged it off and chatted instead with the captain, an elderly, waspish man whose name was Hewitt, and with the first mate, a quiet and scholarly-looking man who seemed a little out of place here. His name was Merrick. Making conversation, he asked:

"You know the waters of the Arabian Peninsula, Captain Hewitt?"

"Yes, Mr. Sequoyah, I know them. They're mighty interesting waters. Provided you can keep off the sandbars, and that's not always easy. Our charts are never up to date. Every time the monsoon blows, they shift, first one way and then the other. We've a draft of twenty-five feet, and we can't always get in as close as we'd like."

Candia said: "I hope the swimming's good." She had put on a lowered wrap-around skirt and halter-top over her bikini, and her skin was shining.

The captain's eyebrows shot up and he looked at her quickly and brandished his knife at her. "But you need a better knife than this, Miss Christie. Sharks. Barracuda. Have you ever met a barracuda in the water?"

"No, I haven't, thank God. Only on a plate, covered over with parsley and slices of lemon. That's not quite the same thing, is it?"

"Keep a good knife in your belt and you'll be all right. If you know how to use it. I hooked a forty-foot shark there once, foul-hooked him in the tail, and he broke my two-hundred-pound line... Forty feet, that's a lot of fish."

Merrick said didactically: "The fossil remains of the Carcharodon, which was a type of shark, show that they once must have been as much as ninety feet long."

"Aye, and if you go deep enough in the gulf, you'll probably still find them roaming about down there. So, if you want to swim— keep close in shore and you'll be all right. Maybe."

Candia said clearly: "My late fiancé, Luther Fenton, was a great fisherman. The best deep-sea man in the Bahamas."

Hewitt was about to say something, looked quickly at Christie instead, and kept quiet. There was a little silence, and then Christie said:

"Your late fiancé, as you chose to call him, was an idiot. Have some more wine and shut up about him."

Watching, Sequoyah saw the color come to Candia's cheeks. Reaching for the wine, she said:

"It takes one to know one, I suppose. And in some things, Father, your ignorance is abysmal. He was a good man. Don't make me sorry I left him."

"That was your choice, not mine."

"Yes, after you..." She sighed and sat for a while sipping her drink, and Christie smiled at her and said softly:

"Anything I do, anything I did, *everything* I do...is for your own happiness, Candia. That's all I want. Believe me. When you're older and more mature..."

"Older?" Candia laughed shortly. "I'm twenty-four, and as for my maturity... Shall I put you more completely in the picture?"

"No, I'd rather you didn't." Christie's glance went down the long table, looking at the others; they were paying great attention to their food, seeming, almost, to know what was coming and not welcoming it.

Candia looked at her father and there was a hard look in her eyes. She said: "You reach maturity, if you're a girl, when you're no longer a girl, do I make the point? It's merely a matter of biology..."

Christie's face was furious, and the captain looked up and said quickly: "You'll be pleased to know, Mr. Christie, we were making nineteen knots when I left the bridge. We're getting closer all the time."

Abruptly, Candia pushed aside her plate and stood up. She said coldly: "If you don't mind, I'd like to be excused. I'm not hungry."

Christie did not look at her, but when she had gone he turned to Sequoyah with a smile and said: "I suppose I should go to her, that's what she wants. But if I do... She likes to feel that when she whistles, I run, and I don't like that."

There was not much he could say. Sequoyah nodded briefly, and Merrick said:

"It's none of my business, of course, but I had the feeling when she came aboard that Miss Christie was not her usual self..."

"As you say, Mr. Merrick," Christie said, "it's none of your business." The smile was still there, and he looked at the first mate and said: "You have one thing in common with my daughter. Extreme immaturity."

"Yes, sir. I'm sorry..."

"Forget it." Christie turned away, put a hand on Sequoyah's arm, and said clearly: "Roger, do me a favor, will you? Will you go with her? I have a feeling you'd be good for her."

"A messenger with an olive branch."

"Something like that. Just don't wave it too blatantly."

"I won't have to. I have a feeling she's a very understanding young woman, but if that's what you want..."

"It's what I want."

Sequoyah said lightly: "Well, in that case...that's what you'll get. But first, if you don't mind, I'll finish this excellent lobster. Be a crime to let it get cold, wouldn't it?" He could feel Christie's surprise, and a little later, when the lunch was over, he found Candia back on her towel in the hot sun, lying flat on her back with the straps of her brassiere undone and a handkerchief across her eyes. She pulled aside the handkerchief when she heard him and said:

"Somehow, I didn't think that would be Father. Did he send you to me?"

"Sort of."

38

"Well, wasn't that nice of him?"

Sequoyah sighed and sat down beside her. "You are a difficult woman, Candia. And he's right, you know. He is thinking only of your happiness. Maybe he doesn't quite know what that entails, but..." He broke off and grinned at her. "And you were rather goading him, weren't you?"

"And what about you, *Mr.* Sequoyah, do you know what my happiness entails?"

"Your own way, obviously."

She was like an animal at rest, almost purring but ready to strike out at him; he could sense it. She slipped on her dark glasses and said:

"This isn't the first time, you know. Every time I bed down with someone I really like, something goes wrong. And if I bother to try and find out why, somewhere in the background there's that fine Machiavellian hand of his."

"Oh, surely..."

She said impatiently: "You're guessing, you know, unless you really understand him better than I do, and isn't that a bit bloody unlikely? He yanked me out of a comfortable, friendly bed..."

"He's your father, after all..."

She said disgustedly: "Oh, for Christ's sake, you think he minds if I get laid once in a while, of course he doesn't..." She broke off and laughed and said: "Where are you from, Roger?"

"From Oklahoma, and we're off the track again."

"Well, that accounts for it..." He felt a touch of impatience with her and she sighed and said: "No, he doesn't mind *that,* he's just afraid of...of a permanent liaison with a man he thinks isn't good enough for me. The old fashioned marriage mart, new style..."

"Surely that's his privilege..."

"But the *way* he does it! He never does anything openly always behind the scenes, pulling strings... Let me tell you what really happened. Luther Fenton isn't a rich man not by our standards, but he makes out all right, and for nearly a year we were very happy together. He's good company, alert, not overly-intelligent but amusing... He had a little trouble over some shares he'd bought, sixty or seventy thousand dollars' worth that turned out to be useless because the company was on the verge of bankruptcy. He'd bought them on margin, and the broker was after him for the money, which he hadn't got, and I was all set to lend it to him. I could have gotten it from Father easily enough, but I was too late, Father got there first. The bankrupt company suddenly merged with one of the minor Christie companies, and the shares shot up again and turned Luther's seventy thousand loss into an overnight profit of just double that, with Luther Fenton as a newly appointed comptroller... And then..."

She laughed shortly and fell silent. Sequoyah said awkwardly:

"Well, that was just a helping hand, surely..."

"The merger cost Father a fortune, but he could spare it, and Luther was suddenly... too busy to see me. He flew to New York for a few days, and at the end of the month I followed him to find out what the hell he was up to. Oh, he was frank enough. He told me...Father had put him back on his feet in exchange for a promise, it was as simple as that. My lover boy said—'We've had a good time, baby, let's call it a day.'"

"Then he was right, wasn't he? Your father. If you'd married a man who was prepared to leave you like that..."

"Who the hell said anything about marriage?"

"I see."

"I wonder if you do. He just...bought him, the same way he'll buy you, if you don't watch out." She sat up with one hand to her breast and turned her back to him. "Fix my bra, will you?"

He clipped the fastener for her, and she slewed round to face him and the sun, her long thighs apart and her heels tucked under her rump, and she sighed and said: "Well, perhaps it's all for the best. I suppose Luther's not the only pebble on the goddam beach." She slipped off her dark glasses again and held his look; again, he was reminded of the fear in the portrait's eyes, and he could find no trace of it now, and she said, deriding her own discomfort: "I'm a hard woman to please, and what about you? Are you married?"

"No."

"I always suspect an eligible bachelor who's over thirty-five."

"Oh? Of what?"

"Does he like to play the field, or doesn't the field interest him?"

"In this case, it interests him."

"Well, thank God for that. Cooped up on this crate for a couple of weeks..."

He smiled at her and said: "Is that a promise?"

"Call it window shopping." Without any conscious attempt to change the subject, she asked: "What kind of a Place is Orassia? Is it going to be a bit dull?"

"Dull? That depends on what you're looking for, doesn't it? There might not be much for you to do there, outside of the capital."

"The capital. Fifty Bedouin in tents."

"No, I don't think so. I've never been there, but it's part of the oil basin that every oilman knows fairly well. There's oil under every inch of the Middle East, more or less, and there's always the hope that each new drilling will find a way into it. Orassia's one of the places where a few exploratory holes were drilled some ten years ago, with no results, but the conclusions of the survey crews are always subject to re-examination. Your father has re-examined them and... Well, he thinks the Shah's belief might just be right."

"That wasn't precisely what I asked, darling."

"Oh." Sequoyah spread his hands hopelessly. "What can I tell you about a place I've never seen? It's on the junction of the Gulf of Aden and the Arabian Sea, a little bit off the beaten track because the main caravan route in the old days was further to the west, along the coast of the Red Sea and across to the Somalia...or else further to the east and across the Gulf of Oman to India and Persia. Along the coast, I suppose, there will be villages, wherever there's a riverbed that might supply water once in a while, but inland...inland, there's nothing but what the Arabs call the Rub el Khalil, which is another way of saying the empty quarter of Arabia. A few oasis, here and there..."

"Dashing sheikhs on white chargers..."

"They mostly ride donkeys or camels, and they're mostly not quite so romantic. There'll be a few date palms, some figs perhaps, a little wild corn growing, a hell of a lot of cactus, and for the rest...as much sand as you'll be able to stomach. When there's a sandstorm, which is pretty often, your only refuge from it is in the water. It gets into your eyes, your nose, your mouth, your hair... You can't hide from it and you can't escape it. It's not very pleasant, a layer of fine

41

sand over everything you touch, over everything you eat..."

"Good God, you paint a marvelous picture."

He grinned at her quickly. "In this business, you get to take it, even not to mind it too much. But if we're living on board I don't imagine it will be too bad. We can always put out to sea for a few miles. I hope." He looked at her curiously and asked: "What made you decide to come, Candia? I mean...there must be plenty of other places you could go to get away from...from any unpleasant memories..."

She raised an elegant shoulder, shrugging off the question, and said nothing.

The land was out of sight now, and the gulls had gone, and the only sound was the rush of the water. He waited a long time, and then said gently:

"May I ask you a rather personal question?"

She looked at him quickly, and he fancied that had she been a cat, the hair at the back of her head would have begun to rise; he almost decided not to ask it, but she was waiting, slipping off her glasses again in a reflex that he found a little disturbing, as though she wanted to read in his face any nuance there might be in his voice, his manner, even in his silence. He said hesitantly:

"There's a portrait of you in the main cabin..."

She laughed. "Oh, that..."

"I thought there was a touch of fear in the eyes, the kind of fear that only a skilled and discerning artist might see. Was I wrong?"

"Yes. You were wrong." She was still smiling. "For fear, read bewilderment. That was a time in my life, one of the many times, when I just didn't know which way to turn. I'd run home again, part of a pattern, and for a while I'd thought I'd stay, stay with Father. My mother died, ten years ago, did you know that?"

"No."

"And Father was left with the job of bringing me up, and for a busy man I suppose that isn't very easy. It was mostly schools and governesses, and long holidays with relatives, and occasional trips all over the goddam world to see what scheme was currently occupying the attentions of the...the rather distant tycoon who was my father. He was always so goddam *busy,* but somehow I always had the feeling that when things got tough I could go to him. And I could, too. He was always there with advice, and with money, and with...with a certain amount of love, I suppose, Christie style. But he never stopped work long enough to let the help settle down. He'd tell me what to do and then get the hell out of there, fast. And, when that portrait was painted, I was thinking: *this is what he wants, an image of me rather than the real thing, something he can carry with him and ignore without complaint when the pressure of other things gets too strong.* It was an alarming thought, a bewildering thought, and I was convinced as I could be that I was right. Bewilderment, that's the key word."

"And now...you still think that?"

"I don't know." She turned away from him then and lay down in the sun again, stretching out her long legs and touching the tight flesh at her waist, as though assuring herself of its excellence. She said, mocking him: "There's a lot about me that's really quite desirable; but you're getting to know the wrong things, aren't you?"

He protested. "I don't think so..."

"Presupposing an intimacy you haven't really earned, not yet."

He looked at her soberly for a while, and when she fumbled in the straw bag that was beside her, he took out a cigarette from the fancy gold case and lit it for her, and she grimaced and said:

"Only gold, it's part of the pattern too." She smoked in silence for a while, and then tossed the cigarette away impatiently and let it lie, still burning, on the deck; he went over and put his foot on it and then threw it over the side. He heard her, behind him, say: "You're a careful man, Roger Sequoyah. I don't think I like that."

Leaning with his back to the white rail, he turned to face her. "A fire at sea, is that what you want?"

"It takes more than a cigarette to start a fire on board this ship. You have an aptitude for putting out fires, Roger Sequoyah, don't you?" When he said nothing, she said coldly: "Next time you come to sit with me, come of your own volition."

He was surprised at the hurt in her voice. He said: "Hey, wait a minute."

"All right, I suppose that was unkind. Come over here."

He crouched down beside her again, squatting on his heels, and she reached up and pulled him down to her and kissed him on the lips;

he felt the tip of her tongue touching his teeth. He lost his balance and fell across her, catching his elbow on the deck so that the tingle ran up to his humerus bone and down to his little finger, and he could feel the angle of her hipbone pressing into his ribs. She was laughing again, laughing at his discomfort, and he said, not quite chiding her:

"You're full of surprises today."

"So get off my tummy."

As he struggled to right himself, a button of his jacket caught in the top of her bathing costume, and she watched, amused, while he tried to free it, not offering to help him, but laughing at him all the time and lying there still while his fingers probed. She said:

"Are you always so awkward?"

"Only when people throw things like that at me."

"But you like?"

"I like."

"Good. So go and make your report to Papa, tell him I'm in a good humor and there's no cause for him to worry. And, when you come back, come back because you want to, not because he sends you."

"All right, I will. If I can get this damned button out of the way." Her skin under his knuckles was soft and resilient, warm to the touch. He felt her fingers touching his, and then the button was free, and he stood up and smiled down at her and said: "I'll be back."

He went back to the dining salon, and only Christie was there, smoking and sitting silently at the head of the table. Sequoyah said:

"She said to tell you she's in a good humor, although I suspect there's a little anger left over. Not very much."

Christie came out of his dream. "What? Oh, Candia... Yes, well... Good." He pushed back his chair and stood up, and said: "I think we'd better check over that sounding gear, you and I. Breck reported a malfunction when he tested it this morning."

"Oh?"

"And there's a bundle of aerial photographs I want you to see, the coast of Orassia."

"All right."

"And then I want you to map out the most likely places for diving. Can you use a scuba kit?"

"Sure."

"Good. We'll survey an eighty-mile stretch of the coast between Ras Hashim and Jebel Qusair, and I'd like you to look out the most promising places." He thumped Sequoyah heartily on the back and said: "That ought to keep you out of mischief for a couple of days."

When they went up to the chartroom, Sequoyah looked out and saw that Candia was gone. And he was conscious that Christie, half smiling, had seen his quick look at the quarter-deck.

The smile reminded him of a word Candia had used: Machiavellian.

# CHAPTER 4

THE SUEZ CANAL was far behind them, and the *Abaris* was heading on a southeasterly course down the Red Sea, its Doxfords pushing it effortlessly along the smooth surface of the water at more than sixteen knots, before Christie raised a point that had somehow (perhaps needlessly, Sequoyah thought) troubled him ever since they had left Marseilles.

The heat was intense. It struck down at them from the burning sky and was reflected up from the water, seeming to be made even hotter in its reflection; there was not a breath of wind, and the sweat was running in rivulets down his bare chest. The thermometer at the bridge indicated a hundred and nineteen.

A few thousand yards on their starboard bow, a small island of sand, treeless and gleaming white in the hot sun, pushed the flat dome of its surface out of the bright blue of the sea, and a small group of dark-skinned men were standing there, waving at them; faintly, they could hear their shouts. They looked almost naked, and when Christie came and stood beside him at the rail, watching, he said:

"They still do it, even today. The twentieth century, by God."

Sequoyah turned to look at him, to watch the expression of scorn on Christie's face. "Do what?"

"Maroon them. A dhow going north to Mecca, they pick up a crew of somalis in Berbera, and when they get close enough to Jedda, they dump them on an offshore island. It's cheaper than paying their wages."

The tiny island looked fragile, almost a mirage, the heat

shimmering above it as though at any moment it would sink below the water or dissolve in the flame of the reflected sun. He thought of the saline water round it, and of the salt-laden air that would drive a thirsty man out of his mind with fear and desperation, and he said:

"We're picking them up, surely?"

Christie shrugged. "You don't know these people as well as I do. The moment the dhow arrived in Jedda, the Arab skipper told the harbor master he'd seen a group of marooned men on an island... The harbor master knows damn well the skipper put them there, and knows, too, that a dhow master can claim he can't stop if the wind is dropping. So he'll pay the old fox twenty rials for the information, and a boat will go out to pick them up. But by that time, the dhow master will have unloaded his pilgrims, and will be on his way to Suez with a load of carpets. Custom, Roger, as old as the hills."

"I would have thought the Somalis would have caught onto it by now."

"But they have, indeed they have. But if you tell a Somali you'll take him to Mecca, and promise him a hundred shillings as well, he'll sail you anywhere in the world, even knowing what's likely to happen to him, because it happened to his father, his brother, and all his goddam cousins as well. But every Somali automatically thinks he's smarter than the next man, so he knows it can't happen to him..."

Roger watched the men for a while with his binoculars. They wore only loin-cloths round their skinny waists. One of them was quite naked; he had taken off his cloth and was waving it furiously at them. He heard Christie say: "Don't worry about them, they'll be picked up. In any case, Breck's on the radio now, calling Jedda." And then came the scrutiny. Without changing his tone of voice, Christie said: "I had a long talk with Candia this morning."

The non sequitur startled him. He was angry with himself for the moment of apprehension that came over him, but he put away the binoculars and said casually:

"Yes? Is she enjoying the trip?"

Christie said: "She's having a ball."

"Good." Roger waited, thinking he knew what was coming and telling himself: What the hell, my conscience is clear... Christie put a hand on his shoulder in a gesture that was almost fatherly, and said, very quietly:

"The hot weather's not good for her. She lies in the sun all day and lets it burn her up."

Roger frowned. "Oh? With a tan like that, the sun won't do her any damage."

He could visualize her now, her long, long legs stretched out, deep gold against the bright colors of her towels, a different bathing costume every day, her skin turning darker and more silky as the days went by, till it was shining brown like the skin of those men out there on the island. Sometimes the globules of her sweat would form at the deep V between her breasts, and she would wipe at them with a towel, casually, seeming always to watch him if he were there beside her. Behind her dark glasses, the startling blue eyes were hidden, and somehow they discomforted him.

Christie said: "I was thinking of what's inside her."

Roger looked away and said: "Fenton? You think he's still...upsetting her?"

"Somebody is. Although I don't think upsetting is the right word."

He wondered if Christie was asking him a question, and decided he was. He said lightly: "My behavior towards her has been immaculate, if that's what you mean."

Christie was smiling. "You're a step or two ahead of me, but I suppose I would have phrased the question sooner or later."

Roger said shortly: "Well, there's the answer if you ever want to be more precise," He looked at Christie curiously and said: "If that's what you thought...you don't seem particularly worried. Or is that my imagination?"

"Put your imagination to better work, Roger. We're the kind of family, Candia and I, you probably haven't much experience of. The acceptance of money and its uses, the knowledge of its power...these things are as much a part of heredity as freckles or a bad temper."

"Now you're ahead of me, Mr. Christie. Way ahead."

"It's because of hereditary money that Candia has never learned the blatant lie that there are some things that can't be bought."

"If you've brought her up to believe that that *is* a lie..."

Christie said quickly: "Oh, but I haven't. On the contrary, I've

48

tried to teach her that it's a truth, even though I don't believe it myself." He leaned over the rail and stared down at the sea. A school of porpoise were curving rhythmically in and out of the water close by the hull, waiting for the daily garbage. He said moodily: "A parent sometimes has to teach his children things he doesn't believe in, if only because he is conscious of the damage his own cynicism has done to him. You still tell a small child that there's a Santa Claus, and it's not wrong, but when the time comes for the child's first doubts...then you find that something charming has gone. It's the beginning of cynicism, a beginning of the understanding that the world is not quite the place you once thought it to be."

"Candia's a long way past the Santa Claus stage."

"Yes, she is. And her first understanding was something that I tried hard not to teach her, not to let her even learn by herself. Her first understanding was that Daddy's money will buy her any toy she wants, even if the toy is..." He broke off and looked at Roger, and said: "Fenton was a toy. I bought it, and broke it so that she couldn't play with it any longer when I found out it was bad for her. So now, a little bewildered, even though it's not the first time I've broken her harmful toys, she is wondering why I don't buy her another. Or why she can't buy one herself. Maybe one of us should...I don't know."

He knew very well what was on Christie's mind, but he grinned, masking his knowledge, and said: "I wish I knew what the hell you were saying."

The smile did not leave Christie's face. He said softly: "I think you do know. And don't try to hide your intelligence from me, young man, I had the measure of it an hour after we'd first met."

Roger was about to answer, and the answer would have been close to anger, but he saw Christie look up over his head, and Candia was there, standing on the deck above them and looking down, her terry cloth wrap thrown loosely over her shoulders. She turned away and came down the companionway towards them, and she put an affectionate arm round Roger's waist and leaned with him over the side, and looked at the porpoises and said:

"All they want out of life is a little garbage." It was a comment directed at her father.

Christie turned on his heel and stalked away without a word.

Candia watched him go and said:

"Well, now you know, don't you?"

Roger turned to look her full in the face. He wanted to maintain his anger, but when she slipped out of the yellow bathrobe and dropped it on the rail, he looked at her long enough, instead, to know that anger was the wrong emotion. He put both his hands at her waist, his thumbs touching the points of her hips, and said:

"Must I tell you the same thing? That I wish I knew what the hell you were talking about?"

She reached up and kissed him on the mouth, quite slowly and easily, as though it were the most natural thing in the world. To his surprise, he found himself wondering about the quick, lithe movement of the ankles that had pushed her body up then let it drop back again, and then she held him by the upper arms and arched her spine back and said:

"When I know you better, I hope I'll know when you're being deliberately obtuse, and when you're just being bloody naive." She said clearly: "My old-fashioned father has just given you permission to make love to me, just in case you need his okay. Good-hearted bastard, isn't he?"

As he stared at her, a gust of wind lifted the bathrobe off the rail and sent it floating down to the water. He made an unconscious gesture to reach for it, but she tugged at his arm and said:

"If he caught you at it, he'd feel obliged to horsewhip you, or something, but take my word for it, darling, that's what he's just done. He feels he's planted an idea in your mind, an idea that would never have occurred to you, and I hope you think it's a good one. Now come and oil my back for me."

She walked away, and he sighed to himself and then followed her, obediently, up the companionway to the deck above where she had heard his conversation with her father. She lay down on her stomach on the bright red towel that was spread out there, and she slipped the catch of her bathing dress top, and rested her head on her arms, and waited for him to go to work. He took the bottle of oil and began to rub it, automatically and in silence, into her golden skin.

He heard someone coming up the ladder and turned to look, and Breck was there, his eyes sullen and angry. He stared at them for a moment and then said: "Your father was asking if there were anything you wanted, Candia."

Without looking at him, Candia said casually: "If that's true, just tell him I don't want to be disturbed right now, will you?"

Roger could feel the anger; he saw the sudden tightening of the muscles on the hard, enigmatic face. And then Breck turned on his heels and was gone. He began to wonder about Breck.

Later that evening, long after the sun had gone down and the brightly lighted ship was a silent ghost cutting sharply through the dark waters, he was pacing the upper deck, with his head sunk on his chest and his hands thrust deep into his pockets, frowning, piecing together the essential extracts of the seismological reports he had been studying, feeling more and more sure, as the time went by, that he knew exactly where to start the drilling and yet forcing upon himself a caution that he knew, from long experience, was necessary. He began to compose, mentally, a cable to the Paleographic Institute in Johannesburg: "*Request structure contour details of 1957 Leborg Survey, with detailed reflection shooting report...*" and began to make his way to the radio cabin.

His rubber-soled shoes made no sound on the deck, and he paused for a moment with his hand on the latch, wondering about security, knowing it might not be wise to alert the Institute of their area of interest, and he shrugged and turned away, meaning to talk to Christie about it. And then, from inside the cabin, there was a sudden, startling sound, the sound of a blow followed by the crash of breaking furniture. He swung round and ran back and threw open the door, and the movement there froze, a moment of violence arrested by his appearance.

Breck was standing in the cabin, white with fury, and across the other side of the room a big, burly man in a dark blue sweatshirt was lying across a table on his back, his arms thrust out as though to help his balance; there was a cut across his mouth and the blood was seeping from it. It was Tagos, the big Greek.

Roger said: "Hey, what the hell..." and then the Greek was suddenly on his feet again, moving with the astonishing speed of the overweight athlete, hurling himself on Breck with his powerful arms flailing. He saw Breck sidestep neatly and bring his fist down across

51

Tagos' neck, and the Greek slithered across the floor again and crashed into the steel cupboard where the codes were kept. For a brief second he blinked the pain out of his eyes and shook his head, and then he looked at Breck savagely and said: "Your own mother, you bastard."

There was a moment of silence, and then he said again, clearly and coolly: "Bastard." He lay on the floor, not moving, waiting.

Breck's face was white. He walked over to him, leaned down as though to pick him up, and Roger saw the Greek's right hand shoot out, the thumb extended, jabbing it viciously at Breck's eye; he saw Breck swing away from the unexpected blow and lose his balance, and then Tagos was on top of him, driving his huge fist repeatedly into his throat, one hand grabbing a handful of hair and the other working like a sledge hammer.

Roger stepped forward, slipped a forearm under the Greek's chin, and lugged him back, feeling the massive weight of the man and swinging him bodily across the room, then stepping lightly round to meet him should he come back; there was a conscious effort to drive away the fear, just a moment of it, and then he was ready...

But Tagos climbed to his feet heavily and wiped at the blood on his mouth, and Breck stood up again and said angrily: "I can handle him, keep out of it."

Roger said coldly: "I won't keep out of it, what the hell do you think you're trying to do, a couple of kids..."

For a moment, no one spoke. The two men, both powerful, angry, tense, stood glaring at each other across the intervening space while Roger waited. And then Breck went to the intercom and pushed the button, and when Christie answered, he said shortly: "Tagos, the man we took on in Marseilles..."

Christie's voice over the speaker was sharp: "Well?"

Breck said: "Calindoris put him on board."

There was a brief hesitation at the other end, and then Christie said: "All right, you know what to do. We need to know if there are any more of them."

Breck looked across to Tagos. "No, there aren't any more, I'm sure of it. He's the only replacement."

"All right. And, Breck..."

"Yes, sir?"

"Keep it quiet. No one must know."

Breck said: "Roger Sequoyah is here."

Again, the silence, and then Christie said calmly: "Roger?"

Roger went to the microphone. "I heard a fight, came in to break it up, what's the problem?"

"No problem, Roger, but you'll oblige me by... Well, we'll talk about it later. A family matter, all right?"

Roger shrugged. "All right."

The intercom went dead, and Breck said to Tagos: "You know where the brig is. Get going."

Tagos said sullenly: "I want a word with Christie. Or the skipper."

"After."

Tagos took a deep breath; it was as though he were resigning himself to what lay ahead of him. He turned and went to the door, and before he followed him, Breck looked at Roger with a sour smile and said:

"You heard, didn't you, a family matter? A good idea if this doesn't get spread all over the ship."

Roger shrugged. "I'm not interested."

"Good."

Roger said dryly: "And don't bother to thank me for the help."

Breck was genuinely surprised. He said: "Oh? If that's what you expect...then, thank you for the help. But take my word for it, it wasn't necessary. All you did was...put off the beating he's going to get."

Tagos looked, but said nothing. And when they had gone, Roger straightened up the broken table, looked around and checked the equipment, slipped the catch on the door, and closed it behind him. He was worried, not by the incident itself, but by the knowledge that behind it, hidden from him, there was something intensely perturbing. And he wondered who Calindoris was.

He hung around on deck for a while, wondering, not liking what he had seen, and then he worked for a while in the chartroom, half hoping that Christie would come in and broach the matter, and at last he put away his maps and analyses, and went looking for the brig.

He found it at last, and there was a sailor on guard there, a slight, cheerful Italian he had spoken to once before. He said briefly: "I want to see the prisoner," and the Italian gestured broadly. "*Ma...non é permesso, Signore...* Mr. Breck's orders..."

Roger said angrily: "The hell with Mr. Breck. Let me in."

The guard hesitated. He sighed deeply and raised both his eyebrows and said: "Well...everybody gives orders, *che vita dura...*" He unlocked the door and opened it, and Roger went inside and found Tagos, lying on the bunk with his hands behind his head, staring up at the ceiling. The sight of the man shocked him. There were dark bruises on his cheeks, and a crude white bandage over his ear was soaked in blood; a plaster patch over one eye did not hide the cut across the eyebrow, and the lips were puffed up and split.

He said, horrified: "Good God, what have they done to you?"

To his surprise, Tagos grinned. He said sardonically: "They? Not *they*, Mr. Sequoyah. *Him.* Breck. He throw a good punch." Roger stood looking at him, and as though reading his thoughts, Tagos said: "No, they didn't tie me down to do this, it was a fair fight, he let me...defend myself. Ha! Defend myself! Not a mark on him, he throws a good punch."

Roger said, puzzled: "And I thought you didn't speak English?"

"Ten years in Liverpool, seven in New York Harbor, sure, I speak good English."

"Then you want to tell me what this is all about?"

Tagos grinned and slowly shook his head. He said softly: "Why don't you ask the bastard, Mr. Sequoyah?"

"And who's Calindoris?"

Tagos began to laugh. "Calindoris? Never heard of him. Sounds like a Greek like me, doesn't it? Never heard the name in my life."

Roger turned and went to the door, but Tagos said suddenly: "Hey, if you want to do something for me..."

He turned back. "Well?"

"If you've got a cigarette is all."

He found a pack in his pocket and tossed it to the Greek. Tagos said: "Matches?" Roger gave him a book, looking around the room instinctively as he did so, and Tagos laughed again and said: "No, it's all steel, nothing to burn, but don't worry, just a smoke."

"What will happen to you now?"

Tagos shrugged, lit a cigarette, and drew the smoke into his lungs. He stretched out on the bed comfortably, enjoying himself. He said: "Doesn't matter a damn what they do with me, does it?"

Angrily, Roger stormed out of the brig and went to find Christie.

He came upon him in the main lounge, studying a book and sipping brandy from a wafer-thin goblet. He looked up as Roger came in and said gently: "A glass of brandy, Roger, to take away the sourness. Come and unburden yourself. That look on your face does not become you."

Roger said: "You should see Tagos' face."

"Oh. So that's all it is."

"That's *all* it is."

Christie closed the book he had been reading; Roger saw the illustrated lettering on its blue Morocco cover: *The Slave-Women of the Shah*. Christie went to the cabinet and poured a brandy and said: "You want to know the why and the wherefore, is that it? You think you have the right to know?"

"No, I don't. I just want to know what's going to happen to him."

Christie shrugged. "He'll be put ashore at Aden."

"And the beating?"

Christie said steadily: "A family matter, between him and Breck."

Roger hesitated. He said at last, taking the drink that Christie offered him, making a gesture of it: "I had the feeling that something...very unpleasant was going on. There was a lot...of hatred in the air. And yet when I saw Tagos just now..."

Christie looked up. "You saw him?"

"I went to the brig."

"I see. To satisfy yourself?"

"Yes." He wondered if Christie would object, and he was ready for a quarrel.

But Christie merely smiled and said: "I'll make a small bet with you. Tagos was as cheerful as a man could be, am I right?"

Surprised, Roger said: "Yes, he was, I wondered why."

Christie raised his glass. "Here's to our secrets, Roger. Tagos was a very happy man, because if you hadn't barged in when you did, Breck would undoubtedly have killed him. And now, he can't, it's too late. So you see...a good thing you're on board, isn't it?"

Roger said angrily: "And you don't want to tell me why?"

"No, Roger. I don't. How do you like the brandy?"

Roger sighed. He knew he wouldn't get much further with Christie, not tonight.


Candia came to his cabin in the early hours of the morning.

He had switched off the air conditioner and thrown open the portholes, and he lay on his bunk with a towel round his waist, restlessly turning, half asleep in the darkness, and the slight sound at the door brought him sharply back to wakefulness. He turned and saw that she was standing there in the shaft of moonlight that streamed in, so bright that it was almost like daylight, standing at the door and leaning back into it with her hand still on the cold brass of the doorknob, and he heard her say: "God, it's hot in here, how can you possibly sleep?"

He reached up and flicked the switch, and the gentle hum came to him with a blast of cold air. He found himself speaking very quietly, as though he were part of a conspiracy. "I never liked artificial air."

For a moment or two she did not move. She stood there, looking at him, and said: "Two days to Arkan, I'll be glad to land."

"It's been a good trip, calm seas all the way."

"Too bloody calm."

She came over and sat on the bunk beside him, and he moved a little to make more room for her. He was conscious of his nakedness under the towel. She wore a long brocaded housecoat, closed all the way up to the neck so that not an inch of her body was showing, the tight collar giving her an almost oriental look. She put a hand on his chest, stroking him lightly with the tips of her fingers. She said:

"They say the Shah of Orassia has three hundred concubines and three wives, is that a good combination?"

Roger laughed. "It's a good way to open a conversation. As a

Muslim, he's allowed four wives, what happened to the other one?"

The fingers on his chest were still exploring. She said:

"Breck told me. He keeps only three so that if he meets a girl he particularly fancies for a wife, he can marry her at once, without waiting the few hours a divorce would take. They have to say, three times, and in front of witnesses 'I divorce you...' and that's the end of it. Did you know that? To say it once, Breck says, it could be in anger; twice even, but three times...that guarantees they really mean it. So, with only three on the roster, he can marry his fourth wife without unnecessary delay, and promptly divorce the oldest to make room on the establishment once more. A smart boy."

"With three hundred concubines, he shouldn't have to worry too much about how many wives he has."

"Purely for the benefit of politics. The daughter of a not-so-friendly chief, a marriage to cement an alliance...that's what wives are for, isn't it?"

"If you have three hundred concubines. I never did. I was too poor."

"Do I hear a touch of disapproval behind your levity?"

Roger shrugged. "Good luck to him. It seems tough on the poor girls."

She leaned down and kissed him gently, on the lips. "I'm glad you agree that a woman needs her comfort more than once a year. And your feeling for the...poor girls...denotes a nice sense of gallantry."

"Merely a very proper feeling for the underdog."

"The underbitch, Roger."

"There's nothing bestial about three hundred concubines."

"And this kind of talk could go on all night, couldn't it?"

He smiled: "Someone will change the subject in the course of time, no doubt."

She said: "You bastard. You bloody bastard. If I had any self-respect, I'd walk out of here right now. Thank God I haven't any." She leaned down and kissed him again, her tongue lingering on his lips, and then she sat up suddenly and said, exasperated: "My God, you need a hell of a lot of persuasion, don't you?"

He reached out and touched her breast, and the heavy brocade was rough under his hand. He said: "Not really. And doesn't that stuff scratch the hell out of you?"

She took his hand and moved it to her throat and said: "There's a zipper there somewhere."

He fumbled with it for a while, and he began to tremble, not wanting to fight the desire for her any more, and he said irritably:

"These damn things, they always stick at the wrong time." He waited for her to help him, gesturing hopelessly, but she said:

"No, I want you to do it."

He put both hands at her throat, and the zipper began to slide down to her waist, and he slipped his hands under the brocade and caressed her, and he heard her breathing coming fast, alarmingly fast, and she stood up and let the gown drop to the floor and she was naked, and when, trembling too, she began to move onto the bunk beside him, he stopped her and said:

"Wait, stand there in the moonlight for a moment and let me look at you."

He could not think what had made him say it, but she told him, saying with a smile:

"You don't have to assert your mastery, you know."

"I just want to look at you..."

Her breasts were small and tight and upward-thrusting, almost adolescent, and she put her hands to her hair and pulled out some pins with an exquisite motion of feminine antiquity, and when it fell around her shoulders, shining yellow and soft, he could wait no longer, and he reached out for her and pulled her, almost roughly, down beside him, clutching at the breasts and finding her lips with his mouth, and he heard her begin to moan, very softly.

The detachment left her, and the tremor that was shaking her began to alarm him, but she clutched at him and ripped at his back with her fingernails, and he could taste the blood at his lip, and then her delirium seemed to transpose itself into his own body and he could no longer hear the whine of the motors nor the sound of the prow cutting deeply into the water, parting the waves and opening up a way for itself, thrusting ahead firmly as though nothing else across the wide expanse of history could matter, nothing but the movement of the moment.

\* \* \*

When he awoke in the morning, she was gone, and only the perfume of her was still there. He felt exhausted, and turned over on his stomach to sleep again, thinking of her, and he did not wake up again until he heard four bells sound, and then he sat up hurriedly and looked at his watch, and dressed quickly and went up to the dining

Candia and her father were there with Captain Hewitt and the senior officers of the deck, and Christie looked at him and said heartily:

"Sooner or later, on board ship, you oversleep. I suppose it's good for you."

He tried hard to avoid Candia's eye, but she said deliberately and calmly:

"Nights like these, you really should use the air conditioner."

He sensed the sidelong look she flung at her father, sensed the note of sardonic mockery in her voice, but Christie's expression did not change. He said:

"The skipper tells me we'll pass Bab el Mandeb at midnight tonight. We've made good time."

"And Aden?"

There was the slightest pause. "We won't stop in Aden."

"Oh?"

In the silence, Captain Hewitt put down his knife and fork, pushed away his plate, and said carefully:

"That's an astonishing decision, Mr. Christie, if you'll allow me to say so."

Christie said coldly: "My decision, Mr. Hewitt, why should it be remarkable?"

"Because there are stores we have to pick up, and we'll need a mite more fuel unless we're to be becalmed in the Gulf with empty tanks..."

"We'll anchor offshore and the tanker will put out to meet us."

The skipper's heavy eyebrows shot up. "Refuel at sea? If you'll be good enough to tell me why..."

"Because I sent a message to Aden this morning, arranging it."

"You have your reasons, no doubt, Mr. Christie."

"Yes, sir, I do."

Hewitt waited. But Christie turned to Candia and said casually: "You don't particularly want to land in Aden, Candia, do you?"

"No, Father, I don't."

"Good. So that's settled." Christie pushed back his chair and stalked out of the room.

Hewitt sighed. He looked across at his first mate and said: "Well, Mr. Merrick, you know what you have to do."

Merrick nodded. "Yes, sir."

Candia looked across at Roger and smiled. The smile widened with genuine amusement, and then she was laughing suddenly, full of good humor, and when Roger stared she said: "The lengths he'll go to..."

"To do what?"

Candia said: "I'll make a small bet with you, Roger. I'll bet you a hundred dollars that Luther Fenton's in Aden."

The captain snorted and poured himself some more coffee. He glowered at it for a while and said, grumpily: "I never heard the like of it."

Merrick said carefully: "It does seem an odd thing to do. I mean, after all..."

The captain interrupted him sharply. "It'll be a lesson for you, Mr. Merrick. And may I remind you of your position? There's nothing odd about the orders given on board this ship, and you'll carry them out without any such comment. Is that understood?"

"Yes, sir."

Candia was still laughing. She said again:

"I'll bet he's in Aden. Something's gone sour with the merger and he's hopped a plane and come running. You want to take my bet?"

Roger shook his head.

But Fenton was not in Aden. When Candia had gone to her cabin, he found Christie in the chartroom behind the bridge, poring over the photographs Breck had laid out for him. He looked worried, ill at ease, and when Roger came in he turned and said:

"You see what happens when you make decisions on the spur of the moment? Hewitt's a good man, the best there is, he runs a tight ship. But he doesn't like a change of plans, particularly when he's not told about it first."

Roger said: "I don't see why he should be worried about refueling at sea. It's not particularly difficult, is it?"

"Of course not. But he'd like to have been told first, that's all. Which would have been the right thing to do, I suppose."

"What made you decide... about Aden?" Christie shrugged.

"Candia."

"So she was right."

Christie looked at him sharply, and Roger explained: "She thinks Fenton must be there."

"Fenton? Good God no! I'd forgotten all about Fenton. I just don't want her to go ashore, that's all."

"I see."

Christie said heavily: "From Aden, she can fly back to New York if she makes up her mind to do so. On the spur of the moment. From Arkan, or the coast where we'll be working, it would take a certain amount of preparation, which would give her time to reflect. That's all there is to it. I want her with me, Roger."

"And I think she wants to stay. Doesn't she?"

"Provided nothing happens to make her change her mind. On board, nothing can happen. In Aden, it can. It's as simple as that."

"But you can hardly keep her...a prisoner...if she wants to leave."

Christie sighed. "I can, you know, though prisoner isn't the right word. It's merely a question of making sure she has time for reflection. In Aden, she'll spend the evening in the club, she'll meet with a score of people who might be...bad for her..."

"Toys?"

"Something like that. She's in a channel now, a channel that can only lead her the way I want her to go. I don't want her to leave it unless she has to. So I'm putting the temptation out of her way. Do you think I'm wrong?"

Roger said quietly: "No, I don't."

"Good." Christie slapped him on the back and said: "You're a good man, Roger. I'm glad we've got you along with us."

"Well...I'm a good geologist, anyway."

"And if this thing comes off..." He looked at Roger and said:

61

"The deal I'm making with the Shah, if we find his oil, you won't have to worry about that Oklahoma project. Compared with this, it'll be peanuts."

Roger could not keep the alarm from his voice. "The reason for the Oklahoma project... my being here..."

Christie snorted. "Of course, I know that. But you'll be making so much money you'll no longer have to think about it, unless you particularly want to."

"But I *will* want to..."

"Oklahoma! What a hell of a place to settle down and make a home!" He was watching Roger carefully.

"I wasn't thinking in terms of spending the rest of my life there."

"Well, I'm glad to hear that, at any rate." He had a trick, Roger noticed, of letting the fire go from his eyes whenever he wanted to appear uninterested, and now—had he won a battle?—that fire was no longer there; it was as though all he needed to answer a question was to raise the point, and then the shrewd mind could go to work, ignore the comments, and make its own deductions.

The fire had gone, and there was a faraway look in the eyes, a calculated look of extreme nostalgia. He said slowly: "Oklahoma's fine, but it's not the only place in the world. You've a future ahead of you, Roger, a good future. I'd hate to see you waste it in the sticks."

The urge came over him to shake Christie out of his complacency, to say coldly: *Even if I did lay your daughter last night, I've no intention of marrying her, and how do you like that, Mr. God almighty Christie?* But instead, he found himself wondering, and he said to himself, startled at the reflection: *But he's probably right, I'd be better for her than most men and he knows it, and who am I to blame him if he wants what he thinks is best for his daughter and doesn't care how he gets it?*

Strangely, there was a sudden bond between them. He smiled, and said:

"I don't really want to put down roots, anywhere, not just yet. There's time, isn't there?"

"For that, there's always time."

"I just hope I'll be as successful at...at wandering, as you have

62

been."

The fire was in the eyes again. "We've a lot in common, you and I," Christie said. "That's why we'll always get on so well together."

"And that couldn't be more flattering." He meant it, even though he was surprised that it came out so glibly.

And Christie was still smiling contentedly when he went out to look over the distant coastline.

*One of the family,* Roger thought. And then: *he's been alone just too long. In spite of his power, the world he knows is going right past him.*

# CHAPTER 5

ADEN CAME, and the refueling passed off without incident.

The *Abaris* lay off the outer harbor, beyond the mud-choked island of Sirah, while the tanker pumped its nauseous cargo into the yacht's huge tanks, and they watched the harsh coastline, the barren rocks that towered precipitously above them, seventeen hundred feet high and broiled to a deadly cinder by the hot sun and the hotter fires of the volcanoes below; it seemed as though the heat of those fires was still trying to burst out through the rocks and spill into the sea to consume them, and the blasts of hot air came to them from the land, and Candia said:

"My God, do people really live in a dump like this? A barbecue pit, and not a tree in sight!"

Breck came up to them, wiping at the back of his neck and grimacing, and he said:

"Your father suggests you ought to go below, Candia, get out of the heat and the stench. I wish I could do the same. The wind, what there is of it, is in just the wrong direction."

The smell of the diesel oil was sour and ripe, and Roger said: "How much longer?"

"Another hour, then we'll be on our way." Breck turned to Candia and said: "Are you sorry we're not putting in?"

"No."

He peered at her and looked quickly once at Roger. "I rather hoped I'd be able to show you the Officers' Club, buy you a drink there."

"There's plenty to drink on board. Thank God."

"Yes. Yes, there is, isn't there?" Breck looked at Roger again and grinned suddenly. "You've lost a little weight, haven't you?"

"Uh-huh."

"You can overdo it, you know." Before Roger could answer, he made a little gesture to Candia, turned sharply, and began to move away.

Roger said sharply: "Breck!"

Breck turned. Roger said: "What happened to Tagos?"

"Tagos?"

"The man you beat up." He could feel Candia's eyes on him.

Breck grinned and jerked his head towards the rail: "Take a look, Mr. Sequoyah."

Roger walked over to the rail and saw a small launch moving away from the ship's side. Tagos the Greek was standing up in it, and he looked round once and waved, and Roger saw him grin. Behind him, Breck said softly: "Feel good to know you saved his skin?" He moved away.

Roger stared after him and said to Candia: "You know, I'm beginning not to like that man very much."

"Breck?" Candia shrugged. "All he is, Father made him. Some people, you hire their labor; others, you hire the man, and Breck's one of those. What was that about...a man he beat up?"

"Oh, nothing, really. There was a bit of a fight."

"A fight, for Breck, means beating someone up. He's quite a man, in some ways."

Roger said, wondering about it: "I've never quite made up my mind... Is he crew, or secretary, or bodyguard...or what? seems to have no authority, and yet...he makes himself felt, doesn't he?"

She shrugged. "A shadow, nothing else. A shadow that jumps when he's told to. Breck is a sort of personal assistant, and let's be fair, he's a useful man. He can boss a drilling rig, he can order a good dinner, and he knows where to find the kind of women my father likes. He'll do exactly as he's told without question, and he knows how to keep his mouth shut. That's a combination of virtues you can't beat, so he's useful. And Father knows it, he pays him five hundred a week and a bonus of ten thousand every Christmas; is that the sort of salary a secretary gets? Or even a bodyguard? Of course not. He gets that because Father has bought him, body and soul. And, anything Father buys, he wants to keep...until he's no longer any use for it. Let that be a lesson to you."

"A lesson? Not the kind of lesson I need, Candia."

She was mocking him again. "He tells me you're the best oil man in the business. Next to himself, of course. How true is that?"

"In all modesty, a fair estimate, though perhaps a little generous. I know my job, and he knows that I do. And he hasn't bought me, he's merely bought my services. Those are always for sale if the price is right."

"He hasn't bought you *yet*."

"And I don't think he ever will. There's a quid for the quo, as always."

"And it pays to know what the quo is." She said softly: "Do you suppose it includes me?"

He tried hard to find a hurt there, but there was none. The smile was real. Taking his cue from her mood, he said carefully:

"First of all, I haven't the biased idea about him that you have..."

"Only because you don't know him as well..."

"...and so I don't necessarily agree that you're right. And secondly, if that were true..." He felt her hand in his and he sighed and said: "Surely, if that were true, you'd be raising bloody hell. Sign on the dotted line for the goods and chattels."

"This chattel will go along willingly until there's a reason not to."

"A reason like...Fenton?"

"Oh, that!" Candia shrugged. "Do I owe you a hundred dollars?"

"No. I didn't take your bet."

"That's another way in which Breck is useful. I had him sneak a cable ashore, to the immigration people. They've never heard of Luther Fenton. And who cares, anyway?"

"You do, apparently. Enough to try and find out, anyway."

"Not for the reason you think. I've spent a lifetime trying to find out what makes Father tick. And I still don't know."

"And you've no urge to go ashore?"

"None. How long before we hit Arkan?"

"A day and a half, at this rate. Apparently we're to stay in Arkan for the day, and move on early the next morning. Have you looked at the maps?"

"All I could see was sand and water."

"There's a big bay along the coast where the mountains come down to the sea, a place called Hafija, used to be a village there till the water went bad. Gypsum, it's no longer drinkable, and the village, such as it was, was abandoned three hundred years ago, as desolate a spot as you could find. Behind it, the desert stretches for a thousand miles into Saudi Arabia, and there's nothing, not a damn thing as far as you can see, except sand... But at Hafija, there's a great rent in the rock formation where the water gathers, the water from the mountains, a dozen riverbeds, mostly dry, and a few underground streams... They've had a crew out there once or twice, a seismological crew, and their reports, at the time, seemed negative. But we've learned a lot in the past few years, and with a little luck and some hard work, I think we might just hit it, right on the nose. We had a long session the other night, your father and I, and we agreed... We might just hit it right on the nose. In days instead of months."

Candia said cheerfully: "I don't really like to see you quite so earnest, darling. But, if it makes you happy... And it's nice to know how many things you and Father agree on."


She had come to him every night since that first time, and her love-making troubled him.

He knew that for her, at least, it was an animal feeling and nothing else, a satisfaction that almost anyone could have given her; and it hurt him to see her lose herself so completely in a passion that was unsupported by anything more than the merest semblance of affection. The third or fourth night, he had woken when she was leaving, and he had reached out for her, urgently, saying:

"Don't go, Candia, please. Lie down beside me and let's talk for a while. Please?"

She said: "You know it's only out of deference to what I think might be your wishes?"

Startled, he asked: "How's that?"

"That I'm not letting this out into the open. I thought you might want it that way. I never found out why the modern American male's sense of morality confines itself to sex, but...that's the way you want it, isn't it? In secret? Hole in the corner?"

"I don't know, Candia. I honestly don't know. I was thinking of you in much the same way, I suppose. I can't believe you want...everyone to know."

"Fifty years ago it was wicked to hold a woman's hand. A thousand years ago, copulation was considered highly respectable. Where the hell are we, up one minute and down the next, the hell with what they think."

"Your father too?"

"Particularly him."

"So relax and talk for a while. Please. Just talk."

She had been unsure of herself, then, but she had lain down beside him obediently, and when he had offered her a cigarette she had shaken her head, and soon she was stroking his body again till he had said: "Not now, Candia, let's wait awhile..."

She sat up and looked at him, and for a moment there was almost a hostility there, but then she was smiling again, so quickly that his fleeting impression could have been wholly wrong. "All right. You're not as insatiable as you'd like to think, are you?"

"I never thought I was. You're hard to resist, Candia, but...goddammit, I'm an empty shell."

"I can take care of that for you easily enough."

"Just give me...ten minutes or so."

She lay down again with a long naked thigh across his, and her face very close beside him, and soon they made love again and she fell asleep, and when he awoke as the sun came in through the porthole she was still there beside him, her eyes open and watching him in amusement, and the first thing she said was:

"You snore, did you know that?"

He looked at his watch. "Good God, it's gone eight, the ship's awake already, you'll never get back to your cabin without being seen."

"So?"

"Well..." He shrugged. "If you don't mind..."

"I don't mind. Now I'll have that cigarette."

He lit one for her and struggled into his clothes, and she lay there on the bunk with the sheet thrown back from her long and shining body, as dark as a Somali's against the white, with the ivory at her breasts and hips in startling contrast, smoking and watching him and saying nothing, and when he was dressed he said hesitantly:

"I'd better get on deck. Will you stay for a while?"

"Unless you expect me to go on deck like this."

"Is there...is there anything you want?"

She shook her head slowly, smiling at him with a sort of very private amusement. "Not unless you want to make my apologies at the breakfast table."

"Maybe I'd better not."

When he went outside, Breck was coming down the corridor towards him, and almost subconsciously he hesitated; but then he closed the door behind him and moved in the opposite direction. But Breck called out after him:

"Mr. Sequoyah?"

Roger turned.

Breck came up to him before he spoke. "Have you seen Candia around, she's not in her cabin?"

Roger did not hesitate and the lie came easily. "No, I haven't. I only just got up. Try the sun deck."

"I did. In fact, I tried everywhere. Almost everywhere."

Roger said politely: "Sorry I can't help you. But she can't have gone far, can she?"

"No. I suppose not. Though you'd be surprised how far she can go, if she really wants to."

Roger turned away, his anger rising. And, when he reached the end of the corridor, he heard Breck knocking firmly on his cabin door. The anger was about to burst out of him, and he swung round sharply and was about to make an angry comment when Candia opened the door. He saw her standing there in her brocaded housecoat, half open, her cigarette between her fingers, her long hair still unarranged and hanging down to her waist. He heard her say lightly:

"Good morning, how's the weather out there?"

Breck said: "Your father was asking for you, Candia. What shall I tell him?"

"Tell him I'll be along in a few minutes, all right?"

"Check."

"And anything else you feel inclined to tell him."

"There's nothing else, Candia. Nothing at all."

She caught Roger's eye as he stood there, watching, waiting, and she laughed and closed the door. Breck turned away, and without giving him a glance, went off back the way he had come.

He did not see her again till just before lunch, when Christie summoned him, on the intercom, down to the main cabin. He could not hide from himself the fact that a fight now would distress him, but Christie was in the best of humor.

The scuba gear was scattered over the cabin, and Christie was carrying an oxygen tank on his back, slipping the straps between his legs and tightening them as Candia watched him. Roger said pleasantly:

"Not going diving, surely? Fully dressed?"

Christie waved a greeting. "Just trying it on for size. I'd like you to teach Candia how to use these things at maximum efficiency. She knows just enough about them to get herself killed. Will you do that for me?"

"Sure, be glad to."

"The guns too. The big ones can be dangerous weapons if they're not used properly. We'll all be doing quite a lot of diving, and Candia wants to join us. No reason why she shouldn't, provided she knows what she's doing."

Roger turned to Candia, trying to see through the mask of her eyes. "But you've scuba-dived before, haven't you?"

"A little. Shallow water only, in the Mediterranean."

"The main difference here will be in the depth. If we go down very deep, it's a question of taking your time coming up. And the fish—shark, barracuda, moray eels, they're the only ones, really, we'll have to worry about. You can't put your hand into holes in the reefs, that's where the morays hang out, and if they catch a finger..."

He was conscious that Christie was listening, trying to catch an indication of his mood. He said, making conversation, showing willing:

"You'll see lobsters by the hundreds, and if you feel tempted to catch one, make sure both his antennae are outside his little cranny. If one curves back behind him, it means there's danger there, probably a moray, so stay away from him. Some of the coral is poisonous, highly so, so try not to cut yourself on it. And never interfere with a fish that looks like a turkey...the feathers are quills and they're tipped with a particularly nasty venom." He picked up one of the tanks and said: "Try it on, it's lighter under water."

She slipped out of her dress and disclosed a neat black bathing costume that was, he thought, rather prim, and Christie took off his gear and went to the drinks cabinet. As he poured them some sherry, he said:

"I had a radiogram from the Shah this morning. He's looking forward to our arrival tomorrow, a most propitious day."

"Oh?"

"I'd half forgotten, it's their national holiday. The birthday of Raidan el Darrah, the poet who wrote the Kandit Oras. Maybe that augurs well for us."

"A good omen."

"Man lost an important part of his philosophy when he stopped believing in omens, Roger, so let us pretend that we still do. Maybe it means that this time, at last, I'll get a look at that book. Nearly fourteen hundred years old, and one of the greatest works of art in the whole of man's history. Four hundred parchment pages, heavily illuminated in gold and in colors so bright that even today they can still dazzle you. Its covers are ivory, enameled in green, blue, yellow, and red, and heavily inlaid with silver, can you picture it? Apart from its historical value, which is anyone's guess, its intrinsic value alone... I'd give my soul for it. If I had a soul, which I doubt."

Roger said: "I believe that book is more important to you than the oil."

Christie was astonished. "You only *believe?* You must know that, surely. Oil is nothing but money, which can be made easily enough in a thousand ways, but the Kandit Oras... That book was already a national treasure before England had her first king. It was already a way of life when the Caliph Abu Bekr's Saracen armies slew over fifty thousand Greeks and Romans in the field and lost less than five hundred men in doing so, when he took Basra, and Damascus, and Jerusalem, and Emessa, and Yernuk, and wrote finis to the ambitions of the Emperor Heraclius in spite of his Roman Legions."

He's off again, Roger thought, and what's he trying to hide this time behind that mask of cheerful inconsequentiality?

Christie sat and watched while he slipped the tanks on Candia's back, showing her how to adjust the straps and the buckles.

He was back in the darkness of history again, glorying with the soldiers who were tramping over the desert, plowing their way through the alien dunes while the sweat ran down their armored bodies and the coarse sand tore at the straps of their sandals... He was with the hidden Arabs who were waiting, their long lances lowered, their dark faces masked against the biting wind, their horses impatiently champing... He said, dreaming:

"Can you believe that a Roman army could be so easily destroyed? Take it as a measure of the strength these people once had. A thousand years of history were being made when that book was slowly becoming the source of inspiration, the statement of philosophy, for a people who have virtually disappeared from the face of the earth." He said somberly: "All that remains of them is out there, in the desert. Grubby Bedouins whose camels and goats can barely keep them alive, and yet, they were once the center of a highly cultured world. And the only record of that culture left is in the Kandit Oras. Yes, that book is more important to me than the oil. Than all the oil in the world, and if I could get my hands on it..."

He looked at Roger speculatively, and Roger said: "If you're thinking of heisting it, count me out. I value my life too highly. Public executions are not my line at all."

Suddenly, Christie was laughing. "Of course! But just to take a look at it, to touch it! A woman's skin never felt richer than the parchment of a thousand-year-old book."

Candia said brightly: "You've been sleeping with the wrong women, Father. We'll have to see what we can do about it."

Christie said evenly: "Don't hold it against me, Candia, that I want something so badly... I can't get quite so easily."

"I believe that's why you really want it. The first thing you've ever found that your money won't buy."

Christie shrugged. "That's part of it, no doubt, but only a small part. I'd give everything I've ever owned for it."

Candia said carefully: "There's nothing you like more than an exercise in academic hypothesis, is there, so..." Roger waited, aware that Christie was watching her carefully. He was aware, too, that Candia was suddenly quite ugly. She said: "In the storybooks, the Shah would be offering it to you in exchange for my hand in marriage, or some such. What would you say, Father dear, if he did that?"

Christie said instantly: "I'd tell him to go to hell, what else? I don't count you as one of my possessions."

"Would you, Father? Are you sure?"

"Yes, of course I'm sure. It's a damn fool question, and you know it."

Candia said laconically: "Well, just let's hope that's a choice you'll never have to make."

Christie said smoothly: "Academic, you said. Remember?"

Without another word, he got up and left the cabin.

# CHAPTER 6

IN THE thirteen hundred years since Raidan el Darrah had built the town of Arkan, it did not seem to have progressed very much.

It lay like a pale gray scar on the hot foreshore that faced the sea, dried out by the salt and the sun, creeping up the slope that led away from the sea wall, hugging the soil, its whitewashed mud houses packed tight together into narrow streets where beggars stumbled along and children, half naked in castoff *fustans* that hung down to their ankles from their skinny shoulders, scrambled about, darting from the dark alleyways that somehow, even at this time of the day, contrived to look sinister.

The main street, if such it could be called, hugged the coastline. Here, a tarmac surface had been put down, many years ago, but had fallen into disrepair and was potted with deep holes where garbage gathered and hawks fought each other over rotting melon rinds.

Here, the open-fronted shops displayed their wares, while their owners squatted on wooden stools in the shade and idly swatted the flies with decorated whisks.

A bent old man with a copper urn slung on his back, suspended by a broad band that went round his forehead, was clinking tiny eggshell cups and calling out: "*Ahawe, ya effendi, ahawe...*" and pausing now and then to pour a measure of dark black coffee, swinging the urn down so so that the coffee ran in a smooth stream from the long thin spout, up once and down once with the cup, and then a couple of tiny coins tucked quickly away into his waistband and the cry again: "*Ahawe, ya effendi, ahawe...*"

Heavily laden donkeys, as frail as toys under their huge loads, and dyed with henna in honor of the day, pushed their way clumsily through the throng, their drivers beating them and cursing loudly, shoving against the placid rumps and sweating, the sweat staining the grease-bands round their heads, their bare feet splayed out with toes that were almost prehensile; and as far as you could see there were people, people packed tight together, people sweating and people cursing, people lazing in every inch of available shade, people so densely crowded together that it seemed the vast desert must have emptied its quota of humanity here by the sea, here by the palm trees that leaned at crazy angles from the dry dust of the broken pavement.

Behind the main street, and separated from it by a line of thick mud walls and heavy wooden doors, lay the market square of the town, a gigantic open *midan* that might, at other times, have been cool and quiet, at least around its edges where round white pillars supported an ornately carved grillwork that had been built there by Persian captives over a thousand years ago and was now interlaced with straggling vines; but today the *midan* also was packed with Arabs in from the desert towns, bringing their goats and their camels to sell, and their moneybags to loosen when the sun would have gone down and the violent entertainment of the night would begin.

Already (and it was only four o'clock and the town was still sweltering), a group of tall Arabs, their white robes covered with chain-mail vests, wearing steel helmets of an eleventh-century design, were parading round with their swords, the long two-handed swords of the Crusaders, holding them high above their heads to show the less fortunate their much prized heirlooms; and a small group of six of them, in heavy armor and riding small gray ponies, was prancing through the mob and yelling the bold battle cries, letting the populace know that the races and the dances and the sham fights would soon be beginning.

Some of the half-naked children had already climbed up onto the rooftops, where they perched perilously and sometimes squealed at the touch of the hot corrugated iron there, and were yelling insults to the warriors from their points of safety:

"Your mother was a camel, and your father yanked you out feet first!"

"Your grandmother was a brothel-keeper and your father was the son of a hundred and seven prostitutes!"

"Your sister's orifice is wider than the door to my house!"

A policeman, thumping at the wall with his long bamboo stick, called up to a small child: "Come down, you son of a blind pimp, come down!" And the child made a gesture and replied: "This in your backside, who do you think you are?"

"Your father, if you were born in a brothel. Come down!"

The child ran laughing across the roof, and the policeman, hearing the sound of an automobile horn, began to lash out with his cane at the tightly packed crowd around him, shouting: "Way for His Highness, way for His Highness..."

Some soldiers came running, their rifles at the port, forcing themselves like battering rams into the crowd, clearing a way.

And soon, the white Rolls Royce lumbered slowly over the broken road and into the square.

Candia lowered a window (which the Arab chauffeur kept repeatedly raising again, electrically, to show what a marvelous thing he could do with this car), and looked out and said:

"Did you ever see such poverty?"

A ten-year-old child took advantage of the open window and clung to the door, both feet dragging from the ground, calling out: "*Backsheesh, ya bint el Sheikh, backslieesh...*" and the chauffeur cursed and lashed out with the back of his hand, calling out: "Get down from there, you son of seven whores!" And the child replied, momentarily startled: "Eh...son? A girl, you camel, a girl...look..." She dug into the top of her ragged dress and pulled out her breast, and said, jeering: "A *girl*." A soldier ran up and pulled her away from the car and clouted her with his cane, and when she ran off, laughing, the chauffeur turned back and spoke in voluble Arabic, caring nothing for the road ahead, and Candia looked at Roger and said:

"How's your Arabic?"

Roger laughed. "I got the sense of that, but not much more. How far to the palace?"

"Twelve miles," Christie said. "Twelve miles out of town, away from the chaos and the noise." He was in a bad temper because the Shah had not come to welcome them himself, or at least had not sent his son. The army officer who had come to meet them in the Rolls was polite and suave and affable, but Christie had said: "Goddammit, who the hell does he think I am?"

All around them, the crowd pressed in. White robes, and red tarbooshes, and the bright green cloth round the fez that proclaimed the *haji*, the men who had made the pilgrimage to Mecca; and everywhere, the sour stench of flesh, and sweat, and dirt, and a churning, pummeling mass of tight-pressed bodies, where each wide-eyed face was just like the next because it too was part of the festering sore that was the city.

It had taken them more than an hour to get through the dense crowd at the wharf, even with the help of the cursing soldiers and police, and one old man had fallen under the rear wheels of the car, and when he had dragged himself off, yelling, and the soldiers had laughed at him, the incident had upset Christie badly. He had growled: "I sometimes wonder how the hell he keeps a hold on this rabble."

But soon, the crowd thinned out a bit, and as soon as they turned away from the square and hit the sandy track that led north towards the palm trees that lined the bank of the old river, now dry most of the year, the chauffeur put his foot down and the Rolls lurched forward, the loose sand spinning from under its desert-tires, and soon they were speeding along at ninety miles an hour, the chauffeur turning back to grin at them, pleased with the speed, using both hands to tell them how fast they were going.

Candia shuddered, and Roger said mildly: "Nothing much we can hit here, anyway..."

As far as they could see, once the town was behind them, there was nothing but sand. Close by, it was hard sand, broken and rocky, and gray-red with volcanic lava; but further away, on both sides of the track, the soft sand of the dunes stretched out into limitless distance, the crests of the dunes touched with feathered sand that the wind stirred up.

Once they saw a solitary rider, mounted on a racing camel, his rifle slung on his back and his face covered against the wind with his white cloth *keffia*, standing motionless high on a dune, and watching them as they sped past him; the chauffeur honked the horn, and the rider swung his camel round and trotted it off obediently down the far slope of the dune, and Christie said, watching:

"A Bedouin. There'll be a hundred of them just out of sight, one man to see what's going on, one man to be killed if the sound of the car means trouble."

Roger said: "They must know by now... The royal Rolls."

"One of the royal Rollses," Christie said. "He's got twelve of them, the round dozen, and only one road in the whole goddam country, and this is it. Twice the size of Texas, and twelve miles of dirt road. But the palace...now, that's something else again."

Roger grimaced. "I hope it's better than the town, at least." He, too, was upset by the incident of the old man. Brooding over it now, he said: "Did you see his arms?"

Christie said: "Whose arms, for God's sake?"

"The beggar who fell under the car. Livid sores from wrist to elbow."

"A leper. Plenty of them around here."

"But, can't they... can't they do something for them?"

"They can, and they do. They give them handouts."

"And among all that crowd on the dock... not a single pair of decent shoes. I've a feeling that the back streets of Arkan wouldn't bear much inspection."

Christie shrugged. "We came to find oil, not to look at bare feet," and Candia said bitterly: "They made the mistake of being born poor."

"Squalor," Roger said. "The word is squalor. Abject, bloody squalor. And the heat and the dust are getting me down, all right, I know it." He felt Candia's hand on his, and he looked at her and grinned. "I'll be glad to get to work."

"But first," Christie said, "the palace."

"And stop that bloody driver," Candia said, "from closing that bloody window."

The room in which His Royal Highness Shah Omar Ammadin

bin Yusuf Amadi received them seemed as big as a baseball field.

It was the main reception room of the palace, and the walls which separated it from the rest of the building were more than eight feet thick, rising to thirty feet in height where the great domed ceiling had been brightly painted with reds and blues and greens and gold. A portico of slender marble columns ran round each of the walls, their peristyles ornately carved, and on them was supported a broad balcony which itself was framed in carved woodwork in a style that seemed faintly Moorish. Looking round him in awe, Roger saw that at each corner of the balcony, a machine-gunner was seated, his gun pointing down into the great hall.

It was dark in here, and after the blinding heat outside it was almost too cold for comfort. The light, he saw, came from black and white arched windows of stone and glass, heavily decorated, that ran down the whole length of one of the longer walls.

The floor, of painted tile, was almost entirely covered by the longest carpet Roger had ever seen, and the only furniture in the room was a single throne set on a dais at the far end, below which was a line of red plastic chairs in a row, set awkwardly there as though they had just been brought in from the local cinema.

The red-robed Sudanese major-domo who had shown them into the hall bowed gravely, and closed the massive teak doors behind them, and at a gesture from Christie the three of them began the long march to the far end of the room where the throne was.

The Shah, Roger saw, was a thick-set, powerfully built and ferocious-looking man in his early fifties, and he wore a long brown robe, Bedouin fashion, but heavily embroidered with gold, and the gold that bound the black rope of the *agal* round his head proclaimed his royal ancestry.

He sat at ease on the massive red and gilt throne, leaning back and watching as they approached, and then, when they were near enough to bow, he stood up and came down with his hand outstretched, and reached out and touched Christie and said:

"No, my dear fellow, let us forget the formalities, I beg of you."

His voice was deep and throaty, heavily accented, as though he had learned his English, though he had learned it well, at second hand.

Christie said: "Permit me to present my daughter, Your

Highness, and my good friend Roger Sequoyah, who has come to show me where to fish."

"Ah yes, of course, the fish..." The Shah made a cursory nod to Candia, then took Roger's hand and held it firmly. "And are you a good fisherman, Mr. Sequoyah?"

"I think so, Your Highness."

"Good. You know what day this is?"

"Yes, I do. The national holiday, the birthday of Raidan el Darrah. A while ago, we were suggesting that this might be...a good omen."

"A felicitous day on which to arrive. And how was your journey?"

Roger shrugged. "Comfortable, Your Highness. The *Abaris* is a very comfortable vessel."

"Yes, I know. And your host has always refused to sell it to me."

Christie said good-humoredly: "I think I'd almost make you a present of it—perhaps in exchange for a look at the book you've hidden from me so long."

"Ah yes, the Kandit." There was the briefest hesitation, and then the Shah said languidly: "Perhaps, just perhaps, I will let you see it this time. But first, a little refreshment after the long drive out from the town. You must have found our one road very tiring after the comfort of the yacht. Unless you would rather sit on those abominable chairs while you tell me the news of the outside world, I suggest we might go in to eat something."

He waved a stubby hand at the machine guns on the balcony. "This place always depresses me. There have been no less than six assassinations in this room, and my ministers insist on rather more protection than I feel is necessary. But in my private quarters...there we can talk without such unpleasing distractions."

Christie said smoothly: "If you would rather my daughter went with your women...?"

"No, no, of course not, my dear fellow, you know me better than that. I will not inflict our backward habits on you, she is most welcome."

"Splendid."

Candia, warned by her father, said nothing. "You're a woman," Christie had told her, "a woman who doesn't belong to him, so don't expect any attention from him. He might just pack you off to his harem to spend the day with his women." And Candia had said mildly: "I wouldn't mind that at all, I might pick up a few tips."

The Shah clapped his hands loudly, and a small door behind the dais was opened, and they went through into a small garden, brick-walled, where the scent of jasmine was heavy and sweet, and where a fountain was splashing into a blue and green tiled bowl. The hot sun struck them again and almost blinded them with its brightness. There were soldiers here too, squatting under the orange trees with their rifles across their knees, and they stood quickly to attention as the Shah passed, and one of them ran forward and opened another iron gate in another red-brick wall, and they went into yet another, smaller garden, where hibiscus and frangipani were flowering, and a tall orchid tree held a solitary blossom, huge and lavender, on one leafless branch. The Shah stopped and touched it lightly, and turned to Candia and said:

"You know this tree, Miss Christie? One of three that were sent to me from Persia. The other two died, but this one...a rare species, one single bloom every three years, and you see? On the day of Raidan, it blooms."

He snapped off the flower and handed it to her and said: "Your father is thinking that I am less of a savage than I used to be because I permit a woman who is not mine to enter my private quarters. So let us show him how much I have changed, shall we, you and I? You allow me?"

He held it out to her, and when she took it and fumbled a little, wondering what to do with it, the Shah drew the beautiful curved dagger that was in his belt, and as she stared he slipped his hand very gently under the upper part of her white costume jacket, and delicately thrust the point of the dagger through. "There, a buttonhole for your flower." He slid the long stem through the hole, and carefully patted the bloom into place.

Candia, her hands at her sides, watching him quizzically, said: "You are most kind, Your Highness."

The Shah turned away sharply, as though the gesture had been made and that was the end of it, and as a soldier ran forward and unlocked another door in the brick wall he stood aside and held out his hand and said: "After you, my friends, please."

They went into a small room that was cool and sweet-smelling, and the door was closed and locked behind them, and there were fountains here too, three of them in a row, the water making a pleasant sound as it fell onto the cold ceramic tiles and trickled through a carved grating and into a small pool. They passed once more through a small garden and into a long hall, and then the dining room was there, with long white tablecloths spread out on the floor, flanked with silk cushions, and loaded with fish and meat and fruit and cheeses.

At one end of it, a Sudanese servant was squatting on his heels, fanning the white-hot stones in the fire-pit, over which the carcass of a trussed camel was slowly being turned on a spit, and the honey he was pouring over it dripped onto the hot stones and burned in a sudden wisp of blue smoke, and they sat and waited, and the Shah said, gesturing:

"If there is something you would like that is not here, no doubt we can find it for you. We have camel, and lamb, and mutton, and goat, and a roast of water buffalo, and seven kinds of fish, and eighteen cheeses in olive oil from my own groves, quite excellent oil, the best you will find anywhere in the world. And there are goat's tongues, and sheeps' eyes, and the livers and gibbets of chicken, and dates, and almonds, and medlars, and loquats, and walnuts, and apricots and peaches, and I trust your appetites are good."

Roger was surprised to see champagne bottles set out on a brass and copper tray in the middle of the tablecloth, and the Shah, seeing his look, said gravely:

"I am regarded as a holy man, Mr. Sequoyah. So holy that alcohol, which is forbidden to us, turns to water as it passes my lips." He smiled gently and said: "And I think there are certain hypocrisies in your religion, too, are there not?"

"Yes, indeed there are. Many of them."

"And none so anomalous as the strictest of all Western inhibitions, one which has always amused our philosophers as much as it has confused yours. The censure of those pleasures which our own people have always found most rewarding. For you, there is no procreation of the species, nor its attendant gratification, without...original sin, I think you call it. I have always found that a particularly fascinating aspect of Christianity. Fortunately, Allah's word came to us through a somewhat wiser man who realized that the indignities inflicted on us by religion would need at least some compensations. And Raidan el Darrah, whose teaching we follow, wrote down for us many of the things that Mohammed, who was an illiterate and thus somewhat at the mercy of Ibn Thabit, his secretary, was never fully able to communicate. Among these writings was a comment that perhaps places what you are pleased to call 'original sin' in its proper perspective."

The Shah regurgitated loudly, muttered a polite "God be praised for the food within me," and said, reciting: "*In the knowledge that a man has of a woman, there is no sin, save that if he deny himself the bounteous pleasure within her body which Allah, in his wisdom, has offered unto him, then shall his repudiation be an offense in the nostrils of all righteous men; her breast is a hill for the fallow deer to graze upon...*" He broke off and looked at Candia speculatively.

Roger saw that her eyes were bright with an emotion he could not place, an emotion that somehow disturbed him, but if Christie had noticed it, he gave no sign. Instead, watching the Shah, seeking his approval, he said excitedly:

"*...and in her loins is the lair for the lion. Let the deer graze where he will, and let the lion go often to his lair.*"

The Shah turned to him and said pleased: "Any man who can recite the writings of the great Raidan will always find a welcome in Orassia."

Christie sighed. "Ah...a verse here, a passage there, there's not much I know."

"The learned Hindu who made your translation was killed before he could complete his work. And the text is... You should learn Arabic, my friend, the Arabic of the sixth century, when it was the greatest of all languages, the language of poets, of philosophers, of mathematicians, and of statesmen."

Roger said: "There was a king once, in England, who was called 'The Great' because he was a scholar as well as a soldier. He translated the first books into the English language. Perhaps, Your

Highness, you should translate the Kandit."

"Perhaps, one day, I will. My son Hafik, whom you will meet tonight, Mr. Sequoyah, has for many years regarded this as one of the prime duties that must be carried out in my lifetime. But I do not entirely agree. The Kandit is a cornerstone for my people; another cornerstone is their insularity. And if we give the Kandit to the world, perhaps we shall open the doors to one small sector of Arab intellectuality which have been kept shut for thirteen hundred years. Perhaps this would not be a bad thing to do, I do not know; but at least, it is not a thing that must be done without a great deal of careful consideration."

Christie said: "And Hafik, he must surely want to open those doors?"

"Yes, he does." The Shah sighed. "Hafik is the last of an old and feudal line, a line of kings that has gone unbroken since our history began. When your Alfred the Great, Mr. Sequoyah, was laboriously translating the *Ecclesiastical History* so that the backward English could begin the rudiments of learning, Raidan's erudition had already been for more than two hundred years the foundation of my people's philosophy. Hafik would like to give this knowledge to the world, and a thousand years ago I would have agreed with him because the world was in need of it. But now, unhappily, the civilized countries have caught up with our culture and perhaps we have fallen behind as well, so the writings of a great man would no longer have their proper impact. The world would learn nothing, and we would lose...that insularity."

"And at the same time, it would put Orassia on the map."

"Yes, of course." The Shah was smiling gently, and Roger was about to say: *The oil will do that,* when he caught the sudden alarm in Christie's look; it was almost as though Christie had read his thoughts and was momentarily distressed by what he thought was to be a breach of security.

He caught the look in time and said nothing, looking up, instead, at an ornamental frieze that had been painted round the lower part of the ceiling. A line of dancing girls, some naked and some in gauze veils that seemed to flow with their movement, carried wine jars on their shoulders; one of them, a young girl who was delicately touching the diadem at her navel, looked, he thought, rather like Candia, except for the tightly braided hair that fell over one breast, in Sassanian style. He was pondering the resemblance, when Christie, misreading his thoughts now and covering up the sudden silence, said:

"In Mohammedan art, figure-painting was only excluded from *public* places, if that's what you're wondering, Roger. And that particular fresco, unless I'm mistaken, is a copy of the Abasid harem fresco in Samarra." He turned to the Shah and said: "Is that not so, Your Highness?"

The Shah shook his head. "You are well informed, Mr. Christie, but you are wrong. The Abasid Caliphs came *after* this palace was built, and it was Haron el-Rashid himself who had my ancestors' frescoes copied for his Samarra harem. And the painting you see there, of the three ages of life, was also copied for the Baghdad palace of al Ma'amun, though they were subsequently lost when Halagu's Mongols captured Baghdad in the thirteenth century. Now these are the only original fragments left of an unknown painter's work which left its mark on the whole of Mohammedan art throughout the next six centuries."

He added slyly: "And the young woman with one hand to her navel is the dancer Abusa, whose life is recounted in the Kandit, the woman who rose to be the favorite concubine of the King Dvandusi. It was she who pitted her sexual competence against his eight other favorites, hoping to demonstrate their incapacity to him and thus cause their deaths; it was well known that the King would slay any of his women who failed to arouse him."

Candia broke her silence. She said casually: "It's not hard for a woman to arouse a man, if she really tries."

Christie glanced at her sharply and was about to speak, but the Shah raised an imperative hand and said: "A well that is used too often will, at the last, dry out. No artifice will bring forth water that is no longer there..." He turned back from Candia and looked at the painting, then back quickly to Candia again, seeing the resemblance, finding amusement in it, fingering his beard and relishing his thoughts.

Christie fidgeted and asked: "And Abusa? The legend is that her scheme was not very successful. In my own translation..."

The Shah said: "Your learned Hindu deserved to die before he completed his work; he was a craftsman of indifferent merit. If I were to read to you from the original the long tale of Abusa and the women, of the wiles they employed to stir the weakening loins, each applying the art for which each, in her own way, was known..." He looked at Candia again and said: "Each with her own artifice... But Abusa had miscalculated Dvandusi's own capacity, and she was unsuccessful. She had forgotten his ample appetite. Only one of the favorites lost her life, when Dvandusi, attempting to mount her for the eighth time, found that his strength had gone. That was Abusa herself, whose scheming thus caused her own death. It is strange, is it not, how the legend of the dancing girl who robbed the King of his strength runs through all our divergent cultures? Once, they must have run together, side by side. Once, there must have been one single legend for all our faiths."

Looking at the gentle features of the dancer's face, Roger murmured: "Delilah..."

And the Shah said promptly: "The same story. But where the long hair of the Sun God Samson was made to represent the eastern rays of the sun that burst through the gates of Gaza, in the case of the Sun God Dvandusi those rays were portrayed in his all-embracing sexual appetite. The peoples from whom the Hebrews took the legendary Samson when popular excitement demanded national heroes, were sun-worshipers who believed that the sun was the origin of all life; even at that time, my people knew that those origins were in the seed of man himself. Is that the difference between those cultures? Is that why one drew away from the other? For someone, at one time or another in our beginnings, the metaphysical concept of the life-giving sun was not enough. Someone, once, demanded a less abstract force; whoever it was—some renegade priest of the Sun Gods?—he knew that with intercourse life went on, and that without it, life came to an end. Thus, our philosophy was born. It was this philosophy that Raidan expanded into a way of life for our people. The Hindus did much the same, and so, perhaps, did the Chinese. And then, the Christians came with their droll little tale of original sin, and now there is a great barrier between us, because what has always been right for us has lately become wrong for you."

Christie said: "If my own appreciation of your philosophy is lacking, it is merely because I have not been sufficiently exposed to the writings of the great Raidan. I am willing to be converted, Your Highness, as you must know."

The Shah chuckled. He said: "Tonight, my good friend, after we have eaten, you deserve to see the Kandit, and tonight, I will show it to you. I will do more. I will read to you from it the story of Abusa's death, a fascinating tale. Because of her cunning..."

The Shah reached for a sheep's eye and handed it gravely to Christie. He went on:

"Because of Abusa's jealous cunning, he amused himself with the manner of her death. He ordered every one of the soldiers of his guard to lie with her till she should die, and his guard at that time was over four thousand men. It is said she died on the fourteenth day, when she had been mounted by just under a third of them. And then the King, according to the Kandit, had her strapped, breast to breast and loin to loin, to the man under whose body she died, and both of them were then exposed on the palace walls until they rotted away. If you are interested in the similarity of legend in our varying cultures, let me tell you that the unfortunate soldier's name was Sams-u, or Shamesh-u, the bearer of the Sun. And you will note that the less complicated Hebrews had Samson perish when his strength was taken from him by a woman; the more wily Arabs made Samson merely the instrument, and the power remained with the King..."

Christie was staring at the Shah. He said: "Tonight, Your Highness? Tonight?" His eyes seemed to be on fire.

"Tonight, Mr. Christie. After all these years, you shall see the Kandit."

Christie was trembling with emotion. He began to speak, but then he leaned back into the cushions and fell silent, staring out into space, ignoring the curious glance that Candia gave him.

The Shah looked at Roger and said: "Anything I want from Mr. Christie, you see? I have only to mention the Kandit Oras. Does it put me in a strong position? I think it does."

# CHAPTER 7

FOR THE REST of the meal, Christie did not say a word, and when the Shah clapped his hands to signal that it was time to move to another part of the palace, the soldiers sprang to their feet and opened the door again and the party was ushered out.

Christie could hardly contain his excitement, and he whispered to Roger: "Now, you will understand..."

When the door had closed behind them, the Shah took Roger's arm and said: "Am I right? You were about to talk about the oil? At one time...?"

Roger nodded. "Yes, Your Highness, I nearly made an...indiscreet reference to it. I was assuming that...here, in the palace, there would be no secrets."

"In the palace more than anywhere else in my kingdom. A feudal kingdom, Mr. Sequoyah, where the opposition that would destroy me must be next to me if it is to have any hope at all of succeeding. In the desert villages, they can do me no harm, because among the tribes I am loved, but here... This is where the vultures congregate, waiting for me to die, waiting for all that I represent to them to die too, and trying, sometimes, to hasten the end. If a man would kill me, it is only here that he can work his way."

"Yes, I suppose so."

"A jackal can only kill at close range. You will not be here long, Mr. 5equoyah, but you must know that those who would destroy me...this is their lair. I cannot trust my own soldiers. Far from it."

They were moving down a steep, ill-lit stairway of smooth

88

stones that curved round into a cavern set in the sandstone on which the palace was built, and at the bottom a guard brought his rifle to the salute and at a gesture from the Shah opened an iron door which led to a whitewashed corridor. Here, three more soldiers sat at a table, half asleep in the cool light of a bare lamp that shone whitely in the ceiling, strung on naked wires that were carelessly looped over rusting nails, but they, too, sprang to attention and saluted, and one of them ran on bare feet to unlock the corridor's only door; and now they found themselves, surprisingly, in a well-furnished chamber, brightly lit, its floors covered with carpets, and its walls decorated with modern paintings. There were comfortable chairs, an antique desk of the Louis XV period, and a huge oak bookcase well-filled with leather-bound books.

A woman was standing at the shelves, her back to them, and she turned when they entered and came to meet them; Roger stared at her, overwhelmed by the unexpected. He thought he had never seen a more striking woman in his life.

She held her pose for a moment, and then came forward toward them, a tall, angular woman who moved with a kind of long-legged, casual ease, and he heard the Shah say affably:

"You have heard me speak of my old friend Maxwell Christie, have you not? This is Madam Simone Caffa, my Minister of Cultural Affairs. Mr. Roger Sequoyah, Miss Candia Christie, Simone Caffa."

Her eyes seemed to search his.

Not a beautiful woman, but a strong one, a woman so poised and sure of herself that it seemed she had deliberately avoided all but the most casual attempts at elegance, and yet was elegant in spite of it; she was a woman whose presence you felt, almost hypnotically.

Even Candia was impressed, and it seemed that the underground chamber took on an air of a formal drawing room in an old French palace, in the eighteenth century perhaps, when the fate of Europe was in the hands of women who looked like this.

The feeling of controlled power was so strong that it almost frightened him.

And then, she was smiling, and her face, almost ugly a moment ago because of that unexpected power, was strangely, hauntingly beautiful; he felt he was gaping at her. As he shook hands (closing his mouth, he felt, with a conscious effort), he said:

"A great surprise, madam. And a great pleasure."

Her voice was soft and low, a little husky. "You are most welcome here, all of you." She looked at Christie and said: "And I am sorry I was not here the last time you came to our country. I was in Paris..."

Christie took her hand eagerly. "Perhaps...is that why I was not allowed to see the Kandit then? Your special province, madam?"

She laughed and shook her head. "My special province is his Highness. But, perhaps, out of deference to me...I do not know. The Kandit is never taken out of the vault except in my presence. This is one of the essential measures of security for its protection."

"You have it here?" Christie was looking round the room, almost ignoring her, but she shook her head.

"First, I understand there are other matters to be discussed." She turned to the Shah and said: "I have sent the guard away, Your Highness."

The Shah nodded, and Simone crossed to the heavy door, closed it, and turned the key. She stood for a moment at the door, her back to it, leaning into it with her hand still on the heavy brass lock, looking relaxed and calm.

She wore a long white gown that clung tightly to her body at the breast, and her shoulders were bare, smooth, and dark, but it was her face that caught Roger's attention. She had the most startling gray eyes, widely spaced and steady; her nose was quite delicate, and there were two lines at either side of her rather large mouth; but it was the air of almost masculine strength which was most noteworthy.

A woman of thirty-five, Roger thought, mature and very sure of herself, and she's never made a mistake in her life... Her black hair was loosely hanging down almost to her shoulders, cut rather shorter than was fashionable, and looking well-kept as though by accident rather than by design.

The startling gray eyes were watching him, and without taking them off his, she said:

"We are alone here, Mr. Christie, none present who may not know why you are here." She looked at Christie then, as though to catch his reaction, and Christie said, pleading:

"Can't we...can't we see the book now?"

"Later, Mr. Christie. Shall we sit down?" She made a broad gesture, and when they were seated she stood by the Shah and put a hand on his shoulder and said: "Shall I talk, Your Highness, or will you?"

The Shah said something in Arabic and she nodded, then sat facing them at her desk, her long hands on its polished surface, sitting poised and motionless and splendidly regal. She looked around the room as though assuring herself of its elegance, and said:

"You start your survey at Haffja?"

Christie nodded. "And then move east as far as necessary."

"You have the 1964 survey report?"

"Of course. It was quite inconclusive, but I'm starting at the same point they did. There was a remark in the report that leads me to believe that we might have better luck."

"The stratigraphic traps?"

Surprised, Christie said: "Yes, among other things. The coralline growth seemed to them to hold no promise, but since the reef extends for twelve miles to the west, the impervious sediment getting deeper and deeper all the time, I feel that insufficient work was done where the reef hits the shore. That's where we will start."

There was a touch of asperity in his voice, as though he disliked discussing the specialized details of his work with an outsider, and Madam Caffa said gently:

"It is only a question of whether your work will be obvious to anyone watching from onshore. We can close off the area quite simply if we have to, but frankly, I would rather not. What do you think?"

Mollified, Christie hesitated. "That rather depends on how you would do it."

"We could announce military maneuvers along the bay area, but sooner or later the Army would wonder...and some of the generals are not quite to be trusted. If you would feel happy without such precautions, always remembering the vital need for secrecy, not only while you are working but until any resultant deal is made..."

"How likely is it that we shall see any intruders?"

Madam Caffa shrugged elegantly, the slightest movement of a

shoulder. "Under normal circumstances, the possibility would be most remote. Occasionally, a fisherman puts in there for water, but in recent years the gypsum content has increased and the water is now almost completely undrinkable, even in emergency. From the land, no one can approach unless he crosses nearly a hundred miles of the Rub el Khali, and not even the Bedouin will do that. However, we do have to contend with the possibility that a suspicion may grow, enough to cause someone to wonder. And those who might wonder, Mr. Christie, have very persistent minds. They could send a boat to see what was going on."

"There will be no activity on the shore that can't be covered up at very short notice. All the work will be done on board the *Abaris*. Will we be able to stop anyone from boarding us? The police, the customs people...?"

"I'll see that you get one of the Shah's private burgees to fly. It's known that you are a friend of his, so that in itself will cause no comment. And it will give you a considerable authority."

"Good. Then let's leave it at that. The story is that I'm out there with a few friends, fishing."

"So I believe. And we are all aware of the necessity for...the utmost discretion."

"We are."

The Shah had remained silent while Madam Caffa was talking. Now, he leaned forward and said to Christie:

"You are aware of my motives, I know. And I know that you will have explained them to our young friend here, but...if you will permit me..." He looked carefully at Roger and said: "You may not have reached the age, Mr. Sequoyah, at which the illusion of integrity gives away before the onslaught of common sense. If there is oil under this land, perhaps you feel it should belong to my people?"

Roger hesitated. The question seemed loaded. He saint carefully:

"There seems to be a political problem involved in the question, and I'm afraid I'm not really...knowledgeable enough of the background to give you much of an answer, sir."

"Then you are simply working because you are paid to work?"

"I suppose so, though I would not have put it quite so bluntly."

"And it may be that you, therefore, disapprove...or at least, withhold your approval, of what you might regard as a selfish action on my part?"

"No, Your Highness. What I do know of the background leads me to think that you are probably doing the right thing."

"Just the right amount of diffidence, Mr. Sequoyah, to show your reserve without letting it intrude."

"I'm sorry, Your Highness, I didn't mean..."

"Let me put the case to you more bluntly than perhaps Mr. Christie has. A certain European oil company is prepared to make a substantial down payment on a long-term lease for the oil rights, if there should prove to be any oil. My arrangement with them is for immediate signing of the charter, and immediate payment of the money. I need that money, sir. My backward country, somewhat more slowly than the rest of the world, is growing out of the feudal state in which it has rested for thirteen centuries, and my only desire is to put off, as long as possible, what I can only regard as an evil day—the day when popular rule comes to Orassia. The growth of a backward people is accompanied by the most atrocious growing pains, and although, in other parts of the Arab world, these pains may or may not have been outgrown, I know that they were never really necessary. If I point to the examples of Egypt, Iraq, Syria...can we honestly say that the people are better off than they were? In place of the old autocracy, there is a new autocracy, and the end result is the same. Oh, in the course of generations, no doubt, the change will come. But it would have come just as surely by more gentle means, without the pains that I am anxious to spare my people. And lest you think that I am feigning a concern for them which I do not feel, let me also admit that I also have no intention of seeing my own privileged position swept away in a tide of violence and civil war. There is only one man who can control my people, and I am that man. Without my strong hand, there is nothing but misery for them...and there is also nothing but death for me. I will not allow a political philosophy, which will pass, to destroy an ancient heritage—which will not pass. I speak of the heritage of rule, Mr. Sequoyah, the heritage I took from my father and which he took from his—and which I will pass on to my son. Forty generations, Mr. Sequoyah, of unbroken authority; I will not see this abrogated by the evil of the twentieth century, which is arrogance. The arrogance of the lower classes, and the evil thought that one man is as good as another, out of which must come the specious idea that no man, therefore, may rule over other men. Perhaps democracy is suitable for some countries, I do not know; I *do* know that it is not suitable for mine. I will not have my people suffer the change from a tolerant despotism to an intolerant one, and that is exactly what it would be. Now, if it becomes known that immense wealth is about to come to Orassia, there are unfriendly elements outside Orassia who will turn this sudden wealth to their own uses; and there are elements inside Orassia which are ready, and anxious, to play into their hands. But if I confront these elements with a *fait accompli* I will be in the position which I want to occupy—as head of a well-equipped and modern army which can fight off the evil that, one day, will come to us. And it is for this reason that I need the money. Do I make myself clear?"

"Perfectly clear, Your Highness."

"I do not ask your approval of my motives. But I believe that you are far enough removed from our realities not to let them worry you even if you disapprove."

He leaned back and folded his fingers across his stomach, and Madam Caffa said, smiling:

"In other words, we are confident that any qualms you may have about our moral propriety will not be strong enough to jeopardize the future of this project."

Christie said shortly: "He understands that. And furthermore, since I have engaged him, I will take the fullest responsibility for his discretion."

"Yes, Mr. Christie, I am sure you will."

Was there a threat there, Roger wondered? He looked at Madam Calla and saw she was half smiling at him, the gentle, composed smile of a woman who knew her own mind and her own power with an absolute assurance. The lines at the sides of her mouth were there, but unmoving, as though a genuine good will would deepen them but that this was not the moment for it; those lines had been etched by frequent laughter, by the full enjoyment of the moment; but this was not one of those moments and the affability was therefore limited.

But, in her eyes, there was an understanding; it was as though thoughts, unknown to the others, were passing between them.

Then she looked away, her eyes darting, and she said to Christie:

"We are in very good hands. And is there anything you need from us?"

"We have everything, thank you. Everything we can possibly need. I'd like to be kept informed of...any outside interest in what we are doing. Rumors, gossip..."

"Of course." There was a momentary pause, and then she said: "And Mr. Breck is still with you?"

"Yes, he is. Why do you ask?" Again, there was a touch of hostility there, and once again Madam Caffa was aware of it. She smiled and said:

"I know how much you rely on Mr. Breck. I have never met him, but... You know that his mother is now married to the Baron Calindoris?"

Frowning, Christie said: "Yes, I do." There was a tightness in his voice, an anger that was startling because it was unexpected.

Watching them, Roger was aware of a strange current of sudden hostility; it seemed as though he were touching a gaping sore that had been opened up and that he had never seen before, as though here, for no apparent reason, a covering had been momentarily laid aside that had hidden something evil from him...

Madam Caffa went on, calmly and unemotionally: "A woman of high intelligence, I am given to understand, and...would artful be the right word?"

For a moment, Christie did not answer her, and the anger, still there, was masked. It's not against *her*, Roger thought, that anger is against *himself*, there's something he wants to keep hidden... Christie said at last, quite coldly:

"As you are obviously aware, Madam Caffa, I have good reason to know of her...artfulness. Is it pertinent to our discussions?"

Madam Caffa was smiling, a secret smile that seemed to say: There, let the matter rest... She said: "Calindoris is the principal shareholder in the Kuwait Development Company, which is currently negotiating for an oil charter in Trucial Oman."

"You are well informed, madam. Those negotiations are supposed to be quite secret."

"They are. But one of the negotiators is...not as honest as his employers believe."

Christie said smoothly: "Then you must also know just who his employers are?"

For a moment, Madam Caffa did not answer. She appeared faintly troubled. She said at last, frankly: "No, I do not. My information stopped short of that point. My informant himself does not know who employs him. A lawyer behind another lawyer...but where the chain of command starts... No, I must confess, I do not know."

"I find that very gratifying."

The battle was won, the glimpse of the secret life was gone, and all that was left of it was the sudden anger on her face. It was no more than a tightening of the muscles at the side of her mouth, so that the deep twin lines there, lines that seemed to show how easily she could smile, momentarily disappeared.

But then, Christie said easily: "Your informant, no doubt, is Michael Haddadi, who has been carefully fed just the right amount of misinformation to lead Calindoris to an interest in Oman when he might feel more profitably employed investigating my own activities. I, Madam Caffa, am the employer Haddadi has never known. And this seems an opportune moment to tell you that I am perfectly aware of Breck's associations with those who might harm this project, and that, although I trust him as much as I trust any man, I am not letting that trust grow beyond the bounds of reasonable precaution."

The twin lines came back, and the smile on the wide mouth spread, and there was genuine amusement in the wide gray eyes; with a slight movement of the head, the dark hair swung in exquisite motion, and she said:

"You must forgive me, Mr. Christie. I know you only by repute, and I think that you will agree—reputation is quite frequently misleading."

"The sooner you satisfy yourself, madam, of my intelligence, the sooner I shall be satisfied of yours."

The Shah looked quickly at Madam Caffa, and his eyes were

very alert. But her smile was still there, and the gray eyes went to Roger, amused and awake and full of secrets. They said as clearly as if the words had been spoken: *Now, I shall withdraw and give him his victory.*

Christie had not missed her look, he was conscious that the Shah was watching him. He smiled, and said lightly: "It's ungallant of, me to quarrel with you, isn't it?"

The Shah's eyes were twinkling. Using his thick, black-haired hands to gesticulate, he said:

"In all the years that she has been serving me, I have never been able to convince Madam Caffa that the Arabs regard a woman's place as differing somewhat from the one she seems...to have so competently arrogated to herself. There was a time, I must confess, when I watched the growth of her intellect with certain misgivings, because in our philosophy, as in that of the Periclean Greeks, a woman who applied her brain was a rarity that deserved suspicious scrutiny. We have always believed that the womanly virtues were centered in the breast, the loins, the lips, the hands... We could never admit that there might be a superior intelligence there too; the intellect is reserved for men. But in Madam Caffa—there is the proof that the times are changing even for us."

"Always a woman," Christie said, smiling, "who takes man out of the rut when he's been there too long. The Greeks you spoke of... One woman, Aspasia, destroyed the myth of man's monopoly of intellect..."

The Shah said gently: "But it was a man, Socrates, who recognized Aspasia's worth. And do not forget, my friend, that the movement Aspasia led to free women from their servitude created in Athens a chaos that even Athens was not equipped to survive. Our own Aspasia, the great love of the great Raidan, was less arrogant..."

Christie said: "Ninea. Of whom he said: '*She has the curious mind of a boy, and the hungry body of a woman, and her name is Ninea, that all men may know that in her there is the seed and the spirit of Raidan...*'"

"And she died," said the Shah, "by her own hand. If she had not done so, who knows what might have become of our history? It might be that Raidan would not have survived, and we...we would be the simple Mohammedans that our neighbors are. But Ninea repaid the great love the Prophet bore for her, and so...”

He broke off, lost in thought, for a while. Roger felt that the composed gray eyes were still on him, and when he looked at Madam Caffa they did not turn away or change their expression; she was watching him thoughtfully, critically, dispassionately. *An Aspasia,* he thought, *watching the world grow around her and ready to seize her chance to mold it more to her liking...*

The Shah leaned back in his chair, his eyes closed. He said slowly: “Somewhere in our history, scattered by the wind and the sand, there are twelve more volumes of Raidan’s works, destroyed or stolen or burned by pagans, and only the Kandit Oras remains, and do you know why? The other volumes concerned war, and statecraft, and death, and husbandry, and the uses of the phases of the moon. Only the Kandit dealt with the ways in which a man may find his pleasure in the bodies of his women, and so it has survived, for love is greater than war, or death itself. Only the Kandit Oras, and thrice, in my lifetime, our enemies have sought to rob me of it. In the lifetime of my ancestors...who knows how many times...? And if a man lives by what is written in the Kandit... There is no other truth, there is no other way to find it.”

The deep, resonant voice trailed away; it seemed that the Shah was asleep. But then his eyes opened, bright and alert and smiling, and he looked at Madam Caffa and made a little signal with his finger.

She rose, then, and said lightly: “His Highness wants to show you some of the treasures of his palace, but let me tell you first where you are, precisely.”

As they all stood up, she opened a door on the other side of the room, and said:

“There are not many people who are privileged to come down here. This chamber is an anteroom to what we might call the maximum security quarters. In case of danger, this is where His Highness and his immediate friends can preserve their lives and so preserve Orassia. When I first came here, seven years ago, it had the air of a fortress, of a dungeon, where the strength was bare and brutal and unwelcoming. Many of our national treasures were scattered about the palace, unnoticed and in danger of perishing through neglect, and one of the first things I did was to bring them down here and use them, use them as they were meant to be used, for quiet contemplation by those to whom they are an important part of our history. In more advanced countries than ours, there are similar retreats for the leaders of government, but since here we do not have vast military projects and correspondingly vast military problems, our shelter is designed merely to hold our history intact, together with the life of its ruler. Above us, the world goes on, the palace, and its servants, its soldiers and its schemers... But down here, safe against intrusion...this is where our history is recorded, and where our history is made."

She had brought them along a spacious corridor and into a large, domed-ceilinged room that had the musty air of a museum. Here, too, there was French furniture, gilt and red-plush chairs and tables, set out in an orderly display, and the walls were covered with paintings, swords, spears, shields, armor, and heavy brocaded cloth; some of the exhibits were enclosed in glass cases, and one of them had been set out on a marble plinth in the center of the room, directly underneath a heavy bronze chandelier.

It was a book.

It was closed, and the covers were slabs of yellow ivory, the luster of them so deep that it looked like alabaster, and an intricate design had been inlaid around their edges in heavy silver. In the lower right hand corner, a line drawing of a semi-reclining woman had been etched in bright red enamel, the lines so fine that they might have been drawn with a needle. The black braided hair lay in a fine coil along the curve of her breast and down beyond her waist. One languid hand trailed along the lower edge of her thigh, and the other, the fingers lightly curled, rested below her navel. The tips of the fingers were etched in green, and her eyes were tiny sparks of bright blue lapis lazuli. Above her, at the upper left, a raised hand grasped a thin sheath of gold that was a pen, and to the right of the hand there were four lines of ornamental Kufic script, tall, upright, and singularly well formed, that were decorated with delicate curlicue lines of green and blue enamel. The last horizontal of the lower line trailed to one side, twined itself round a slender phallic emblem of embossed silver that ran down the side of the cover, and finally attached itself to a delicately beaten gold lock that was riveted to the ivory boards.

Roger heard Christie catch his breath; the voice was a whisper:

"The Kandit Oras..."

And, when he looked at Christie's eyes, he was shocked to see the greed that was there. It made him shudder. Almost in reflex, he glanced at Madam Caffa.

Watching Christie, her eyes were hard, and cautious, more watchful than ever; he thought, for a moment, that they looked almost cruel.

The hours slipped slowly by in the cool of the underground museum.

Guided by Madam Caffa, Roger and Candia looked at the exhibits that were laid out there as she took them back through the centuries to the beginnings of Orassia's history.

Her voice was low and controlled her movements smooth, relaxed, and restful, as she told them briefly, with pride in her voice, of the great past which was so much part of her:

"...a leaf of the original Koran in Kufic script, from the eleventh century... A bronze mortar from Persia, about 1250, can you see the Sassanian influence? It's quite priceless... An amphora found off the shores of the Red Sea, still filled with honey and preserved in wax; a Tyrian ship caught fire and melted the beeswax it was carrying, and so, some of the cargo was preserved, even after more than two thousand years in the water... A portrait from Baisonqur, also priceless, etched by the great Sala Abbasi, eighth century... The sword of Raidan himself, the legend of its blade reads: 'By the Lance, Life; and by the Sword, Death...'"

As they listened, they could hear the deep, guttural Arabic of the Shah as he stood at the plinth and turned the parchment pages of the Kandit, reading the verses and then translating them to Christie:

> *"And he lay on his left side, for this was the month of the Gazelle.*
> *And she was a Dove and her wings were spread..."*

Roger heard Christie say excitedly: "Vatsayana too, he speaks of the left side, the Gazelle and the Dove..." He heard the Shah say didactically: "Of course, my dear fellow, Raidan too, he attached the greatest importance to the left side, the side of the heart, especially when you are behind a woman, it is most important, really, the right hand for the breast, and the throat, and the navel, and the left hand for the rest. Only in the position of the Lute, when both hands are used together, and then only if the woman's caste is sufficiently high." He said gravely: "The position of the Lute should never be used with a slave girl, or a bearer of water, or one who has labored in the fields. You understand, of course, the development of the thighs..."

Madam Caffa was showing them a suit of chain-link armor, and Roger saw that Candia was paying her no attention at all; she was listening to the eloquent flow of the Shah's explanation, and he heard Madam Caffa break off, saw her look once at Candia and smile, and then she said to him, gently:

"I do not think Mr. Christie will be easily persuaded to leave this room just yet. Shall we go and look at the gardens?"

Roger nodded. "I think it might be a very good idea." He was conscious of Candia's excitement, and he did not like it.

They followed Madam Caffa out of the museum room, up the whitewashed stairway, and out into the cool of the highly scented gardens.

# CHAPTER 8

PRINCE HAFIK did not come to the palace till after midnight.

The great hall was hung with rugs and carpets that draped from ceiling to floor over the whitewashed walls. A seventeenth-century *Ushak,* cherry-red with cartouches of blue and yellow silk, with arabesques and floral forms in yellow, white and rose, hung over the black and white stone windows at the far end of the room, and the deep crimsons of a long line of Tekke-Turcomans covered the eastern wall.

The Ministers were standing in a solemn file, moving up slowly, one by one, to shake hands as Madam Caffa introduced them.

Roger saw that Christie was paying them little attention; his thoughts were elsewhere as he took their hands, mechanically, not bothering to smile.

"This is Mustafa bin Ashad, the Minister of Construction...Hassan el Ferragi, Minister of Transport...Suleiman Hafifi, Minister of Finance and Redevelopment...Osman Kabbaj, Minister for the Welfare of the People...General Fali bin Sassara, Minister of War..."

One by one they stepped forward and bowed, and shook hands, and murmured polite clichés; tall, agile men who moved with dignity in their long white robes; only the General, a thick-set, heavily built man who seemed, by virtue of his weight alone, to be not one of them, wore Western clothes, a tight-fitting khaki uniform that gleamed with polished leather and shining brass. He carried a swagger stick under his arm, and when he saluted and bowed, he said:

102

"I feel I should suggest to His Highness...a military escort for you. The Rub el Kbali is a dangerous place, even for fishermen..."

Christie merely grunted, and Madam Caffa said smoothly: "An excellent idea, General Fali. I will take it up with His Highness."

And when they had all gone, and the party was being escorted once more to the Shah's chambers, Roger whispered to her, worried: "A military escort? Will he insist?"

Madam Caffa laughed. "Of course he will! Until I tell him that the Shah would consider it a personal affront to his benevolent administration, and then he will be forced to admit that there is no danger, and that an escort is therefore not necessary."

"And *is* there any danger?"

She hesitated for no more than an instant. "None at all."

He smiled at her and said: "You sound a little unsure. So, if there is, we'd better prepare for it. It would help if we knew what form it might take."

She looked at him for a long while before she answered. She said at last, somberly:

"In your business, Mr. Sequoyah, you play for very high stakes, is it not so? And you must sometimes, no doubt, accept proportionate risks. It is the same in governing a highly volatile people like the Orassians. There are certain sections of the public who do not agree with our own estimation of His Highness' benevolent administration. Sometimes, their disagreement turns to violence, so there is *always* danger."

She hesitated, and he wondered if she were debating just how much she should tell him. She said:

"Three of General Fali's senior officers were arrested this evening, on charges of plotting to overthrow the government."

When he began to speak, she interrupted him with a gesture:

"It's not the first time we've had this sort of trouble, and it probably won't be the last either. But the movement against us is strong. It is largely directed against His Highness personally, and, therefore, by implication, against his friends—among whom you must be numbered." She gestured at the lowered gardens and said: "Within these strong walls, it is very easy to acquire a sort of deceptive well-being... There is so much that is worthwhile here that it is easy to forget what there is out there in the desert. The palace is cool and comfortable and...luxurious; out there, the desert is burning, on fire with more than the heat of the sun."

Christie was listening, worried. Roger said: "But surely, it's in the desert, among the Bedouin, that the Shah is best loved..."

"Yes, yes it is. The nomads are all on his side because he is one of them. But the townspeople—in Arkan, in the oases—they are all against him because he is not one of them. Some of them have learned a little more than is good for them, and... I can never be sure just how strong popular resentment against him, in the villages, really is."

"And the dissident officers?"

"You are a shrewd man, Mr. Sequoyah. Yes, the dissident officers control—or did control—the southern area of the Rub el Khali. The seacoast where the fish are rising."

"I see."

"It means merely—what we have always insisted on. The accent on secrecy."

She threw open the door in the red brick wall where the orchid tree was, and there was Hafik.

The night was cold, and the garden was lit by tallow flares around which a thousand moths were fluttering, and the air was heavy with the scent of the incense that was meant to keep them away.

Prince Hafik stood over an open brazier of charcoal, his slim hands over the red coals that lit the thin, surly features of his face. He turned and smiled and showed his white teeth and came forward quickly to meet them. He looked at Candia first and said:

"My father told me you were beautiful..."

He took her hand and shook it quickly, then turned to Christie: "Will you forgive me that I was not here to meet you? There was a little trouble in Radija, and I was unfortunate enough to be there at the time. My horse was hamstrung..."

Christie said: "It's good to see you, Hafik, and I'm glad to learn you've still a penchant for trouble. My daughter Candia, Mr. Roger Sequoyah, His Highness Prince Hafik bin Omar Ammadin bin Yussuf Amadi."

The Prince took Roger's hand, and his grasp was surprisingly firm. He was a good-looking young man, slight and wiry and a little over-elegant, and smelling strongly of eau de Cologne. He was dressed rather too smartly in the uniform of an air force commander, and his thin chest was covered with four rows of medal ribbons—among them, Roger noted, the Croix de Guerre and the Legion d'Honneur. He said, smiling quickly:

"And to you, sir, also...my apologies. I planned to be back in time, but..." He shrugged and left it hanging, and Roger said: "Hamstringing? They still do that?"

Hafik was still clasping Roger's hand. He said, smiling: "How else would you unhorse a good rider?" The smile faded, and he said, more soberly: "One of my favorite ponies, half Arab, half Irish. I shall miss him."

"It sounds as though Radija might be a good place to stay away from."

There was a brief hesitation, and then Hafik said: "In theory, I suppose you are right. But I must go back, of course. Tomorrow." He glanced at Candia approvingly, his eyes shining, and said: "Today, I took with me a bodyguard of forty men, good soldiers all of them, and they threw stones at us. Tomorrow, I will go there alone and dare them to do it again."

Roger pulled his hand away and said, frowning: "An excellent principle, Your Highness, but an alarming prospect."

"Not if you know my people as well as I do. They must be taught that there is no fear in those who guide their destinies."

Roger saw that Madam Caffa was watching the Prince, her eyes very thoughtful, as though she were waiting for him to say something of which she would disapprove.

It seemed that Hafik sensed this too, he looked at her and smiled, and said gently: "You agree, do you not, Simone?"

She shook her head slowly. "Agree? No, I do not. But I would not argue the need for caution at the expense of dignity."

Hafik laughed quickly and turned to Roger. "You see? My mentor. Wisdom, reflection and always the delicate touch of prudence. And yet... Do you read Nietzsche, Mr. Sequoyah?"

"Er...not very often, I'm afraid."

"Then let me commend him to you. He saw vice in virtue, and virtue in vice. He found infamy in the dogmatic teachings of his

ALAN CAILLOU

church, and the seeds of evil in patriotism. And in a lighter moment he suggested that a man of courage needs a little danger from time to time...or the world becomes unbearable. Come with me, Mr. Sequoyah. Come with me to Radija tomorrow, just the two of us, alone and unarmed."

Madam Caffa said sharply: "As a guest of our country..."

But Hafik, excited now, interrupted her. He held up a flamboyant finger and said: "The Americans have a special kind of courage that is all their own, did you know that? They are cowards until they see the need for bravery, and then...then, my friend, their resolution is astounding. I have noticed it often, a truly remarkable thing that is peculiar to them and to no one else. The British will face any danger, however stupid, merely on principle. The Germans will face it because they are too dull to recognize it. The French...because it is intellectually stimulating. Am I right?"

His enthusiasm was surprising. Roger tugged at an ear and said doubtfully: "Well, I'd say that's a rather sweeping statement..."

"Of course it is! I'm merely asking you to show me that you will expose yourself to peril...even when it is *not* necessary. Besides, I'd enjoy your company."

Roger said: "A bad argument, followed by a good one." Hafik clapped him affectionately on the shoulder and said: "A good argument is one that cannot be denied. So that's settled."

Surprised, Roger began to speak, but Hafik promptly changed the subject. He said: "And meanwhile, what do you think of my father's palace. Has he made you comfortable?"

Resigned, knowing there was no argument, Roger said: "Yes, very comfortable, thank you."

Hafik said: "Hedonism is almost his only fault." He shot a look at Candia and said: "I too like the good things in life, but perhaps my interpretation of the phrase is a little different from his."

The incipient objection was stillborn. Roger looked at Christie and raised his eyebrows, but Christie only smiled, enjoying the exchange between them, and said: "Just make sure you don't get hamstrung yourself, Roger, it might cramp the operation."

Hafik turned to him and said, gesticulating: "It is their misery that makes them violent, and this I understand. And they must be

106

shown that even when it is understood it will not be tolerated, that if they hate me for the position I hold by right of birth, then my position is none the less such that I can spit upon their hatred. For only by doing this can I ever hope to overcome it. Do you understand what I mean, Maxwell? Sequoyah?"

Christie said dryly: "I only know that where there's trouble, there goes Prince Hafik..."

"Look at Simone," Hafik said. "She knows. She fears for me, but she knows."

Roger saw that her steady gray eyes were on him, watching, composed, and somehow distant; it was as though a secret thought were passing between them. He heard Hafik say again, very softly: "She knows."

Christie slapped him on the back in a rather forced gesture and said: "When this young man takes his father's place, we're going to see a lot of changes."

Roger wondered at the familiarity, and Hafik's handsome face was suddenly brooding, almost sullen. He said:

"We need many changes, and one day, they will be made. Too many of my people—" He broke off abruptly and looked at Candia again and said: "You must have seen?"

"Yes. Yes, I did."

Christie said, shrugging it off: "If you're talking about distribution of wealth, it's a common enough problem, all over the world."

Hafik said swiftly: "And in your part of the world, Maxwell? If you recognize it as a problem...?" He left the question dangling, and Christie said smoothly:

"What am I doing about it? Nothing. Just recognizing that it's with us, and will always be with us. It's the natural result of the competitive spirit, and unless you are going to presuppose identical talents, you can't demand identical results."

"You're right, of course. It's an argument Simone habitually uses." He looked at her affectionately and said: "She believes that when I feel the suffering of my people, I am denying my heritage."

But Madam Caffa refused to be drawn. She held open the gate to the Shah's quarters hand said: "Shall we go in?" As they passed through, Hafik took Roger's arm and said affably: "I understand you come from Oklahoma, Sequoyah, a cattle state. That means you're a good horseman."

"I was once, I suppose. But I traded my horse for a jeep, a long time ago..."

"I have just the pony for you, a seven-year-old Barb, fourteen and a half hands, not as pure-blooded as my Arabians, but very fast, and good in sand. If we leave in an hour, we'll be there by daybreak..."

Roger pulled up short. He said, almost in alarm: "In an hour? But..."

"Of course, my dear fellow, it's a long way. But don't worry, we'll have you back by tomorrow afternoon, you'll have another eighteen hours before you sail." He smiled quickly and said: "We'll push the horses hard, you'll enjoy it."

And when the daylight came, just as Hafik had said, the oasis was there in the distance, shining red in the early sun, its palm trees brightly green, with the small white houses, thatched with leaves, standing out clearly against a sky that was rapidly losing its gold.

He slumped wearily in the saddle, his bones aching, his knees rubbed raw under his light-weight trousers where the ornate leatherwork, heavily embossed in silver, had worked its way, seemingly, deep into his flesh. Even in the cold of the night, he had sweated so heavily that his clothes were soaked through, and the sour smell of the sweating animal was thick in his nostrils; he could not bring himself to think of the trouble that might be waiting for them in the deceptively charming oasis out there, and he said to himself wearily: *Just to get off this goddam horse...* And then he thought of the long ride back, in the heat of the day, and he groaned aloud.

Hafik was ahead of him, way ahead, reining in now and turning back, riding fast back to him and shouting out: "Radija, a splendid sight in the morning!"

Roger forced a smile and said: "I don't suppose we'd find a bottle of bourbon there...?"

The horses stood for a while, panting, their flanks heavy with white foam, and then the Prince dug in his spurs impetuously and shouted: "Follow me in, Sequoyah!"

The hard sand flew up, and the Barb flew forward, and soon they were riding side by side again, riding hard, and Roger called out: "We'd better walk them awhile," but Hafik only laughed and urged the horses on, and soon they came to the oasis and the crisp cold air that hung over the water there.

They reined in their mounts then, and rode slowly among the deserted, ramshackle buildings. A black-robed woman stood at a dark doorway, a terra-cotta jar balanced on her outthrust hip, staring at them; a goat at her feet brayed loudly; some scraggy red chickens dusted themselves in the fine sand; a small child darted out and stared at them too. Three camels were squatting on the ground nearby, their ungainly necks raised, their eyes attentive.

Hafik looked down on the woman as he rode past and raised a hand and said: *"Nurik sa'id, ya bint esh Sheikh*...may your day be peaceful, daughter of a Sheikh..."

The woman stared, and turned back and said something quickly in a low voice, and then she hoisted the jar onto her head and moved off, and when Roger looked back, a tall bearded Arab was coming out of the tiny, one-roomed house, rubbing the sleep from his eyes and staring. They rode slowly on, and then another man appeared from nowhere, and then another and another.

They walked their horses slowly over to where the palm trees hung gracefully over the pool, the heavy hands of dates gleaming red in the early sun, and Hafik looked up at them and pointed with his crop and said: "We call them *bronzes,* the best dates in the world."

The water was clear and cool-looking, and the horses lowered their heads eagerly and drank, and Roger took his water bottle and drank too, and when he found it nearly empty he said: "I think I'd better fill this..."

But Hafik stopped him as he began to raise a tired leg over the saddle, and said quietly: "No. A rule the horseman must always remember when he is among his enemies. He must never dismount. I have water, plenty, for both of us."

All night long Hafik had not touched his bottle during the hard, sweaty ride. Roger grimaced and eased himself in the saddle again, and when he looked back towards the houses he was astonished to see how many white-robed men and black-robed women were standing there, keeping their distance but gathering in little silent groups and watching them, twenty, thirty, maybe more of them, standing and watching and not speaking. A few others were drifting in, and they were beginning to spread out, almost as if the instinct of the hunter were dictating their actions; there was something incredibly menacing in their stealth.

The women among them began to turn away, and still no one spoke, and soon they were gathering about the edge of the water, looking up at the Prince with no expression at all on their faces. The Barb snorted and stomped a forefoot in the wet sand and tossed its massive neck, and Hafik said, smiling: "He smells danger, shall we run from it?"

Roger thought: *I wish to hell we could, but I'm beginning to know you better.*

The Prince pointed his crop at one of the men and said: "That...that one, is the man who hamstrung my horse." He twisted round in the saddle and spoke to him sharply, in Arabic, and the man said nothing; but there was a muttering among the ethers now, and Hafik said: "I have told him that soon my police will come and take him away and that he will be whipped, and you see...he does not dare to answer me."

As calmly as he could, Roger said: "I think maybe the others might...when we begin to ride away."

"We will ride away when we are ready, and they will not touch us. They are afraid." There was a terrible scorn in his voice, and he said: "If my own soldiers, my own tribesmen were cowards like these, there would be no hope at all for my country's future."

Roger looked over the heads of the small crowd. It had grown now, and still there was near-silence, fifty or sixty of them gathered at the edge of the pool with only an occasional mutter to show their sullen anger. He saw that three more men were striding towards them, a tall, white-bearded man flanked by two others; and one of them carried a sword.

It was a long, heavy, two-handed sword of Crusader design, unsheathed, and carried like a cudgel, and he looked quickly at Hafik

110

and saw that he was watching the new arrivals too, a faint smile on his handsome face. He called out suddenly, sharply, imperiously, and the men stopped short and the old one, the one with the white beard, answered him.

And when he had finished, Hafik said: "I told them it was unlawful to bare a sword in the presence of the Prince, and you see...they are not sure of themselves. They are trying to muster a courage they do not have."

"And this game can finish badly for both of us."

"Not a game, my friend. To rule firmly, it is not a game."

"What did the old man say? I only understood the half of it."

"He said his sons were of a new generation that would not respect the old laws. But you see...they respect him, and since he will not move against me, they will not."

"When a man waves a stick, you can never be sure that he's not going to use it."

The Prince smiled and began to speak, but Roger saw the look of sudden fury in his face and swung round quickly. The man with the sword was advancing on them, his two hands on the long hilt, and it was raised above his head; the expression on his face was of uncontrollable fury. Not stopping to think, Roger swung the horse round and dug in his heels, hard, and the thick-set Barb pranced sharply forward, its shoulder muscles rippling, its ears laid back. He threw himself back and tugged on the reins, knowing how the cruel Arab bit would lacerate the tongue, and the horse reared up, its forefeet flailing, prancing on its hind legs. He heard the old man shout, and then the swordsman was falling under the pounding hooves and the other two were falling back, and the horse was in among the crowd and they were scattering...

Roger reined in tight and swung the pony round, away from them, and saw that the Prince had not moved, but was still sitting where he had left him, straight in the saddle, with a light hand resting on the pommel, smiling sardonically; it was almost as if he were enjoying the spectacle.

Languidly, and with affected casualness, Hafik touched a rein to his horse's neck and said lightly: "Well, shall we go now, it's a long ride back..." He walked his horse slowly, unconcernedly, towards the houses, and the people moved aside to let him pass, paying no attention at all to the swordsman who lay on the ground, not moving.

Roger cantered up to ride beside him, expecting an outcry at any minute; but there was nothing but an angry silence behind them, and they did not once look back towards the muttering, threatening crowd.

Soon they were clear of the cool oasis, and Hafik said easily: "And there is one more favor I will ask of you, Sequoyah."

Roger looked at him and asked: "One more?"

"Yes, another one. When we reach Arkan, do me the favor of forgetting the incident, will you? I will say... I will say that we rode there together, that the people welcomed us, and that we rode back again. No one will believe me, but...for Simone Caffa's sake, you know. She worries so much."

"If you wish, Your Highness."

"Good, then that's settled." He looked at Roger sideways and smiled, and said: "Could you have done that with a jeep? Of course not! And now, let us exercise the horses again." He dug in his spurs and pulled away, fast, and Roger sighed and took off after him. All round them, there was nothing but hot sand as far as a man could see.

And farther, too; within the whole scope of his imaginings, it seemed that there could not be a tree, a bush, or even a blade of grass, nothing but hot dry sand that was like powdered lava, still on fire, under their horses' hooves.

And when they reached Arkan, true to his promise, Roger said nothing of the incident at the oasis. When Christie looked at him questioningly, Roger shrugged and said: "A long ride and a very hard one, but I must admit it did me a lot of good."

Candia said: "Tired, darling?"

He shook his head. "What did you do while we were gone?"

"I slept. Alone, darling." Roger looked quickly at Christie, but he seemed preoccupied, and Candia said with a grimace: "And Daddy stayed up half the night reading erotic Arabic poetry. And now, he's a poor man, because he's finally seen something he can't buy, or beg, or steal."

Christie turned away. He said dryly: "If you think in terms of the things I want and haven't got, Candia, then I am indeed a poor man." He turned back and said abruptly: "We have to see the Shah, he's waiting for us."

They did not stay long in the presence of the Shah. He was distant, preoccupied, and angry, and they felt it.

Not liking the mood, Christie said, smiling pleasantly: "As an old friend of the Royal House of Ammadin, let me remind Your Highness that this is an auspicious moment, a moment for very considerable satisfaction. We're about to begin something we've both been planning for a long time..."

And then, the Shah looked off as though someone he had been expecting was entering, and the door at the far end of the long room opened and an officer strode in.

He was carrying an old piece of burlap, a grubby, blood-stained piece of sacking, and he strode to the throne and dropped to his knees in an obeisance that the khaki uniform seemed to make ludicrous.

Madam Caffa looked momentarily startled, as though the poise had unaccountably been driven away, and she said quickly: *"Ba'aden, ba'aden..."*

But the Shah raised an imperative hand and said, in English: "Not later. Now."

She looked at Christie, and at Roger, and then, for a long time, at Candia. Her face was tight with anger.

The officer stood up and held his heavy lump of sacking out for the Shah to see, and the Shah made a gesture. The officer unrolled it on the floor.

Three heads, bloodied, ghastly, sickening, lay at the Shah's feet. The skin over the cheekbones was taut as parchment, and the eyes had the film over them that the fish eyes had in the open-air markets down on the beach. Roger stared, sick to his stomach, and he heard Candia scream and saw Christie quickly take her arm, and then the Shah breathed deeply and leaned back in his throne with his eyes closed, and gave an order, in Arabic, and the officer gathered up the heads (there was blood all over the sleeve of his neat uniform) and put them back in the sacking, and bowed, and began to move backwards towards the door.

Simone said quietly: "I am sorry."

The Shah opened his eyes and looked at her, and then closed them again.

Later that night, when Roger went to the room they had prepared for him, he paced up and down impatiently, unable to sleep and waiting for the day to come and to drive away the fears and the horrors of the night. He thought of Candia and of something Christie had told of him...

Christie had said, making a sardonic joke of it: "...they chop the hands off a thief, and you'd think that would be enough, wouldn't you? A quick cut with a sharp sword and there's an end of it; but no, it's not like that at all..." There was almost a relish in his voice. "The poor bastard is held by a couple of soldiers, another soldier slips a cord over his middle finger and pulls it tight to hold the arm out straight, and then another takes a knife and saws away till the hand comes off, hacks through with a dagger that may or may not be sharp. The time I saw it done, he was screaming and struggling, and it took more than fifteen minutes and they still hadn't made a good job of it, and he got away from them and ran off across the parade ground with what was left of his hand dangling from a tendon that wouldn't break, so they shot him down with a machine gun, escape from custody..."

Roger had shuddered at the image of it. "I'd just as soon not know about it." And Christie had said quickly, smiling a little:

"But you must know about it. Just in case you get the idea that champagne with dinner means...civilization. It doesn't, and it behooves us never to forget it. Once we land on that shore, all the consular protection you may imagine we have...that's all a hell of a way behind us, and we're in a country where absolute rule means despotism in the old-fashioned sense, off with his head, whoever he is."

Roger had said angrily: "I've been in the Arab countries before."

"They're not all like this one. Just don't forget it."

"I won't, don't worry." He had had the feeling that Christie was pushing him, saying: *now there's time to get out if you want to,* and he

114

could not decide just why he should want to do that.

It seemed that the night would never go, and he wondered if Candia too were pacing her room, or lying asleep and forgetting... There was a sound at the door, a gentle knock, so quiet that he might have imagined it, but he switched on the light and went over and opened it, and Madam Caffa was there, still fully dressed, although it was past five o'clock in the morning, and he looked at her in surprise and she said:

"The guard at your window...he said you were not yet sleeping. May I come in?"

He stood back for her. "Of course."

She went to one of the ivory-inlaid rosewood chairs and sat down, and he stood looking at her for a moment, knowing why she had come and waiting for her to speak, and he said at last, offering her the gold case Christie had given him:

"Do you smoke?"

She took a cigarette and he lit it for her, and she inhaled deeply and said: "You know why I'm here, of course. What he did was...unforgivable."

"You mean cutting off their heads, or letting us see that he had done so?"

"There's something you should understand about him. He's...all right, there's no other word for it, he's a despot, and we all know that. But you mustn't judge the harsh and ruthless people you find here by the same standards you would apply in the gentle refinement of the West. We're savages, and we know it."

He said, feeling angry with her for the apology: "And you're his Minister of...Culture. Is this what that culture entails?"

"No, it isn't. I regret the whole episode as much as you do, and I can do about it precisely what *you* can do about it—nothing."

"Nothing except apologize. The world's made up of apology, isn't it?"

She said carefully: "Mr. Sequoyah, the Shah is the only judge of what is best for his People. If that means cutting off the heads of dissidents who are actively planning to assassinate him, then that is what he must do."

"And must he also be so...so goddam blatant about it?"

"The officer had his duty to do, and he did it. The timing was unfortunate, but had His Highness told him to wait... He's not the kind of man who will say: *'Not now, but later, when our savagery may not be so clearly shown.'* If he were, he would be a lesser man."

"Public executions!"

"In your country, you merely invite the press. Is that any better?" Her voice was soft, her English impeccable, with only the slightest trace of an accent that he found fascinating.

"No. No, it's not." He sighed. "Instead of raising hell with you, I should be grateful that you...bothered to offer your condolences, shouldn't I? Perhaps I was worried about Candia. It must have been a terrible shock for her."

"Oh, it was." Madam Caffa almost smiled. "But take my word for it, she will have recovered from that shock already."

"You sound very sure."

"I am sure."

He looked at her curiously. "May I ask a rather personal question?"

"Please do." When he was about to speak, she stopped him and said: "What am I doing here, where did I come from, what is my relationship to the Shah?"

He shook his head. "Right on the first two counts only."

"And the third?"

"None of my business, is it?"

"No, I suppose not. May I have a drink?"

He looked surprised, and she gestured. "A cupboard behind the panel there."

He went to a heavily ornamented rosewood grill and fiddled with it till he heard her laugh and say: "Just slide it to one side." And when he opened it, there was a bottle of whisky and a single glass there. He poured her a drink and she said:

"If you want to join me we'll have to share the glass, it wasn't really expected you'd have guests."

He shook his head and sat down opposite her, watching the way the lines at the side of her mouth deepened when she smiled. She

116

sipped the whisky and said:

"I was born in Italy, but my father was an Orassian diplomat, a very fine one, Mohammed Caffa, you may have heard of him?"

"No, I'm afraid not..."

"He was killed here ten years ago, during one of our perennial riots. A good man, a very good man. He married a French opera singer, Magda Deynse..." She broke off again, and he smiled and said:

"Yes, this time I know who she was." He said suddenly: "Yes, I saw her once, I must have been...oh, not more than ten or twelve, at the Paris Opera House, *Lakme*. I hated every minute of it, but it was...you know, my father took me, part of the grand tour." He grinned. "The good things a child is bored with. Twenty years later, my appreciation had a better edge to it, I hope."

There was a little silence, and then he said:

"You know, I can still visualize her. She was tall, and slim, and wore a white dress that sparkled every time she moved, and I remember how my father frowned at me when I yawned, I was out too late and we'd walked and walked and walked with that...particularly American desperation to see *everything,* not tomorrow or the next day or next year, but now, today, before it all disappears... She was very beautiful, wasn't she?"

"Not really. The lights...the sparkle..."

"I suppose so."

"She was short and rather dumpy, as a matter of fact. But in those days, every soprano who didn't weigh more than two hundred pounds was considered quite svelte."

He said suddenly: "It seems very natural that we should be chatting about...inconsequentialities like this."

"And that surprises you?"

"Yes, it does, a little. Out there, you seemed so...so formal, so much the Minister."

"And now?"

He shrugged, smiling, making a joke of it. "Now, so much the woman."

She held out her glass. "I wish you'd join me."

"All right." He took the glass and drank a little and handed it back to her, and she frowned and said:

"I don't believe my parents were very happy after he brought her back here. My mother died when I was eight, and then my father went off to Washington and left me with a governess here, and then he came back a few years later and was sent to Switzerland, and then... Schools in England, and Italy, and Greece, and then Cambridge for two years and after that the Sorbonne, while he was in Geneva. Always moving around, like a cat on a hot stove..." (It was strange to hear the fluent idiom, so lightly accented) "...and we both came back here, and for a while he was Minister of Finance, and then...they killed him. In Radija."

"Radija? Isn't that where Prince Hafik...?"

"Yes. A constant source of trouble. It's too close to our neighbors' borders, and I'm afraid the Arab dream of a united Greater Arab World too often means a world ruled by one or another of the thousand widely segregated tribes who have nothing in common but the one word, Arab. And even that, among some of them, is a name and nothing else."

He shrugged. "In the States..."

And she said swiftly: "That's not the same thing! For a fair analogy, you must imagine a united Greater Caucasian World, and who would rule it? The Americans? The Germans? The English? The French?"

"One day, they might all do as we did."

"It will be enough, in my lifetime, if I can help unite the warring tribes of Orassia. This means a long lance to keep at bay the rest of the Arabs who want to bring us under their own protective cloak, a cloak that would only smother us." She looked at him somberly and said: "You have seen tonight that we are a very backward people. I ask you to remember that the backward peoples need more help, more tolerance...and a great deal more understanding."

"Now you are the Minister again."

His anger had gone, long ago, and when she asked: "Have I made my point?" he smiled at her and said: "Yes, indeed you have."

"Don't let your...distaste turn you away from us. We badly need the money, and the security, that the oil will bring us."

"If it's there."

"If it's there." She smiled again and said lightly: "Find the oil for us, and the Heaven of the true believers will be yours. You will pass over a bridge as fine as a hair and as sharp as the sharpest sword, and on the other side there will be feasting, and music, and perfume, and fine garments, and doe-eyed maidens waiting for you, just as Gabriel told Mohammed."

He could not tell whether or not she was mocking him, and he said laconically: "I'll be satisfied with our agreed cut of the proceeds."

A thin, reedy voice came to them through the open window, and Madam Calla stood up abruptly and went to the embrasure and looked out for a while in silence, and then she turned to him and said:

"Come and look, Mr. Sequoyah."

He went over and joined her.

Far away to the horizon, the dunes stretched out one after the other, just becoming visible in the deep red glow that was no more than a thin streak in the east. The streak broadened as he watched, and the dunes became astonishingly gold-colored, with a red-gold that seemed to have depth to it, so that if you could imagine you were digging into the limitless sand, you would also think that nothing would come to the surface but the same red-gold light itself, that the harsh dry sand had been strangely turned into something precious by an alchemy that was not quite worldly.

She said: "Have you ever seen anything so beautiful?" He shook his head.

"And the call to prayer has broken the silence. We should have listened to it for a while, while it was still there to be enjoyed."

The thin voice of the muezzin was still calling. She turned to him and said: "A sleepless night for all of us. Will you soon be sailing?"

"At ten, I think."

"Then I will not see you again before you leave."

"But we'll be in touch?"

"Of course."

"Will we see His Highness before we go?"

She shook her head. "Neither the Shah nor the Prince."

"A pity."

"I'm afraid they've had a bit of a fight...over what happened last night. Hafik is more impetuous than his father, but he's also considerably more Westernized. He's not averse to extreme punishment where necessary, but he would never have permitted a show of it. He *would* have said: *'Not now.'* It was only out of deference to his father that he kept silent. You may have seen the anger on his face."

"No. I was...too busy worrying about Candia."

The faint, almost derogatory smile was there again. "As I said, unnecessarily."

"I'm sure you must be wrong."

"Perhaps. I think not. Tell me, Mr. Sequoyah, is she a little...psychotic?"

"Good Heavens no!" Roger laughed shortly. "That's the last thing in the world I'd attribute to Candia. Impulsive, perhaps, unsure of herself, but psychotic? Definitely not."

Abruptly, she held out her hand. "I must say goodbye to Mr. Christie. And his daughter. It was good talking to you."

Her hand was warm and soft, and the gesture was a little awkward, like the handshake of a woman who is more accustomed to having her hand kissed but who wants to avoid a too aloof formality. He was even aware that she felt the subtle distinction herself, as though, because they had shared a few thoughts together, they were no longer really strangers any more. She held his hand firmly and said:

"I hope it will not be too long before we meet again. I hope it will be soon."

"I'm sure it will be. Goodbye."

She turned, and was gone, and he rubbed a hand over his chin, feeling uncomfortable about the stubble of beard there. He looked out of the window for a while, watching the gold turn to yellow and imagining he could already feel the promise of the day's heat. And when the muezzin began to call again, he said irritably:

"Oh, shut up, for Christ's sake."

# CHAPTER 9

THE PREPARATIONS for sailing were well under way.

The yacht rode at anchor in the shallow, steaming waters of the bay, and the white-robed crowds had gone, seemingly melted away, except for the few curious Arabs who sat lethargically in the open-air cafés by the wharf, where small boys ran nimbly among the tables carrying smoking twigs of charcoal in brass tongs for the *narghilehs*; they sat squatty on wickerwork chairs, and sucked the smoke through the rose-scented water out of long, ornately decorated tubes, some of them idly playing backgammon, (they could hear the monotonous clicking of the dice), some of them daydreaming, some of them just sitting. Even on board you could smell the sickly scent of hashish.

An ill-nourished child wandered among the cafés, carrying a wooden box in which there were shoe brushes and cans of polish, clattering the brushes against the sides of the box and hopefully calling out: "*Sumal, ya effendi, sumal...*" (He looked without dismay at the array of bare feet and sandals, and when he found someone wearing shoes he squatted close by and waited, with infinite patience, for an order to begin.)

On board, there was an air of impatience. The seismographic crew, their equipment checked over for the third or fourth time, because there was nothing else to do and they were anxious to start, hung around the lower decks, leaning on the rail, watching the flying fish jump, looking for signs of shark; one of them had dropped a steak deep down into the water on the end of a length of wire, a six-inch hook at the end of it, and was waiting to see what would happen.

121

Roger and Candia stood together on the upper deck where she liked to sunbathe, watching the shoreline with the tolerant patience of those who are about to leave a place they can live without, making small talk and not really saying anything of importance; and then, suddenly, they heard the insistent blare of the car's horns, and the royal Rolls came lurching to a vicious stop near the wharf.

It was still an incongruity against the whitewashed walls of the city and the harsh dry yellow of the dunes beyond. A uniformed dragoman jumped out and ran to the wharf, shouting and waving his arms, and from the bridge Christie said: "Hold it, Mr. Hewitt..."

The skipper gave an order into the speaking-tube, and then Breck appeared at the gangplank to meet the dragoman, and in the background the chauffeur, dressed in a dark blue suit in spite of the sweltering weather, leaned against the car among the sleepy houses, lit a cigarette, and waited. Some children came and stared at the car, silently, not daring to approach too close.

Roger watched, but he could not understand what it was that was being said. Breck was talking fluent Arabic, and in a little while he turned and led the dragoman up to the bridge, and Candia, watching, said:

"Hell, if this means a delay..."

Roger shook his head. "Who knows?"

He looked at her obliquely, and saw that there was no more than a trace of impatience on her face, and she laughed and said shortly:

"I want to get out of these damned clothes and into a bikini." She gestured towards the shore. "I'm supposed to defer to their highly advanced ideas of morality while we're in their highly advanced harbor."

"I thought for a moment you were still worried about the business last night."

Candia looked at him blankly for a moment. "Oh, that... God, it was awful, wasn't it?"

Roger looked at her curiously. "And I believe you've quite shrugged it off."

Candia said: "The hell with it, if he wants to chop off a few heads, that's his bloody business. Just as long as mine isn't one of them."

Thinking of Madam Caffa, he said nothing, and then Christie hailed them from the bridge. "Roger? I'm going ashore for a while, I won't be long." There was no word of explanation, but the irritation was marked.

They leaned over the rail together and watched Christie climb into the Rolls, and then it took off fast along the dusty road to the palace. From below, Breck looked up at them and grinned, and called out:

"An urgent summons, maybe we're not going after all."

Candia said: "Oh, God..."

Breck came up and joined them then, and Candia said with a sigh: "Are we going to be long in this dump?"

He shrugged. "Your guess is as good as mine. All we can do is wait in patience. A royal command from the Shah."

"What the hell does he want, anyway?"

"I haven't the vaguest idea." He leaned on the rail with his back to it, and crossed his ankles and looked at them with a slight smile and asked: "Did you hear the news?"

Roger shook his head, and Breck said: "No, I suppose if you don't know much Arabic... I listened to Radio Quatar last night, and again early this morning. There was considerable trouble over at Radija yesterday."

Candia said: "Radija? Prince Hafik was there, he said his horse was killed..."

"He was lucky to get away with his life." Breck said, as though the whole thing amused him: "Apparently, it started off as nothing more than a *rhazzu,* a Bedouin raid, their idea of a noble sport, ride into town and beat up the citizenry, then ride out again with all the loot they can carry, they still do it. But there was a detachment of the Shah's Camel Corps in the oasis, and a small battle started. The people sided with the Army, and the Bedouins began to have a bad time, and then Hafik, apparently, tried to stop the Bedouins and persuade them to go back to the desert, and the Army turned on him. The noble sport had become a trifle...political. The Bedouin side with the Shah, automatically, because he's one of them... According to Radio Quatar, it was an army officer who fired on Hafik, though Radio Aden says it was a civilian.... Take your choice of stories,

123

there'll be plenty of them."

Candia said: "I bet it was a general," and when Breck raised an eyebrow Roger told him about the executions.

Breck frowned. "And the radio said nothing about that. Well, it figures. No one outside Orassia wants to give the impression that there's any strength in the old man's government, it pays them to play down the efficiency of his secret police."

Roger said: "Three generals...beheaded. I'd be happier if they were of lower rank. Generals usually have large forces behind them. A dissident Army..."

Breck shrugged. "Only part of it."

"And apparently the dissidents may control the southern areas of the Rub el Khali, might make it awkward for us, don't you think?"

For a while, Breck said nothing. He took off his sweat-soaked shirt and threw it over his shoulder and said gently, enjoying it:

"There are some stores on board you may not have seen, Sequoyah. Eighteen machine guns and a great deal of ammunition. And every man jack of the crew is handpicked. We've nothing to worry about."

Roger said sharply: "I came here to look for oil, not to fight a bloody war."

"Scared?" Breck's voice was mocking and unpleasant.

Roger looked at him coldly. "If you care to think that, it's your damned privilege." He turned and moved away, and Candia called after him:

"Roger, wait!" She ran to catch up with him, and when they had gone below she said: "Don't let him worry you, it's all part of his goddam neurosis."

"Yes? Well, one of these days I'll punch his bloody nose."

She laughed and said: "He'd take you apart with his bare hands if you tried it."

"It would still be worth it." He was walking, not really caring where he was going, towards the big main cabin, but she took his arm and said:

"This way, there's something I want to show you."

He went with her to Christie's personal quarters, and she poured him a drink, in spite of his halfhearted protest that he didn't want any, and said:

"Sit there and be comfortable, I want to read you some poetry."

"Poetry? This time of the day?"

"Sit down, and listen."

She slid the tall mahogany ladder along on its silent runners, and climbed to the top and looked back at him, and then reached for a half-bound leather volume that was gold-tooled in an intricate oriental design, and came down with it again and lay down on the sofa with the book balanced on her breast. She said:

"Light me a cigarette, will you?" He lit one for her and gave it to her, and she patted the sofa beside her and said: "Sit here, there are some marvelous illustrations."

He sat beside her, smoking and waiting, with one hand laid lightly on her hip, and when she found the place she began to read:

> *Her Breasts were like twin Towers of white marble,*
> *On which the Sun, the Right Hand of the King,*
> *Still lingered,*
> *And her thighs were an opened gate of alabaster*
> *To welcome the rampant Lion to his Lair*
> *In eagerness,*
> *And that Staff of pleasurable strength, proud and Majestic,*
> *Long as the spear of the noblest Warrior*
> *Who was the King,*
> *Made ready for play by the liquid touch of the Rose,*
> *Searched, and found, and drove full length,*
> *And the dew*
> *Falling gently on the grass-covered mound...*

Roger said impatiently: "If your father found you reading that..."

She put down the book and laughed. "You don't want to see the pretty pictures?"

"No, I don't."

"And he won't see me, he's dancing to a tune the Shah plays, a pretty tune on a reed pipe that says: 'Come back, Mr. Christie, come back and dance for me.'"

He looked at her curiously, ignoring the venom there. "Do you often do this? I mean...sneak in here and go through his books?"

"His private little collection? Yes, I do."

She closed the book with a snap and jumped up, brushing past him and sliding off the sofa with a quick, lithe movement, an animal in flight. The leather volume dropped to the floor, and he picked it up, feeling the smooth texture of the ancient leather that was as soft and delicate as the petal of a camellia; and when he looked at Candia she was at the top of the ladder again, rummaging through the highest shelves. She looked down at him and said:

"They're all here, the *Khama-Sutra,* illustrated, and the *Shastra* too, have you read the *Shastra?* It's much more detailed, exciting... He's got the *Satyricon,* but a lot of that is dull, isn't it? And here's the original *Samosata,* in Greek and English, not the one that, who was it, Apuleius? Not the one Apuleius cleaned up, but the original..."

"I'm surprised you even know about that."

"Oh, I know," she said, "I've read it a dozen times, do you know what really happened when she got in there with the Ass, it wasn't the way Apuleius put it at all, boy he really messed it up. And you know that little piece about the serving girl Fotis? Well... Ah, here we are..."

She had found what she was looking for, a big square book, very thin, with a green leather cover decorated in gilt lettering. She said excitedly: "The most marvelous copy of the Kingdom of the Lotus, illustrated by..." She was flipping over the big pages, her eyes alight. "Illustrated by Anton Viladi, almost the only copy in existence. Look." She opened the book to show him, and then slipped down the ladder and sat beside him on the sofa again, spreading out the book on her knees. She said again: "Look."

He began to feel acutely uncomfortable, and she turned the page and showed him a painting in delicate pinks and greens and blues, a detailed painting in water color of a young Hindu prince on his royal bed, with five young women gathered closely round him in attitudes he could only think of as extraordinary. The ornate script of the caption was in French, and she said:

"How's your French, lover?" Not waiting for him to answer, she translated it for him: "The Prince...how would you translate *besognant?* Working over? Setting to work? There's a much better word, isn't there? The Prince at work with five of his women at the same time. How would you translate that, Roger Sequoyah?"

He said angrily: "I wouldn't translate it at all, I'd leave it alone, and that's what you ought to do."

She said mildly: "Oh? But I'm only catching up on my education. What's the use of an erudite father if a little of the erudition doesn't rub off on his daughter?"

"There are other things you could learn from him."

She said maliciously: "These are the things he knows best."

"Candia..."

"Well, so he does too, just ask him."

He sighed. "Put that stuff back and come and have a drink."

"Or a cold shower?"

"Candia!"

"Well, you wouldn't want me to remain just a backward child, would you, with no knowledge of...what did Vatsayana call it? The Great Delight? Just a question of education, Roger, that's all it is."

He sighed. "In that direction at least, I'd say your education was fairly advanced."

"Then let's take some of the pretty pictures to my cabin."

"No. Put them back."

"Roger, I told you before, you're a bloody prude. And there's a note in your voice that tells me you're getting tired of me."

"No, it's not that..."

"You're driving me out."

He protested: "No, I'm not, it's not that at all..."

"And you want me to find some animal seaman down on the lower decks, is that what you want? Someone with better staying power?"

He began to get angry with her. He stood up and said: "Put that bloody book back where it belongs, I'm going out for some fresh air."

The laugh had gone, and there was as ugly line to her beautiful, childlike mouth. "You're not only a prude, you're not half as good as you think you are in bed, either." She sat up suddenly, picked up the book again, and unexpectedly threw it at him, violently. She snapped: "Catch up on some of your own education, it might make a more satisfying man out of you!"

The leather cover of the volume had hit him under the eye and hurt him, and he bent down to retrieve it and put it down on the desk. He said:

"You want your behind spanked, it should have been done a long time ago."

She began to laugh again, the anger gone as suddenly as it had come. She lay back on the sofa and said:

"And I like that too, why don't we try it some time?"

He turned away and went out.

It was not till late that night that Christie returned. Dinner had been served, and cleared away, and the night had turned unexpectedly cold, and they were listening to the radio in the after lounge, worrying a little over the news.

The announcer from Aden said:

"...and the incipient revolt seems for the moment to have been put down, though not without considerable loss of life. In the troubled Oasis of Radija, and around the Jebel el Ghaida, more than three hundred persons have been killed, but it appears that the security force of His Royal Highness, Shah Omar Ammadin, is firmly in control of the situation. A small section of the Army has joined forces with the Rebel Committee for Progress, but they have been driven out into the desert where, unless further help is sent from the surrounding Arab countries, which they expect, they will certainly be wiped out by the armed Bedouin who are still intensely loyal to His Royal Highness.

"Diplomatic sources in Jedda have stated that the frontiers have been closed to deny the rebels access to outside supplies of arms and money, and Radio Arkan has appealed for the restoration of order in the affected areas..."

Breck switched off and said: "Help from the surrounding Arab countries, the usual picture, the maximum of mischief all round. But, if you ask my opinion, I'd say it was all over."

Roger, wondering, looked at him and Breck turned away. There was something there, Roger thought, that he could not easily define. Was he hiding something? Was it a lie? Breck went on:

"I picked up a call for help on the shortwave radio a while back, the rebels were recounting their losses to...I don't know who they were talking to, but they sounded pretty exhausted."

Roger said, frowning: "What's this Committee for Progress?"

Breck grinned. "Better known as the Awlad Yussuf. The one has emphatically denied any connection with the other, but that's all part of the political picture; since Yussuf is an Orassian figure, they need a more...a more International aspect to their name, or our friends across the border wouldn't be so anxious to move in with their so-called help. Hence...now it's the Committee for the Arab People's Progress, and what self-respecting Arab could turn down an appeal from a bunch with a name like that?"

"The Jebel el Ghaida, that's not too far from where we'll be operating."

"Fifty miles or so from where we start, the nearest settled area, but it doesn't mean a damn thing."

"I hope you're right."

A steward rapped on the door and put his head in and looked at Breck and said: "The Rolls is out there, Mr. Breck."

Breck got quickly to his feet and grinned at them. "Well, now we'll know."

He went out, and they waited, and when he returned Christie was with him. He seemed tense and excited, and he said:

"We have guests..." He turned and said: "Come in, my friends, come and meet my officers."

Roger looked at them in surprise. Simone Caffa was there, and Prince Hafik was with her. As Christie made the introductions, Roger watched him, looking for some sign in explanation, but there was none.

Madam Caffa was gracious and formal, and Prince Hafik seemed cheerfully casual, smiling quickly and shaking hands heartily, his bright eyes smiling and his teeth showing quickly white, and at last Christie said:

"The Shah has suggested that some governmental authority on board might be a useful thing, and I agreed with him. So..." He turned to Madam Caffa: "Let me show you over my ship, I think you'll find her exciting." He looked at Roger and said: "Roger, come with us, would you like to?"

Roger got to his feet and looked quickly at Candia. He

129

wondered if there were a pointed snub there, and if so, what was the reason for it, but she was looking at Hafik and smiling gently to herself, as though to say: *Never mind, there's a new interest here...* Speaking to Hafik and almost ignoring Madam Caffa, she said pleasantly:

"It's going to be good to have you both aboard. I'm the only bystander at the moment." Then she said to her father: "I wonder if Madam Caffa would like my cabin, it's the nicest..."

But Simone shook her head. "I'm not at all demanding." And Christie said affably:

"There's plenty of room for everyone, but it's a good idea. Shall we go?"

They wandered together over the yacht, and when they came to the bridge Christie said to the waiting skipper: "Any time, when you're ready, Mr. Hewitt, you know the course."

The captain nodded.


Later, Roger said to Madam Caffa, trying to probe their relationship:

"The Prince is a very serious young man. Underneath that cheerful affability, there's a searching mind, am I right?"

They were sitting—the three of them, Christie, Roger, and Madam Caffa—in the small forward lounge that served as an observation cabin; a quiet intimate room that had been cunningly slipped, as it were, into the rounded stem when the remodeling had been done. The long drapes that covered the curved windows had been drawn, and the lamps, peach-colored, cast a warm glow over her face as he watched her.

She nodded. "And highly intelligent, a product of some of the best schools in Europe." She looked into her glass and smiled and said: "While his mentor sits here watching the night go by, he sleeps, and do you know why? He sleeps because this is the quickest road to tomorrow, and Hafik wants tomorrow more than anything else in the world."

Christie sighed. "The process of growing up, too slow, and then...much too fast."

"Each new day brings him closer to a vision, a vision he has of a greater, better Orassia. There is so much he wants to do."

Christie said dryly: "I always fear visionaries," and Madam Caffa answered swiftly: "You are one yourself, Mr. Christie. So am I. So is Hafik. He studies, he learns, he waits. And one day, he will make a great Shah, greater than his father or his grandfather."

There was a great deal of pride in her voice, and Roger said, not so much wanting to agree with Christie, but knowing what was behind the cynicism:

"A country grows more slowly than a man. Sometimes, great damage can be done by sweeping changes."

She looked away. "Yes. Yes, I know that too."

For a while she fell silent, worrying over something, and Christie got up and pulled aside the drapes and looked out over the water, then flung open the windows and let in the cool night air. And when Madam Caffa looked once at the lamps, Roger switched them out so that the room was flooded with the white moonlight which streamed in.

He said: "The moon over the Red Sea, I've seen it a hundred times and it's always brighter than it was the last time." He turned to look at her, remembering the gold of the desert that she had shown him, looking at her and admiring the calm that was there, the almost statue-like quiescence.

She was not, he saw, as young as he had first thought. Her features, her body, her movements were those of a woman of less than thirty; but there were tiny wrinkles under her eyes that gave her face a certain maturity, that seemed to add to the self-assurance. *A women who has worn well,* he thought, *who has kept herself physically perfect through, perhaps, that will power that shows through so strongly.* He was surprised that he had not seen before an essential animalism in her, in the way she moved, in the way she sometimes stayed perfectly still, as though all the energy were constantly controlled and ready. It made her seem unexpectedly desirable, as though the great long step between the stranger and the friend would be a short and easy one to take. He was aware, for the first time, of her body; the small, lithe hips were smooth and sleek, and it shocked him to realize that he was mentally undressing her.

131

He pulled himself away from his reverie and looked at the calmness in her eyes. It occurred to him that had she used make-up she would have looked almost like a teenager, almost younger than Candia. He wondered if those almost invisible lines were part of the proclamation of maturity in a woman who knows that age is better than youth. And yet, there was a purity to the skin that was quite remarkable, a depth of texture like that which the great painters had sometimes shown when they were painting the women they loved.

*This was the point,* he thought, *it was a face on which, somehow, past and future love was clearly defined.* In spite of the almost regal assurance, an ancient, almost lost concept of femininity was clearly there. It was a face that, on a canvas, would make a man stop and look more deeply, and then turn back again to discover what it was that had made him stop. There was a confident set to the mouth, too big and too strong, that added to the confidence in the eyes. There were moments, when she moved her head, in which she looked almost masculine; and then, suddenly, with the slightest movement or change of expression, there was a haunting, feminine beauty. Above all, there was the repose.

He thought of Candia's disjunctive volatility, and the comparison left a strange disquiet on him; he began to wonder if he were perhaps beginning to fear Madam Caffa. He thought of strength and violence, and he said suddenly:

"Radija, is it all over now?"

She turned to look at him, and the hesitation seemed to say, without too much offense: *It's not really your business, is it?* Her eyes were quite cold.

"Yes, Mr. Sequoyah, it is over. A few noisy dissidents, nothing more."

He pressed the point. "The Committee for...what was it? The Arab People's Progress?"

Again, the cold hesitation. "I prefer to think of them as the Awlad Yussuf. Yussuf himself was a popular leader of the seventeenth century who fought against the Yemenis and was killed trying to replace one king with another. And yet, the men who claim to follow his teachings are only concerned with the establishment of a kind of nihilism. Do you believe that any good can come from...from anarchy?"

Roger said deliberately: "The first of the anarchists were rebelling, surely, against cruelty and injustice. Out of the initial pains, there came lasting good."

"And nihilism too."

Christie said flatly: "No. The nihilists were considerably more pessimistic. The anarchists merely wanted to demolish the current political, economic, and social institutions, and then start from scratch..."

Beginning to mock him, she said: "Carrying their ideas on the acquisition of property so far that equality was to become a law, imposed on the people by whom? By what form of government? They denied the necessity for *any* form, whether imposed or elected, since it was not, they said, compatible with the exercise of complete liberty. Yet that nebulous government they denied was to impose a new set of laws, a new tyranny... Property is theft, they said..."

"Only in the metaphysical sense that slavery is assassination. And by the same token. The one destroys human personality, the other separates the creator and his work, it's a solid enough theory. In theory."

"...and like the Communists, they presupposed an ideal state in which a political philosophy might work that did not take into account the basic truth that men, like the other animals, are seldom equal one to the other."

Roger said: "And if the Awlad Yussuf started from scratch?"

She smiled. "Some say that Orassia would have an exarchy. A government from Cairo, or Baghdad, or Damascus, or Jedda, or even Riyadh—anywhere except Arkan."

Christie said: "Then you are sure that their financing comes from abroad?"

"No, Mr. Christie, I am not. The Awlad are a secret society. And they have kept their secrets well."

"Even from you?"

"Even from me."

"The point is," Roger said, "are we going to have any trouble with them?"

"No."

133

"Well, thank God for that, at least."

Madam Caffa finished her drink and looked at her watch. "In an hour, it will be daylight, another tomorrow for Hafik, a day nearer his accession."

She was about to rise, when Roger said curiously: "Do you look forward to that day, Madam Caffa? Might it not mean the end of your own authority?"

She was momentarily startled. "Oh? Why do you ask that?"

Christie was watching them, his eyes alert and amused. Roger shrugged:

"I had the impression that you were perhaps the Shah's link to a world he doesn't really belong in, a world that is quite foreign to him. Prince Hafik is quite obviously closer to that...larger life. And, therefore, perhaps, he would not need your help as much as the Shah does. And does it offend you that I raise the point? It's merely academic."

She laughed. "No, it does not offend me, and it's more than academic. When the Prince takes over control of his country's affairs, I will be there if I am needed. If not..." She said gently: "If not, my work will have been completed. I have spent my life helping a boy to become a man. His more liberal thoughts are an extension of my own. In a sense, all that Hafik is today, is the end product of my own intelligence. When the time comes for him to rule alone, I hope that he will be capable of it. If he is, then my own authority will not die; it will merely be passed on." She looked at him with sudden interest and said curiously: "When we met, I was introduced as the Minister for Cultural Affairs. And yet...you seem very sure that I have so much power."

"I would have said influence, perhaps, but...yes, you gave me that impression."

Christie said: "He's a perceptive young man, Madam Caffa, and there's one thing we have in common; we both know the benefits of power, and therefore we both recognize it easily."

She stood up and said lightly: "I will accept that as a tribute. And now..."

"Bed?"

"I think so. The night has passed very pleasantly."

134

They walked with her, the two of them, through the silent ship to the cabin which Candia had vacated for her, and they left her there; and as they passed through the main lounge on their way to their own quarters, Christie growled:

"Who the hell put the lights out?"

He switched them on and pulled up short with an expression almost of shock on his face.

Hafik and Candia were sitting quietly in a corner, close together on one of the leather sofas, and Candia was looking at her father and smiling gently.

Hafik said: "Time for bed? I suppose it is. You have a lovely ship, Mr. Christie. And a lovely daughter too."

Candia looked up at her father and it seemed to Roger that she was enjoying the brief moment of shock. She said softly:

"It's not always quite so easy, is it?"

For a moment, Christie did not answer. He merely stared at his daughter, his face dark with sudden tight-lipped anger. And then he said curtly: "Good night." He turned and walked quickly away, leaving Roger standing there and sensing a touch of awkwardness.

Suddenly, Candia laughed. She said: "Yes, time for bed, I suppose."

She jumped up quickly, reached up and kissed Roger on the cheek, turned, and was gone.

Roger looked after her, and Hafik stood up and said cheerfully:

"She's an interesting girl, isn't she?"

"Uh-huh."

"And rather young. But very attractive." He said ruefully: "Did I sense a certain...annoyance in her father? Sitting here in darkness..."

Roger said diplomatically: "I don't think so. He's had a hard day."

"Yes. Yes, of course." He smiled quickly and said: "I'll say good night, Mr. Sequoyah."

"Good night, Your Highness."

Hafik said deprecatingly: "Outside of Arkan, the formality is not really necessary, you know."

"I'd say you carry a title very well."

"Sometimes, it irks a little."

135

"Madam Caffa suggested you had...shall I say, democratic inclinations?"

Hafik laughed. "We all do, the sickness of the generation."

"You don't really believe that."

"Oh, but I do! If Simone has taught me nothing else, she has taught me that a poor and backward people need the help that only authority can provide."

"She is a remarkable woman."

Hafik said somberly: "Without her, my country would be in the most abject state of chaos. One day, she will help me make it a Paradise." At the door, he turned and said: "You were talking in there a long time. Did you like her?"

"Yes, very much."

"I'm glad. Good night, Roger."

"Good night."

When he went to his cabin, Roger found Candia's clothes strewn all over the floor, and she was in his bed, waiting for him.

# CHAPTER 10

THE NEXT DAY, when they were alone, Christie asked Roger: "Are you deliberately avoiding the question?"

His dark, shrewd eyes were probing, watchful, giving the words an importance which the voice seemed to be trying to hide. It was almost as if Christie were prompting him to assume an interest which he really wanted to avoid, trying, as it were, to bring out an intimacy by the sharing of secrets. There were several questions in Roger's mind, but he knew that there was an obscurity here that was deliberate; without being sure of the reason, or even searching for it, he knew he would not get the right answers.

He was aware, too, of a sudden spasm of guilt in his own mind, a guilt that was all the more sharp because he could not believe that Christie was completely unaware of what he was doing with Candia; or rather, he thought wryly, what Candia was doing with him...

But Christie, watching him closely, had other things on his mind. He said, insisting and trying to mask the insistence:

"You haven't asked what Hafik and Simone are doing on board."

The relief was considerable. Roger grinned at him. "I thought you'd tell me, in time, if you wanted it generally known. Since you hadn't yet done so... I thought you rather enjoyed the little mystery."

Christie shook his head. His look was earnest, sincere, completely trustworthy. "No mystery. They both have a huge stake in this operation, don't forget. If it comes off..."

"Uh-huh."

Christie looked at him sharply, and Roger avoided his eye. "Moreover," Christie went on, "if there should be any trouble down there, then their presence will be invaluable.

"Or a considerable embarrassment. Any trouble will come from the anti-Royalist group, the Committee. Not from the Shah's own forces, with whom Simone and Hafik might have some authority."

"Maybe." Christie shrugged and changed the subject, and Roger knew that the lies had been tried out and put away as useless and the hell with it. He did not pursue the matter; but he wondered what it was that Christie was trying—so successfully—to hide from him. He could be sure of only one thing; the emotion that was being skillfully hidden was a sort of jubilation. Somehow, he was sure, the presence of Simone and Hafik represented, for Christie, a considerable triumph. And in that triumph, he was sure, there was something that would not bear too close inspection.

They went down to the main lounge together, where Breck had prepared the maps for them, and Christie tapped a wiry finger on the pale brown strip that ran along the blue of the water and said:

"We'll set up a camp on shore, in tentage, just about here, a more or less permanent camp. The men can range along the coast as necessary and report back to the ship constantly. But our guests will stay on board at all times."

"Oh? They might prefer it ashore..."

"I've already discussed it with them. They agree that it's best."

Roger sat down and said carefully: "If you think that they are in any sort of personal danger, Maxwell, I wish you'd tell me about it. If there's something up your sleeve..."

Christie said coolly: "Nothing up my sleeve, and no personal danger. It's a question of convenience and nothing else."

"I see."

But he did not. He knew damn well that something was going on that would smell sourly if brought out from under cover.

Christie turned to Breck and said, as though there had been no interruption to his train of thoughts:

"You'll be in complete charge on shore, Breck, and I think you'd better make the camp your H.Q." He grinned quickly and said: "Since Roger here is sure that the Bedouin are going to ride in over the dunes and massacre us all, you'd better put a small post up in the mountain, four or five miles back, a couple of men with a radio to keep an eye open..."

Roger said coldly: "You know as well as I do that we are in no danger at all from the Bedouin. It's the Committee we have to worry about."

For a moment, there was a sharp anger in Christie's eyes, but it went away and he said mildly:

"Yes, of course, the Bedouin are on our side. Am I being short-tempered today?"

"Yes, you are."

"Then, I'm sorry." He looked at Breck, and Breck silently gathered up the maps and went out, and when he had gone, Christie sat down and rubbed a hand over his eyes. He looked up at Roger and said ruefully: "I'm very fond of young Hafik, very fond of him indeed. And you know how I feel about Candia."

"So, that's it."

"That's it."

Roger said: "Dammit, you mean because they were sitting in the dark together? If that's all that's going on..."

Christie interrupted him. "That's all that's going on now, maybe, but... She made her intentions pretty plain, and I don't like the looks of them. My...fondness for Hafik is...it's an intellectual thing, he's a bright young man with a future ahead of him that's important to me, and so...so I like him. But that's all it is. He's the kind of man...you can like him or hate his guts, and the border's an easy one to step over. Has it ever occurred to you that for a man who lives by his intellect it's a great deal easier to dispense with his...friends?"

"No, but I'm glad you pointed it out."

Christie waved an airy hand: "Oh...in our case, emotion and intellect, together they can't be broken..."

"I hope you're right."

"You know I am. But with Hafik..." He said darkly: "He'd better keep his distance, I'll carry my responsibilities just so far."

"If I know you as well as I think I do, you'll carry them all the way."

"I wish you wouldn't try to confound me with my own

strength."

"And I wish I knew what the hell you were talking about."

"You heard what Candia said."

Roger shrugged. "I heard, but I didn't understand her, either. I obviously wasn't meant to."

Christie smiled, a slow, amused smile that spread to his eyes.

"No, it's me she's after this time. *'It's not always quite so easy,'* she said, and she was very sure I'd understand. It was a direct jibe, a reference to our old friend Luther Fenton and what I did about him. And it means, quite clearly, that she's deliberately going to throw herself at Hafik. For kicks. She wants to find out what I propose to do about it."

Roger felt extremely uncomfortable, listening to what seemed to him a confession of weakness, even though he knew that the weakness was deliberately shown. But he could feel the hidden anxiety, and he said slowly:

"First of all, I don't think Hafik would...well, he seems a serious sort of young man, not the type to... He's apparently not the hedonist his father is."

"No, he's not. Not as wise as his mentor Simone. He's liable to get involved with Candia even against his will. For him, a woman...is just a woman, in spite of that civilized veneer."

"It's a bit early to make an assumption like that, isn't it?"

"Perhaps." Christie said moodily: "But better now than when it's too late."

Roger felt he was being dragged into a discussion he could not easily tolerate. He stood up and said:

"Well, there's not really a great deal you can do, is there? After all, Candia knows her own mind, she's not a child any more, even if... She thinks you regard her as rather younger than she really is, did you know that?"

"Yes, I know, and I'm right. She is younger than she really is."

In the silence, he was sure that Christie was waiting for him to say: *If there's anything I can do to help...* He said, instead:

"I think you're worrying unduly."

Christie nodded, and when Roger looked at him he was surprised by the expression of acute misery there, and he could not hide the momentary shock. He grimaced and said:

"Hell, I feel like a father confessor."

"So go and see what she's up to, will you? Do me a personal favor."

Roger snorted. He said sourly: "I don't really relish the role you're trying to force me into, but if you think it will help..."

The image of their quarrel, of Candia's sudden access of temper, was still acute; reasoning about it, he knew that it would have passed, that now it would be for her no more than something to laugh about.

He shrugged and went out, and he found her alone on the sun deck, lying on her stomach with her long legs spread out and the top of her bikini lying carelessly beside her; he picked it up and handed it to her, and she put down the book she was reading and swung round as he sat on the polished deck beside her. She raised an eyebrow and said coolly:

"Where are our guests today?"

"Simone Caffa? She's still sleeping."

"At eleven-thirty in the morning? But I mean Hafik, as you well know."

Roger said: "Hafik is in the chartroom, learning a little something about his coastline."

"On a day like this he should be lying on the deck in the sun, with an attractive young woman." She looked at him obliquely and said: "You don't like Hafik very much, do you?"

He was surprised. "What on earth makes you think that?"

"Oh, I don't know. I sensed it."

"You're quite wrong."

"I think he's cute."

"Not a word I would use, but I suppose I understand what you mean."

"Are you jealous?"

"Hell, no. Should I be?" She sat up and he gestured at the bathing costume top and said with a sigh: "I'd be happier if you put that on..."

She let her hands gently touch her own breasts and said: "You liked them last night, you said the nicest things about them. Is it only

141

in the sunlight that my body worries you?"

"It'll sure as hell worry your father if he comes along."

"You want to bet?" But she put the top on and swung her back to him and said: "Fix it for me, then you can breathe again."

He fastened the catch and she lay down on her back, and squinted up at him and said: "But you were cold last night."

"Was I?"

"Are you getting tired of me? So soon?"

"You know I'm not."

"And I know that it doesn't mean very much to you, does it?"

He said carefully, smiling at her: "Not as much, perhaps, as it would if it meant something to you."

"Well, I suppose that's fair enough. What's Father doing?"

"Worrying about you. And Hafik."

She reached out and found her dark glasses and slipped them on, and put her hands under her head and said nothing, and he wondered if, behind the green lenses, she were watching him. He decided she was, and he said lightly:

"You're a bit of a minx, Candia, aren't you? You like to punish your father."

He was surprised at the sudden venom in her voice. "I've got a lot to punish him for."

"Don't make Hafik a party to it."

"Why not?"

He said patiently: "We're all going to be cooped up together here for a good many weeks. Too many conflicts... Besides, he's not really quite the man for you, is he?"

"Oh? You're quite wrong, Roger Sequoyah. Anything handsome and virile is the man for me. And the key word is virile."

"You'd be hurting him just to hurt your father, that's a pretty lousy setup."

"You're moralizing, Roger Sequoyah, and it doesn't suit you."

"It's time someone did moralize a bit."

She sat up suddenly and said: "Well, coming from you...! Is this because you couldn't make it last night?"

He took out a couple of cigarettes and lit them, and passed her one, and she took it and said:

"Well, is it?"

He lay down beside her and said without rancor: "I thought we'd come to that, sooner or later."

"If you tell me I've drained the life out of you, I won't believe it."

"No, it's not that."

"Oh? Then the reason is even more fascinating. I'm no longer the only woman on board."

He said angrily: "And you know damn well it's not that either."

"So? I'm listening, darling."

He grimaced, knowing that anger could be dangerous. "I'm told it happens, once in a while."

"Not to my men, it doesn't, not without a damn good reason." She laughed suddenly, turning to him with genuine pleasure, her anger gone. "You remember the story of Queen Balavruda?"

"Remember it? I never even heard it."

"Your education's been sadly neglected. Eighth century, Persia or somewhere, she ordered the castration of every man at her court who couldn't satisfy her seven times in one night, and she was astonished to find that not a single one of them failed. So she put the number up to ten, and then to twelve, and still there were no victims. She then came to the obvious conclusion that her own physical perfection was responsible for her lovers' frenzy, and would have lived happily ever after, just like in the fairy stories, except that a discarded lover told her that the Grand Vizier had been feeding them all aphrodisiacs. So she had the Grand Vizier executed, and then discovered, when it was too late, that no one could satisfy her anymore because the secret of his love potion had died with him. Poor Balavruda was never quite the same again, and neither, with that wonderful aphrodisiac gone, was the poor old world."

"Well, there's a moral there somewhere, I suppose. But, take my word for it, my...hesitancy last night..."

"Hesitancy!"

"For want of a better word. It was not the result of a change in my diet. I'm beginning to ask myself questions, and I don't really like the answers too much. And it's nothing to do with *your* physical perfection, either."

143

For a long, long time she said nothing, but lay there, thinking. "Then it was an exercise in self-control, and I hate you for it."

"I wish you'd take off those damned glasses so that I could see your eyes when you talk to me like that."

She turned to him and slowly took off her glasses, and said: "Is that what you wanted to see, Roger? Do you know me so well, do you hate me so much?"

Her eyes were red with suppressed tears. The unexpected sight of them shocked him. Suddenly hurt, he put a hand on hers and said: "Nothing I told you could possibly have hurt you." His voice was low and gentle, and he felt her hand tighten under his and she whispered:

"Am I ill, Roger? Do you think I'm ill?"

"No, I don't."

"I'm a bloody nympho."

"According to the Hindu poets you seem to like so much..."

"Yes, I know, the ultimate excellence. But the man who wrote that was only looking at it from his own point of view, you think he stooped to wonder about the woman's? Of course not, he was lying there, satiated, knowing that when he was ready again she would be too, ready to try harder the next time because... Could a woman think up a phrase like that? The ultimate excellence? If it meant, for her... No, Roger, it's not like that for the woman, I know, I can tell you just what it's like... You search, you strain, you try hard and you cry out and it's not with relief, it's with pain, because the relief hasn't come and it's too late now and wait till next time and try again, and all the while it's...it's a grinding at you, a tearing at the flesh and no relief, and... And still you hope that maybe the next time, and you try again, and again, and again, each time harder than before and there's the ultimate excellence, but it's not for you, because something stops the flood from coming, and you let them batter away at the dam and still it won't come, it's dry, and you try again because there's nothing else to do but hope that one day the dam will break and the flood will come... And it never does, Roger. It never does."

He said very gently: "All I asked, Candia, was that you should not use Hafik to hurt your father, that's all. And nymphomaniac or not, I don't think you're ill. And I'm very, very fond of you." He leaned over her and kissed the wet eyes quickly, and said, changing the subject so that she could not pursue it: "We'll be putting ashore some time tomorrow, did you know that?"

"Breck told me." Grateful for the change, she said: "What are our chances, about the oil, I mean?" She touched her wet eyes with a finger and brushed away the tears.

He shrugged. "The reports have been consistently unsatisfying but our methods are changing so fast, improving so much... I just don't know. Perhaps we'll be lucky. Every once in a while someone goes over the ground again, ground that has long been passed up...they did that in Bahrein, and now it's producing something like eighteen million barrels a year."

Her mind was very far away. She said, brooding: "How many women have you loved, Roger?"

"Oh... I don't know. My fair share, I suppose."

"And how many have made you happy?"

"Even for a moment?"

"Long enough to remember."

He laughed. "That's a good yardstick. Even if it's only for a moment...you remember. Sometimes, more than others, you wish it were for longer. I don't like to forget, but...gratitude's not enough, is it?"

"I'd give my soul for the sight of New York."

"Bored?"

"Not yet, but I will be pretty soon, cooped up in this...this factory. Oil is all that anyone really thinks about, cares about, you can smell it on their breaths, the hell with it!"

"Once we go ashore..."

"I know, the burning sands, the romantic dunes, the hell with them too."

"There's going to be a lot of scuba-diving, you said you liked that."

Candia said: "The way I feel right now, a dip in the water might be just the thing."

She stood up, looked at him once, went to the rail and was gone.

For a moment, he could not understand what she had done, and then he leaped up and ran quickly to the side and yelled at the bridge: "Man overboard!" And then he kicked off his shoes, cursing because they wouldn't come off fast enough, and then he leaped over the rail and dived after her.

As he went down he heard a bell ring, and then the water came at him fast and he knew that in his urgency he had misjudged the great height, and the water hit him with a solid blow that knocked the wind out of his body and wrenched his back, but he rolled himself over and kicked out, and when he reached the surface, the yacht was already turning in a sharp circle, the water churning behind it, and he heard someone on board shout, and when he looked round for Candia, she was treading water a little way away from him, looking at him and laughing wildly, with her long hair slicked down at the sides of her head. A long arm came up and cut the water as she swam towards him, and she said, laughing and shaking the water from her eyes:

"That was a lousy dive, you should have seen yourself."

He was furious. He shouted angrily: "You bloody little fool, you could have been killed, what the hell are you trying to prove?"

She wouldn't stop laughing. "Prove? I'm not trying to prove anything, just feel like a dip in the nice warm water, I'll race you to the shore." Her eyes were galvanic, decrying the laughter.

He shouted; "Don't be an idiot! Candia, for Christ's sake...!"

She turned and began to swim away, with long, easy strokes, and he put his head in the water and struck out after her, and when he came up for breath she was a long way ahead, and he swore loudly and struggled out of his confining trousers and shirt, and set off again, looking back once, up at the ship that seemed so far away now... He was glad to see that it had stopped, that several of the crew were running towards the davits.

He said aloud: "You stupid little bastard," and flayed at the water savagely, using the eight-beat crawl that once he had been so good at, holding his head low and wondering how long he could keep it up. The shore, from down here, was not even in sight, and as he raced he tried to figure out how far it would be, and thanked God that a boat would be coming after them...

He began to worry about sharks, and took a quick look around him, and he saw her more clearly now, losing ground to him but still a long way ahead, and he got his second breath and slowed to a six-stroke, swimming well and feeling all the old vigor come back, because he needed it and this was part of his upbringing too, to bring all the forces to bear when they were wanted...

He swam easily now, his body straight and smooth, and when he next looked ahead there was a moment of alarm because he could not see her, but he found her quite close by, a little to one side, flailing her arms desperately now and gasping for breath, and he changed direction and swam over to her and said gently: "It's all right, Candia, there's nothing to worry about, they've stopped, there's a boat coming..."

He put an arm round her waist and felt her go limp, and then she began to struggle savagely, putting a foot in his groin and trying to push him away, and he wondered whether he should hit her, a quick hard blow on the jaw that would quieten her down. He decided not to, and instead slipped round behind her and held her firmly by the upper arms, and then rolled over onto his back, feeling her struggles growing weaker and knowing that she was very close to exhaustion.

He heard the roar of the motor launch, and he trod water and waited, and when it came, Breck was there with two of the crew, and Candia opened her eyes and looked at them blankly, and suddenly all the life was there again, and she almost laughed once more.

She said: "So, my father didn't come."

Breck shook his head as he helped them aboard. "No, Candia, he didn't."

"Is he angry?"

Breck grinned. "Not half as angry as the skipper. First time in years I've heard him forget he's a gentleman." He was unfolding a blanket for her, and she said irritably:

"You don't really think I need that, do you?"

When they climbed up the rope ladder to the deck, Christie was waiting. He looked at Candia and said harshly:

"Are you all right?"

She nodded and walked right past him, and when he went to follow her, Roger put a hand on his arm and said: "It might be wise to leave her alone. She asked why you weren't in the boat."

"You know why I wasn't."

"Yes, I do. And if you try to make something of it now, you'll spoil it. She'll realize why, soon enough, and be grateful for it. Just give her time."

Simone Caffa was there, watching him obliquely, and her eyes remained somber when he smiled at her. Christie walked away, frowning to himself, and when Breck went to get the launch aboard, he stood there with Simone, looking down into the water for a while.

She said at last: "You must have something to say, Roger."

He shook his head: "What is there to say?"

"What would have happened if you hadn't gone after her?"

"No one would have known what happened to her."

"And you think this is what she wanted?"

"I wish I knew."

He was surprised at the ease with which he spoke to her, as though, with her, there were no need for the demands of discretion, of a discretion that Christie, full of pain and worry, had gone to such lengths to ensure. It was hard to stop himself from saying bluntly: "*She tried to kill herself...*"

He was aware that she, too, knew how close they were, as though they were partners in this thing that was trying so hard to break out and distress them all.

She said slowly: "It's strange...Maxwell Christie is as strong a man as I've ever met, and yet when the launch was ready, Breck looked at him and asked: 'Are you coming, Mr. Christie?' And he answered: 'No, it must remain just a prank, nothing more, you must laugh it off...' And when he turned away, I swear to you, Roger, he was as close to complete collapse as a man can come to. Hiding it well, but on the verge."

"Because he knows it *wasn't* a prank."

"When I told you, before, that she was...psychotic...you did not believe me."

"I think now that you were right. And I was wrong in other ways too, I never fully realized what a child Candia really is. It's pretty easy, isn't it, to confuse sophistication with maturity. But Christie was right too, it's got to be...played down. If the thought of suicide was really there, then that's where it's got to stay, in her mind."

"I'm glad you're not afraid to use the word." They were talking very quietly, almost conspiratorially. She looked slowly all over the deck, as though to make sure they were alone, and said: "Were you talking to her when she made up her mind?"

"If you can call it making up her mind, yes. One minute she was laughing, the next she was gone. It wasn't till I saw her face out there that I thought it might be something other than an irresponsible joke. And even then... I just don't know, Simone. What I saw could have been...plain fright. Maybe that's all it was."

"Then that's the assumption we'll all make." Simone sighed. "All the world needs, really, is a little more...backbone. It would make living so much more pleasant. Let's go and find Hafik, shall we?"

They found him in the chartroom, at work on the maps with compass, protractor, and slide rule, and he looked up eagerly when they came in. He said: "The British naval charts, we've been trying to get them for years, and here they are... Christie has promised me a set, they're the best I've ever seen." He grinned quickly and added: "Top secret, and there's nothing there but sand and water."

Simone said: "Sand and water and oil."

Hafik laughed: "Let's hope so." Roger was aware that he was waiting for something, and as though reading those thoughts, Hafik said lightly: "They tell me Candia went for a swim, wasn't that rather foolish? Is she all right?"

Roger said: "Sure." He had draped a towel round his waist over his shorts, and he felt the incongruity of the still wet socks. He said: "I joined her, didn't know how strong a swimmer she is."

"She should know better than to dive off a moving ship. The screws could have cut her to pieces. I suspect that all our talk of oil was beginning to bore her, she wanted a little diversion to brighten the day."

"Precisely what she said," Roger told him, and Hafik flashed his quick smile and said:

"Quite a girl, and a handful of trouble for her father, I'll bet. When do we reach the headland, at midnight?"

"About then. Have you had word from the bridge?"

"No. I made a few calculations. If we maintain this speed..." He said to Simone: "Christie wants us to stay on board, do you think that's necessary?"

She said quickly: "No, I don't, but let me talk to him first. I'm sure he's being unnecessarily cautious."

"Admirable, but presumptuous. Did he talk with General Fali?"

"Only briefly. Why do you ask?"

Hafik grinned and looked at Roger and said: "Fali bin Sassara, our Minister of War, he sees hidden armies lurking in every oasis, waiting to destroy us. A good soldier, but a schemer."

"Whose loyalty," Simone said, "has been proved conclusively."

Hafik nodded. "Yes, I know we can trust him."

Roger wondered if there were a note of uncertainty there, and he said: "But I understood the entire coastal area of the Rub had been cleared?"

"Oh yes indeed, and not by my father's forces, either. By nature, Roger. When the wells went sour... Today, not even a passing fisherman will put in there. A desolate, dreary stretch of emptiness where nothing moves."

"Except the fish."

The quick laugh again. "Of course, the fish. Can you fit me out with scuba gear?"

"Sure, there's plenty on board."

"Good. And there's the gong for lunch."

There was a forced heartiness in the air when they sat down to eat. The skipper was silent and morose, and Merrick, the first mate, cast anxious glances at him from time to time.

But Christie was in good form, chatting easily and lightheartedly about the work that was ahead of them. In answer to a question from Hafik, he said:

"The currents affect the distribution of materials washed into the sea, and so does the configuration of the ocean floor. With samples of sediment, and cores from the underlying bedrock, we can deduce, with a certain amount of accuracy, the stage in which the oil migrated from its source sediments into its present traps. We know the traps are there, we know the rock stratum is porous enough, all we don't know yet is how to get at them, whether it's economically feasible."

"We also know," Hafik said, "that oil of some sort has been readily available here for thousands of years. The Zoroastrians knew that three thousand years ago..."

"Pitch," Christie said promptly. "Asphalt, naphtha, go back as far as the fire-breathing Chimera of the early Greeks, and we've got definite evidence of oil under every square mile of these coasts. There were asphalt roads in Ur of the Chaldees, and the Tower of Babel was built with tar instead of mortar, and so was the Great Wall of Babylon. The Code of Hammurabi fixed the price of calking a boat with bitumen..."

He looked at Simone and said: "The oil business was pretty well organized even in those days. They floated their cargoes of naphtha down the rivers in coracles of hide stretched over reeds, and then they dismantled their boats and carried them back overland for the next trip down on the current; even today, there's no such simple solution to the problem of the empty tanker on the return trip. When I was young, just starting out in this business, I put in a few years in Kirkuk. Did you know that Alexander the Great reported on the burning oil there? The barbarians laid a trail of naphtha along the path that lead to his lodgings, and fired it to impress him with the power that lay under their soil. Where your people came from, Hafik, when your Zoroastrians were trying to find the causes, and the uses, of the underground fires, the oil down there was as inviting as it is today, just waiting to be used. And the problem remains the same—how to get to it. That's our only question."

Roger looked at Candia and saw that she was smiling to herself. He said lightly: "Oil, nothing but talk of oil, it's becoming an obsession." He turned to the captain and asked: "How far offshore do we drop anchor?"

Captain Hewitt's eyebrows shot up. "I wish I knew, Mr. Sequoyah," he said darkly. "I planned to bring her under the lee of the cape before the moon went down, but"—he glared at Candia—"we lost a mite over two hours this morning, so we'll be standing out until daybreak, and I'll take her in as soon as the sun comes up. There's a shifting sandbar we have to worry about..."

"Two hours," Christie said with a touch of asperity. "What the hell does it matter, Mr. Hewitt, if we lost two hours? Or two days, or two weeks?"

Hewitt reddened, and then he glanced quickly at Candia and said gently: "Your father's a wise man, Miss Christie, if he'll permit me to say so. I agree, the wishes of the owner and his family are as important as the welfare of the ship, but, I'm an old man, and I'm set in my ways, and if you were my daughter I'd put you across my knee for what you did this day, and spank your bottom till it was red as a lobster's tail." He added gravely: "Don't ever do it again, young lady, a moving ship is a murder weapon. If someone hadn't shouted in time, the screws would have got you as sure as my name's Matthew Hewitt, and it would have been a sad, sad ship we'd be working on. There's a lot of love for you on board this vessel, Miss Christie, don't take it away from us by...carelessness."

Roger said, watching Christie carefully: "Well, that was quite a speech."

And Candia said with a sigh: "And I promise you I won't forget it, Mr. Hewitt."

Roger caught Simone's eyes, and knew what she was thinking. She was thinking: *how long will she remember?*

But Candia suddenly laughed. She looked at Roger and said: "If only you could have seen your face!" It was as though the worry had never been there, not even for a moment. She stood up abruptly and pushed back her chair and said: "Well, I'm for the sun deck, take care of my tan. Who wants to join me?" She was looking at Hafik when she spoke, but Roger got quickly to his feet and said: "Yes, a good idea..."

She did not take her eyes off Hafik, and she waited, but he shook his head and said: "May I join you later? There's some work I'd like to do in the chartroom..."

She said calmly: "Then, perhaps this evening... Roger, let's go take some clothes off." She turned away and went out.

Roger looked quickly at Christie, searching for any sign of understanding there; he was momentarily surprised at the smug look on Christie's face. He saw that Simone was avoiding his eye, and he said, almost (but not quite) laughing: "Why don't you join us too, Simone? There's a good breeze blowing..."

For a moment, she did not answer, and he was aware of an unaccustomed uncertainty in her. But then she said: "All right, I will. Give me a few minutes to change."

"Good."

As he went out, he could feel Christie's eyes on the back of his head.

He caught up with Candia and took her arm, and went with her up to the sun deck, and as she took off her fold-around skirt, he said lightly: "No more games like the last time, okay?"

She shook her head. "I've had my lesson. But make me a promise."

"All right."

"Scuba-diving as soon as we're there."

"It's a promise."

"Good." She said idly: "Hafik wants to take me down under the reef, but I don't think I quite trust him."

He looked at her and said nothing. She lay back on the deck and handed him the oil bottle. "Do my legs for me, will you?" He sighed and unscrewed the top and began to rub the lotion into the long brown thighs.

He had just finished when Simone arrived, and he stood up and began to lay out a towel for her, but she shook her head and pulled up a deck chair instead, and sat there silent for a long time, leaning back and settling easily into a kind of quiet that was so much a part of her. He saw that Candia had slipped on the dark glasses and knew that she was watching her, watching and waiting and wondering, and there was a tenseness in the air, as though a fight were about to begin. He found himself waiting for it; and soon, its beginnings came.

Candia said carelessly: "Is it true that the Shah has three wives and three hundred concubines?"

He thought to himself: *Oh-oh, here we go...* But Simone said quietly:

"No, not quite true. The number of concubines is probably a great deal smaller. No one really knows at what point a woman becomes, in the technical sense, a concubine. The word presupposes something more than a single...episode, doesn't it? If you count all those, then of course the figure is considerably higher. But in the palace harem, there are currently two hundred and twelve women, most of whom belong to the Shah. The others, of course, are for his son."

*A slow withdrawal,* Roger thought, *and then a right hook to the side of the jaw. Nice.*

Candia asked innocently: "And only three wives?"

"Three."

There was a pause, and then Candia said: "Which of the two categories do you belong in, Simone?"

Simone said quietly: "Neither, my dear." She stood up and said: "And, if you'll excuse me, I find I have other things to do."

As she walked away, Roger got quickly to his feet, looked after her in dismay, and said to Candia coldly: "That was a lousy thing to say. And why, for God's sake?"

She was laughing, and he did not wait for an answer, but turned and followed Simone. When he caught up with her, he went with her to the companionway without speaking, waiting for her to say something, trying to gauge the anger there, but Simone looked at him and smiled and said quietly:

"Is it wise to leave her alone?"

He said roughly: "She's not alone."

And when Simone looked a question, he jerked his head towards the boat deck; Breck was there, leaning back against the rail and smoking, paying no attention to anything, and Roger growled:

"You don't see Breck doing nothing without reason. I don't like him very much, but I won't deny his competence. Candia's safe enough."

"I see. Why did you want to come with me?"

He shrugged. "Taking sides, I suppose."

"It's good of you, but..."

"I know, you're perfectly capable of shooting Candia down in flames..."

"Of course. If I were to worry over little things like that... I was trained in a good school, Roger, the school of diplomatic necessity. Nothing touches me. Nothing."

"I can't believe that."

"It's true, but it's nice of you not to believe it."

"Are you going anywhere in particular?"

"No, not really."

"Then let's go aft and watch the water."

"All right."

They went to the lower deck and leaned over the fashion pieces, looking down into the white froth that was churned up behind them, and across to the distant shoreline where the sand was low on the horizon, yellow-bright in the afternoon sun. It was an isolated, lonely spot on a busy ship, and the soft sound of the screws and the bubbling water was the only sound that came to them. Down here, close to the sea, it seemed they had left the rest of the vessel far away, that nothing was there but a small platform poised above the flat white water. There were not even any sea gulls.

Simone said, watching the shore: "One of my earliest recollections is of the Italian coastline. My father took me sailing out of Portovenere when I was just a child, and the boat overturned and we hung onto the hull for three hours, watching the shore get further and further away as we drifted out to sea. He was so angry... And I was so scared... But the shoreline there is dark with trees and bright with houses. And look at ours...nothing, nothing but sand."

"Once, there were great cities there."

"Yes, I know, and I still find it hard to realize it. If it were not for the occasional ruins...an old fort, a collapsed copper mine, a broken sea wall, I would say that all history, all our history, is a lie. When you look at the gypsum desert today, you can only ask yourself, how was it ever possible for this wasteland to support the great cities that we know the Sumerians built here, and the Phoenicians and the Nabateans after them? Have you been to Hafija?"

"No, never."

"There is a dry crack in the sandstone of the bluff, where you will find seven coconut trees, one date palm that no longer bears fruit, a dried-up riverbed, and the shells of three buildings. Nothing more. And yet, Raidan el Darrah once wrote: *'We fed our armies on the fruit and the sheep of Hafija, and we quenched our thirst with the good wine that we found there, and their women brought us garlands of flowers with which they made beds for us to rest on while they bathed our wounds in an abundance of water.'* That was only thirteen hundred years ago, and Hafija was a fortified city which Raidan held for two years against eighteen thousand horsemen led by Ali Othman, the son of the Caliph, who was killed, at last, by a Persian slave girl whom Raidan had converted to the Faith. He was a great soldier, Ali

Othman, but he was destroyed, as so many great men have been, by the love of a beautiful woman. Her name was Ninea, and they say that she loved Raidan and was the mother of two of his sons... She was young, and lovely, and wise, and one night during the great siege of Hafija she dressed herself in gold-embroidered robes of red silk, and carried a golden amphora of wine out of Hafija to Ali's camp, a present of good will for him. Fearing it was poisoned, he made her drink it, and when she did not die he took her to bed, and in four days he was so much in love with her that he would no longer leave his tent to lead the forays against Raidan's defending armies. And on the fourth night, while he slept beside her, she took a sword and struck off his head and gave it to her servant, and left the camp, saying she was going into the desert to pray for him, and she took the head back to Hafija and gave it to Raidan..."

Roger said, startled. "Judith and Holofernes!"

"Of course, the same story. But our Judith, Ninea, killed herself because she halt defied the love of the great Prophet Raidan. But with the death of Ali Othman, the siege was lifted, and Raidan went to Arkan, where he founded the Faith that has been ours ever since. And Arkan too...it is no longer the great city it once was. There is nothing left of it but dirt, and squalor, and misery. And a few memories."

Sensing the sorrow, he said: "Your country means a great deal to you, doesn't it?"

"It is my whole life. My country, my Shah, my Prince. For me there is nothing else."

"It's not enough, Simone."

"Yes, Roger, it is enough. It's all I have ever wanted."

"And the things that...any other woman gropes for, wants so badly, spends her life trying to reach...?"

Simone looked back to the deck above them. "Up there, a young girl is looking for all those things... No, I don't want them."

"Your determination presupposes a...a kind of coldness."

"Perhaps. If my thinking is wrong, that is something I will never find out until it's much too late to do anything about it."

"You are a very disturbing woman." He laughed shortly and said: "I was talking with Hafik about the honorifics. I never even began calling you 'Excellency,' did I? Should I have done that?"

156

"I think you would have found it incongruous, to say the least."

She began to laugh, and he felt very close to her. He said slowly: "I feel you would make a very good friend."

"Friendship has never been very much of my life." She was suddenly very somber again, her gray eyes troubled. "Perhaps my life could have been fuller with a little more of it, I don't know. Outside the court, the people I meet—diplomats, officials, apologists for every government in Europe and the Middle East—in a dozen different languages, there's seldom the language of friendship."

"And in the court?"

She hesitated: "Are you asking me the same question?"

"As Candia?" He said quickly: "Good God no."

"But I will answer her, for your benefit. I am not, nor have I ever been, the Shah's mistress. Once, there was speculation that he would make me his wife, and when this was first brought to my attention I began to think about it very carefully. Of course, I could not refuse, even if I had wanted to, but... I thought about it and decided that he would do this if, and when, he began to feel that my talents as a diplomat were waning. I knew that while I held the power I had earned he would not add to it by increasing my popularity with the people, which would be the immediate result of such a marriage. He is a shrewd man, His Royal Highness, and he knew that if he made me his wife he would create a figure to be reckoned with perhaps too much, a figure which would add a greater wisdom to the strength he has established. He has never doubted my loyalty, but..."

When she broke off, Roger said, prompting her: "The despot must always fear the popular image."

She nodded. "Yes, I will even allow you the word despot. The people of my country would see, in me, a giant step towards something that many of them want, a Western trend to their culture. Progress, if you like to call it that. But while the culture I represent remains subjugated entirely to the whims of the Shah, it is, in the public mind, not strong enough to lean upon. And so, his position is stronger."

"As a figurehead."

"Not really. He is the Shah, and he rules completely. He listens to me, but the decisions are his."

"And you find that position...satisfying?"

"Yes. Yes, I do. It is enough to serve him."

Roger said: "If I were as close to you, Simone, as I would like to be... I feel I wouldn't quite believe you."

She said nothing. Her gray eyes were clouded over by something he could not clearly understand.

Pressing her, he asked: "Does that worry you? Should I apologize?"

She said quickly: "No, of course not. Shall we join the others?"

# CHAPTER II

FOR THE FIRST time in what seemed a lifetime, Roger slept alone that night, and his primary feeling was of relief. He was still asleep when a tap at the door roused him, and he turned over, tousle-haired, and looked at his watch and said: "Six o'clock, oh God..."

But it was Baines, one of the stewards. He brought in a cup of coffee and said:

"Mr. Christie's compliments, sir, and would you join him on deck as soon as possible."

The engines had stopped, and the faint thrumming noise was noticeable by its absence; the air was still and hot, and he switched on the air conditioner while he dressed, and when he went on deck, Christie was there, leaning over the rail and looking out at the shore, a little more than four hundred yards away.

The tall red bluff that was called Hafija was a little to one side, and in its early morning shadow he could see that all that was left of the once great fortified city Simone had told him of—a few yards of crumbled wall and the crookedly leaning, water-starved trees with the empty shells beside them.

And stretched out under the lee of the bluff, in long, untidy rows, were line after line of military pup tents. Among them, some soldiers were moving around, in various stages of undress, some putting on their khaki uniforms, some washing in portable basins, some squatting over charcoal fires and cooking, some lying in the early morning shade and doing nothing.

A group of officers was standing on the beach, staring out at the yacht, and when Roger took the binoculars that Christie, in silence, offered him, he saw that one of them was General Fali.

He said: "A headache."

Christie nodded. "A godawful headache."

"What are you going to do about it?"

Christie looked at him and grinned. "I'm going to fish. But first we'll have a little conference."

"We've got the authority on board to get rid of them."

"Sure we have, but let's not use it too quickly. I'm waiting for Simone Caffa. When she comes up, I want the three of us to sit down and talk this out."

"Not Hafik?"

"No, not Hafik. This is something Simone must handle. Technically, General Fali outranks the Prince, who's only an air force commander, and in any case... Let's play it off the cuff."

"It doesn't seem to worry you too much."

"It Intrigues me. I want to know what the hell made them disobey the orders I know they had, and a little bit of intrigue never worried me."

Simone came to join them, her face tight with anger, and Christie said quickly:

"I'm sorry to call you so early, but this is something I thought you'd want to know about."

She nodded briefly. "May I have the binoculars?"

When Roger gave them to her, she stared out across the water for a long time, and then she said:

"General Fali bin Sassara, Colonel Osman Kibbaj, Colonel Mansour, all of the Southern Command. Eighty tents, no transport except three staff cars, that means they marched here."

Christie said: "And they can bloody well march out again."

"Of course. I promise you, there'll be no difficulty about that."

"Good. But there's only one question: why are they here? If we could find that out before they leave, I'd be grateful."

She handed the binoculars back to Roger. "Does the Prince know about this?"

Christie said: "Not yet. I thought it better to leave it to you. Unless..."

"No, I'm glad you did. He'll have to know, of course."

"Of course."

"I suggest we invite the General over for breakfast."

"Is it possible the Shah has confided in him?"

"No. Quite impossible."

"Good. Then breakfast it is. Now?"

Simone nodded. "The sooner the better."

Christie called out: "Breck!" and when Breck came running, he said: "Madam Caffa would like to send a message ashore."

Breck waited, and Simone said carefully: "Mr. Christie joins His Highness Prince Hafik in presenting his compliments to General Sassara bin Fali, and in requesting the pleasure of his company at breakfast, have you got that?"

Breck repeated the message, and Christie said: "The colonels?"

Simone shook her heart. "No. Just the General." To Breck, she said: "Perhaps you'd be good enough to wait and bring him out in the launch? Let him know you're waiting for him, will you do that discreetly?"

Breck said: "Yes, Your Excellency."

There was a flicker of a smile on Simone's face as she looked once at Roger, and then she turned away to watch Breck lower the launch.


The General was effusive, charming, immaculate, and full of an inexplicable menace.

He was a short, stubby-shaped man, with a bull neck and too much flesh on his body; on his face, too, Roger thought, the jowls plumped-out and heavy, the lips fleshy and mobile. But the eyes were hard and shrewd, the black liquid eyes of an animal, that were permanently wary of any danger that might lurk, unseen; a woman's eyes, he thought, set in the face of a fat, middle-aged man, but eyes, nonetheless, that showed an extraordinary awareness of what was going on. On the surface, a fat, placid laxity; but underneath, a sharp and perhaps ruthless intelligence.

Roger remembered the first time they had met, when he had known at once that the smooth, courteous affability was a mask for a strong-willed competence. He saw again now that under Fali's apologetic stubbornness there was something it was vital to conceal; he wondered what it was, and the ignorance disturbed him.

He had said to Christie, as they watched Breck coming back with the General: "Things like this always worry the hell out of me when I can't figure out the reason for them."

But Christie had laughed off his discomfort: "Isn't that an arrogance? In this part of the world, if you can figure out what an Arab keeps tucked away under his head-cloth, you're a better man than I am. The wheels are turning in their minds, always, and the Western intelligence is seldom sharp enough..."

Watching the General now, Roger was aware of those wheels.

His pudgy thighs were spread apart as he sat on the leather sofa, with cigarette ash falling down over his khaki-covered paunch, and there was a heavy gold ring on the little finger of his hand as he waved it at Simone, gesticulating, making a point. He said:

"My orders, Your Excellency, came from His Royal Highness himself, and they were quite explicit. He said *'A withdrawal of all forces from the Southern Area.'* Surely this must mean not only our own Armed Forces, but also any dissidents as well. You must realize that the rebels we have been chasing dispersed into the desert. Some of them took refuge on the Gebel el Ghaida, and until we have cleared them out I cannot in all conscience withdraw the troops. Meanwhile..." He waved a hand airily. "Meanwhile, we are evacuating the area, in stages, in accordance with my orders."

Simone said clearly: "We are aware of your good intentions, General Fali, but your sagacity is not so apparent. His Royal Highness' intentions were surely obvious?"

Fali brushed aside the reflection on his intelligence. He shrugged and said:

"Of course. His Royal Highness wanted to be sure that Mr. Christie's party would not be disturbed, that an empty shoreline would remain empty. So that he could fish...unwatched by prying eyes. To this end, an Army is to be moved."

Roger could feel the tension between them. But Simone was only smiling. She said gently:

"No, not really. There was merely an expression of the Shah's wish that no unannounced maneuvers would intrude on his seclusion, and if you care to call it a whim, then I will agree with you. But the whims of His Highness, General, are your orders, and my orders. And they will be carried out to the letter."

For a long time, Fali did not speak. At last, he turned to Christie and said:

"I wonder...would it be discourteous of me to ask Madam Caffa ashore? Some of my officers, learning that she and Prince Hafik were to join your party, evinced a certain anxiety for their safety. It would be useful if she could assure them, personally, that she is totally in agreement with His Highness' wishes."

Christie frowned, but Simone said quickly: "I will be happy to talk to them, and the sooner the better. Shall we go now?"

"Of course."

Again, Roger was aware of an undertow of suspicion. Christie, he saw, was not comfortable, and the frown deepened when Simone added:

"It would be better if the Prince stayed on board, I think...?"

Hafik had not spoken. He had listened to them, his eyes alert, his handsome young face expressionless, knowing too that there was a duel going on between two strong people, a duel he could not fully understand. He said now:

"My authority, General, is limited, as you know, but I will expect to see your troops moving out within the hour. By midday I will expect to see nothing but a cloud of dust over the dunes. And I will not expect you to return. My father's...whims...are not subject to question, whether you understand them or not. As for Madam Caffa..."

She interrupted him quickly, putting out a hand to touch his arm. "No, Hafik, it's all right. Let me speak to them."

Looking at the General, Roger was shocked to see the venom in his face, the expression of cordial hatred that was there. But it was gone almost instantly, and if Hafik were aware of it, he made no sign. He stood up and said:

"All right, Simone, if you think it's best..."

"I do." Only her mouth was smiling.

Breck took them ashore in the launch, and Hafik joined Christie and Roger on the bridge, looking out at the tents through their glasses. Christie said somberly:

"A lot of fuss about nothing." He turned to Hafik and asked: "How much do you think he really knows? About what we're doing?"

Hafik said flatly: "Nothing. But in the mind of a soldier... At the palace, nothing would have been said at all, and there would have been no suspicions, but when the rebels unexpectedly ran to Gebel el Ghaida, then it was immediately necessary for the Army to pursue them. My father's insistence that the area should remain empty, when in fact it was not, could only arouse suspicion in the mind of a man like General Fali."

"When I first saw them out there," Christie said, "I had the idea that he wanted to assure himself that we hadn't...kidnapped you, spirited you off for purposes of our own."

"He is not so loyal to me." Hafik grinned quickly and said: "Had you done that, one barrier to the General's advancement would have gone, and he would have welcomed it."

Roger said: "I sensed a certain reserve in his attitude towards you."

Hafik laughed and put an affectionate hand on his shoulder. "You are always a diplomat, my friend. What you mean is that you saw he hates everything I represent. He does." He added dryly: "But his hatred has at least one virtue; it is not unreciprocated."

Roger said: "And Simone...is she safe with them?" He felt uncomfortable with the question, as though he were attributing to the situation a danger it did not have.

But Hafik, he saw, was as worried as he was. He nodded, unsure of himself, and said slowly:

"I almost insisted that she stay on board, but..." He turned to Christie and said, groping for the words: "Am I right, Maxwell? Never to start a fight without the assurance of victory? If we had denied Simone her talk with the colonels, and if Fali had stood firm, I am not sure that he would have respected my authority. I felt it was better to give way, since she was so confident that it would be better. Among my people, this kind of thinking is regarded as a heresy out of the hated West, but it is something the West has taught me to believe."

Christie said promptly: "Of course, and you're right. This is the essential difference between success and failure. It's a fine and noble thing, no doubt, to break your head against a brick wall, but it's a hell of a way to knock the wall down. You were wise not to test it. And don't worry about Simone. Her ability to stay on top of a situation is phenomenal. She is in no danger, and she knows it, or she wouldn't have agreed so readily. But tell me why you think Fali's out there in the first place? If it's not to assure himself of your safety...?"

But Hafik only shook his head. "I understand Fali the soldier. Fali the politician is a little more devious. Our timing is unfortunate. We left Arkan for this empty stretch of coast just when the rebels were leaving Radija for almost the same pinpoint on the map. It's a pity that the two activities coincided, but there's not much we could have done about it. Had we waited...who knows what might have happened?"

*Then the rebels,* Roger was thinking, *are a hell of a lot stronger than we're been told, and that oil money is needed in a desperate hurry.* Money for arms, money to put down a popular movement that might, or might not be worthy, that might, or might not be attempting a fairer distribution of the country's wealth.

There was not even a sardonic satisfaction in knowing that he, by *force majeure,* was on the side of the wealthy.

The bright white paint and the gleaming brass of the luxury yacht was spread out there below him, and beyond it was an arid, worthless land inhabited by how many millions of close to starving nomads who grubbed in the dirt of the scattered oases to find a shred of sustenance and then move on, hoping always to find food enough, water enough, peace enough...   Their children had empty bellies, and they themselves had empty ambitions, ambitions that meant the acquisition of a pair of sandals, or a castoff rag to drape a virgin with at marriage, or another camel to feed a hungry mouth...   Always   the problem of mouths to feed and sores to heal, and water to wash away the dried-out sickness of the desert...

Candia came and joined them, a glass in her hand, her long slim body browner than ever in a white bikini; she reached out and took the binoculars Hafik was using, and he turned and smiled at her quickly and dropped his eyes once to her body, and showed her his white teeth and said:

"You look beautiful today. I think our Orassian sun is good for you."

She handed him her glass and said: "Try some of our special brandy, that's good for you too."

He grimaced: "At this hour of the day?" But he sipped from her glass, and Roger looked at Christie and saw that he was frowning.

Candia said: "Is our Minister spreading her culture out there? If so, she's enjoying it."

Roger used his glasses and saw Simone emerge from the General's tent. She was laughing, and the officers that came out after her were smiling too. He watched while they all shook hands and bowed and made silent comments, and then she was walking towards the launch where Breck was waiting. He saw Breck move to carry her through the ankle-deep surf, but she shook her head and splashed through the water unconcernedly; she looked like a soldier returning from a battle that had been easily won, moving lightly, straight and strong, without a backward glance. He heard the motor start up, and soon Simone was climbing up the ladder to the deck.

He went down with Christie to meet her, and she said at once:

"No more trouble, they'll be gone in an hour or two."

Christie looked back at the bridge once, where Candia and Hafik were looking down at them, and then he asked:

"The one thing I want to know..."

Simone laughed. "He was quite sure that my presence on board was not entirely voluntary. He wanted to know what pressures had been put upon me to make me come with you. I told him that I had merely joined an old and dear friend for a well-earned holiday, within easy call, and that my Prince was with me at my insistence."

"And he was satisfied?"

Simone shrugged. "The truth is always satisfying, when it is properly explained. Now, they're pulling out."

"And the rebels?"

"Their strength has been grossly exaggerated."

"Gebel el Ghaida?"

"Deserted. An empty mountain, as it always was. If there should be any of the...dissidents left there, they have no transport, no supplies, no arms. And fifty miles of waterless desert lies between us and them. In your world, fifty miles is not very much. But here, without water, it is as far as the end of the world."

"Then we can go to work?"

"By tomorrow, the crew can land, they can set up their camp... Yes, we can go to work."

Breck was hovering in the background, waiting. Christie turned to him and said:

"All right, as soon as they've gone, send a party up on the mountain to keep them in sight for as long as possible, two or three men, well-armed, self-supporting, with supplies for a week at least. During the night, move the seismographic crew ashore, open up the laboratory first thing in the morning. I want to see the contour maps daily, and I want some results in the first ten days."

Breck said mildly: "Fifteen to twenty square miles, that's assuming we're going to be very lucky."

"You can do better than that. Push them, three shifts a day, we might not have the time we planned on." He turned to Roger; "I'll be counting heavily on you, from now on in. Once we find the anticlines, you take over the analyses. There's not going to be much sleep for anyone..." He broke off and said to Simone: "I'm afraid it's going to be rather dull for you. I won't be the perfect host, but the ship is yours."

Simone said nothing. She was looking across the water to the shore.

The soldiers were already breaking camp.


They had gone by the middle of the afternoon. All that was left of them was the cloud of dust hanging over the dunes that Hafik had spoken of, and three men, led by a tall and rangy Swede named Folkhagen, were slowly moving off up the slope of the sandstone mountain that was on their flank, carrying heavy packs of water, and food, and their radio.

Every boat on board was pressed into service to carry the crew ashore, and now that he saw them, as it were, en masse for the first time, Roger was astonished at the huge number of them that had been scattered over the four decks of the yacht; it made him feel somehow ashamed of the distance which had always remained between Christie's intimates and his employees.

He had had a word with Folkhagen before the little team set out, and the Swede had said, in answer to his question: "Don't you worry, Mr. Sequoyah, nobody come within twenty miles of this place we don't know about in good time. Mr. Christie choose me because he knows he can trust me, fifteen years I work for him."

"You know about the rebels, of course?"

Folkhagen had laughed, pulling out a Luger. "This gun go with me all through the war, save my life in Morocco, another time in Venezuela, you got no worry on my account, not from rebels."

"Keep in hourly contact, every hour on the hour, day and night."

"I know, Breck told me."

"And if you need help, we'll find the men for you."

"We don't need no help, but thank you. Just you don't worry about us."

He was aware, with annoyance, that he was trying to assert his own usefulness, knowing that Breck had done all the work with his customary competence, knowing that he was a bystander until the reports started coming in, and knowing that the need was overwhelming, the need to get his teeth into something and get the job done.

The feeling had been strong, and it had started when he climbed up on deck that morning and saw that they had arrived, a feeling of urgency that always seemed to come with the knowledge of a new place, however empty, a new place that held the imponderable promise of all the earth's richness under its cloak of silence, or of nothing...

These are the shores, he thought, on which the Sabean merchants sunk their deep wells and dragged up oil and asphalt and salt in goat-skin bags, and separated them by sedimentation, more than twenty-five centuries ago. Remembering what Christie had said—*the secret is to take yourself back in time, to touch the antiquity*—he thought about the Sabean warriors, armed with spears and javelins, lying in wait for the caravans of balm and incense that were crossing the desert that led to the Land of Canaan, of the slaves who labored under the whip to build the Marib dam, of the Queen of Sheba and the caravan from Ophir...

Was this the shore of the legendary land itself? Was it from here that the Tyrian sailors brought the great ships laden with gold to Solomon? So much of history was forever buried by the encroaching sands of the terribly dunes that moved, a few feet a year, relentlessly and inexorably southward, with the winds, to dry out and to destroy, till all that was left was an empty, dreadful desert where only the ghosts now stirred, where only the imaginings could conjure up again, out of the silence, the vision of the bustling prosperity that had once been there. All through the evening and well on into the night, the supplies were ferried ashore, and the tents were set up where so recently the army tents had been, and bare-chested men were sweating, even in the cool of the night, to fill the great tanks of prefabricated aluminum plates that had been bolted together to hold the water supply, a supply that in turn was ferried out from the yacht's freshwater tanks...

He stood among the great piles of supplies and listened to the sounds of construction, alien on the desert air, and knew that for him the excitement was beginning again, as it had begun a dozen times, when the failure of his predecessors was a challenge that demanded more than his best efforts to prove himself; and he did not leave the beach until the first red streaks were broadening in the eastern sky, and then, he stripped off his shirt and his shoes and left them on the sand, not caring about them, and walked into the gentle surf and swam out to the ship that lay motionless at anchor three hundred yards offshore.

The water was warm, almost hot, and he swam slowly, with easy, gentle strokes, feeling its freshness after the dust of the beach, and when he climbed on deck and padded silently towards his cabin in the stillness, he saw a shadow move in the darkness and he stopped, peering.

Candia was there, lying on a mattress under the lee of the sternpost where he had talked with Simone. She pulled a towel over her naked body, where the white breasts gleamed against the dark or her skin, and he heard her say softly and clearly:

"Good night, Roger Sequoyah."

He hesitated, waiting, trying not to look towards the red glow of a cigarette that had been in the shadows beside her a moment ago and now was there no more, knowing that Hafik was there, not moving, not speaking.

He said: "Good night, Candia," and turned and walked away.

# CHAPTER 12

HE WAS NOT able to analyze satisfactorily the violence of his own emotions.

He stood alone in the bow of the yacht, leaning against the housing of the anchor winch where the stainless steel cable stretched tautly down to the water, staring out at the narrow streaks of red in the sky and thinking about Candia.

He wanted to tell himself: *Hell, if that's what she wants, she's welcome to it,* but he could not convince himself; he knew that there was a question of wisdom here, knew that if Christie found out, there might be trouble ahead for everybody, including Candia herself. He had no doubts at all that he *would* find out; he had come to believe that Candia was waiting for just that. He did not relish the prospect of a personal explosion that could come at a time when every thought they would have should be concentrated on avoiding the more prosaic troubles that seemed to be in store for them. If the matter of General Fali had not really been solved, and he was sure it hadn't, then all their energies and devices would be needed for this matter alone, and if Candia...

He looked round quickly, smelling an unaccustomed perfume, and Simone was there in the gray light, a ghost that had come up to him soundlessly in the half-light. He looked at her in surprise and said: "Simone! I didn't expect to see you at this hour of the day..."

"I saw you come here, I saw the worry on your face and knew it wasn't just Fali."

"You saw me?"

171

She gestured. "I was watching them."

He looked back towards the deck where he had seen Candia. "I see."

"And I saw that you had seen them. Then, I was worried not so much about them, as about you."

Surprised, he said: "About me?"

She said carefully: "Yes, Roger, about you. And I welcome the surprise in your voice. Is that presumptuous of me?"

"Not presumptuous. Gratifying."

"I thought perhaps...that what my Prince is doing would be harmful to a friend. Was I wrong?"

"Most certainly."

"She's a very proprietary young woman."

"I'm afraid so. I don't like it any more than you do, but...not for the reasons you deduce."

Simone moved over to the rail and looked away. She said quietly: "That Candia Christie should seduce Hafik would not normally alarm me, because in spite of his...his natural honesty he's a very shrewd young man and he must know that—to her—it means nothing at all, any more than another drink means much to a dipsomaniac. But the timing is wrong, and so is the reason."

"If he knew the reason..."

"Oh, we know it all right." She turned to face him, and he was aware of the distance between them. He went over and stood beside her, close to her, and he said:

"You may have come to the same conclusion I have, it's fairly obvious. Kicks, they call it."

"No, there's a stronger reason." She did not press the matter when he refused to ask her what that reason was, and he knew she was aware that he already knew it. She said at last: "Did you stop to wonder why she tried to quarrel with me yesterday? The Shah's concubine?"

He shrugged. "A perverse sense of humor."

"No. Almost the first thing she said to me, when she was so graciously moving out of her cabin, was 'Everything on board this ship is yours. Except Roger Sequoyah.' Does that surprise you?"

Astonished, and a trifle embarrassed too, he said: "Well, I'll be damned..."

"Then she was wrong?"

"I'll say she was wrong! Good God!"

"There's a gap in your ages that presupposes a deeper understanding."

"I understand her well enough...her reasons for..." He broke off, and when she waited in silence, he turned away from her and said slowly: "You said yourself, these things don't matter a great deal to her. Yes, I made love to her. I wanted to, and I did."

"And now?"

He hesitated, and said wryly: "You're very easy to talk to on matters that ought not to be spoken of."

"Only because I want to know."

"Why, Simone? Why is it so important for you to know?"

She said gently: "I think you know the answer to that."

"If I do...then I'm afraid of it."

"Afraid?"

"I'm afraid my...my motives may be wrong. I feel I can see something I want but dare not...not reach for in case my arms aren't long enough. Is that putting it too bluntly?" He put his hands on her shoulders and said gravely: "How shall I put it? I'm on the edge of something, something that means so much to me that I'm scared of letting myself believe that I want it, I'm scared that if I reach out and touch it—like a child staring into flames for the first time..."

She smiled: "You want to be sure they won't burn?"

"It's not that. I want to be sure I know *why* I reach out for them."

She said gently: "A question of comparison?"

"Yes. Of comparison, of...of relative maturity. You're a very perceptive woman."

To his annoyance, he found he was trembling. Her gray eyes were searching his, looking for any pain there. He said again:

"On the edge of something... I have been...for a long time..."

She smiled with sudden amusement. "A long time? A few days."

"A few days can be a lifetime."

"And just as slow. I was waiting for you to tell me. I'm still waiting."

"It would be so easy to say, and I would mean it, and yet..." He grimaced and said: "The fear of rejection too, it never mattered a damn before, not a damn."

"And now, it does?"

"It matters a lot."

She reached up and kissed him gently on the mouth, a kiss that was affectionate and friendly, and she smiled again and said:

"I'm glad that it matters. And no woman minds being compared with another, not when she is as sure of herself as I am. Sometimes, she's grateful for the comparison."

He was still not sure. He felt his grip on her shoulders was tightening, and there was an intimacy in the touch of her that was almost compulsive. He said urgently:

"A man looks around, at women, and sometimes he forgets...to look *up,* and when he does, he wonders... It's like reaching for something that's too far away."

"I'm not distant from you, Roger. I'm very close. As close as you will ever want. And I will give you more than Candia could ever give you." She said fiercely: "Much more."

He said: "I want more."

He pulled her close to him and kissed her, crushing her body to his, feeling her stomach tight against his, feeling her moving her thighs against him, and he slipped an eager hand down to her breast, astonished at its hardness, clutching at it tightly, feeling the nipple under his fingers, knowing that suddenly there was here, in his arms, all that he had ever really wanted, knowing that the flesh had taken on almost a secondary importance so that the sudden realization of his desire for her astonished him, and he wanted to tell himself, surprised: *But it is not this that I want, it's something more.* Holding her breast, kissing her throat, he said it aloud:

"It's not this I want, it's something more, a lot more..."

Her hand was moving down his side. She said: "This, and something more as well, we'll have it, Roger, both of us, it's not enough for you or for me either, but we'll have it all, and this is part of it, an essential part, and I will show you just how essential it is... When the time comes—if the time comes—when there are things about me that you will not accept, then I will teach you that in physical love... I will show you worlds you never dreamed existed, worlds that will make you forget there is anything else outside, worlds in which nothing will matter but the flesh, and the body, and love. When there is pain..."

"There never will be pain. But I will accept the remedy. Always, always..." He said suddenly: "My God, what's happening to me... Never before, Simone, never like this."

Her hips were almost painfully tight against him, and her hands were searching, searching but soft, unlike anything he had ever felt before; his own strength astonished him, gratified him, lifted him to a height he had never before experienced.

He said again: "My God, what's happening to me...?"

The first yellow tip of the sun was showing over the blood-red of the water, and suddenly there was the sound of a muffled explosion on shore that brought him back to prosaic reality. Simone, startled, broke away from him and said:

"What...what was that?"

Roger grinned at her, holding his urgent need in check. He said: "They've started blasting, the first step..." He looked down at himself and said: "I was close to exploding, myself, God, I feel an idiot standing here...like this."

"The daylight comes very fast."

He grimaced: "I know. Perhaps it's even better that it does."

There were running feet on the deck, and he heard someone shout: "They've started blasting!"

He raised his hands helplessly: "I need a couple of minutes."

She was smiling, her eyes alight with pleasure. He said: "You were wrong in one thing. I will *always* accept."

Her eyes were suddenly grave. "Perhaps. But if not..."

He kissed her again, quickly, on the cheek. "Your world is the one I want, Simone. And the hell with everything else. With *everything* else."

There seemed to be no time for all that had to be done, just as there was no time for their love to grow.

175

Christie came and went in energetic silence, hurrying between the yacht and the shore, abstractedly at work in the chartroom one moment, then on the beach with the crew the next; a lithe, agile, tireless figure, always hurrying, always preoccupied, always alert.

At midday, Breck brought Roger the first of the contour maps, and said: "The first batch. They look pretty good to me."

Even Breck seemed a good man to know today, and Roger felt vaguely ashamed of his dislike. He said cheerfully: "Well, I don't want them yet, give them to Christie."

Breck grinned. He said smoothly: "I wouldn't dream of showing them to you before he's seen them. He's examined them, he's started drilling, he'll have the core samples for you by six o'clock this evening."

"Good, that's fine then. And Breck..." Breck looked at him. Roger said: "You're right, of course, to report first to your boss. Just let's not make quite so much of it, okay?"

Breck hesitated. The smile did not leave his face. He said at last, easily: "Sure. Did you get any sleep?"

"Nope. What's the word from Folkhagen?"

"Not a soldier within a thousand miles of us. They've just...disappeared."

"I hope that's not as bad as it sounds."

"He watched them right through till dark, and in the morning, they'd gone. Either they marched all night, or they're out there in the dunes somewhere."

"And we'd better know which it is."

Breck nodded. "We're putting a jeep ashore. Folkhagen is going after them to find out. We'll know soon enough."

"I've not seen Prince Hafik all day, do you know where he is?"

Breck's mouth was twisted into a sour smile. "He's with Candia, over on the headland, scuba-diving. They're looking for lobsters in the reef."

"I hope he knows what he's doing. The sharks'll be coming in after the garbage."

Breck's expression did not change. "I've got a man on the hill with a rifle."

Roger said: "And do they know that, Breck?"

176

"No, they don't." Breck turned away and said softly: "What they don't know can't hurt them, can it? I figured that the Prince might not like it, and that Mr. Christie would, so I did what I thought was necessary and kept quiet about it."

"Is the small launch available?"

"Yes, it is. Something you want?"

"No, not really. I'll take a run out and see how they're getting on."

"The samples..."

"Six o'clock, I think you said?"

Breck said nothing, and when he had gone, Roger went to find Simone.

She was in her cabin, reading, and she put down her book and moved over on the sofa so that he could sit beside her, and she said: "You're a busy man."

"And I'm not even going to apologize to you for it. With anyone else in the world, I would. With you..." He said helplessly: "I've *never* felt like this before. We're suddenly...so quickly I don't believe it...so close together that... I'm the happiest man you ever saw in your life. And that...that damned composure in your eyes!"

She laughed. "Have you come to rest a while? A little sleep?"

"With you, I want more than a little sleep. Until tonight..."

"Whenever you want."

"I want all the time. But a minute is not enough."

"I know that. And I'm glad of it. Shall we sleep together tonight?"

"Yes. In my cabin, or yours?"

"In mine. Unless..."

He laughed, knowing what she was thinking, and she began to laugh again with him. She said: "The scent of her perfume might still be there." But she offered him her mouth, and when he had kissed her, she said gravely: "It's good that we can laugh about it."

Her skin was unbelievably soft, her eyes calm and gentle, and he thought he had never seen a woman change to beauty in so short a time. He let his hands caress her for a while, feeling her tremble under his touch, enjoying the postponement and knowing that something fine was waiting for him that should not be hurried, and he pulled himself away from her and stood up, rubbing a hand through his hair, forcing a control on himself.

He said with a grimace: "I can't even sit close to you, not any more, for God's sake what's it going to be like when we're together in public? What the hell am I going to do, I feel like an overripe teenager..." He turned back to look at her and said at last: "I think I need your help. As a conspirator."

"Oh?"

"Hafik and Candia are out there together, swimming, under the headland, where the reef is..."

There was a moment of anxiety reflected in her face, and he said quickly:

"What they're up to is their business, but we've got to keep this from Maxwell, you and I, until...one of them gets tired of the other."

"The headland is out of sight of the camp where Maxwell is..."

"Breck put a man up on the hill, with a rifle, to watch for sharks."

She sat up quickly and arranged her dress. "Can we take the launch?"

"Get into a bathing costume, and we'll swim. Almost my last few hours of leisure..."

"Then, let's put them to good use."

"Shall I wait for you on deck?"

She said gently: "No. Wait for me here."

She went into the bathroom while he idly flipped over the pages of the book she had been reading. It was a small volume bound in soft green leather, well-worn and tooled in golf leaf, and it was in French, entitled *A Short History of the Persian Wars and Their Consequences,* by Feisal bin Suleiman Caffa. There was a dedication on the first page, and he struggled with the French and read: *"To my daughter Simone, in the knowledge that what lies ahead is the result of what is past."*

He heard the sound of the shower, and glanced at the open bathroom, forcing himself to stay where he was, and in a little while she came out, wearing a bathrobe and holding out two bathing costumes for his inspection. She said gravely:

"This...or this?"

"The black one."

Watching him, she took off the robe and stood there for a moment, naked, her eyes on his, and he stood up and went to her slowly and put his arms round her and held her for a moment, and she kissed him and said:

"I have had lovers before, Roger."

"I never saw so lovely a body."

"When you want, for as long as you want."

"I want...now. But I'm going to wait. I want to wake up beside you."

She said: "*Touche-moi...ici...*"

He stroked her gently for a while, and then she shuddered and pulled herself away from him and said: "To wake in the morning, with you beside me, waiting for my love..."

She moved away and shook her head, and he picked up the bathing costume she had dropped and watched while she stepped into it, and she kissed him again quickly and said:

"Let's go and see what other secrets there are to be kept."

They went out hand in hand, like lovers, and Breck was there at the head of the ladder where the launch was gently bobbing up and down in the water. He said, with a twisted smile: "If you need me, Madam Caffa..."

She shook her head, and Roger said sourly: "We'll be back long before six."

They set off across the water towards the sandstone bluff, and Simone looked at him and said: "You don't trust Breck, do you?"

"No, I don't."

"I think you're wise. But he's very close to Maxwell."

"I know, and I can't think why."

She said: "If you were to ask him, he'd probably tell you. If not, perhaps, one day, I will."

He did not press the point, and soon they reached the stark red rock of the headland that jutted sharply up out of the bright blue sea. The waters broke over the reef in small white waves, and Candia was there, standing waist-deep on the coral, a spear gun in her hand, a tank on her back and her goggles pushed away from her eyes, her long hair clinging to her shoulders. She waved at them cheerfully as they approached, and called out:

"I thought the work had started? Come on in, it's marvelous."

Hafik surfaced ahead of them and pushed back his goggles, and swam to them as Roger cut the motor. He pulled himself half out of the water and looked at Simone and began to laugh, and then he said:

"Simone! It's good to see you relaxing, you should do it more often, are you coming in?"

Roger tossed the anchor overboard, and Candia called out: "Better watch out for sharks, I think we saw one out there a while back."

Simone said lightly: "Don't worry, there's a guard up on top of the hill."

There was a moment of concern on Hafik's face, and he looked round quickly towards the shore, then back at Simone. He said: "You're a good friend, Simone, but I think you came a little late. Does it matter?"

"I don't know."

Candia was swimming toward them, and he was wondering if she had heard. He looked at her carefully, but her expression had not changed. She hung on to one of the rowlocks and tossed the wet blond hair from her face, panting and looking up at them, and Hafik turned to her and said:

"Don't overdo it."

Roger asked: "Were you ashore?"

She nodded: "Under the headland there, the sand's red-hot."

"Anyone around?"

Candia's eyes were bright with good humor: "I didn't see anyone, but then, I wouldn't, would I? What was that about a guard?"

He said casually: "Someone with a rifle up there, watching out for the sharks."

"That's what I thought you said."

She dropped onto her back, her fine breasts thrust out of the water, and began to backstroke towards the shore, the droplets gleaming as they fell from her long brown arms, her legs thrashing.

Hafik turned to follow her, and Roger said to Simone: "I'm going up the hill, coming?"

She nodded. They dived together into the water, and swam to

the beach where the white sand was hot under their feet.

There were tiny crabs scurrying back and forth, and larger ones that watched them cautiously, impatient of the intrusion; a lobster lay sullenly in a small pool of water, its antennae waving, searching out the unknown danger, and Simone looked at it and said: "Hafik's caught his supper..."

She was hopping from foot to foot on the hot sand, like a child, dipping her feet in the water to take the sting out of them, and Roger asked: "Shall I go back for your sandals?" But Simone shook her head. "It doesn't matter. Let's get up there."

They found Breck's man sitting in the shade of an outcrop of rock, a rifle cradled on his knees, and he stood up, grinning, as they approached, and stubbed out his cigarette; a big, ungainly slob of a man in a baseball cap and rolled-up trousers that were already too short, with his belly hanging over his belt and a white sweatshirt tight over his bulging chest. He was tossing sunflower seeds into his mouth, spitting out the shells on the sand; his jaws worked rhythmically, automatically, and he gestured at the rifle and said: "Sharks, Mac, you never know..."

Roger said sourly: "I know all about that." He bent down and picked up the binoculars and trained them on the two beach towels that were spread out on the sand below, just in focus. He said clearly: "Let me make it plain. If you've seen anything down there that I wouldn't want you to see, you'd better forget about it."

"Just a lot of empty water is all, Mac."

Roger put down the glasses and turned towards him. Simone was standing a little to one side, her lips showing her distaste. He said: "Look, I don't know what your name is..."

"Carl. Carl Jubot."

"...and I don't want to know. But when Breck asks you the question he's going to ask you, you'll tell him you have nothing to say. And you'll tell him that's what I told you to say, is that understood?"

Jubot stared at him, a beefy handful of sunflower seeds arrested in its rhythmic way to his mouth. He said: "Look, Mac, you keep to your department, I'll keep to mine, okay?"

Roger's hand shot out and grabbed the white sweat shirt,

twisting it up into a knot and pulling it in close. He said: "Look, Mac, you want I should beat the bloody hide off you? Right now?"

The sunflower seeds in their paper sack went spilling all over the ground, and Jubot held his look for a moment, his beefy face flushed and angry. Then he shrugged. "Okay, okay, if that's the way you want it, and look what you done to my lunch."

Roger released him and said: "You can tell Breck that my orders superseded his, and that my orders to you are to say nothing. Now, get back to the ship where you belong."

Jubot dropped to his knees, his ankles sticking out incongruously from the calf-length trousers, and began scooping up the spilled seeds, pouring them back into the sack. He said:

"Hell, they didn't do anything much, only once, it ain't the first time I seen it done... Okay, okay, I didn't see it." He looked up and said: "But he's quite a boy, that Prince, I should have his luck." His eyes were on Simone's thighs, and Roger felt like driving a fist into the heavy, sullen face.

He said sharply: "Watch it!"

"Okay, okay, take it easy, Mac."

"Get back to the ship. Go on, beat it."

Simone took his arm and said urgently, knowing the height of his anger: "Come away, Roger, let's get down there and join them."

"All right." He waited till Jubot had slithered off on his heavy rump, sliding down on the other side of the hillock, and said, growling: "The way he looked at you..."

"I know. It doesn't matter. Men have wanted me before. But there's only one man now who matters."

"Not like that. The bastard, I should have kicked his teeth in." He sighed. "I wonder if he'll tell Breck what he saw?"

"I'm sure he will. But I think Breck will know better, now, than to talk about it to Christie, now that Christie can so easily learn it was deliberate. It's one thing to mention casually, that Hafik and Candia were seen...and really ought to be more discreet. But to admit that he was spying on them, waiting for that very thing to happen...not even Breck could explain it away."

"I hope you're right, Simone."

"Oh, I'm right," Simone said. "Only I don't think Candia cares whether her father knows or not."

"I'm sure she does."

"No, Roger, she doesn't. Last night, when they were on the deck together, I heard them talking..." She looked at him quickly and said: "It was very distasteful, but I listened. Hafik is very dear to me, and I have to know."

"I understand that. It's precisely how I feel myself. Distasteful, but essential."

"He told her. He said: 'I don't really like being quite so indiscreet, Candia,' and she answered: 'I don't give a damn who knows.' I nearly made my presence known, for Hafik's sake, but instead I moved away, knowing what they were doing and hating it, and knowing too that nothing I could do would stop it. Oh, I could have...delayed it, I suppose, but Hafik would never have forgiven me, and I've never before tried to stop him from doing what every virile young Arab must do. And I know that it would have been useless."

"But Candia knows her father...how shall I put this? I don't think Christie really *minds,* can you understand that?"

"You're wrong. Quite wrong."

"I have cause to know that I'm right."

She said quietly, insisting: "No. With you, it's another matter altogether. For Maxwell, you represent something he admires, you're probably one of the few men he can bear to think of as part of his family, Candia's part. Hafik merely represents something he can use. In you, he sees himself, an image of the man he once was and who is going in the same direction he himself took so successfully. In Hafik, he sees merely a means to an end, and the end is his share or...whatever there is under these beaches."

Roger listened in silence, knowing that she was right; knowing too that there was no rancor there at all as she spoke so casually of his affair with Candia. It was easy to brush aside and think no more about something which, with anyone else, he would have felt acutely embarrassed about. But he was worried about Christie. He said at last, heavily:

"In his own way, he loves that child, and she won't even bother..." He broke off, looking down at the beach where Candia and Hafik had come ashore and were running along the sand together, hand in hand. He wondered where Jubot had disappeared to, and looking for him he saw him further off, walking in the dune grass, heading for the distant camp.

Simone said: "It's not that she won't *bother*. What she is doing, she is doing deliberately. She's trying to punish him, whether she knows it or not."

He looked at her, frowning. "I hope you're wrong, Simone."

"I'm not wrong. You will see. Let's go down, shall we?"

Worrying about what she had said, he followed her down to the shoreline.

Later that night, when he was checking over the analyses, Christie came in and perched on the edge of the table, and said:

"I think we're going to be lucky, how does it look to you?"

Roger grimaced. "A little early for guesswork. I told the crew to move four hundred yards to the northeast, right above the old shoreline. There's a salt dome, according to my reckoning, less than half a mile offshore..."

"I know, they're moving already."

Good. That's a pretty good crew you've got there."

The best in the business. We're going to be lucky, I can feel it, I can smell it, that feeling you always have...You know what I mean?"

Roger grinned. "I know enough not to be misled by it. I want three or four more days, a lot more samples..."

"You'll get them." Without changing his tone, Christie said: "Haven't seen Candia all day, what's she up to, is she getting bored?"

"Not as far as I know. I was out swimming with her this afternoon, she seemed to be enjoying herself."

"With Hafik?"

"Yes. And Simone. We went over by the bluff..."

"Breck said you had a little trouble with one of his men."

"Oh?" He tried to take the edge from his voice. "What did he say?" He waited for Christie to answer, but Christie was waiting too. Roger smiled quickly and said: "You mean the guard he put up there? I didn't think it was necessary, and believe me, we need every man we have just now..."

184

"I see."

"After all, there were four of us together and we were well inside the reef. Had Candia been alone, of course I'd have insisted on having someone up there to keep an eye open, but she wasn't alone, and a guard was merely a waste of manpower when we need every man we've got." He said lightly: "I seem to have hurt Breck's feelings, I must apologize to him."

"No, not really. I think he was..." Christie sighed and said: "Let's not play games, Roger. Breck just wanted to make sure that that bloody little pimp didn't get out of hand."

Roger was shocked at the unexpected epithet. He said: "But, for God's sake, I thought..."

"That I liked Hafik? So I do, just as long as he remembers he's a guest on board my ship."

"But..."

Christie said irritably: "All right, I didn't choose my words as carefully as I might, but I don't want Hafik sniffing around Candia, and neither, I should think, would you. All right, he's a good fellow, sincere, intelligent, well-disposed, all that bloody crap, but he's also the spoiled son of a goddam despot who is used to having his own way a damn sight too easily. In the world Hafik lives in, you whistle and the women lie down and open their legs, because he's his God Almighty Highness the Prince, the son of the Shah and the Heir Apparent, besides being too goddam free with his father's money and his own good looks. I don't want him whistling for Candia."

The temper was rising. Christie's face was flushed with anger, and Roger said: "I'm quite sure that Candia has a great deal of your own common sense, she knows how to behave, she knows how badly it would worry you if there were anything... Hell, I'm sure you've absolutely nothing to worry about."

He saw that Christie was watching him closely, trying to discover how much of what he said was the truth. He said cheerfully:

"And there's nothing more alarming than the rampant parent, especially when he's ramping about for nothing."

Christie turned away. He said: "You've changed, Roger. A few weeks ago, I could read you like a book. Now, I can't any more. I can only...hope that you're telling me the truth."

185

"I am. And we've other things to worry about."

Christie was suddenly relaxed again. There were heavy bags under his eyes, but the eyes were bright. He looked at his watch and said:

"Two in the morning. Did you get any sleep last night?"

"No, none at all. Did you?"

"I didn't even want any. But now... Shall we meet again at daylight?"

"The next batch of samples will be in by then, and I'll be looking them over."

"Batch number four, that's the promising one."

"Yes, I think it is. Have you heard from Folkhagen?"

"Folkhagen?"

"The man who went to find out what happened to the Army."

"Oh, Folkhagen... Yes, the Army's still moving north. They're well out of our way now." He was peering at Roger. "Something worrying you about them?"

"No. I just want to be sure they're out of our hair. I don't have your taste for trouble."

Christie laughed. "They're out of our hair. See you at six. Get a good night's sleep."

Thinking of Simone, knowing that she was waiting for him, Roger said gravely: "I will indeed. Good night."

When he had gone, he went to his own room and took a quick shower, and slipped into a dressing gown, and walked quietly over to her cabin.

He found her asleep, with a lamp on the bedside table still lit and the curtains drawn over the windows. She lay on one side, curled up like a child, her elbows out over the sheet that covered her, and her shoulders were bare.

He stood looking down on her for a moment, and then she stirred and her eyes opened, and she was suddenly wide awake. She looked up at him and smiled, her eyes bright and sleepless, and said nothing, moving over to make room for him. He leaned down and slowly pulled the sheet away from her, and looked at her naked body for a long time, and she waited, and at last she put out a hand and touched his, and he slipped out of his robe and lay down beside her, his hand on her breast.

He could hear her rhythmic breathing, quiet, slow, composed, and her body was warm beside him, warm and soft and somehow...belonging.

It seemed that he had known her all his life, that this was not the first time but was merely the completion of something that had happened, many many years ago, when he had first become aware of the physical needs, when first he had known a kind of immature love with some now forgotten child-woman who had then, perhaps, seemed as important to him as Simone was now.

All the rest no longer mattered, not the past, not the future; there was only the present and the exciting new worlds that she had promised him.

Her hands were moving lightly, slowly over his body, and the urge was irrepressible to love her now, quickly, and he reached for the lamp to put it out, but she pulled his hand away and whispered: "No, the light is good..."

And then, the delirium began to engulf him, and the heat was burning him alive, and his body was racked and twisted and tortured, and the sweat was pouring from it, and he could not believe there was anything in the world but the sweet flesh that was brushing his body, that anything else could exist but the frenzy that was on him.

He found he was fighting for breath, fighting for relief and begging for more at the same time, hearing only the moans that were his own, blinding himself to everything except this strange and wonderful new thing that was all about him, driving out every thought except that of the fury of her love.


Later, much later, he said, panting: "I'll never leave this bed, never..." She smiled, and leaned over and kissed him, and he said: "Hell, I'll never be able to." He looked at her gravely and touched her breast and said:

"For all my life, Simone, for all my life. Nothing must ever come between us, nothing, nothing, nothing."

She lay curled up beside him, a hand on his chest, her face close to his, her eyes solemn and composed. She looked strangely childlike and innocent. He kissed her and said again: "For all my life, Simone. I want you forever, the two of us, just you and me, and nothing else in the world."

She was strangely silent, looking into his eyes with that calm and peaceful look that seemed to deny the violent flush that had so recently been on her; it was a look that seemed to mask something she did not want to be seen, as though, in her world, there never had been a forever. But she said, her voice very low and soft: "Whenever you want, for as long as you want. I love you, Roger."

The heat began to rise again, and she slowly turned over onto her back, and the child was gone and the woman was there. And when he stirred, she reached up and very gently, very slowly, began to stroke his face.

# CHAPTER 13

FOR MORE THAN seven miles along the beach, and for a thousand yards inland, the electrodes had been sunk into the soil at eight-hundred-foot intervals, and the black cables from the big generators snaked over the sand like giant worms that had come up on this desolate shore to die in the heat of the sun.

The geophysical team, backing up the drillers who were bringing up the constant flow of core samples, were working round the clock, checking the resistances between the electrodes, measuring the drop in the potentials, sending their calculations by radio to the ship, where the charts and graphs were being sorted, classified, and evaluated. And everywhere there was an air of urgency. Breck was driving the men hard.

All through the afternoon, a tremor of excitement had been felt on board. At midday, one of the geologists had called Roger ashore, and there had been a meeting out among the dusty dunes, where the wind was beginning to whip up a fine spray of biting grit that found its way into their eyes and ears and left their faces coated with a fine yellow dust. Christie was there, trying hard to contain his excitement, handing to Roger one chart after another, waiting for confirmation or denial of something he felt must be true.

The wind whipped at their clothes as they stood there, sweating, ankle-deep in fine sand, with the bustle of the camp pulsating all about them, a camp that had grown like a living thing till more than two miles of beach were covered with stores and tents and water barrels, and the prefabricated aluminum huts that housed the magnometers, the seismographs, the explosives. The ubiquitous cables coiled on the sand, and the constant pounding of the drills was a constant cacophony around them.

Their faces were burned red by the sun and blistered by the wind, and it seemed that there was no time even to wash or get cool, as though time were running out and that today, or tomorrow, or the day after, would surely be the end of all their planning and all their hopes.

Christie waited, his eyes bright and darting, looking at the others and trying not to show his excitement, and the senior physicist stood by smoking calmly, drawing on his pipe and muttering: "It's still not sure, it's nothing more than an assumption..."

Roger looked up from the charts and stared out across the beach. He pointed and said: "Give me some samples of the topsoil from the ridge there, take a line, a foot below the surface, a thousand yards or so. Get the lab to analyze them for wax content. Go down a bit deeper and see if we can find traces of ethane, I think we probably will. Have them pinpoint the spot where the hydrocarbon content is lowest, then look for the halo round it..." He turned to Christie. "I like the looks of it. I think we're in business."

Christie said eagerly: "How sure are you?"

Roger shook his head. "We can count on the electrodes, they don't lie..." He indicated the chart he had been given. "This fits in exactly with my own calculations. I'd estimated the crest of the anticline just about there, but we can't be sure till we see what it's like down below. It won't take long..."

"Can we call the Shah?"

"Not yet. Let's wait a few hours."

"He's mighty anxious to get word from us, he'll be sitting on his radio day and night."

Roger said: "Let's be sure first. I'll get back to the ship and put the computer to work."

"All right, if you think so. We'd better bring the crew down from the hill and put them out along the ridge."

"Good."

"And meanwhile..."

"Meanwhile, we wait. There's nothing else we can do." Christie slapped him on the back heartily and said: "I'd almost forgotten that Oklahoma project of yours..."

Roger said quietly: "I hadn't."

"...but you're getting closer to it every minute. Maybe I'll even come along with you and give you a hand, would you like that?"

"I'd like it fine."

"Then that's what we'll do. We might fly back to the States from Aden..."

Roger said dryly: "Don't you think we might at least tidy up the beach here before we go?"

Christie laughed: "All right, you're not certain, but I am. As you said, the electrical system doesn't lie, and neither do my bones, put the two together and we've got oil, all the oil we want. And that's all there is to it."

He looked up towards the top of the dunes. During the day, the wind had covered the coarse grasses that were struggling where the dunes met the beach, and further along, towards the headland, the lonely coconut palms were bent towards the water. He said:

"I don't like this wind."

"Wind and sand, it's a lousy combination." Roger turned to one of the men who was hovering near by, waiting to take the good news to his fellows: "Tell Breck there's a sandstorm coming up, by the looks of it."

The man nodded and moved off, and Christie said: "Don't worry, he knows."

Roger grinned. "Yes, I suppose he does, there's not much he misses, and I've an idea something is building up that we're not going to like..."

"On the other side of the mountain. We had word from...what's his name, the fellow out there?"

"Folkhagen."

"Yes, he sent word, a dust storm moving across the dunes, he thinks it's going to hit us if the wind holds in this direction."

"That's all we need. We'd better get these charts over to the lab."

"And I need a shower."

They had to shout against the wind, and as they went over to the launch, Christie stopped and said: "Are you keeping an eye on Candia for me?"

Roger turned in surprise. "I didn't think she needed it."

"This thing with...with Hafik."

"Hardly my business, she's old enough to know what she wants."

"I'm making it your business, I want you to break it up before it goes too far."

Roger said: "Look, first of all I've got my hands full with more important things, the things you brought me here for. Secondly, I don't think Candia needs a wet nurse and if she does it's not going to be me. And thirdly, you're only going to aggravate matters if you turn away from your work, just once in a while, to impose a discipline on her that she's obviously never had."

He turned angrily and went on down to the launch, and Christie came running after him and took his arm and said, pleading: "All I'm asking is for you to help see she doesn't get hurt, is that asking too much? Roger, please..."

He sighed, his anger gone. "All right, I'll do what I can, but don't expect a bloody miracle."

Christie's fear was gone too, gone so fast that the show of it might have been deliberate. He said quickly: "That's all I want, Roger, you're in a good position to apply the gentle pressure that's needed, that's *all* that's needed..."

"And what's that supposed to mean?"

Christie said earnestly: "It means, Roger, that I rely on you more than I ought to. Don't let me down. Please."

"Okay, okay."

"Good, then."

They splashed through the ankle-deep surf together and pushed the launch into deeper water, and as they swung aboard Roger said carefully: "But you must have spoken to her yourself about Hafik, surely?"

Christie hesitated. "Not...very forthrightly, I'm afraid. I dropped a hint. Anything stronger would only precipitate matters, that's the kind of child she is. Tell her she mustn't touch the candy and she won't eat anything else."

"And?"

"And she told me to go to hell, more bluntly than she's ever done before. She gave me a bad time."

"Well, you're not the most tactful father in the world, are you? If you applied some of your...your business acumen, you'd make out a lot better with her."

"I don't have the time to do that."

"No. That's just the trouble."

Christie looked at him angrily for a moment, but said nothing about Candia. Instead, he asked: "What do you think of our chances?"

Roger said patiently: "I'm not going to try and evaluate them till I see those samples, you'll have to wait, that's all there is to it."

"I know. At a time like this, on the edge, right on the edge, it's always the worst time. All our planning was aimed at just one thing, hitting it right on the nose, right away, and it looks like we've done just that. And I can't believe we haven't." He shook his head, muttering to himself.

He was nervous, anxious, restless, and when they reached the chartroom and found Hafik there, sitting alone and making out a graph, he said irritably: "We've got experts for that sort of thing, you know."

Hafik looked quickly at Roger and back to Christie. He put away the chart and said, shrugging it off:

"I didn't realize my interest in your work would disturb you. I find the sketches very interesting. Sand, shale, limestone, slate... Am I right in thinking there was a river here once, below the bluff?"

Christie said: "Where's Candia, have you seen her?" and Roger said quickly, seeing the sudden flash of anger: "Yes, a long time ago, a deep river that came down from the Jebel Hauta..."

Hafik did not wait for him to finish. He said to Christie coldly: "I'm afraid I haven't seen her all day."

Christie muttered something under his breath and went out, and Hafik looked at Roger and said:

"That was very rude of him, wasn't it? And I'm sorry you should have thought it necessary to come to my rescue."

"It's a difficult time for him. We've just found very strong indications of a sizeable trap, the very thing we hoped to find, just where we hoped to find it, and now we're waiting for the proof. A lot hangs on what happens in the next few hours, and all we can do is wait so...it's a bad time for all of us. It's no longer any use for him to worry about the analyses, and so he worries about his daughter instead."

"And me?"

"Yes. And you."

"You're very blunt."

"I'm sorry. I have to be. It's important to all of us to avoid...family squabbles just now."

"A tight and happy ship?"

"Something like that."

Hafik went and closed the chartroom door. They were alone. He sat down, leaned back and put the tips of his fingers together and said:

"Let's talk, shall we? If there's something on your mind, we may as well fight now and get it over with."

"Fight? There's nothing to fight about."

Hafik said: "I suppose in the crudest terms it could be said that I took Candia's mind off you for a while, and if you dispute my right to do that, now's the time to say so."

Roger went to the cabinet and took out the bourbon bottle that was there. "Whisky?" Hafik shook his head, and Roger poured himself a drink, watching the Prince, not liking the sardonic expression very much. He said quietly: "I said there's nothing to fight about. If you'd...taken her from me, I suppose there would be. But there's not."

"Then would you mind telling me why you're making it your business?"

"Candia is merely flaunting an affair with you in the hope that her father will find out, and disapprove. And raise hell about it."

"And that's supposed to worry me?"

"I thought it might. I thought it might put you in a position of less than regal dignity."

"It doesn't. I'm not even sure it's true, though I have an idea it might be." He shrugged elegantly, and said: "An academic question, Mr. Sequoyah... In your world, you don't talk about the women you've bedded down with, do you? Why not?"

Roger shrugged: "I'd say that's a pretty solid attitude."

"For the inhibited Western mind that has not yet brushed aside the dirt of its cave-man origins, perhaps it is. In my world, a man's merit is reflected in his sexual abilities—just as it is in yours, if you bothered to think about it. But we haven't muddied up the issue with the puritanical hypocrisy you try to live with. In my world, a man will not hide his prowess, and I will not hide mine."

"Are you trying to impress me because you made Candia? I can't imagine it was very difficult."

"No, it was easy." Hafik said calmly: "By virtue of my privileged position, I have never really had to try very hard. In my own country, I merely command. I see a woman I like, and she is ordered into my father's harem, where she awaits whatever attentions I might be prepared to give her. And in Europe, I've never found it very difficult either, for reasons which are probably apparent. So, you see, I've never had the struggle that I am told is so important if you find it necessary to assert your masculinity. I don't have to assert mine, I know it's there." He said, brutally: "And so does Candia."

"What are you trying to goad me into, Hafik?"

"Goad you? Into nothing. But I want to make it clear that what I chose to do with Candia is none of your damn business."

"It is. Whatever affects the well-being of her father...and hers, too..."

"You think I'm bad for her? I'm not, you know."

"That isn't really the point."

"No, it's not. The point is that I will do what I damn well please, with her or with any other woman. Candia pleases me. I find a great deal of pleasure in the contemplation of her body, which I find extremely beautiful. I've always had a weakness for that...that luster she has to her skin, have you noticed it? And as long as it pleases me, I will continue to put her body to its proper use. For as long as I like, and without interference from you, or from anybody."

"Its proper use, that's the crux of the matter, isn't it? What *you* regard as its proper use is not exactly acceptable to the more civilized world."

"Ha!" Hafik pointed an over-manicured finger at him and said: "A conflict of philosophies! You make love to Candia in dark corners, hoping no one will find out. I make love to her openly, with no attempt at concealment. And somehow, in your distorted mind, that makes you more civilized than I am. I suppose you can rationalize that too?"

"Discretion, good manners, I don't give a damn what you call it."

The temper was beginning to rise, the academic interest going. Hafik said tightly: "Are you telling me not to make love to her any more, or are you telling me to keep it a secret?"

Holding his anger in check, Roger said: "I began by asking you to use a little discretion for Christie's sake. Now I'm telling you to leave her alone."

"Telling me?"

"Yes, Your Highness. Telling you."

Hafik said clearly: "Did you know that Candia is insatiable? I imagine you didn't. She told me you weren't particularly expert in bed, so you probably never had a chance to find out, but I did. The first time, it was of no great consequence, pleasant enough, but really only for the sake of adding one more to the list. But then I found out that she could not be satisfied, and you know, an insatiable woman is very exciting, because she tries so damned hard, all the time, again and again and again, and to a hot-blooded man... But you wouldn't know about that, would you? To a man of my temperament, a soft and beautiful body like Candia's, that is always there waiting for more, never tired, always demanding, begging for more, begging on her knees... On one occasion at least, that's what she did, went down on her knees and begged, you find that amusing?"

Roger put down his glass, stepped forward, grabbed Hafik by his collar, and yanked him to his feet. For a moment, there was a look of shock on the spoiled, handsome face, as though iconoclasm had never been known before, and then Roger drove his fist home and hit him under the side of the jaw, hard, sending him sprawling back onto the divan.

Hafik stared at him, shocked and furious, and wiped a hand slowly at the blood that was staining the side of his mouth. He took out his handkerchief and wiped at it, and then stood up and went slowly to the window to look at the shoreline. There was a dignity in his movements, in the way he held his body straight, his shoulders well back, his hand steady. He turned after a moment and said:

"Technically, we are in Orassian territory. Technically, you have committed a crime for which..." He broke off and looked at Roger strangely and said: "Do you know what the punishment is for a physical assault on a member of the Royal Household? On the heir to the throne? Can you stretch your imagination as far as that?"

"Yes, I can. I've already seen your idea of justice graphically demonstrated."

"And it doesn't frighten you?"

"No."

"You think in terms of...of consular protection? That an American citizen is above the laws of such a backward country? Is that what you think?"

"No. I don't."

"Then you will, at least, attempt to save your skin by an apology."

"No, I will not."

"Even though it would do no good."

"The hell with you."

Hafik had made no effort to hide the astonishment. He said again: "Not even to save your neck? A simple matter of an apology? The good manners and discretion you were trying to impress on me a moment ago?"

Roger said stubbornly: "I will not apologize, and if you talk like that about Candia any more, or about any other woman I know, I'll do it again, and keep on doing it till you get the point, is that clear?"

For a moment, Hafik just stared at him. He shook his head slowly, and dabbed again at the corner of his mouth, then looked at the tiny bloodstain on it. He said again, frowning:

"Not even a token apology? You don't have to mean it."

Roger said nothing. Hafik shook his head. "I don't understand, I just don't understand." He raised his voice and said angrily: "I am the Prince, dammit!" The silence was unendurable. Hafik dabbed at his mouth and said: "Royal blood, it looks like anyone else's, doesn't it?" He suddenly began to laugh, and said: "And why shouldn't it? All right, Roger Sequoyah, if you refuse to scuttle away at the thought of my vengeance..." He said clearly: "I was wrong in speaking so frankly, and...yes, I was goading you, I wanted to find out what kind of man you are. I found out, didn't I, so out of defeat, allow me a little victory. I was wrong, and I apologize. Moreover, I apologize sincerely. And now, I'll have that whisky you offered me."

Roger poured him a drink in silence and handed it to him. He was not at all sure of what was going to happen now, but Hafik turned away with a short laugh and said:

"Not since I left school...Oh yes, they used to beat me up there once in a while, there was always the school bully... He beat me up for different reasons, because I was a dirty wog, or because I was a Prince who had been clearly told he was just like any other student. But not since then, Roger, not since then. I suppose it's wrong that a man should be...impregnable through other virtues than his own. Wouldn't you say that?"

Roger said: "I'd say it's a hell of a way to put it, but I suppose I'd agree with you."

Hafik swallowed his drink quickly and put down his glass. He said awkwardly: "Another thing they taught me in school... I always thought it rather foolish..." He held out his hand and said: "Shall we shake hands?"

Roger took the firm grip, feeling a trifle unsure of himself, feeling more than ever remote. He said: "Goddamit, and now I'll apologize, too. There should be better ways among civilized men to settle an argument. I'm sorry."

"Then, shall we forget it?"

"I will."

"Good. And for what it's worth..." Hafik laughed shortly and said: "All right, for what it's worth I'll use a little of that discretion. You're a good man, Sequoyah, I like you. I suppose a punch on the nose is good for the royal soul."

There was a knock on the door and one of the radio men was there, looking worried. It was Hendricks, a young Englishman Roger had spoken with before. He said:

"I was looking for Mr. Christie, sir..."

"In his cabin, I imagine."

"No, sir. At least, I knocked, there was no answer. The cabin was locked, sir "

"Oh?" It didn't sound right. He said: "He may be sleeping, it's been a tough haul... Something I can do?"

Hendricks handed him a paper, torn from his pad, on which he had scribbled a message. He said anxiously:

"It just came in from Folkhagen, sir... Miss Candia, out on the dunes, alone..."

Roger said quickly: "Let me talk to him." Followed by Hafik, he hurried with Hendricks up to the radio shack, and when Hendricks handed him the microphone, he said: "Folkhagen? Roger Sequoyah, where is she?"

Folkhagen's voice came back clearly over the speaker. The other operators were waiting, looking at him. "Mr. Sequoyah? She's walking out into the desert, about three miles off, heading north, and I don't like the looks of it, sir... Can't see her now, she's behind a dune, I've sent a man after her but I thought Mr. Christie better be told, we're having trouble catching up with her..."

"You have the jeep out there?"

The voice was doubtful: "Don't know whether the jeep can make it over the dunes, it's pretty soft out there, we tried it before..."

"Still quicker than on foot. Send it down to the beach."

Folkhagen's voice came through excitedly: "There she is! I can see her now, she's climbing up a dune, hold it, I'll get the range finder..." Roger waited a moment and then: "Hullo, are you there? Is just under three miles, I don't see my man but he must be a long way behind her... She just fell down but she got up again, she seems all right, but... You know what it's like in the dunes, I don't know how she got so far."

Roger said: "Wait for me. Try and keep her in sight. Signing off."

Hendricks was changing the frequency on a walkie-talkie. As Roger hurried out of the shack he handed it to him and said:

"This will keep you in touch with Folkhagen, sir, shall I get Mr. Breck?"

"No. I'll take care of it."

He hurried, with an anxious Hafik, down to Christie's cabin. He said irritably: "Christie must be there, he's waiting for the stuff to come in from the beach..." He hammered on the door and called out: "Maxwell? Roger. Are you there?"

Christie's voice came back to them irritably: "What the hell is it, Roger, I'm busy?"

"It's Candia. We've got trouble."

He heard a chair scrape, and the door was flung open. Christie was there, his face suddenly white. "What do you mean?"

Roger said: "A message from Folkhagen. Candia's wandered off into the dunes by herself. I'm going off to get her."

"I'll come with you." He thought he could sense relief in Christie's voice, and Christie said hesitantly: "I thought for a moment that you meant she'd..." He said quickly: "Just a moment, I'll come with you."

He stepped back into the cabin, and as Roger was about to follow he saw that the wall safe was open, but Christie stood there, blocking his way and saying again: "Just a minute..." He closed the door and left them there, and Hafik looked at Roger, puzzled, but Roger shook his head.

In a few moments, Christie came out, smiling at them and saying: "I'm sure it's nothing to worry about, but we'd better take a look."

Roger said casually: "Did you lock the safe?"

"Yes, I locked it." His eyes were hard. He said almost accusingly: "Did you tell Breck?"

"Breck? No, I didn't, we don't need him."

"No, perhaps you're right." He looked at Hafik and said: "Roger and I can handle this, I'm sure."

Hafik smiled. "If you wouldn't mind... May I come with you? I'd be grateful."

Christie shrugged. He said sarcastically: "Regal gratitude is always worth something, I suppose. Yes, of course you can come if you feel it's important."

He said no more, and they walked in silence to the ladder and down to the launch that Breck was sitting in, waiting, knowing, as always, where he was needed, and they sped over the deep blue water to the shore and rammed the boat hard into the wet sand. As Breck busied himself with the anchor, driving it into the sand, Christie looked once at Roger and said:

"Breck? We don't need you, wait here."

Breck looked his surprise. He nodded, lit a cigarette, leaned against the boat and waited.

The wind had risen, and the drive up to the steep mountain was murderous. The wind was carrying a heavy spray of sand off the tops of the dunes, whipping it into an almost horizontal stream of grit that drove hard into their faces as they slowly climbed upwards.

The driver was Folkhagen's close friend, a thick-set man from Denmark who spoke very little. He plowed the jeep fast into the dunes, racing up them as far as he could go, and when the wheels began to spin, in spite of the four-wheel drive, Roger jumped out and slipped the canvas sand-mat under the wheels, while Hafik pushed, watching it shoot forward again and then struggling through the soft sand to catch up. At last, the Dane looked at Christie and said: "Maybe you take the wheel, Mr. Christie...?" and when Christie nodded and moved over, he slipped out and put his heavy shoulder to the metal body, broiling hot in the sun, forcing his weight into it while Roger repeatedly slipped the sand-mat into position, again and again as the jeep edged slowly forward.

When they reached the top and the blown sand-spray was at its fiercest, Christie, panting even at the wheel, said: "Hell, let's walk, it's quicker..."

Hafik nodded. His slender body was cool, no perspiration staining his clothes. He pointed and said: "When we reach the bottom..."

They drove fast down the other side of the big dune, forced the jeep up again as far as it would go, and then left it with the Danish driver. Christie said to him: "Get it back to the beach, tell Breck we might need a few men, have them fan out and move north."

The Dane touched his cap. "Yes, sir."

Christie said: "Let's catch up with her."

He took off his white jacket and his shirt and dropped them in the jeep, and set off through the deep soft sand, and when they reached the top again, they could see Folkhagen, high above them and far away on the jagged rock they called the mountain, waving his arms. Roger switched on his walkie-talkie. He said:

"Folkhagen...can you see her?"

"Yes, Mr. Sequoyah, she's ahead of you, a little to the left, a long way ahead, beyond the dunes."

Roger said: "Give me a compass bearing."

Through the binoculars, he saw Folkhagen taking the reading, and then the voice came out of the box again: "Three hundred and twenty degrees, seven thousand yards, she's still moving."

He swung the binoculars round. There was no sign of her.

As far as he could see, the red sand stretched out into the distance, red and brown and yellow, with no sign of a tree or a blade of grass, with only deep gashes of purple where the *wadies* lay, deep scars in the sandstone where once rivers had flowed, where once the Nabateans had flung up their miraculous dams to catch the vital flow that watered their crops and gave them life and now was gone. There was ridge after ridge of dark, interminable mountain, a limitless vista where nothing moved, where there were no animals because there was no food, and no life because there was only silence.

It was hard to believe that in this arid land, somewhere, there were wandering tribes of Bedouin, searching in patience for water which would keep themselves and their camels alive for another season, living always on the edge of death and sometimes dying, their deaths unrecorded, because there just wasn't any.

The mind could not fully grasp the immensity of the desert; the mind could only sense the heat that consumed it all, the blistering sun that broiled it from above, and the volcanic fires that burned it from below.

The land was caught between the two fires, and nothing could live there. And around them, the wind and the dust were gathering, joining forces to drive them out of this inferno.

They stumbled down the steep dune again, falling sometimes and rolling over, then staggering up and plunging on. Roger muttered: "Seven thousand yards...in this..."

Christie said, angrily: "Four miles, what the hell's she up to?"

Hafik was worried. He said: "We'd better catch up with her, fast, it doesn't take long in the dunes, she can dry out in an hour and she must have been there longer than that." He pointed to the side. "If we keep to the foot of the dunes, go round them..."

Christie said: "No, over the top will be quicker."

"We'll never make it over the top. Four, five, half a dozen dunes is all a man can climb before he's exhausted..."

Christie swore, and Roger said: "He's right, let's keep on the level as far as we can."

Christie glared at him: "Then you're not as fit as you should be."

But he did not argue any more, and they hurried off together, following the crescent-shaped foot of the dune that towered more than three hundred feet above them.

Down here, the wind was gone and the heat was intense, but above them the sand-spray was still being carried through the hot air like a power-blown blast of grit, gray-yellow where the sun could not find a way through it. The sweat poured off their bodies for a while, and then they were sweating no more, and Roger held out the first of the water bottles and said:

"A long drink each, or we'll have other worries."

He never ceased to wonder, even after years in the hot deserts that covered the oil beds, at the speed with which dehydration set in.

Christie flopped down on the sand and drank greedily, then handed the bottle to Hafik. He said irritably:

"For God's sake, there's a goddam camp within a mile of us, all the ease and comfort you could want..."

Roger knew he was driving away a fear, using a rationalization to drive off the specter that was always in the desert, in every desert, a specter that had never lost its power, because the word itself denied the presence of anything but the emptiness of death, however close to safety...

A man could die within hailing distance of all the help in the world, close to the ease and comfort he was used to, separated from it only by sand, by a mountain of sand that was high enough, and impenetrable enough, to reduce him to a shriveled, empty sack of leather and bone, with all the moisture gone, taken by the sun and the hot sand that would make him brittle in a few hours, as though there never had been water in his body but only dust and powder and dried-

203

up phosphate. Sometimes, there was only the will there, and sometimes the will was not enough.

Looking at Roger, knowing what he was thinking, Hafik said:

"The desert has always frightened the Europeans. But to us...we are Bedouin, Roger."

"I know. Let's get moving." He helped Christie to his feet and said: "Would you rather go back?"

But Christie shook him off angrily and said: "Once I get my second wind...the penalties of the life I lead."

The determination was there too, and Roger knew that there would be nothing to worry about from Christie. He got on the blower again to check with Folkhagen, but there was no signal coming in. Christie laughed shortly and said:

"Maybe it's easier down here, but I still say over the top, we'll keep in contact."

Forcing himself to move faster, he headed up the next dune, Roger grimaced and said to Hafik:

"He's got a point there, we ought to keep in radio contact."

"The wind will kill you both up there."

"You mean..."

"Yes. I'm going round and I'll be there before you are. But go with him, Roger. On his own, he's just stubborn enough to get himself killed."

"All right. If you're sure."

Hafik said easily: "This is my desert, I was born in it. Walk along the top as long as you can, it's the climbing that takes the strength out of you. And don't worry about me."

Roger nodded and set off after Christie.

The sand piled up as high as his calves, filling his shoes, and he dropped down and took them off, letting the sand burn his feet rather than suffer the added drag of them as he labored heavily upwards. He fell again and again, clawing at the sand and making little holes with his hands out of which the sand dribbled slowly, pulling himself upwards on hands and knees.

He saw that Christie was still on his feet, moving closer to the dark, frightening layer of wind-blown sand that was howling over their heads at the higher levels, a virulent cloud of sand that was dense and heavy, moving fast in an interminable, horizontal blast off the top of the crest. He saw Christie stop and look at it, then put down his head and struggle up towards it. He was moving well now, with something that Roger knew was only will power.

The blown sand hit him as he reached it and tore into his eyes, his nose, his mouth, a biting, acrid sand that seemed to smother him. He could see nothing, and there was a moment of panic. He took off his shirt and wrapped it round the lower part of his face and called out: "Maxwell! Where are you?" There was no reply, and he yelled louder and then he heard Christie calling: "Here...behind you..."

He dropped to the sand and crawled back, and there was Christie, pulling himself to his feet again, knee-deep now in soft sand, struggling to get his balance and being blown over by the wind.

Roger ripped his shirt in two and handed half of it to him and said: "Use it...it might help..." Then he spoke into the walkie-talkie again: "Folkhagen? You can't see us, but we're half a mile to the west of you. Where is she, can you see her?"

Folkhagen sounded worried: "I can see her, but I can't see you. She's stopped now, she's lying down, it's hard sand over there, the same course you were on."

"Which way to get out of this sand? Is it all round us?"

"A big patch, a mile across by the look of it, a dust devil."

"I hope that's all it is."

"Yes, and it's moving north, but I don't like it, there's another one joining it, from the southwest, moving fast, building up into something that looks pretty nasty. Mr. Sequoyah, sir..."

"I think maybe we'd better join you first."

"No, keep on the same course, you'll never climb the mountain on this side."

"All right, the same course. She still there?"

"Not moving, Mr. Sequoyah."

"If necessary, can you get down to her?"

"Not in time. Is a long way from up here, you're closer, maybe two miles."

Christie said: "An hour to reach her, we'd better move down, an hour or more at the rate we're moving."

"No, we keep moving straight. Hafik's down there, trying the way round, and I think he's going to beat us to it."

Christie laughed. "If that's meant as a jibe, it's deserved, so let's get moving. Come on."

It was good to see the spirit returning to him.

They stumbled on, their heads down into the wind, moving off course to keep to the ridge and save the hard climb up again, suffering the wind instead of the labor, counting the minutes and correcting the direction when the ridge veered round in its crescent course.

The sand and the wind were blinding them, suffocating them, stifling them. And suddenly they fell, almost together, rolling over and over down the steep side of a dune, slithering to a stop in a dust bowl full of quicksand and clawing their way out of it together, sharing their fright and their efforts as it seemed to suck them down.

The air about them was suddenly still, and the light was gray, a yellow-gray light that filtered through the storm above them, and Roger fumbled for the walkie-talkie that had slipped from his hand, knowing that without it they were in trouble. He found it under the sand, and switched it on and was relieved to hear Folkhagen's calm voice: "I can see you now, you've just cleared the dust devil, you should be able to see her...about eighty degrees east of you..."

Roger stumbled to his knees and swung the glasses round, and there she was, lying on her back in the sand, with her arms flung out; she was not moving. He saw with horror that the driven sand, falling from the edge of the storm, was beginning to cover the white silk of her dress. One long bare leg was already completely covered, and more of it was moving up close to her face.

He dropped the binoculars and pulled at Christie and said in something approaching panic: "My God, we've got to hurry..."

There was more than a mile to go, a mile of deep, ankle-tugging soft sand that fought them every labored step of the way.

He looked at his watch and was astonished to see that they had been nearly two hours out in the desert. Another dune lay between them, and they stumbled down, always down towards its next point, in a strange sort of stillness that was aggravated by the wind which howled over their heads.

As they groped their way lower, the sound lessened till it was only a distant moan. He checked his compass and headed up the weary slope again, moving up three paces and falling back two, knowing that this was the last and that there wasn't much time.

The wind hit them again as they reached the top, and the storm was stronger now, the dust thicker, so thick that it was a dark cloud round them, hiding them even from each other, forcing them to hold hands as they pushed a way through it. They stumbled on for more than two hundred yards, sinking deeper into the sand, buffeted by a wind so strong that it seemed it must surely blow them out to the desolate center of the desert... "The Empty Quarter," Roger said, shouting to make himself heard, and Christie yelled back above the wind: "What?"

"Nothing... Keep moving..."

They came out of the wind and the dust suddenly again, as though a miracle had cleared the air for them, and when Roger looked back, the dust was an impenetrable curtain of gray, seeming not to move, seeming to be too dense to move at all; only the roaring sound of it told them that it was alive, alive and vicious, ready to cut to pieces anyone foolish enough to enter it.

He turned again and used the glasses to check the direction, to check the progress of the stifling sand that was covering her, and he muttered: "Thank God, thank God, she's all right..."

Hafik was out there with her, bending over her and wiping away the blown sand that was piling up over her. He passed the binoculars to Christie and Christie watched for a while and then sank down on his knees in the sand, with the moving curtain still roaring close behind him, and stared out into the desert and said:

"For a while there, it seemed important that we should get there first, but it wasn't, was it?"

"No, of course it wasn't."

"And now...now I'm indebted to that..." He said bitterly: "Now I'm in his debt. I owe him my daughter's life."

Roger said furiously: "What the hell does it matter who got there first? Another few minutes and she'd have been dead, her mouth full of sand, can you bear the thought of that and still worry about...about your golden image? Is that all she means to you?" He leaned down and yanked Christie to his feet and shouted: "Another few minutes and your troubles with Candia would have been over, would that have been better?"

He was shocked at the look of distress in Christie's eyes. He helped him to his feet, his anger gone, and said: "I'm sorry, Maxwell, forgive me... For a moment, it seemed that... Hell, I'm sorry."

Christie took the binoculars and used them, and soon he said, quietly:

"I'm a pretty lousy father, Roger. Sometimes it's good to be reminded of it. Not good, but...necessary. I've a lot to thank you for. And to thank Hafik for too."

Roger put hand on his shoulder. "We'd have been there in time."

Christie said: "Fifty men on the beach, a couple of miles away, and she could have died, she nearly died." He handed Roger the binoculars and said: "She's all right now. Shall we try and reach them, or go back to the beach?"

"We'll go back to the beach and wait for them."

"All right, whatever you say."

Roger watched them through the glasses for a while. Beside him he heard Christie gulping down a drink of water, and he said absently: "Don't drink too much too quickly..."

Watching, he saw Hafik tear off a strip off the white dress and fold it, and then soak it in water from the bottle he was carrying, and lay it carefully over Candia's face. He picked her up, a limp brown body in startling white, and began to walk with her in his arms, carrying her easily round the crest of the dune, the dune that they had labored so hard to climb, walking lightly and with no effort at all and moving in long, deliberate strides, like the Bedouin he was.

He flipped the switch of the walkie-talkie: "Folkhagen? Is he heading in the right direction?"

He knew it was a useless question. He could almost hear Folkhagen grin. "Yes, Mr. Sequoyah, right on the nose. Can I call the others in?"

"The others?"

"Yes, sir. Mr. Breck's out below the dunes with a dozen men, I'm in touch with them."

"Good, signal them in. We'll move down and join His Highness."

Folkhagen said: "Highness is right, Mr. Sequoyah, he got there just in time, another few minutes would have been too late, you'd never have made it..."

Roger switched off. Christie's mouth was hard, and he said nothing. Roger put away the glasses and sighed. "It doesn't matter a damn, does it? Just as long as someone got there in time. Anyone."

Christie did not answer.

# CHAPTER 14

CANDIA WAS still unconscious when they got her back to the ship.

Simone was there, waiting on deck, her gray eyes steady but full of apprehension. Some of the crew had gathered at the head of the ladder, anxious to help.

Breck said: "All right, get back to work, there's nothing to see."

Roger carried her up the ladder to the deck and down to her cabin, and Simone stood beside him while he gently sponged water over her face and throat, and then Hafik came in with a big bundle of towels and went into the bathroom and turned on the shower, and when he came out he was wringing them out all over the expensive carpet. He said:

"Pick her up a minute, put these under her..."

Christie was standing in the doorway, watching, his fingers twitching. He said: "You'll give her pneumonia."

But Roger shook his head: "No, it's the best thing to do, she's dried out."

Christie said nothing, and when Roger looked again, he was gone.

Simone helped him move her off the bed while Hafik laid out the towels, and they put Candia on top of them and spread more wet towels over her, and Simone said gently:

"She'll be all right, don't let her drink when she comes round."

She made as if to leave, but Roger said: "No, stay with me." He saw Hafik throw Simone a quick glance, and he looked to Breck and said: "Bouillon, chicken soup, something like that?"

Breck nodded and went out, and then Candia opened her eyes and looked around the room blankly; it seemed that she trembled for a moment, and there was fear in her eyes, and then she saw Roger and looked at him and he said, watching the clarity come back to her:

"It's all right, Candia, it's all right."

She blinked, and then the veil was gone and she said: "Well..." She looked around the room again and back to Roger and said: "Well, whenever I'm in trouble, there's Roger Sequoyah, gentle and solicitous and not understanding a bloody thing."

He said: "Don't kid yourself, I understand better than you think. How do you feel?"

"Awful. Cold. For God's sake, pour me a brandy."

"Some chicken soup coming up."

"What a godawful thought."

She moved to push away the wet towels, and Roger said quickly: "No, leave them, you'll come out all over in blisters, and that wouldn't do, would it?"

But she pushed them away anyway, and sat up and said: "For Christ's sake, why do people always make so much *fuss?*"

She was looking around the room, and Hafik smiled and said: "Your father? He's getting re-hydrated too." He looked quickly at Roger, smiling, and said: "Your father carried you back through the dunes, right through the middle of a sandstorm, a dust devil. If he hadn't... He saved your life, Candia."

She stared at him. "Daddy did?"

"That's right."

For a moment, she said nothing. Then she lay down again and said softly: "Well, good for him, I'd never have believed it. These wet towels are bloody awful, can't I have just a small brandy?"

Hafik stood up and went to the cupboard and took out a bottle and a glass. "Just a small one, then. Sip it slowly, drink a little water with it, all right? And keep those towels around you."

She said meekly: "If you say so."

Simone looked at Roger. "We'd better see how Maxwell's getting on."

He nodded. At the door he looked back at Candia and said: "I'll tell him you're all right now, had a job making him lie down, he's anxious for you..."

She said clearly: "I'll bet."

He sighed. "One of these days, you'll find out just how much you mean to him."

He took Simone's arm and they left, closing the door behind them, leaving Candia and Hafik alone together, and in the corridor outside Breck was hurrying up with a tray on which was a bowl of bouillon. He took it from him, knocked on the door, went inside and put it down, and when he came back, he said to Breck: "She's all right now. Just leave them alone." As he turned away with Simone, he could feel Breck's eyes on his back.

Christie's cabin was locked again when he knocked briefly and tried the door, and Simone said in surprise: "Locking himself in, is he all right?"

Roger said: "Something odd going on, I don't know what it is."

He knocked again, and Christie called out: "Coming." He opened the door for them and said casually: "Is she all right?"

"All right and asking for you."

"Come in."

Simone said: "I think you ought to go to her, Maxwell."

"Is she alone?"

Roger said: "No, Hafik is with her."

Christie turned away. "Then she's in good hands. Come and have a drink."

He stood back and waited, and then Roger followed Simone into the cabin.

In spite of the brightness of the day, a desk light was on, though the desk was bare except for a large magnifying glass. Christie slipped it into a drawer and said again:

"She's in good hands. Hafik knows how to take care of things like that, a Bedouin. Knows how to turn them to good account, too."

Roger said carefully: "He told her you'd carried her in from the dunes yourself, a fiction you'd better keep up."

Christie stared at him, his eyes alive with sudden fury. He said explosively: "What the hell would he do a thing like that for?"

"Just an impetuous gesture. Not a wise one, but...a generous

212

one. He's not really mature enough to remember that...one lie leads to another. He found an occasion to give Candia something she desperately needs, something you won't give her, and he took it. He was well aware you were trying to save her...he just...pushed it along a little, hoping it might do her some good. And it did."

Christie sulked for a moment, his eyes sullen. He said at last, sourly: "Well, I suppose that in his position I might have done just the same sort of thing, and with just as little cause. And, when she finds out it was a lie..."

"There's no reason why she *should* find out."

Simone had gone to sit in one of the leather chairs, her long legs crossed, her hands in her lap, quite unruffled and calm. Looking at Christie, she said: "Of course she'll find out, if you tell her."

Christie said nothing. His hand shook as he began to pour himself a long drink of whisky. He gestured with the bottle, almost absently, at Simone. She shook her head, and Roger said: "I think we all need a drink."

He went to the cabinet and Simone said: "All right, perhaps a little brandy."

As he took out the bottle and the fine, tissue-thin glasses, Christie said to him, frowning:

"Roger? Tell me if you think Simone is right. She thinks it would be beneath my natural dignity to pass the word around, that I'm too weak—or too strong, perhaps—to say: *In spite of what happened, the story is that I was the one who saved my daughter's life, and every man jack on board this ship had better remember it if he knows what's good for him.* She thinks the...the image you spoke of is more important to me." He sipped his drink and said: "You think she's right?"

Roger sighed. "Yes, I suppose she is. Somehow, I just can't see you attaching more importance to Candia's welfare than to...your own dignity."

Christie flushed. He looked at Simone and said: "Is that truly your opinion of me?"

Sitting there, poised and completely self-assured, she said gently:

"I don't know, Maxwell. Word is all over the ship, no doubt,

213

that it was Hafik. It's equally sure that you could change it if you wanted to. Very few people would understand the rightness of your motives if you did. *'Everyone must pretend it was I who saved my daughter's life.'* As you suggest, it's not an easy line to take, is it? You'd earn a lot of contempt from a lot of people, people whose respect you have earned, whose respect you probably need. On the surface, it would appear to be a terrible, contemptible thing. But that has never worried you before, has it? And this time...the stakes are considerably higher. I think you know that."

Christie walked over to the intercom and pushed down the switch. He said:

"Get Breck on the line."

Roger had poured the brandy and taken a seat close to Simone. He said to her, worried: "We're crucifying him."

But Christie merely laughed. He said: "I don't think it's as important as all that. But perhaps I'm wrong. We'll find out, won't we?"

Breck came on the line and said: "Mr. Christie? I'd better come and see you..."

Christie said: "Wait." He looked at Roger and spoke into the microphone: "Breck, there's to be a new story on board, a nice new comforting story. To wit, I went out into the desert and I brought Candia in, and Hafik had nothing to do with it. I brought her in myself, is that understood?"

There was a momentary silence at the other end. Then: "Yes, sir."

And don't be so damned smug about it, that's the story from now on in, and God help anyone who lets her find out otherwise, including you."

"Yes, sir."

"And what do you want to see me about?"

"I'm trying to get the preliminary report on the radio to the Shah in Arkan. We can't raise them."

"Oh? Why not?"

"I don't know, sir. There's just no answer. Arkan's off the air."

"All right, keep trying."

He switched off the intercom and Roger asked, frowning:

"Preliminary reports? Already? Isn't that just a little previous?"

Christie grinned. It seemed he had forgotten the moment of distaste. He said: "I think you're too cautious, Roger. I went over the facts and figures again, there's only one chance in a thousand we're wrong. And that's exactly the extent of my message. *I said overwhelming evidence, yet to be confirmed,* and that's all I said. He'll expect to hear from us...just what I expect to hear from you." He looked at his watch and said: "Any hour now, they'll be calling you down to the lab."

"I'll be ready when they are. But meanwhile..." He hesitated unsure. "Meanwhile, I think we ought to get Candia out. Radio for a plane to come and pick her up and take her to...Paris, New York, anywhere but here."

Christie stared at him. "What the hell good would that do?"

"Why do you think she wandered out into the desert all by herself?"

"You tell me why."

"And why did she jump overboard the other day?"

"All right, I'm listening."

Simone reached out and put a hand on Roger's arm. She said quietly: "No, Roger, you're wrong. And I think Maxwell already knows what she's trying to do."

Christie said shortly: "Yes, I do. Tell him, Simone."

Roger waited. Simone said at last: "She wasn't trying to kill herself, Roger. Nothing was further from her mind."

He said dryly: "Two damn-near successful attempts at suicide, and she wasn't really trying?"

Simone nodded. "Each time, she knew someone—probably you—would turn up in time. On the first occasion, you were right there with her, ready to leap in after her, just as you did. The second time, she already knew she was being watched, she knew there was a man out on the mountain who would surely see her in plenty of time to call for help. She knew that she could push herself to the edge of suicide and that someone would drag her back."

"And why should she do that, for God's sake? Simone, you must be wrong!"

"No, Roger, I'm not. Just think about it, you'll see how right I am."

He looked at Christie, astonished. Christie was nodding slowly. "She's right. Candia's trying...to get at me, to prove to herself that she means...nothing to me at all. And that's a neurosis I'm not prepared to pander to."

"Then show her, for God's sake ..."

"I've shown her often enough. She's never believed me. If I go to her now, and say *Please don't do that again, Candia, because I love you*... What effect do you think it will have?"

Roger said promptly: "You'll convince her."

Simone said: "No. She'd be convinced only that her father was scared. A major triumph. And the next time..."

Roger interrupted her. He said, choosing his words carefully, making sure they would understand there was no doubt at all in his mind:

"There is nothing more certain, Maxwell, that if you take that line—if you don't give in when she's pushed herself so far—then the next time you won't be able to save her. I am sure of this, completely sure. It's a battle between the two of you, and someone has got to give in. And that someone must be the strongest. That's you, Maxwell. There's not a shred of doubt in my mind about it."

Simone was frowning, wondering, trying to gauge all that was in Christie's mind. In Candia's mind too. And when Christie said stubbornly, "My way is best," she said slowly: "Roger, I think he's right. I'm not sure, but...I think he's right."

Roger said urgently: "Go to her, Maxwell, for God's sake go to her, now. *Now*. If not, she'll do something...something terrible."

"No. I won't."

And Simone, a strange kind of desperation on her face, said: "Maxwell...how can I help you? I just don't know her well enough."

Christie shook his head. He said bluntly: "No one knows her well enough, not even her own father. All I can do is...what I think is right. And I think she's got to work out her own happiness. She's got to stand on her two feet like the rest of us, and until she does that..."

Roger said, resigned: "That's a hell of a prospect."

"The alternative is a great deal worse."

Again, a long silence, and then Christie snorted; he said:

216

"Women are a goddam pain in the neck, aren't they?" He lifted his glass to Simone. "Here's to you, Simone, a few more women like you around, and the world would be a hell of a lot better."

There was an urgent knock at the door, an insistent, impatient knock. Roger went to open it, and Breck was there, a message form in his hand. He looked past Roger at Christie and said briefly:

"I think you'd want to see this right away. From Hassan, in Aden, I signaled him..."

Roger stood aside and Breck entered the cabin. Christie took the message from him and his face went white. He looked at Simone and handed her the paper in silence. She read it and stood up quickly and went to the big radio console and said:

"Aden, it's Aden we want, where is it?"

Roger said: "For God's sake, what is it, what's happened?"

Simone said: "It's come, at last it's come." She handed him the message form and Roger read: *"In answer to your enquiry, we have not been able to raise Arkan either. We have just monitored a report from Radio Mecca that heavy rioting his broken out in Arkan and that army units have joined with the rebels and are now attacking the Palace there. The situation is confused, stand by for further news as it comes in."*

Christie had joined Simone at the console radio. The clipped British accent of the announcer was calm and matter-of-fact:

> *...and, although the battle has by no means been decided, it seems clear that the Palace has fallen. His Royal Highness Shah Omar Ammadin seems to have escaped, and there is a suggestion that he may have left Arkan by air. The airport is still in the hands of loyal troops, but is also under attack at this minute. The Minister of War, General Fali bin Sassara has called for the country to stand by for an important message, though it is not clear whether or not he has sided with the rebels. Radio Radija claims that he has, but Radio Arkan, already known to be in rebel hands, is silent. Stand by please for one moment...*

There was a long pause, and they waited. Roger looked hard at

Simone, trying to find any trace of alarm there, but there was none; those cool gray eyes were as composed as ever. He said quickly: "We'd better get Hafik..." But Christie shook his head. "Wait, let's see what's going to happen." He turned back to Breck. "Get Aden on the wire, pipe it here on the intercom, I want to talk with Hassan personally." Breck nodded and hurried out, and Christie switched on the intercom again and left it open.

The flat, disinterested voice of the announcer came on again:

> *Here's a message that has just come in. General Fali bin Sassara, broadcasting from Radio Arkan, has announced the formation of a Provisional Government, headed by the Committee for the Arab People's Progress, of which he is now disclosed as the apparent head, with himself as Prime Minister and Minister for Defense and Foreign Affairs. In his short, rather confused speech, he has stated that the Shah, warned in time of the impending revolt, has made his escape from the airport, taking with him eighty-five pieces of luggage filled, according to General Fali, with jewels and currency. It is not quite clear when this could have happened, if indeed it did, since the first outbreak of the revolt in Arkan itself only took place a few hours ago. The whole picture is, I'm afraid, quite unclear, though reports from the rebels themselves are being sporadically broadcast from Radio Arkan, which, having been heavily shelled, is not now functioning as well as perhaps it might...*

Christie said: "For God's sake...!" And then Breck's voice came over the intercom:

"I've got Hassan, Mr. Christie."

Christie said: "Good, put him on." He signaled to Roger, indicating the radio. "Turn that damned half-wit off."

Roger switched off the radio, and stood by Simone, trying to gauge the anxiety that must be there and finding no sign of it. She picked up her glass and sipped from it, not looking at anyone, sipping quietly as though nothing at all were happening. Then Hassan came on the air, a soft, effeminate voice touched with excitement, a disembodied ghost speaking on the intercom, with an obsequious deference that could be strongly felt:

"Mr. Christie? Are you there, sir?"

Christie said impatiently: "Of course I'm here, what have you got?"

"It's all very confused, Mr. Christie, but it seems that Arkan is fairly firmly in the hands of the Committee for Progress. There's been a great deal of fighting, and a large number of people have been killed. We are fairly sure that the Shah got away in his personal plane, taking a lot of money with him, but there seems to be no one else left alive at the palace, it's in ruins, they shelled it. They must have moved very fast indeed..."

Christie growled: "You can say that again, go on."

"...and General Fali has already announced the death of Prince Hafik..."

Christie said: "That's nonsense, he's with me, on board this ship."

"Yes, Mr. Christie, I was aware of that, but it seems that Fali isn't..."

"Fali is too, what's he got up his sleeve?"

"Oh? Are you sure about that, Mr. Christie?"

"He was here, having breakfast with Hafik only a few days ago, so he knows he's all right, what's he trying to do?"

"Then there is only one possible interpretation, Mr. Christie. The General is afraid that certain sections of the Army, and of course the Bedouin, would rally round Hafik if they knew he was still alive. He is trying to forestall that. It also means that the general must ensure that Hafik does not return to Arkan, and there is only one way he can do that. I suggest..."

"All right, all right," Christie said impatiently, "We'll be out of here before they can reach us, long before. What about their planes, the Air Force?"

"For the most part, they are loyal to the Shah, but the rebels have the airport."

"Then we can possibly expect a visit. Would they dare bomb me?"

There was a pause. Then: "It is a distinct possibility, Mr. Christie. Perhaps Hafik should speak to his people from your radio, could you do that?"

Christie said coolly: "I could, no doubt, but I won't." He was fully in control of himself again, all the distress and anxiety gone. "If I did, we'd be asking for trouble. Whatever consular protection we may have now...if I let Hafik rally the troops from this ship... No, I won't do it."

"Then let me announce that he is with you. Then, I think, they would not dare attack you, even to get him."

"Let me think about that, don't do it yet. Do you know where the Southern Command is?"

"They spearheaded the attack on the palace. The Southern is General Fali's own command."

"They have a Navy, three frigates, what are they doing?"

"We've no information on them yet, but they are all somewhere in the Red Sea, on maneuvers, they have been for the past month. If they have word from Arkan already, they are probably heading for Egyptian waters now."

"Then, all we have to worry about is an air strike. Hold on." He turned to Simone. "What do you think, would they dare?"

Simone shook his head. "No, Maxwell, they won't dare. An American ship...the rebels will want all the outside sympathy they can get."

"If the Commies are behind it?"

"Even if they were, but they're not. They won't dare touch you, not openly."

He was watching her closely, enjoying the intellectual exercise of her appraisal. He said shrewdly: "You must know the Committee very well, Simone, I'll have to take your word for it."

She nodded. "I know them well. I watched them grow from...from a handful of uneducated beggars in rags to...to what they are today. General Fali is not a fool, he'll be very careful."

"You're taking it well, Simone. It does you credit."

"There is no other way to take it. I'm glad His Royal Highness got away."

Christie spoke into the microphone again: "This is a tough one,

Hassan. Where will the Shah go?"

"To Paris, Mr. Christie, I imagine. He likes Paris, he'll be welcome there."

Christie said dryly: "Yes, with all that loot... Who are you in touch with? In Arkan, I mean?"

Hassan said: "No one, not any more. Both my men were in the palace, and the palace is a ruin now. More than eight hundred killed, Mr. Christie. My last report came through less than twenty minutes ago, but I think... I don't think there will be any more."

"Other sources?"

"I have a man in Radija, and of course the rebels will be talking to Mecca, Cairo, and Raydah, I have men in each of those places, we should manage to keep well informed."

"All right, find out how long I've got before I can expect some sort of action against Hafik. I'm going to pull out, but I want time to get my crews aboard. Stand by, keep listening, I'll call you when I need you."

"Very well, Mr. Christie. I think in a few hours, the situation might be considerably clearer. If I could have a little time to evaluate the reports that are coming in. A lot of them are quite confused..."

Christie said dryly: "Take all the time you want, Hassan, the damage has already been done. Irreparably. I'm signing off."

"Signing off, sir, I'll call you as soon as we know something more."

Roger said: "He seems to know what's going on, who is he?"

Christie said: "Hassan Lafera, Britain's Number One spy in the Middle East. He likes to live a little above the standard the British allow him."

"I'm surprised he didn't foresee this, then."

Christie only grunted: "I said their Number One, I didn't say he was any good." He passed a hand over his forehead. "Just at this moment, they couldn't have chosen a better time. If they'd just waited a few more days..." He went to the door. "I'm going to see Candia. We'll meet back here in three hours; you, Roger, with Simone and Hafik. We'll decide just what's got to be done."

Roger nodded. "All right. I'd better see about getting the crews aboard."

Christie smiled wryly: "Look out of the window."

Roger went to the wide bay window and looked out.

The men were gathered at the shore, waiting, and three of the ship's boats were heading there to pick them up. He heard Christie say: "I know you're not fond of Breck, but there's his value. He doesn't have to be told."

He was gone.

Roger went to Simone and took her by the arms, pulling her close. He said:

"That's a pretty lousy break for all of us, isn't it? For you most of all."

"Yes, a pretty lousy break."

"You saw it coming, didn't you? Isn't that why you're here?"

Surprised, she shook her head. She said urgently: "Don't try to guess, Roger, you'll find all the answers...are wrong."

"Kind of puts you out of a job, doesn't it?"

She did not answer. He kissed her and said: "It's an ill wind...This isn't the time to speak of it, but when the time does come, I'll be glad you're free. I told you, forever and ever."

She did not speak, and he looked at her curiously, trying to find the answer in those veiled gray eyes:

"You didn't answer me before, either. What is it, Simone? You want less than that? Am I asking for too much? It's got to be...forever..."

"I know. I want that too, so badly. But...in my world, you see what happens...so easily."

"It need not affect us any longer."

"The Shah will still need me." She sounded, for the first time, unsure of herself, as though the confusion had at last reached her too.

He kissed her again, holding her tight. "You want to spend all your life mollycoddling a king, is that it? There are better things ahead for both of us."

"Let's talk after...after the meeting with Maxwell."

"All right. We'll do that."

"I love you, Roger, more than anything in the world. I want you to understand that as you've never understood anything before."

"I will. Nothing else is important to me."

"I have never wanted the things you have offered me, never. I want them now."

He said lightly: "My boss is talking to your Prince, we've a few hours, there's nothing we can do but wait. Will you come to my cabin?"

"I told you before, Roger, I said...whenever you want."

"I want now."

He took her arm, and they went hand in hand out of the cabin.

# CHAPTER 15

ALL THROUGH the dark of the evening, the evacuation of the shoreline went on.

On Breck's orders, the big floodlights that had served the second and third shift crews were dismantled first, and the rest of the work was carried out in darkness. Until the moon came up, men stumbled over each other as they dragged the cables down to the launches, stripped down the water tanks, struck their tents, gathered the stores in untidy piles along the sand. The movement from shore to ship was heavy and constant.

A few moments before the scheduled meeting, Roger came out of Simone's cabin, and Christie, his head bowed, was walking along the sycamore-paneled corridor. He called after him, and Christie stopped and half turned.

He said: "Maxwell? Did you talk to Candia?"

Christie put both hands to his eyes and rubbed at them, rubbing away a sort of weariness. "Yes, I talked with her."

"And?"

"I tried, Roger, I swear to God I tried. But...I just couldn't...couldn't humble myself. I told her...I told her to pull herself together and stop playing games, there were more important things I had to worry about..."

"A hell of a good choice of words..."

"I told her I'd...I'd talk to her again when this was all over, when we were back in the States, or France, or wherever...when my work here was finished. I promised her..."

"And she said: *'Now, Daddy, now.'*"

Christie raised his eyebrow and said coolly: "As a matter of fact, that's almost precisely what she said."

"And you still wouldn't climb down and show her that your...your love was more important."

"I wouldn't crawl! That's what she wanted me to do." Roger turned and walked on, and Christie hurried after him and said urgently: "Roger, there are decisions we have to make, difficult decisions..."

Roger said tightly: "All right, let's go make them."

The anger was back in Christie's voice: "Can't you understand? You think I'd have got where I am today if I let...my personal worries interfere with my work?"

Roger threw open the door to Christie's cabin. He said quietly: "If you're satisfied with what you are today, then there's no more argument, is there?"

Simone came down the corridor to join them, and he touched her arm as she paused by him, and there was a great understanding between them.

They went inside together and they listened again and again to the reports that came in from Hassan, and from the beginning it was very apparent; their only safe course was to go out of the territorial waters of Orassia as soon as possible. Hafik, his eyes averted, sat and listened in silence. The muscles at the side of his jaw were tight, his lips compressed. It was as though he were ready for their sympathy, and waiting to reject it.

But there was a considerable surprise from Christie.

His hands spread out flat on the table, his dark eyes alert and darting from Roger to Simone and over to Hafik, Christie said:

"We're in no danger, because all that has happened has been foreseen. We know what we have to do, so let's do it." He glanced at Roger and said carefully: "It seemed necessary at the time, to hide this from you, Roger, and don't ask me why because I don't know..." He grimaced. "The results of a lifetime spent in circles where secrecy is sometimes vital if a man's to survive. Let's say no point would have been made if I'd told you, and leave it at that." He turned to Hafik and said: "And you only know the half of it too." He looked over to

Simone: "Shall I? Or will you?"

She nodded, and Christie said:

"Your father, Hafik, was half convinced that the rebels were a lot stronger than most of his advisers believed, and that includes, I'm afraid, those closest to him..." He shrugged. "He told me privately that it was almost the first time, Simone, that he'd not been in complete agreement with you. He was almost convinced there was going to be a nasty uprising that he might not be able to handle, and he wanted you, Hafik, out of the way. Ostensibly, there was good reason, as we found out. Your presence on board, in case of trouble with the Southern Command... But the real reason, as he explained it to me, was much more simple. His idea was that if a rising should take place, then he would attempt a compromise with the rebels, offer to abdicate in your favor, and let those who support you—a considerable section of the country, I believe—form a coalition government, with you at its head. He felt he could only achieve this if he could be sure, and the rebels would know too, that you personally were out of harm's way and immediately available to head the counterrevolutionary movement. Obviously, if anything happened to you, his bargaining position would be untenable, and he wasn't taking any chances. Simone didn't like the idea very much, did you, Simone? But she was overruled by the Shah."

Simone shook her head. "My objection was a formality. I felt Prince Hafik's place was by his father's side in the event of trouble. When the Shah insisted, I gave way, readily. I have always readily given way to him."

Christie went on: "But now...how can we be sure what happened? Probably, the rebels moved too fast to permit any discussion, any bargaining at all. The Shah felt obliged to get out, and the fact that he took with him a sizable part of the country's gold reserve..."

Hafik said sharply: "I don't believe that!"

Christie raised a placatory hand. He said smoothly: "The fact that he apparently took so much currency with him probably indicates his determination to suppress the revolt, and eventually defeat it, from exile. There could be a less laudable reason too, but let's assume an honest one..."

226

Hafik's face was flushed. He said softly: "You know that my father is an honest man, Christie."

Christie said quickly: "Yes, I do, as honest as I am, and if I were in his position I'd make sure I lined my pockets well, whether I were contemplating a fight or not. He's accustomed to luxury, he's almost a professional hedonist, and I don't imagine he's about to live in a garret in Paris and leave all that loot to a bunch of hotheads whose prime allegiance is almost certainly to forces outside Orassia. But that's neither here nor there. The point is, our obvious duty now is to take Hafik the hell and gone away from here. I propose to warn Hassan that we're coming to Aden, just as soon as the loading is finished, have him arrange for a plane to take Hafik to Paris, where he can join his father and work out with him whatever they think is best. As far as we're concerned, our job here is close enough to completion to justify my asking him for at least our prearranged percentage of the down payment he will receive from the European Oil Amalgamation—if he should be able, from exile, to re-establish his— or Hafik's—position. We'll put in our incomplete report, which may be inconclusive but is none the less highly favorable, and hope that we can get paid off. Your own position, Simone, is less clear..."

She said quickly: "Oh? Why do you say that?"

Christie said bluntly: "Rightly or wrongly, Fali has proclaimed a government. Whether your loyalties are to a deposed Shah or to a non-elected government...that's entirely your business, and I'll say nothing about it except that if you want to go to Paris I'll see that you get there. It's up to you."

Hafik was staring at Simone in consternation, as though the idea had never occurred to him that her prime concern might now be for a country torn by revolution rather than for the Royal House itself. He began to speak, but she looked at him and smiled; Roger saw that the accustomed calm was not there. Or rather, it was there, but only on the surface, hiding an anxiety that her gray, steady eyes could not entirely conceal.

She said: "Hafik knows that my loyalties are to him and to his father."

"Then you want to go to Paris?"

"Of course."

"Good. I'm glad. I don't know much about this fellow Fali, but frankly, I didn't like his looks. There's going to be a lot of bloodshed in Orassia before this thing's over, and I'd hate to think that some of it might be yours."

Roger said: "There's another thing we have to worry about."

Christie turned to him: "Oh?"

"If the Shah does not succeed in re-establishing his position...if the revolution succeeds completely and there's a new government...what then? It's something we ought to discuss."

Christie said clearly and calmly: "There's no discussion necessary. If the Committee becomes the legal government, I'll deal with them. I'm in a strong position. Amalgamated won't make that down payment, and it's a lot of hard cash, unless they get a report from me that the investment will be worth their while." He said dryly: "The distance between a revolutionary committee and a legal government is a very short one. The Shah, or the Committee. Whichever comes up, they'll have to deal with me, and I hold all the cards. No report, no oil. No oil, no money."

Roger saw that Simone's lips were tight, but she said nothing.

The tiny red light over the intercom was flashing, and Christie looked at his watch, and said:

"Hassan, five minutes late again." He crossed over and opened the circuit, and said: "Come in, Hassan."

The softly effeminate voice came out of the speaker: "Mr. Christie? Forgive the delay, sir, it seemed wiser to wait for the end of the report ..."

Christie frowned: "What report?"

"From Radija, Mr. Christie. The plane in which the Shah escaped was supposed to land in Athens for refueling. It didn't make it."

"What?"

"No, sir. It's more than an hour overdue..."

"The kind of pilots he's got, they probably hit Calcutta instead..."

"No, sir. A Turkish coast guard station reported an explosion aboard an unidentified plane flying at ten thousand feet just off Gilindire, they're out looking for the wreckage now..."

Christie said sharply: "You must have more than that!"

"Yes, sir." They could almost hear the disapproving sigh in Hassan's gentle voice. "They're out looking for the wreckage now, but it won't tell us anything we don't know. I checked with Radija. They put a bomb on board his plane, timed to drop him in the middle of the Mediterranean."

Roger looked at Simone. Her face had gone white.

Hassan's voice droned on: "It seems that General Fali is pretty well in command of the situation already, the provisional government has already been sworn in, and recognition by at least four of the Arab states is expected momentarily. The Bedouin are gathering out in the desert, but there's not a great deal they can do against Fali's tanks and armored cars. Arkan is ringed with troops, martial law has been declared, and I suggest, Mr. Christie, that you act with the utmost dispatch. They are firmly convinced in Radija that Prince Hafik is dead, and Fali must realize that if it becomes known he's still alive, his own position will be very considerably weakened. He must know that there's only one man who could rally any kind of popular support for the Royal House, and Hafik therefore represents a constant danger to you personally."

Christie said: "Hassan...get this straight...I want a plane for Hafik and Madam Caffa, standing by at Aden when we get there, give us...forty hours."

Roger said: "You'll never make it in that time."

"Yes, we will. If we have to leave the heavy equipment ashore, we'll do that." He pushed the alternator button and said: "Mr. Hewitt? Under way in an hour, no more. Tell Breck to have everyone aboard by then, as much equipment as he can salvage, leave the rest of it behind. Full speed for Aden, as fast as you can push her, and let's really push. All right?"

The skipper's voice sounded resigned and weary. "I'll have you there in forty-four hours, Mr. Christie."

Christie went back to the main circuit. "Hassan? We'll be there in forty hours. I want the utmost secrecy, don't even talk to Paris, no names, no hints, nothing. Is that understood?"

"Yes, I understand."

"Good. I'm signing off, but keep in touch. Let me know if

anything startling happens."

He came and sat at the table again, and looked around at the others. "Now, are we all clear as to what we're doing? Roger? Simone? Hafik? Any questions, now's the time for them."

Simone looked at Hafik questioningly. She said slowly: "I think Hafik has something on his mind."

Hafik stood up and began to pace the room, his head sunk on his chest, his brows drawn together. He said heavily:

"In spite of all his faults...he was...he was such a good man. He loved me more than anything else in the world, and that's all that counts, really, isn't it? The rest...the rest is nothing. And now..." He said bitterly: "A dirty, unshaven, uneducated rebel, a sans-culotte, a filthy bomb... A good, good man, the best father anyone could wish for."

Christie was watching. Roger said, with a gesture of hopelessness: "If I can offer my condolences... I'm sorry, Hafik. There's nothing anyone can say, is there?"

He saw that Simone's face was taut, an anguish there under the calm. She shook her head and said nothing, and he saw how strong was the effort to control herself.

Hafik said, pacing: "Abdication, in my favor...do you know what he meant by that? He meant that there was one thing he wanted more, much more than the...the despotism he's always been accused of. He wanted a continuation of the royal line. It's lasted a long time, and now... Simone is right, there is something on my mind." He turned to face her and said, with great dignity: "You know very well what I must do. I must return at once to Arkan."

Christie said impatiently: "Don't be a fool, you wouldn't last five minutes!"

"Not to the city itself. Put me ashore ten miles up the coast, on an oasis there called Bir Minsula. The Bedouin there are my own family, my cousins, their sheikh would lay down his life for me, gladly..."

"And you think Fali won't be expecting that? Don't be a fool, Hafik."

"Take me to Bir Minsula."

"No."

"You must!"

"I won't." Christie turned to Simone. "Tell him how wrong he is, Simone, make him understand that Fali's troops will be out there watching every move the Bedouin make, waiting for just this kind of thing. He'll listen to you."

Simone said quietly: "No, I think he's right. I think that he might have a chance of success, not a good one, but a chance, at least. It might be the right thing to do."

Christie hesitated. He said at last: "You know how highly I regard your intelligence, Simone. But I think this time you're way out. Roger?"

Roger said bluntly: "I had a couple of hours with General Fali on board this ship, a couple of minutes with him at the palace. I'd say Fali is a shrewd and highly competent man. I say he'll be sitting outside every oasis within a hundred miles of Arkan, waiting for Hafik. If he weren't so completely sure, he'd never have announced that Hafik is already dead. That statement he made can mean only one thing. That he's estimated Hafik's reactions perfectly, and is lying in wait for him to do...just what he hopes we'll let him do."

Hafik said stubbornly: "You can't stop me. If I have to swim ashore and walk all the way to Arkan..."

"I can stop you," Christie said, "and I will. You'll stay on board this ship till we reach Aden, and then you'll get on that goddam plane if I have to lug you on board myself."

He turned to Simone again. "I'm sorry to insist, but...you can both carry on the fight from Paris, you might have a chance, maybe even a good one. But I have a responsibility to the old man, and I'm going to carry it out." He said, his eyes glinting: "He paid me well enough."

Roger frowned. "He *paid* you?"

Christie was gloating; there was malice all over his face. He laughed shortly and said: "Yes, I exacted a heavy price, to keep his son out of danger, and that's just what I'm going to do."

Roger threw up his hands. He said: "Simone knows more about it than any of us. I hate to disagree with her, but..." He looked at her hopelessly. But her face was expressionless.

Christie said: "You and I agree, Roger, they're both overruled.

Now, all we can do is wait."

The door opened suddenly, and Candia was there. She stood in the doorway smiling at them, mocking their seriousness. She had been drinking, and her voice was a trifle slurred. She said: "It's all over the ship, and...and all I want to know is...is it true? My Prince doesn't have a kingdom anymore?"

Before Christie could speak, Hafik said: "The Prince is a Shah, Candia. They killed my father."

Candia said: "Well, that's life. Did they chop off his head and roll it out over the nice red carpet?"

"No. They blew up his plane over the Mediterranean."

"And you couldn't dash to his rescue...like you dashed to mine?" She looked at her father and laughed. "It's all right, Daddy, it doesn't matter anymore, it doesn't matter a damn who saved your darling daughter's life for you. But I'm interested that you tried to take the credit for it."

Christie had not moved. He sat staring out into space with a slight smile on his face, and Roger said harshly:

"All right, Candia, who told you?"

Candia did not take her eyes off him. She said softly, using the same words again: "Some animal seaman with better staying power." There was a touch of hysteria in her laugh: "I don't even know his name, I don't even want to know it. What I want to know is, what made you think you could get away with it, *Daddy?* An out-and-out bastard shows himself sooner or later for what he really is." Her voice was rising.

Simone said desperately: "Candia, listen to me..."

Candia turned on her. "Shut up!" Her voice was full of loathing. "Shut up, you filthy whore! Were you in it too? Oh, I've got your measure, you cheap bloody hustler! Did you know I'd find out, were you waiting for me to find out? Were you hoping it would cut your precious Prince down to size, is that it? You think I can't see through you? You want him for yourself, is that it?"

Hafik said sharply: "Candia, no! Be quiet!"

She looked at him and the fire went out of her. She said gently: "Can't you see what they're trying to do to us?" She turned back to her father; he was sitting there silent, a distant look on his face. She said softly: "You didn't really think a secret like that could be kept for long, did you?"

Christie said mildly: "No, I didn't really think that. I just...hoped, that's all. I've spent all my life hoping, haven't I? Hopelessly. And I know that it never pays off."

Candia shook her head. "No, Daddy. It pays off." She said quietly: "You'll see that it pays off."

She slammed the door shut behind her. Christie leaned forward on the table and sank his head in his hands. And when Roger looked at Simone, the expression in her eyes said clearly: Let's leave him alone for a while.

Together they moved towards the door. And then, muted, distant, but distinct, there came to them from the shore the ominous rattle of machine-gun fire.

It was a sudden, startling burst, repeated, repeated again, and then taken up by two, three, four more guns. Christie's head came up with a snap, and he lunged for the intercom and switched it on, and almost immediately the skipper's voice came over, calm, restrained, laconic: "They're fighting on shore, Mr. Christie..."

Christie said: "I'm coming."

He snapped down the switch and ran to the door, and when the three of them reached the bridge, Hewitt was calmly watching the shoreline with his binoculars. He handed them to Christie and pointed. "Breck's men, but I can't see what they're firing at."

Roger went to the rail and leaned against it, watching, his heart beating fast. The bright flashes of the guns were clear against the dark of the dunes, and then there was the ponderous, threatening boom of a heavy gun further away in the distance, and Roger said: "My God, that's artillery...!"

They saw the exploding shells on the beach to their right; they could feel the sudden compression of the air around them.

The heavy boom came again, and then a third, and he heard Christie say, behind him: "How many men still on shore?"          '

Hewitt answered him: "Breck, the rear guard of six men, and two more boatloads."

"And we're ready to sail?"

"Aye, we're ready."

The high-pitched roar of the light launch broke over the sound of the guns, and there was a thin white streak on the dark water as it headed towards them. The heavy, explosive sound came again, and three shells splashed in the water far beyond them and to their left, and Christie said, without emotion: "They're looking for the range."

One by one the lights were going out all over the ship, and soon there was only darkness, and Roger looked up at the bright moon and said: "A searchlight for them, we shine like a beacon..." He looked at Christie and said: "There are guns on board, what are they?"

But Christie only smiled and said: "Nothing big enough to cope with artillery."

Simone was watching the launch as it spun in a wide circle, its outboard motor dying, and then Breck was there, looking up at them from bellow, his teeth shining white, his bare chest dark against the dark of the sea. He called out cheerfully, enjoying himself: "Three tanks, Mr. Christie, General Pershings, I think, still a mile away and trying to get over the dunes. We fired to try and halt them." He added dryly: "They've halted."

Roger said quickly: "Pershings? Ninety-millimeter guns, a nice thought, isn't it?"

Christie ignored him. He called down to Breck: "Can you get everyone aboard in time?"

"Sure, no problem there, I'll stay behind with the outboard and one machine gun till the beach is clear, better swing her around, she's broadside on to those guns."

Hewitt had already given the order, and the yacht was moving slowly on her single anchor chain. Christie shouted: "All right, get them in as last as you can, we're ready to pull out."

Roger looked down over the railing and called out: "Breck...wait for me, be right with you!" He turned to Christie and said: "I suppose it's too much to expect any anti-tank rifles on board?"

Christie looked at him, frowning, and said: "Leave it to Breck, Roger..."

And Roger said calmly: "No. He's going to need help. Those tanks won't stay halted for long."

Simone was staring at him, and he said with a smile: "Just how good are they?"

She was worried, and she showed it. "Not very good, by your standards. General Fali's own preserve, but..." She grimaced. "We rely for our arms on...the Americans, the British, the Germans, the Russians...anyone who will sell to us. It's sometimes hard to keep them going." She said again: "Not very good."

"That's what I thought. But the Pershing carries a pretty good armament, if they know how to use it, a twelve-mile range or more, and one shell from a ninety-millimeter will blow this ship up like a matchbox." He was already sliding down the companionway, and he heard Simone's anxious voice, saw her start forward towards him: "No, Roger, no!"

He said: "I must. A dark night, but a white ship."

A shell landed far off to seaward, sending up a tall column of water, and he heard Breck call out, angrily: "Well, if you're coming, Sequoyah..." and he answered: "Keep your shirt on, they're still lobbing them over the dunes..."

He slipped down to the lower deck, went quickly to the storeroom, and when he came out he ran down and jumped into the outboard and said to Breck:

"All right, flat out to the beach."

Breck looked at him and said nothing, and the motor roared and soon the bow ran full tilt into the sand and they clambered out together. The big launch was beside them, and the men were piling in, and Breck said with a touch of aspersion:

"One boatload, you see, you're wasting your time."

"Am I? What about the equipment?"

Breck stared at him. "Good God, you're worrying about the equipment? At a time like this...?"

"Worrying about it, no. But get it aboard."

"For Christ's sake..."

"You heard what I said." He felt Breck's eyes on him as he walked up the steep slope of the beach towards the dunes. He stopped and called back: "If you have to-cover me," and without waiting for an answer he turned and went on, hurrying now, hurrying towards the dreadful rumble that was the sound of the tanks moving up in the darkness on the other side of the dune; he was grateful for the darkness.


The tanks had stopped.

Here, deep among the dunes, no sound came from the beach, and he fancied he could hear the guttural Arabic of the tank crews. He lay on the black sand and watched; there were three of them, as Breck had said, and one was way ahead of the others, almost to the top of the ridge, and as he lay there panting with the exertion he wondered why they had stopped, wondered whether the terrible risk he was taking was going to be wasted after all. And then a heavy Cadillac motor started up with a roar, the rear tank to the right, and it began to slew round in the sand, not moving in a straight line but crabbing its way forward, and he thought: *A busted tread or else it's patched up with baling wire, but if it does get to the top...*

The gun of the leading tank fired again and the explosion of it deafened him, and he leaped to his feet and ran, slithering, down the dune to a point midway between the leader and those in the rear. He could see now that the hatches of the two tanks were open, and he thought there were shadows crawling over the huge black monsters; he ran on, falling in the soft sand that came over his ankles and sometimes up to his calves, and once he dropped the bundle of dynamite sticks he was carrying.

Another motor roared to life, and then another, and the beach vibrated with the sound of them. He heard a hatch clang loudly, and then a voice shouted out, in Arabic, something he did not understand, and in a moment of something like panic he pressed himself deeper into the soft sand, lying flat on his face and waiting. But then the hatch clanged shut again, and he looked up to see that the rear tanks, both of them, were coming towards him, fifty feet apart on each side of him... He squirmed deeper into the sand and prayed, holding his breath and waiting, watching, hoping.

Neither of them was moving straight, and one of them, the one on his left, passed within ten feet of him; he did not dare show the relative white of his face, but kept it buried in the sand, knowing that the rest of him was dark as the dark sand itself and that, with luck, and if he kept dead still, he might not be seen.

The lead tank was stationary, and the others were catching up, getting into position for a broad assault over the top of the dune. A gun roared again, and the flash of it was blinding. They kept moving, and soon he could tell that they were far enough ahead of him, and he got to his feet and ran, stumbling and trying to catch up. He thought: *If only they'll keep going now, just long enough...* He struggled towards the nearest one, coming up on it from the rear.

He could not hide from himself the fear as he touched one of the great steel hulks, forced himself to touch it in an effort to drive the panic away, an effort to prove to himself that the crews were locked inside there, separated from him by nearly seven inches of armor. And then he jumped aboard, his heart beating fast, and lit the long fuse of one of the dynamite sticks. He leaned over and thrust it under the tread, and then slipped down again and raced as fast as he could towards the second one, over the swallowing sand that seemed to clutch at his feet, to hold him back, to send his blood racing and to cause his heart to pound...

It was close to the top now, almost lined up with the lead tank, and he thrust another stick under the tread quickly and raced away, struggling along the crest now, towards the leader.

And then, the first blast went off, much too early, and he said aloud: "God damn..." and pulled up short as the hatch of the lead tank went up with a clang and a figure struggled out. And not stopping his motion he turned and fell, rolling down the steep slope towards the beach again.

There was a quick burst of fire behind him, just one, and then another blast went off and he struggled to his knees and lit a fuse with his lighter, flicking it two or three times before it would catch, and he hurled the stick far behind him, and then he heard Breck's answering fire and thought: *Well, thank God and Breck for that...*

One more stick now, and he lit the fuse and hurled it, and he heard the muted sound of the outboard starting up, heard Breck's voice calling angrily: "Well, come on, for God's sake..."

One of the improvised bombs went off, much closer than he thought it would be, and he felt the sudden rush of air as he struggled on, half running, half sliding, stumbling all the time. He kicked off his sand-laden shoes and ran barefoot, not sliding so much now, and in a moment he was falling into the launch, feeling Breck's hands pull at him as the boat shot forward into the light surf. He looked back and saw one solitary tank moving down the dune, its machine guns firing, the tracer bullets cutting through the air high above them.

Breck said casually: "Pretty lousy shots," and Roger tried to catch his breath and said: "Well...the others?"

"We're the last two, everybody else is already on board."

"And?"

He could feel the restrained anger, and then Breck laughed shortly, a sharp, sardonic grunt of a laugh. "The equipment, yes, we got most of it, one boatload, the launch piled high. The seismographs, magnometers, most of the special tools. You didn't expect to salvage the heavy stuff, did you?" He jerked a thumb at the beach and said sarcastically: "Like the rigging...?" When Roger did not answer, Breck said dryly: "We can afford to lose every bit of it, but...it's a matter of principle, isn't it? They could have killed both of us, and we saved a few thousand bucks, was it that important to you?"

Roger said calmly: "They could have, they didn't, and yes, it's a matter of principle. But not the one that you're thinking of. I just don't like people throwing shells at me and doing nothing about it."

The churned-up water was a white streak behind them, a bright marker on the dark sea, but when the tracers started up again, they still cut through the air high above them, and soon they came to the ship and Breck called up: "Okay, we're aboard!"

He could see Christie's white face, and as he swung for the ladder the face disappeared and then the heavy Doxfords increased their tempo from idle to full speed and the screws were turning fast and the yacht was lurching forward and out to sea.

Clinging to the ladder, he looked back towards the beach. The machine gun had stopped firing, but the solitary tank he had failed to stop was still rumbling down from the dune. It was five hundred yards off and still moving, and he looked at Breck and said heavily: "And all that trouble might just have been for nothing." He began to climb, and when he reached the bridge, Simone ran to him and put a hand on his arm, saying nothing, but looking at him with all the worry still in her solemn gray eyes.

They waited a while, listening, and then Roger took the glasses and looked at the shore.

The monstrous dark shadow he could see there was the solitary Pershing, standing silent and menacing now, close to the edge of the water, a huge and brutal mass of steel that, somehow, seemed an anachronism on the deserted beach that once had known the shuffling feet of other armies, long ago... It was like something from another world, watching them and keeping silent.

The yacht sped away into the darkness, but the firing did not start again, and there was only the silent shadow there, growing smaller and smaller as they increased the margin of safety that lay between them.

Christie looked at Simone and said, his eyes alert and very watchful: "You were right, they don't want to hit us. At this range, they couldn't miss."

Simone shrugged. "As I said, an American ship, they can't risk an incident, not even to get the Prince."

Christie persisted: "And if we had stopped?"

"They would have boarded, taken us off, and let you go."

Christie nodded, and said nothing. He looked at Roger and smiled. There was a wealth of gratitude in his look.


When the danger of the beach was far behind them and Simone had gone to her cabin, it seemed a natural thing that Roger should follow her.

He sat beside her as she lay full length on the divan, and he put a hand on her breast and caressed her gently, and she held his hand still and stared at the ornate ceiling for a while in a silence that he found heavy and oppressive.

The thrum of the Doxfords, pushed to their maximum, vibrated gently, and they could hear the upsurge of the white water as the rounded stem pushed through the waves. The sea was rough, and the yacht was beginning to roll a little.

He said gently: "A long night ahead of us."

Simone turned her gray eyes on him, and they were somehow veiled and distant. Her voice was troubled. She said: "How much do you love me, Roger? Truly?"

He said impulsively: "More than anything you can dream of, ask me, ask me, ask me anything, Simone. Anything at all..."

"If I asked you to give me up, to forget about me?"

"I know that you wouldn't ask that."

"No, no I wouldn't. It's something...far worse, perhaps."

"There could be nothing worse."

"If I asked you to know me as I truly am? For what I am?"

He began to laugh. "The old, old story, and the old, old answer. No matter what you are, I love you. And I know what you are."

"No, Roger, you don't, not all of me."

"You're the woman I love, forever, remember?"

"Only part of me is a woman. The rest is...diplomat, politician, Machiavellian schemes, call it what you like, but it's not woman."

"I don't care. I'll take the part of you I want, and learn to love the rest. It won't be hard. I know you so well, Simone, much more than you think..." He frowned; her eyes were full of tears. He said urgently: "There's a whole new world for us, Simone, you can forget all this, put it behind you..."

"Not what I have to do."

The silence was heavy. He said at last: "It will make it much easier, if you tell me. The Queen can do no wrong."

He leaned down and kissed her, but she pulled herself away and stood up and said: "No, Roger, I have to tell you, even have to ask your help for something...something you will not be able to do. I'm counting on what I know is your love, even though I know it may...it will...destroy it—even though it means to me...more than you can even imagine." She brushed a finger across her eyes and said: "I don't remember when I last wanted to cry, when I had to...to force away from myself the knowledge that I am a woman and to think only of...of other things."

He waited a while, and took out the gold cigarette case Christie had given him and lit two cigarettes and gave her one, and when she still did not speak, he said steadily:

"Whatever it is, Simone, it's no good waiting. You know that I will help you, you must know that."

"I know it because I am a woman, and that's what I'm afraid of." She turned away to hide her face from him, and took a deep breath and said: "I must go back to Arkan. With Hafik."

He said lightly: "There's no great problem there. I'll just argue you out of it. You know the facts better than I do, let me put them in their proper perspective, and you'll see how wrong you are. And, if you still insist, then I'll talk to Christie. In this, he'll do what I suggest. All you have to do is convince *me;* and meanwhile, I'll try to convince you. It's as simple as that. Now..."

She said quickly: "No, it's not simple. I must take him back...for other reasons than those you know. For terrible reasons. I cannot explain them, and yet...I must. And I will."

He frowned. "I thought I had all the facts."

"No. Not the essential ones."

"All right, tell me this; if Hafik goes back to Arkan...what do you estimate his chances of survival to be? I'd put them pretty low."

Her voice was almost inaudible. "He has no chance at all of survival."

He stared at her blankly, not understanding. "At least we've found a basis for agreement there." A pause. "And you still want to take him back?"

"I must."

"Then...just tell me why?"

She turned to face him now, and her eyes were hard, her lips tight. She said clearly: "For the very reasons that Christie pointed out, that you agreed with. In Paris, he can mount a counterrevolution. It would destroy my country."

He began to speak, but she raised a hand and said: "No, wait, it is my turn for the perspective. The rebels, as you call them, and as you heard, are much stronger than you previously assumed. They comprise, or at least have the sympathies of, more than half the country, much, much more. The desert nomads, the Bedouin, whose contributions to our culture has always been negligible...they are the only ones who will fight for the old regime. In the cities, almost the entire population will welcome the Committee, they've been waiting for them, praying for them, and now...if Hafik mounts a counterrevolution, as from Paris he would, it will mean only one thing—the complete destruction of our cities—such as they are—and a reversal to the savage, nomad life out of which Raidan el Darrah led us more than thirteen hundred years ago. All that he lived for, all that he left for us in the thirteen volumes of his Kandit, all this would be destroyed, and Orassia would be a desert again. This is why I say that Hafik, who is as close to me as my own son, must not be allowed his freedom."

He was staring at her in horror, waiting for her to say what he knew she must say.

She went on, gesturing, groping for an easy way to say it: "Apart from my personal...wishes, my personal love for...for you...there is only one thing in the world greater than my loyalty to Hafik, my love for him if you like, and that is my loyalty, my love for my country. To save one, I must destroy the other. It is not an easy choice, Roger."

He said harshly: "But you've made it."

"Yes, I have made it. I must sacrifice Hafik. I must take him back with me to Arkan."

"They'll kill both of you! You must know that!"

"No, not me... Perhaps it would be better if they would. But they will not."

He said, and there was a new anxiety flooding over him, an anxiety that was more painful because he could not understand it: "You said...the entire population of the cities will...will welcome the Committee? That they've been waiting and praying... and yet...if this is the truth, Simone, then all that you yourself represent...is it so wrong?" He waited.

She said at last, speaking very slowly and carefully: "I planned this uprising, together with General Fali, nearly nine months ago. Like a child in my womb, the seed grew, just as painfully, and when it burst forth...I ask you...only to understand...my pain... It has cost me, already, the life of the Shah, whom I admired...and it will cost me also the life of his son...whom I love."

The hard shell had broken, and there were tears staining her face, but her voice did not falter. She said again: "I must take Hafik back with me to Arkan, and I must ask for your help, in the knowledge that you know why I ask for it."

Roger began to pace the room, forcing himself to think clearly. He said at last: "You could easily have lied to me, Simone, told me that his chances were good. A lie would have been...all right...if you really believe in what you are doing."

"You think because I have lived a lie for so long...because I had to...that I could include you with all the others who had to be deceived?"

"I would have believed you, Simone."

"I know that."

He said vehemently: "Thank God you chose to tell me the truth. Then this... Committee knows all about the oil?"

"Yes, of course."

"And they didn't move until they were sure...relatively sure...that it was there, that the down payment from Amalgamated Oil would be forthcoming?"

"Not till then."

"They found out pretty damn fast, Simone."

"Breck sent a message."

"Breck? But why, for God's sake?"

"I had hoped that Christie would tell you about Breck, but I see that..." She stubbed out her cigarette, and took up his cigarette case and took out another, and when he had lit it for her, she said: "Breck has always believed that he is Christie's son. He's just...uncertain enough to feel that he has a duty to him, a duty that may or may not have been put on him by deceit... There was a woman once, thirty years ago, she told him..." She shook her head and said: "What does it matter now what she told him? Nobody, not even Christie, knew the truth. One day, perhaps, Christie hoped he would find out. Meanwhile, there was the son of a woman he had once loved, a woman who tried to trick him, a woman he had grown to hate, and yet...he could not bring himself to hate the boy he thought just *might* be his own son. Either his son, or...someone who had been planted on him by a scheming woman, like an evil reminder of a weakness Christie would like to forget. So Breck became...what? A shadow, hoping for substance one day? He has never known whether or not his mother was telling the truth when she said that Christie was his father, and the one thing he's lived for, for many, many years, is...proof, one way or the other. His mother remarried, a man named Calindoris, a schemer like Christie himself..."

243

Roger said: "He put a spy on board, a Greek named Tagos."

"Yes, I heard. And Breck found out. It solved the question, didn't it, of where Breck's loyalties lay...to his mother, or to the man he hoped was his father. It's a sordid story from beginning to end, and I used it... I used Breck's urgent need to know... When your first report was made out, a precis of its essential elements was radioed to Radija even before the copies had been distributed on board this ship." She looked hard at Roger and said: "You see the kind of world I have been brought up in? In my dealings with Calindoris, I learned the truth; Breck is Christie's son. And I gave Breck this knowledge in return for his help. I extracted a price. That's the kind of woman I am. And now, I am using even your love."

Roger said quietly: "Sit down, Simone. Sit down with me and...let me think."

Obediently, she sat beside him and waited, not looking at him, and he thought for a while and then said: "The bone of the matter. You want me to...to forgive you what you have done, and..."

"No, not forgive. Understand. And agree that it was necessary."

"It comes to the same thing, doesn't it? And you want me to let Hafik die...a man you love far more than I do... in exchange for what? For the knowledge that I will stand by you? Even when I think you are wrong? Is that it? Is that the deal?"

"No." She said quietly. "It's not a deal, Roger. I don't want to sell my love. I want to persuade you that I am right."

"To *murder* Hafik? That's what it amounts to. In exchange for a political triumph?"

"If only that's all it were! No, it's not that. I want you to tell me that I was right in the choice I made, and to understand the pain—the pain that the choice brought on me. I want you to understand how hard it was and to...to strengthen my...my resolve. A man I love, a country I love, one of them must be destroyed. One, or the other."

He said: "I know that I must agree with you, and yet...I can't bring myself to do it. A man...the abstract concept of a country I don't even know..."

She said gently: "The Greek progression... First, the love of a human being, and through that love a better love, the love of the universe and then a love of God himself. Perhaps, because of us, so much of what I once felt for Hafik has been lost, and now the resolve has gone."

He said harshly: "Were you his mistress, Simone?"

She said incisively: "No! Never! No, it was...something quite different. In him, I saw...an extension of my own hopes for my country. It was never more than that."

"And when General Fali came?"

"He came because he was afraid the Shah had learned of what I was doing and had arranged to get me out of the way. There was no time to tell him earlier of the true reason. That I came to learn from Christie, and to tell the Committee, the moment the oil report came in favorably. We need that money as much as the Shah needed it. For him, it was to be used against us. For us, it was to be used for Orassia."

"And your position on the...what's its fancy name? The Committee for the Arab People's Progress?"

She said steadily: "I am its President. If you like, I am its...brains."

He stood up and began to pace the room, knowing that the problem was insuperable. He said slowly: "I know you well enough to be sure, absolutely sure, of your motives. No jealousy, no greed, no...evil, I'm sure of that. But...how can I be sure that you are right, Simone?"

"You have seen my country at close quarters. The poverty, the disease, the sickness...You saw the haunted luxury of the palace too."

"I come from...from a group I suppose you'd call it...to us, we're always on the side of the underdog, that's the way we've been conditioned. But we're also conditioned to distrust this kind of talk about...distribution of wealth."

"Maxwell finds an easy way out. He chooses to think the Committee are Communists; that's conditioning too."

"And he's wrong?"

"Very wrong."

"I will not doubt your motives, and I cannot doubt your intelligence. You make it very hard for me. I wish to God you'd chosen to deceive me too, to let me find out when it was too late..."

"It would have done no good...to us."

245

"And that's a comfort, of a sort." He said bitterly: "Why don't you just ask me to take Hafik into a dark corner and beat him to death, it would be easier."

Is it because...you don't really like him? Would it be easier to stand by and watch a *friend* be killed for sake of a million stricken people?"

"Perhaps."

"There's not much time, Roger, one way or the other."

"I know. Force majeure, they call it, the dictates of necessity. I think it's easier for you to admit them than it is for me. Means to an end, I can't accept the principle quite so readily."

She did not speak, waiting for him to continue, holding herself in check. He said: "Don't wait for the answer, Simone, because I don't know what it is. If I...murdered this boy for your sake, because that's what it amounts to, you could forgive me, in time, because *force majeure* is something you've been brought up to believe in. But if I let you murder him, it would always come between us, I'd never be able to forget it, not even to justify it. Intellectually, I'd sooner or later be able to admit that it was necessary. Emotionally, I never could. And between you and me, Simone, it's both these things, intellectual and emotional, and I won't sacrifice either of them. I'm going to stop you. I'm not going to let you kill that boy...or our love either."

She made a last desperate effort. "Then don't help me. Just...just believe that what I am doing, without your help, is right! Just say at least that you can understand...that you can at least feel the anguish I've had to...to bring on myself."

"Yes, I can do that, I can feel it, and anything that hurts you... I hate. But there's a gap between us, Simone, that I can't easily bridge. I know that...to argue with you wouldn't help, but..." He said stubbornly, but gently: "I'm going to fight you, Simone, and I want you to know why. I'm going to fight you hard, because I'm fighting for something I want more than anything else in the world. I want you. The two of us together...with nothing, not even this, that might ever come between us. For that, by God, I'll fight the whole world."

She did not speak. Her mouth was tight, her eyes full of pain. He kissed her once, very gently, and then went out of the cabin.

For a long time he stood there, leaning against the door and trying to realize the import of all that she had said, trying to readjust his thinking. At last, he opened the door silently again and said softly: "Simone?"

She was lying on the divan, face down, and her body was shaking. The sound he heard coming from her, the long slow moan, was the most terrible sound he had ever heard.

He closed the door quietly, and went to find Christie.

# CHAPTER 16

HAFIK SAID SLOWLY: "You cannot, by argument, ever convince intelligent people who know that they are right."

"Goddamit," Roger said, "she's *not* right."

"But she is. There's a difference between her thinking and yours that you'll never be able to overcome. The totality of her instinct, you know what I mean by that?"

"It's not an instinct. She has coldly reasoned it all out and come up with the wrong answer."

"It's reason *and* instinct. Her instinctive knowledge has merely been strengthened by her rationalization. She is a strong woman, Roger, stronger than either of us, and she has examined her instinct and found it to be right. Can you understand the torment she must have gone through?"

Roger, thinking about it, shuddered. He said: "Yes, I can feel it for her. I understand it...more than you'll ever realize."

Hafik turned away, not meeting his eye. "And you yourself, Roger... I know how close you are. Was it hard to...to come to me and tell me that the woman I have so long...admired, yes, loved if you like...to tell me that she is demanding my death? Was there torment there too? There was, wasn't there? Considerable torment."

For a long time, Roger did not answer him.

Hafik turned back and looked at him shrewdly and said: "Is it because...my death would come between you? Is that it? You must love her very much."

Roger could feel the generosity and could not understand it. He

248

sighed and said: "Sometimes, Hafik, you're too wise for your years. You won't even...condemn her?"

Hafik said swiftly: "Do you?"

"No. No, I don't. I just...expect you to." He said heavily: "It's your life, not mine."

Hafik shrugged. "It's easier to pay with your own life, than with someone else's, much easier."

"There's a gap between us too, Hafik. They've overthrown your government, they've murdered your own father, you find that your closest friend is...is a traitor to all you've ever believed in, and yet..." He gestured hopelessly. "It's a bloody great gap a mile wide, and I can't even see across it."

Hafik said: "Because you examine only the results, not the motives. When you disagree with someone you admire, you have to ask yourself who is right? With a lesser intellect than Simone's, the answer would be easy. But Simone is sure enough to sacrifice everything she loves, for an ideal, in spite of all the pain and suffering that ideal is now causing her..."

"For a political philosophy!"

"No," Hafik said impatiently. "She stated the choice fairly. A man, or a country, when she loves both. Call it politics if you like, but it's a great deal more than that."

Roger said flatly: "All right, are you telling me you're prepared to go along with what she wants? To let Fali put you up against a wall to satisfy his own ambitions?"

Hafik sighed. "And it's more than his ambitions, too, you're looking only at the end result again, you're forgetting the larger picture. All my life I've believed in the autocracy my father has always represented. All my life I've known that there were forces, not only in Orassia, not only among the Arabs, but all over the world, that denied the morality of that philosophy. In your own country, would you permit it? Of course not! With us, it's always been different, and I used to think it always would be. But now...now I see myself as the heir to a tyranny. I see the tragedy through Simone's eyes, because my eyes are hers, and it has put the aims of the rebels in vastly different light..."

"Eight hundred people killed, and God knows how many more

to come..."

"A small price to pay if they are right."

"Thank God for that *if*."

They stood together in the darkness on the deck, the cold night air dark and silent around them, detached from the throbbing ship that was pulsing with the steady sound of the motors. The moon hung low over the water, the stars were bright; there were no clouds. Further out to sea, another ship was passing, gliding silently along, brightly lit, and they watched it for a while.

Hafik stood motionless, listening to the silence. He said: "I too must do what I think is right. I have found a respectability in the revolution that I did not expect; nonetheless, I cannot agree with its aims, and I will fight it, even if it means fighting Simone."

"There's not much she can do, you know."

"No, there isn't."

"Unless," Roger said unhappily, "unless she persuades Christie. Do you think he'd listen to her?"

Hafik said ruefully: "He's not very fond of me. He might."

Roger thought about it for a while. He asked: "I wonder why he agreed to take you on board so readily? He said the Shah had paid him, does that make sense to you?"

"My father was a wealthy man, even by Christie's standards. Does it matter?"

"If he was paid hard cash to take care of you, that's exactly what he will do, he's that kind of a man. If he made a bargain, he'll keep it, whatever happens."

"In spite of his hatred for me?"

"It's hardly a hatred," Roger said, knowing it was a lie. "But in spite of his...his dislike...yes. His whole life is built round the concept of a *quid pro quo*. Even if he hated your guts..."

Hafik said quietly: "He hates my guts so much he'd do anything to see me dead. Anything."

Roger laughed. "No! With Christie, business before pleasure."

"All right, then let's go and see him."


Maxwell Christie was locked in his cabin again.

He seemed irritated when he opened the door to them; there was an impatience in his look that made Roger think there was something radically wrong going on, something Christie wanted to hide from him, and somehow the thought annoyed him. Without beating about the bush, he said:

"Simone has just told me... Did you know already?"

"Know what?" Christie asked. He looked blankly from Roger to Hafik.

"She's President of the Committee, the Arabs for Progress bunch. She's in cahoots with General Fali."

Christie stared. "Simone? I don't believe it!" He said wrathfully. "Are you sure? She told you so herself?"

"Can we come in?"

Christie said: "Just a minute." He half closed the door and they heard him unlock the wall safe and lock it again, and then he came back and opened wide the door and gestured them into the cabin. He said harshly: "I want to hear this from Simone herself. If it's true... What did she tell you?"

Roger said simply: "She made no bones about it. To be fair, she offered a...a justification, of sorts. But that's not the worst of it. She wants to take Hafik back to Arkan, and that means..."

"I know damn well what that means," Christie said angrily, "it means the firing squad, at best. But... Good God, I can't believe it." He sank down into a chair and said: "Yes, I *can* believe it, it would account for a lot of things. I never quite understood how she got rid of Fali so easily that day. It wasn't Hafik's presence he was worried about. It was hers. And why she agreed so readily to come along in the first place." He looked up at Roger. "There's no doubt about it, I supposed"

"None. And what are we going to do about it?"

Christie stood up quickly and pulled down the big coastal chart from its roller. He stubbed his finger on it and said: "Here, a sandbar, a mile or so across, eighteen miles offshore." He looked up to catch Roger's puzzled expression and said: "Don't try to stop me, Roger. Unless she's got some damned good excuse on that glib tongue of hers, I'm putting her ashore on that sandbar..."

Roger exploded: "For God's sake...!"

251

And Hafik said quickly: "No, we can't possibly do that."

"We can, and we will." Christie said wrathfully: "If you knew Simone half as well as you think you do, you'll know she'll stop at nothing, a strong woman, Roger, and there's nothing more dangerous in the world..."

Hafik said: "Then confine her to her cabin, she can't harm us on board."

"No. She goes ashore." Christie went to the intercom and called the bridge. "Mr. Hewitt? There's a big sandbar four miles or so ahead of us, just offshore, the one they call Ra'adus. Stop the ship there, and have a launch ready."

There was a hesitancy in Hewitt's voice. "Aye, aye, sir. But we'll lose a lot of time."

But Christie did not answer. He switched off the microphone and raised a threatening finger to Roger. He said again: "Don't try and stop me."

"But why, for God's sake? Tell me why?"

Roger stood there and waited. He was aware that the Prince was watching Christie, a puzzled look on his face. Hafik said:

"You're going to be responsible if she dies, and she probably will, a sandbar...! Just tell me why you can't simply confine her on board? Even that's too much, if you ask me."

Christie said coldly: "I don't ask you." He seemed to have recovered some of his poise. He said: "All right, since you must know more than is good for you...I was handsomely paid by the Shah to take care of Hafik in case of an emergency. If I renege on my obligations, apart from any other consideration, whatever government finally emerges in Orassia has got to be shown that I completed my part of the bargain..."

"You can afford a goddam refund. Give them back their money if they ask for it..."

"...and I want my position to be impregnable. If I abandon Hafik now, it won't be. If that means putting Simone Caffa ashore, marooning her, whatever it means...that's what I'm going to do."

He spoke into the intercom again: "Breck? Give Madam Caffa my compliments, ask her to step into my cabin for a moment."

"Yes, sir."

Christie sat down and looked at them, and when Roger opened his mouth to speak, Christie said: "No, it's no good arguing! My position is going to be...impregnable. I made a bargain, she's not going to stop me from keeping it, nobody is."

Roger said: "I will, if I have to!" His voice was sharp.

"Don't try it!"

Roger said quietly: "I'm not going to let you get away with it, and that's all there is to it."

When Simone came in, her face was pale and drawn, but the composure was there again. Christie said, not getting up:

"I just want to know one thing..."

"It's true, Maxwell. If you want my reasons, I'll give them to you." She looked searchingly at Roger, trying to see what was behind his expressionless eyes. He shook his head.

Christie said coldly: "I'm taking Hafik to Paris. I'm putting you ashore on Ra'adus. What happens to you then... I'll radio Arkan when I'm ready to tell them you're there, and it won't take them too long to get to you. By then, Hafik will be out of the Middle East and well on his way to France. And if you have anything to say...?"

Simone shook her head. "Nothing." She turned to Hafik and said: "I'm sorry, Hafik, sorry you had to find out and sorry for what I had to do. If this is what you want..."

"No," Hafik said, "it's not what I want." He raised his hands hopelessly. "Everything I've ever believed in...all gone! Surely...surely, Simone, if the rebels' aims are...are justified, worthy enough to merit your support...couldn't you at least have...have tried to reason with me? It might be, might easily be, that you would have convinced me. I've always, always listened to you, done what you advised..."

She said evenly: "And turned you against your father? No, Hafik, that would have been a great deal worse."

"Yes...yes, I can see that..."

Simone turned to Roger. "And you, Roger? Is this what you want?"

There was no appeal in her eyes, no asking for help or sympathy. Behind the veil, he thought he could sense a kind of shock, well repressed because it was only one of many, as though the pain had lessened because it was constant and unyielding and she had grown into the necessary strength to fight it.

Roger held her look. He said quietly: "It's not what I want either. And I'm not going to allow it to happen."

He turned on his heel and stalked out of the cabin.


The captain listened to him in shocked silence. Roger said at last: "So you see? It's up to you, Mr. Hewitt."

Hewitt shook his head slowly, his red, weather-beaten face showing the heavy lines. He turned away, frowning, and said:

"In all these years, I've never disobeyed a single one of his orders."

Roger said gently: "A record you'll have to break now. There's no other way, is there?"

"In other words, Mr. Sequoyah, it's not up to me, is that it?"

He wondered if the skipper were playing for time, time to sort out the confusion and make a painful decision, and he answered: "The decision must be yours, you're the captain, I can't interfere with the running of the ship. But the reason Christie wants you to stop..."

"Aye. It could be murder, and I'll have no part of it."

Roger turned to go, but Hewitt put out a hand and stopped him, and said: "And if you don't mind, Mr. Sequoyah, I'll tell him myself, he may as well hear it from me."

Roger nodded and stood back, and then Breck was coming up the companionway, hurrying, his face sullen and angry. Hewitt's mouth dropped open, for there was a gun in Breck's hand. The mouth snapped shut again, and Hewitt said furiously: "Mr. Breck, I'll have no guns brandished about on board my ship, put it away..."

Breck stood there, his eyes cold and hard. He looked at Roger and said: "You're right, you can't interfere." He turned to Hewitt: "You know the orders. We stop at the sandbar."

The moment of alarm, of shock almost, had gone. Roger said: "Breck, you're a bloody fool, put that gun down and shut up."

The barrel of the revolver swung around to point at him. It was a long-barreled Bayard, a thirty-eight. Breck said stubbornly: "This ship is going to stop, Sequoyah, at the sandbar. We're going to put her

ashore. Those are the orders, and by God they'll be carried out."
There was a sudden, flaming rage on him.

Roger said slowly: "Madam Caffa has just told you...something
you've waited a long time to find out, something you've waited thirty
years to hear..." He looked quickly at Hewitt's tight, angry face, and
he saw the momentary puzzlement there, and then he went on: "And
now, in gratitude, you're a party to her murder."

"Murder!" Breck snorted. "She'll be picked up within a few
hours..."

"Maybe, maybe not..."

"And for what she told me...she extracted a price, a heavy
price." The fury had turned to pain now, and as though conscious of
the hurt Breck said sharply: "More than ever now, my loyalties
are...where they've always been." He looked once at Hewitt, but the
skipper's face showed no curiosity, only a dark anger.

Hewitt said: "We're not stopping, Mr. Breck," and Breck said
sharply: "Stop the engines."

He moved forward to call the engine room, and Hewitt, furious,
stepped towards him. And then Roger, more sure than ever that Breck
was bluffing, shot out a hand and took hold of the gun, holding it by
the chamber, gripping it tight with every muscle he could bring to
bear, not letting it revolve, knowing that in the struggle the trigger
could be pulled, even accidentally, and that this was the only way to
stop the gun from firing

The scuffle was brief; it was almost as if Breck were reluctant
to resist, though the violent anger on his face was not lessened. And
then the gun was in Roger's hand, and he said quietly: "It's no good,
Breck, just take it easy." He thought for a moment that he would have
trouble with Hewitt too; Hewitt's face was purple with rage as he held
onto Breck's shoulders, and Breck shrugged himself free with an
impatient gesture, and the captain turned away as though to hide the
apoplexy.

The fight had gone out of him, and Breck said heavily: "He's
still the owner, and whatever he wants..." He broke off, and Roger
asked: "Right or wrong? Is that what you mean? You'll support him
even in this?"

Breck said stubbornly: "In everything."

Roger broke open the gun and checked it, found it fully loaded, then closed it with a snap and held it out for Breck to take. Breck took it slowly, hesitated a moment, and then thrust it into his belt. He turned and moved towards the companionway, and Roger said: "Wait...let me make a point."

Breck stopped. He did not turn back, but stood there with his hands on the polished mahogany rails, not moving. Roger said: "Now that you know...what Madam Caffa told you..." Breck looked back at him, and Roger said: "No one doubts your loyalties. But they should persuade you to stop him from making a terrible mistake, from doing something he'd regret for the rest of his life. If he can't take hold of himself, if his anger is blinding him to reason, then he's got to have help. Right now, there's no one more important for him to turn to than you."

When Breck did not answer, he went on, speaking very quietly: "If you admire a man, it's not enough to do everything he wants; if what he wants is wrong, then you've got to fight him. A new identity, Breck, it needs a new kind of strength."

Breck said nothing. In silence, as Roger watched him, he went slowly down to the deck.


You could feel the tenseness all over the ship.

Hewitt's talk with Christie had been violent and explosive, and had left them both in a towering rage. And the word had quickly spread. The seamen, those who were not on duty, were gathering in little groups, worrying about their paychecks; it was as though a muttering on board were growing into an open rebellion. He could not be sure for Breck, and he knew that the time had come for a heart-to-heart talk with Christie.

He found him pacing up and down the boat deck, smoking furiously and muttering to himself. He turned at Roger's approach and pointed an angry finger at him. His voice was a snarl. He said: "You know what you've done to me, Sequoyah? You know what you've done to yourself?"

Roger said calmly: "I've saved you from something you'd regret for the rest of your life. Why don't you just accept it?"

"Accept it?" Christie was shouting, his temper boiling over. "Do you know what you've done? If their new government makes any claims against me..." He broke off and muttered to himself, and Roger frowned.

"Claims? What sort of claims?"

"Oh, shut up, the damage is done."

Roger shook his head. "I wish the hell I knew what goes on in that mind of yours..." Christie had thrown away his cigarette, and a smell of burning was coming from somewhere. Roger growled: "A fire on board, don't you know better than that?"

He searched and found the end of the cigarette, ground out under Christie's heel, and Christie was looking round, anxious and puzzled.

And then, a wisp of blue smoke was carried by the wind past their faces and Roger said: "My God, there's a fire..."

Christie looked at him blankly: "There can't be, the best sprinkler system in the world..."

They ran together for the companionway and slid quickly down the handrails, and the corridor below was clouded with smoke.

Breck was running towards them, fast and light on his feet, and he leaped up and grabbed at the rail that carried the sprinklers and wrenched at one of them till it came off in his hand, and he dropped down again and said: "They're dry...the pipes are empty."

The smoke was coming heavily now, through the closed doors at the end of the passage, and Breck raced towards them and began to struggle with them, trying to force them apart.

Roger put his fist through the glass on the wall and pulled out the ax, and shouted: "Let me do it, get the hose down..." He drove the ax hard in the crack between the two doors, and threw the weight of his shoulder onto the handle, and the lock broke and the doors flew apart. Beyond, there was nothing but acrid blue smoke, and now an alarm bell began to ring, insistent and loud, and they could hear running feet on the decks above them.

Breck had the hose out and was turning the valve, but it was dry and he shouted: "The main valve, someone's turned it off." He ran down the passage and they followed; and when they came to the heavy bronze valves that controlled the flow of water to the fire equipment, they found that a chain had been passed through them and padlocked.

Breck stared at it and yelled to Roger: "The ax, for God's sake...!" They could hear a heavy, desperate pounding on the heavy door beyond them, and Breck stared at it, startled, and said: "My God, they've got to get water through there... For God's sake..." He raised his voice and yelled: "Break it down, put an ax to it, break it down, hurry..."

Roger said: "Stand aside." He took the long ax in a wide arc and brought it down hard on the chain that held the valves, and he felt the sting of it shaking his arms, and he struck it again and again, and the sparks flew, and then Breck found a crowbar and slipped it under the chain, and they heaved at it together.

While they struggled, Roger shouted to Christie: "Go see where it's coming from!" And Breck yelled: "It looks like the main lounge."

Christie stood there blankly, almost in a daze, and Roger yelled again: "Go on, the main lounge!"

Christie turned and stumbled off, and one of the officers came running up and said: "It's all over the forepart, what happened to the water?"

Roger had taken the ax again and was attacking the valve.

The officer said calmly: "Someone locked the fire doors before they went to work, we're trying to get them open now."

Breck said sharply: "No, we'll confine it down here, keep those doors shut..."

Roger wiped at the sweat that was pouring into his eyes. "Who else is down here?"

The officer said: "We're checking that now, thank God most of them are on deck."

"Prince Hafik?"

The officer smiled: "On deck, trying his damnedest to get down here, two men holding him, skipper's orders..."

"Keep him there."

"Yes, sir."

The fire alarm was clanging, and now there were flames at the rear end of the corridor. Roger swung at the valve again and it came off and clattered to the floor, and the rush of water came out at him and threw him off his feet, and he stumbled up and said to Breck grimly: "There goes the water pressure we needed, can we get it into the pipes?"

Breck shook his head. "No, we can't." He looked round at the closed fire door; someone was hammering on it, and he heard Simone's anguished voice calling: "Roger! Roger!" He ran to the door and shouted through it: "Are you all right, is there any fire there?"

"There's no fire, Roger, let me through..."

He shouted: "No, stay there...it's a furnace in here..."

He turned and ran to find Christie, cursing at the water that was running free and finding its way down the stairway, where it was not needed. A white-jacketed figure collided with him in the smoke-filled corridor; it was Baines, the steward. He grabbed him and said: "Baines! How many down here?" and Baines grinned at him through the smoke, coughing. "Just checking now, sir, the captain's orders."

"Any fire on deck?"

"No sir, just in this section, they'll control it...but...we'd better get out in a hurry...and we've got to get water here..."

Breck was attacking the single fire door with the ax, calmly, rhythmically swinging it against the steel casing where the lock was, and Roger ran past him, slipping in the water and coughing the smoke out of his lungs.

He found Christie hammering on the locked door of his own cabin, his face white, his eyes wild. The smoke was pouring out under the door, and the heat here was intense.

Roger grabbed at his shoulder and said desperately: "Is anyone in there...?"

Christie shook his head, he beat at the door with his fists, trying to force it open, and Roger shouted: "Candia... Where is she?"

Christie yelled: "I don't know... I don't know..."

Breck came running up and Roger yelled: "Where the hell is Candia? Have you seen her?"

Breck stood there, panting, his clothes soiled with soot and sweat. He said: "She must be in there...there's nowhere else, they've checked..."

"Water?"

"They're trying to fix that valve now, get it under control..."

"And the fire door?"

"One's open, there's water there, not here where we need it..."

The paint of the molding round the door was beginning to blister, and Roger said: "Get some buckets then, a chain of buckets..."

Breck said: "They're coming now, Sequoyah..." Simone came running down the corridor, coughing, stumbling in the smoke, and Roger said: "Thank God...Get up on deck ..."

But she shook her head. "Candia, I can't find Candia..."

Roger brushed her aside. He raised his ax and brought it down on the heavy timbers of the door, driving it home again and again, and Christie leaned against the door jamb and wept openly, hammering at the wall with his fists. Again and again he brought the ax down, close by the hinges, and at last one of them went, and he reversed the ax and hammered at the other, feeling the shock of his blows running the length of his arms.

The heat was building up intolerably, and the thick smoke was blinding, and someone sloshed a bucket of water at him and he saw that the flames were licking at the door where he had forced a way through; the door hung drunkenly on its hinges, and he stepped inside where the smoke was thicker and the heat was murderous.

He looked aghast at the burning ruins of the cabin, sure that no one could survive there, but from high on the bookcase wall where the smoke was worst and the flames were racing from the drapes up to the shelves, he heard the choking, lung-tearing cough, and Candia was there, on top of the ladder, her clothes torn and black with smoke. ...And in the center of the big, luxurious cabin, a large pile of books was on fire, and Candia was pulling more off the shelves and throwing them onto the pile; he could smell the sickly scent of burning gasoline, and then Simone was beside him and he tried to push her back out of that inferno that was the cabin.

The smoke was so thick that he could see nothing, nothing at all, and a gust of wind blew up the flames into his face and singed his hair. He could dimly make out the form of a man—was it Breck or Christi stumbling into the room.

He heard Simone scream somewhere, and he yelled: "Breck! Breck! Get Simone up on deck!"

He could not believe that anyone could live in the furnace, and he stumbled towards the ladder and found that the ripe mahogany rungs were on fire, and through the smoke he could see nothing, but he could hear Candia still up there, coughing her lungs out; a row of books came hurtling down on him as he tried to clamber up, and he struggled and reached for her legs and found them, clawing at them as she kicked at him.

He reached out again and fastened his hand on her ankle and climbed up higher and grabbed her round the waist, and she kicked out at him and hit him hard in the face as he balanced himself there; and as he tried to pull her down he felt that she was clinging to the bookcase itself, holding on tight with a strength he did not know she possessed. He put both his arms round one of her thighs and slipped his feet off the rungs of the ladder, and let his whole weight hang there, pulling her down, clawing at her and trying to break her grip, and then he felt a blinding blow in the face as her bare foot caught him in the eyes, and he yelled: "Candia...let go..."

He reached up again and clawed a handful of hair and pulled himself up by it, coughing and spluttering with his lungs full of acrid smoke, and he used his free hand to hit her, hard, on the side of the head, and at that precise moment the flaming bookcase came away from the wall and the ground came up and hit him, and there was a searing pain in his side, and Candia was lying on top of him, dress torn almost off, and the massive mahogany bookcase was lying across their bodies.

He wrenched himself round and kicked out a burning spark that was lying on Candia's thigh and firing her dress, and he ripped at the cloth and tore it away, and the smoke cleared momentarily as a gust of wind came in from a broken window. He saw Breck struggling with Simone, trying to pull her away as she tried to get to him, and the flames were spreading fast, and he yelled out:

"Get her out of here, Breck, get her out...!"

He heard her scream: "No, Roger...no!" and saw Breck dragging her away. He saw Christie, stumbling blindly, pulling out the desk drawer where the key to the safe was kept, spilling its contents into the flaming debris and then dropping onto his knees among the flames and groping, groping around in the smoldering embers, his eyes wild with a sort of terror in which there was the wild look of the maniac...

The pain smothered him, and he opened his eyes again and saw the pages of an open book burning close by his face; he had a vision of the picture Candia had showed him, the Hindu Prince with his five women, and then the flames were creeping along the naked thighs and the paper was curling as though the bodies themselves were writhing, and then nothing was left of it at all, nothing but the smell of burning leather and the acrid scent of the smoke.

There was water all around now, black water in which burned timber was sizzling, and the heat was deathly, and the smoke was blinding him. He pulled himself free and tugged at a heavy wooden spar that was wedged firmly under a flaming stanchion; its other end was lying over Candia's leg, and he knew by the twisted form of it that the leg was broken. His hands were on fire with the pain, and he struggled to his knees and thrust his shoulder under the wood and yelled: "Christie, pull her out! Pull her out...quickly...!"

The spar was alight, burning deep into his shoulder, and he looked back wildly, feeling it crushing him, and he saw Christie at the safe, pulling it open and reaching in.

He yelled, in agony: "Christie! Jesus Christ, for God's sake, Christie! Grab her!"

Christie looked back once, and turned back to the safe, reaching deep inside and pulling out a heavy, ivory-covered book, and for a moment he stood there, dazed, not conscious of anything round him, clutching the book to his chest and muttering.

Roger yelled again, desperately: "Christie...Christie! Help me! Drag her free, for God's sake! Quickly!" He could feel the weight of the red-hot spar crushing him, burning its way deep through his flesh. His head was reeling, and the room was coming and going, with the vision of Candia lying there limply and the flames licking at her torn dress and the black water swirling round her....

And suddenly, Hafik was there, throwing himself forward, forcing his slight body against a board he was carrying and using as a lever, and Hafik said calmly: "Hold on, Roger, it's coming up..."

They strained together, laboring, and Hafik looked at him, smelled the sour stink of burning flesh, and pushed harder and said, gasping: "They tried...to hold me back...hold on...a little more..."

The flaming stanchion moved, and pivoted over, and crashed again to the floor, and Candia was free. Roger collapsed, moaning, to the ground, and the water lapped at his face, and dimly he saw Hafik pick up Candia again and stumble with her out of the cabin and into the corridor, and then he was quickly back again and helping Roger to his feet and saying urgently: "Are you all right, Roger, are you all right?"

The clarity returned, and he gasped out: "What a...what a damn...damn fool...question..." He reached at Hafik and pulled himself up and said shakily, gripping him by the shoulders: "Candia...Candia, I think she's dead..."

He heard Hafik say quietly: "No, she's not, she's hurt, a broken leg...Simone is with her..."

There was a strange look on his face, a hurt, puzzled look. He began to pull Roger away, and suddenly the cabin was full of men with buckets of water, and the sound of the sizzling flames was fierce behind them as they fell over each other into the corridor.

He groped on his hands and knees, and found a clear patch of air and drank in great draughts of it, and Simone was there, bending over him, and he said again, weakly: "Candia...is she alive?"

He heard Simone say: "She's alive, my darling, it's all right, it's all right."

The fire in his shoulder was boring into him, and he could smell the burnt flesh; it sickened him. A man came running up with a small canvas case, and was bending over him and sticking a needle into his arm, and soon the pain went away a little, not entirely but enough to take the clouds away from his eyes. He looked up and Hafik was standing close by him, looking down with that strange, almost angry expression. Simone was aware of the tension there, and she looked up, puzzled, and said: "Hafik?"

Hafik said slowly: "Before anything else, Roger, before anything else...did you know?"

Roger grappled with the coma. "Did I know? Did I...know what?"

"The book."

"What book?"

Hafik said steadily: "Did you know that Christie had it?" There was a terrible edge to his voice.

The clarity came, and with it there was a vision of Christie, standing by the safe and clutching the ivory-bound book to his chest, ignoring the flames and the suffocating smoke and everything else that was round him, ignoring too his daughter as she lay there, helpless, pinned down by creeping flames that were licking at the body he had given life to....

His head fell back. He said: "My God, it was the Kandit Oras." He could feel Hafik's eyes on him. He looked up and shook his head. "No, Hafik, I didn't know." Simone's hand was on his cheek, and she was crying. She said, over and over again: "Roger...my darling...my darling..."

Hafik said nothing. He turned and started to move away, and Roger said: "Hafik! Wait!" He tried to get to his feet, but he stumbled and fell again, and then Simone was holding him up, and he stood there for a moment, clutching at her for support and swaying wildly while the paneled walls, stained now with smoke, came and went and pulled him with them. He heard her say, urgently: "Come with me, Roger, with me..." and he tried to push her away and fell against her instead.

He held his arms tight around her slim body, feeling the strength in her, and he said again: "Wait, Hafik...wait..."

Hafik was waiting. He said at last, very quietly: "No, Roger, what I have to do... I have to do alone." He looked at Simone. The tears were gone, and the calm was there, but terrible now.

Roger looked at her and said: "I must go with him. I know...I know..."

She nodded. "All right, my darling, if you must. If you can..."

"I can."

He walked unsteadily from her and followed Hafik down the long smoldering passage. The water was back in the pipes again, and was pouring down uncontrolled, and he heard someone say, irritably: "Turn that bloody water off, we don't need it now..." and someone else said, far away, "We can't, the valves have gone..."

He staggered on, stumbling, trying to keep up with the striding Hafik, and the water poured down all round him.

They came upon Christie in the after lounge. He had found

Candia at last, where she lay stretched out on a divan, moaning slightly and twisting her head from side to side. Christie stood above her, looking down on her, one hand groping at the air over her face like a blind man, and the other, with the Kandit Oras clutched tight to his chest, caressing the ivory boards of the covers. She was looking up at him and saying: "Daddy? Daddy? Oh God, Daddy, I'm sorry, I'm sorry...Daddy?"

A trickle of saliva was at the corner of Christie's mouth, and his eyes were quite blank; the groping right hand did not stop its weird, hypnotic movement, and then Hafik said, very clearly:

"The Kandit, Christie. Give it to me."

The slowly moving hand stopped; all movement stopped. It seemed as if even the unchecked flow of saliva stopped. And then Christie's head came up and there was a wild light in his eyes and the veil over them had gone, and he was no longer an animal but a strong man, and he shouted once, very sharply: "No! It's mine! I made a bargain!"

Hafik said again, very quietly: "Give it to me, Christie."

Roger moved forward, and stopped; there was a gun in Christie's right hand, the hand that had stopped its groping, it was pointed at Hafik's chest.

For a moment, a moment so short that it might not have existed at all, the picture held. And then Christie fired, again and again and again, and Roger lunged forward and tried to wrestle the gun away, knowing that he was too late and hearing the gun still firing. He heard Candia scream, and as he fell, he saw her roll from the bed onto Hafik's body, and some men came running up, shouting, and grappled with Christie; Breck was one of them.

Roger fell back, helplessly, falling to the floor as the pain came sweeping over him, falling clumsily to the ground and feeling the white-hot fire in his shoulder driving its way into his head. He saw Breck taking the empty gun from Christie's shaking hand, and then Simone was helping him to his feet again, clutching at him and looking down at Hafik as he lay on the floor, quite still. Candia was crawling over him, dragging her broken, twisted leg, clutching at his head and pulling it tight to her breast, holding him to her and moaning, weaving her head from side to side and never seeming to stop.

Simone bent down and held Hafik's wrist for a moment, and when she stood up she looked at Roger and said nothing. He heard the long breath escape from her body.

Breck was lifting Candia up, very gently, holding her wrists when she tried to fight him, putting her gently down on the divan again and wiping at her forehead with a wet rag, trying to stop the interminable side-to-side motion of her head.

Roger felt he was falling. He clutched at Simone and she held him, and all the pain was rushing back into his shoulder, an intolerable agony that welled up inside him till he wanted to scream. He felt Simone's hands round his waist, and then there were other hands too, and suddenly there was nothing round him but a world of blackness that was lit with flashing stars that went out when he tried to focus his eyes on them, and he could hear his own voice, very far away, saying over and over: *Forever and ever, Simone, forever and ever...*

And then, even the voice was quiet, and there was nothing left at all.

# CHAPTER 17

THE SQUAT, WHITEWASHED houses of Arkan gleamed brightly in the sun as the ship steamed slowly towards the tiny harbor.

The minarets were slender needles piercing the hot blue of the sky, and even out here, the faint, high-pitched wail came to them across the water as a muezzin called his stricken, impoverished and excited people to their midday prayer.

The sea was calm, and deep blue, and silent. And the first slight winds were blowing, the winds that soon would bring the great brown-sailed dhows down from the Red Sea with their cargoes of carpets, of oil, and of dates, and hides, and spices.

They stood together in the bow looking out towards the shore, Roger and Simone, and the only sound that came to them was the gentle scraping of a holystone, the flat stone they sometimes called the prayer book that was used for bringing the decks to a sparkling brightness, as, behind them, a seaman was on his hands and knees with a bucket of water beside him. His work finished, the scraping sounds stopped, and the man stood up and looked at the shore too; it was the Frenchman whom Roger had first heard singing, a long time ago, when he stood here once with Candia.

He turned back, and the Frenchman touched his cap and grinned, and said: "*Hein...dejà, nous sommes arrivés ...*" He wandered off, with the water splashing out of his bucket, padding along silently on canvas shoes.

Simone said: "Yes, we have arrived. I wonder what it is we shall find there?"

Roger's hand was at her waist. "Whatever it is...as long as we are together. Forever, Simone."

"I know. Forever."

"And Hafik has come home."

"A martyr."

The body of the young Prince lay in state in the well of the main staircase, in a coffin of heavy walnut which the carpenters had made, with handles of beaten silver which had been stripped from the ornate decor of the burned-out cabin. It was covered with a flag that Breck had produced from the lockers, the gold and green flag of Orassia, with its white crescent and its strange, mystical upright bar of purple which, some said, was the phallic emblem of Raidan el Darrah.

And on it, in a box of polished oak, lay the Kandit Oras, the heavy price the Shah had paid for the safety of his son... Once more, it was on its way back to the country that gave it its birth.

Roger said, worrying: "I wish I knew what's going to happen to Maxwell, now. They must never know, ashore, just how Hafik died."

Simone said: "He died trying to save Kandit Oras from the fires. It's all they need ever know. If ever the truth comes out... Maxwell will be out of our reach, Roger. It's better that he should be. Breck will take good care of him."

Christie, and all that he had stood for, the power, the eagerness, the driving force that now was shattered, was a cloud that darkened the days that were behind them. It was a nebulous, wandering cloud that might, one day, be dispersed by the clarity of reason, but now was a dead and hopeless thing.

He stayed in Breck's cabin, with a guard at the door, and Breck was there with him, tending him, listening to his ramblings, feeling his anguish, knowing that never again would Christie be a man.

Roger said slowly: "It doesn't seem fitting, Simone, for a man like Maxwell Christie... There must be worse men than he, who better deserve madness." He shuddered. "That dazed, frightened look, the look of an animal that has been half killed in a trap, it's...it's too much to suffer."

"One day, perhaps...who knows?"

He nodded. He turned the binoculars on the shore, on the tiny wharf, and he said: "General Fali, three other officers, a platoon or so of troops, an honor guard. Their rifles are reversed."

"The burial party. There will be a great sadness in Arkan tonight, in the whole country. Even those who feared his father most...they loved Hafik for what he might have brought them. A forlorn hope, perhaps, but a strong one."

Beyond the town, against the yellow of the dunes, there were small black figures, lined up along the high crests, almost shadowless in the midday sun.

He said: "A hundred Bedouin, more perhaps...perhaps a lot more."

Beyond them, he could see the black tents they had brought with them, to pitch near the outskirts of the town.

He said: "Will there be trouble from them?"

"Not if they brought their tents. On a *ghazzu*, a raid, they bring only their camels and their guns. *Raffiq* has been declared."

"*Raffiq?*"

"When I spoke on the radio with General Fali, he told me. A truce, an institutional meeting to settle differences. He is a wise man, Fali, the Bedouin will give him no trouble. May I look?"

He passed her the glasses and waited, and in a little while she said: "No tanks, no armored cars, the officers are wearing their swords. There will be no more fighting, Roger, I promise you. No fighting. Just a lot of hard work." She touched his hand and sighed. "It will be good to know you're beside me."

"At your feet, if you wish."

"It may not be easy for you, at first."

"Nothing worthwhile ever is. But...if Orassia joins that select little group...the oil states...you're going to need me."

"Yes, I know."

She looked at him. "And Oklahoma?"

Roger shrugged. "A whimsy that's gone. Something better has taken its place. Something to take pride in."

Her hand was on his, and the touch of it sent a tremor through him. She said quietly: "A new life for you. I'll show you things you never knew existed."

His arm tightened round her waist, and he said nothing. The pain in his shoulder was still there, and his face was white and drawn.

The burn had gone down to the bone, and now...he sighed, and said: "Now, the pain is all coming back. I need you more than you need me, Simone. Love, love, love, I never knew it could be so strong."

She touched gently the great mass of white bandage on his shoulder. "Let's go and see how the other cripple is getting along."

They went together, slowly, up to the sun deck.


Candia put aside her book and looked at them. She said: "My God, what a mess you look, Roger Sequoyah."

He grinned. "How's the leg?"

"It tickles, it weighs a ton." She lay back in a deck chair with a crutch beside her, and her arms and shoulders were covered with bandages where the flames had burned her.

Simone said: "You really ought to be still in bed."

"Bed is for babies and old, old women. I'm neither. I'm somewhere in between, I suppose, not quite grown up and only old...in parts." She looked at Simone and then at Roger, and there was still a touch of the old malice there, in her sullen eyes. But she sighed and said: "What a godawful mess..."

Roger said: "Have you seen your father today?"

"Yes, I saw him." She turned her face away and said again: "I saw him. Every day, I will see him, for as long as I live, long after he's gone, I'll still see him, just as he is today."

He said, frowning: "What will you do now, Candia? Will you be...alone?"

Her eyes brightened a little. "Alone? You know me better than that. Another Luther Fenton..." She looked at Simone. "Another Roger Sequoyah." She turned away again and said heavily: "Or another Hafik."

There was a little silence, and he looked for a trace of tears in her eyes; there were none. He sighed. "Did you have lunch?"

She grimaced. "That godawful broth, that's all Breck can think of. A broken leg, and I'm supposed to eat broth, does that make sense to you?"

"No, not really."

"Broth. Jesus..." She looked towards the shore and said slowly:

270

"It gets closer, there's nothing more...more relentless than a ship approaching a harbor."

"Yes, I know. Sometimes, you get the feeling you wish you could stop it, not for any good reason but just because it *is* so relentless. And then you know that there's nothing you could, or should, do about it."

Simone was standing aside from them, letting them feel a little together. Candia looked towards her and said: "I hope you know what you're doing, Roger Sequoyah."

"I know what I'm doing."

"You think it's going to be easy?"

"Nope. It's going to be tough as hell." He could feel Simone's eyes on him. He said to Candia, making a joke of it: "Commensurate with the rewards, which are quite considerable."

He was pleased that she did not answer the gentle goading; was she aware of what he was trying to find out and denying him the satisfaction of knowing, of ever knowing? He hoped she was.

There was the beginning of a smile at the corner of her spoiled child's mouth, and she said: "Are you going to miss me?"

"Of course."

She shot a glance, an envious glance, at Simone again. "Like hell you will."

Breck came slowly up the companionway, moving heavily, the lightness gone from him. He stood for a while looking out at the approaching shoreline, waiting. He said at last:

"Another few minutes, Roger. If you have any final instructions..."

Roger shook his head. "No. Just drop us off and be on your way."

"Sure."

"You've a hard time ahead of you, I'm afraid."

Breck nodded, his eyes brooding and serious. He looked quickly at Simone and back to Roger, and there was just a slight touch of a grin there. He said lightly: "And so have you."

Simone moved in and crouched beside Candia, one hand on her knee. Her touch was gentle, her eyes were grave. She asked: "Do you want to go below when...when they take him ashore?"

271

Candia shook her head and reached for her crutch. "No, I'll stay up here, by the rail. I want to...to see how they receive him."

Simone said: "They'll receive him like a Prince."

There was pain in her voice: "A Prince...riddled with bullet holes."

"No one will ever know. We dressed him...in full uniform...he looks like the Prince he always was." Candia did not speak, and Simone said: "He's coming home, bearing the Kandit on his body, and our history will go on, unbroken."

She helped Candia to her feet, and let her lean on her shoulder while they went over to the rail, and Breck came and stood beside her. Candia said lightly: "Maybe I'll marry Breck one of these days, you think that would be a good match?"

Simone's expression did not change, and Roger looked quickly at Breck and saw that there was a warning in the eyes, a warning to say nothing. He thought: *My God, here we go again...* But he kept quiet, and then Breck began to laugh softly. He said: "Perhaps not a good match, but...interesting."

Roger thought: *Well, it's none of my business, if there really is a problem there, Breck can handle it, Breck can handle anything. Maybe after all, it might be the best thing for her...as long as she never knows. And from Breck...she never will know....*

The shore was close now, and they heard the motors lower their note, and a raucous brass band struck up on shore, not very much in tune, and Roger said: "My God, is that your national anthem?"

Simone nodded. "That's it, I'm afraid."

"Well, you said it wouldn't be easy for me." He put out his hand. "Good-bye, Breck. Good luck."

"Good-bye, Roger. And you're going to need the luck more than I do."

"Perhaps." He kissed Candia gently on the cheek. "Good-bye, Candia."

Simone took his arm, and they went slowly down to the lower deck where the bo'sun was putting out the gangplank.

The honor guard marched raggedly aboard, and the band struck up a dismal march, and soon the coffin was being carried ashore, the bright flag fluttering about it. And then a new sound came to them from the town, where a thousand black-robed women were gathered, watching the cortège as it marched up from the wharf.

It was the high-pitched, frantic roll of a thousand tongues ululating as the women began their formal wailing, the sound of it growing as the men took up the stylized cry, the sound of it swelling till it seemed as if there was nothing in the desert but the ancient lamentation that had sounded there since history first began.

Beyond the white buildings, the black spots against the dunes that were the Bedouin had grown, and now there were thousands of them lined up there, and they were waving their rifles and firing them into the air; and then they took up the lamentation too, far away, until it was a monstrous, drawn-out sound that filled the air and brought the dry, dead desert to life again, a desert that was burned into silence by the hot sun and that only at times like these could show that in reality the life was still there, struggling, sometimes winning, and sometimes losing.

The dunes of the desert, crescent-shaped and brilliant yellow, dotted here and there with the life it so unexpectedly showed, were a backdrop against the burning blue of the sky, and below them the tiny town nestled forlornly, seeming to grow out of the sand where the water was, the white houses and the green shrubs showing that here, too, the struggle was always going on, and was sometimes being won.

They watched from the deck while the funeral cortège wound slowly along the single street, and the policemen moved among the crowds, flailing their long canes and pushing them back, and the soldiers broke their ranks and dropped to their knees and took up the lamentation, and the General was waiting there with his colonels, grave and silent, and somehow dignified by the sadness all around

Beside him, Roger heard Simone's long drawn-out sigh. She took his arm and looked at him once, and said: "Shall we go ashore now, Roger?"

He nodded, and took her arm. Together, they moved down the gangplank and onto the wharf.

THE END

# ABOUT THE AUTHOR

Alan Lyle-Smythe was born in Surrey, England. Prior to World War II, he served with the Palestine Police from 1936 to 1939 and learned the Arabic language. He was awarded an MBE in June 1938. He married Aliza Sverdova in 1939, then studied acting from 1939 to 1941.

In January 1940, Lyle-Smythe was commissioned in the Royal Army Service Corps. Due to his linguistic skills, he transferred to the Intelligence Corps and served in the Western Desert, in which he used the surname "Caillou" (the French word for 'pebble') as an alias.

He was captured in North Africa, imprisoned and threatened with execution in Italy, then escaped to join the British forces at Salerno. He was then posted to serve with the partisans in Yugoslavia. He wrote about his experiences in the book The World is Six Feet Square (1954). He was promoted to captain and awarded the Military Cross in 1944.

Following the war, he returned to the Palestine Police from 1946 to 1947, then served as a Police Commissioner in British-occupied Italian Somaliland from 1947 to 1952, where he was recommissioned a captain.

After work as a District Officer in Somalia and professional hunter, Lyle-Smythe travelled to Canada, where he worked as a hunter and then became an actor on Canadian television.

He wrote his first novel, Rogue's Gambit, in 1955, first using the name Caillou, one of his aliases from the war. Moving from Vancouver to Hollywood, he made an appearance as a contestant on the January 23 1958 edition of You Bet Your Life.

He appeared as an actor and/or worked as a screenwriter in such shows as Daktari, The Man From U.N.C.L.E. (including the screenwriting for "The Bow-Wow Affair" from 1965), Thriller, Daniel Boone, Quark, Centennial, and How the West Was Won. In 1966-67, he had a recurring role (as Jason Flood) in NBC's "Tarzan" TV series starring Ron Ely. Caillou appeared in such television movies as Sole Survivor (1970), The Hound of the Baskervilles (1972, as Inspector Lestrade), and Goliath Awaits (1981). His cinema film credits included roles in Five Weeks in a Balloon (1962), Clarence, the Cross-Eyed Lion (1965), The Rare Breed (1966), The Devil's Brigade (1968), Hellfighters (1968), Everything You Always Wanted to Know About Sex* (*But Were Afraid to Ask) (1972), Herbie Goes to Monte Carlo (1977), Beyond Evil (1980), The Sword and the Sorcerer (1982) and The Ice Pirates (1984).

Caillou wrote 52 paperback thrillers under his own name and the nom de plume of Alex Webb, with such heroes as Cabot Cain, Colonel Matthew Tobin, Mike Benasque, Ian Quayle and Josh Dekker, as well as writing many magazine stories.

Several of Caillou's novels were made into films, such as Rampage with Robert Mitchum in 1963, based on his big game hunting knowledge; Assault on Agathon, for which Caillou did the screenplay as well; and The Cheetahs, filmed in 1989.

He was married to Aliza Sverdova from 1939 until his death. Their daughter Nadia Caillou was the screenwriter for the film Skeleton Coast.

Alan Caillou died in Sedona, Arizona in 2006.

# LOOKING FOR ACTION & ADVENTURE
# AUTHOR ALAN CAILLOU
## DELIVERS !

## AVAILABLE IN PAPERBACK AND EBOOK

# ADDITIONAL ACTION & ADVENTURE
# FROM ALAN CAILLOU

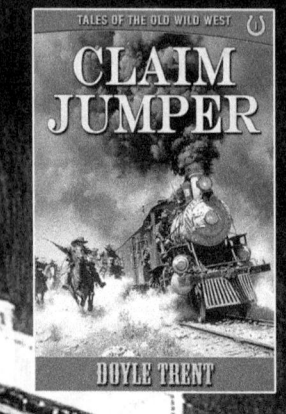
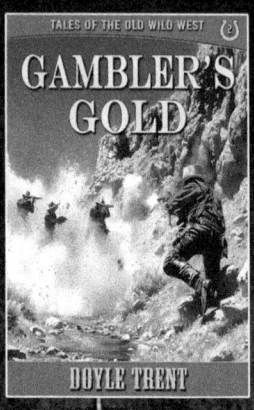

# FROM FANTASY AND SCIENCE FICTION
# AUTHOR ROLAND J. GREEN
## THREE EPIC SERIES

## FROM CALIBER BOOKS IN PAPERBACK AND EBOOK

# DON'T MISS ANY OF NEIL HUNTER'S NOVELS FROM CALIBER BOOKS

Reporter Les Mason is completing an expose on the Long Point Nuclear Plant. But before he can finish he dies an agonizing death. The doctors are baffled—and there are similar cases to follow...Chris Lane, his girlfriend, and organizer of the Long Point Protestors, discovers Mason's notes, and decides to find out for herself what the plant has to hide.

## 2 BOOK SERIES

In middle of the 21st century America – over-populated decaying cities are ruled by hi-tech gangs pushing every vice and wastelands are controlled by bands of mutants. Ordinary citizens are oppressed and face a hopeless future. But Marshal T.J. Cade is a new breed of law enforcer. Teamed with his cyborg partner, Janek, Cade takes on these criminals and works in the gray areas of the law to get the job done.

## 3 BOOK SERIES

The village of Shepthorne England wasn't being gripped, but strangled by a winter's blanket of heavy snow and Arctic temperatures. The trouble began innocently enough with a massive pile-up of autos on frozen roads leading to and from the village. Then, from the sky, a military transport plane with its top secret cargo of devastation crashed down towards the center of the village. Hell was just beginning to touch Shepthorne and its unsuspecting citizens...

## FROM CALIBER BOOKS

www.calibercomics.com

# CALIBER COMICS GOES TO WAR!
## HISTORICAL AND MILITARY THEMED GRAPHIC NOVELS